## Praise for The Dream of the Turquoise Bee

*. . . the touching and gripping tale of Tibetans who escape over the mountains to India, pray for the return of His Holiness the Dalai Lama to Tibet, live under the brutal oppression of the Chinese government, and teach their children to love, herd animals and read—this describes my parents and their parents and their parents before them in Tibet. More than a great adventure story you cannot put down, this is an education about our culture--written by someone who has been on the inside learning and experiencing it for years.*

-Lobsang Tsering (Tibetan Living Communities-TLC)

*A rich and powerful novel that combines romance, mysticism, and politics in the mysterious world of Tibet. A thrilling and intelligent story unfolds as artist and botanist Erzebet Pelletier sets out to find wildflowers — and to discover what happened to her journalist husband who vanished years earlier as the Chinese moved into Tibet.*

-- Sasha Paulsen, Napa Valley Register



*Somewhere between your eye and these pages lies a story of love without borders in a country who's own were trampled, one where there … a spiritually sensitive storyteller who brin… I loved it.*



*Charlie Parker once said if you don't liv… woven from Aigaki's unique perspective … lived with the same fearless originality that Bird blew, and I found this book to be as noteworthy as its author.*

--Caroline McHugh, CEO of IDology, Author

*" . . . this story is the Tibetan story, including the complex Tibetan-Chinese dialogue, that not only happens in Halls of State, but also in the homes of every citizen. It is thoughtful and beautiful and took me back t… and the mountains of Kham. I recommend it to anyone who is interested in Tibet, including Tibetans … to remember … homeland."*

-No…



*'The Bee is a travel agent guidin… and cajoling us through time and geography. France in the 50s, Tibet in the 70s and London in the first decade of the new century. Spanning the course of 50 years, the mystery of a journalist's death is explored, revealing karmic intersections that are plausible and heartbreaking. At the story's core is a nation's struggle for independence from a foreign power, with the struggle reflected in the lives of its characters.*

*Dianne Aigaki*

*Tibetan culture, language and tradition is woven so tightly into the story that we scarcely detect the lessons that expand our basic knowledge of this remote region. The story is told through divergent eyes and dialect, capturing the feelings of key characters as they intersect, then move away from one another—an archetypal theme, but not often seen played out in a remote culture. The book leaves just enough unsaid to make us yearn for a sequel."*

-Donna Deweerd, Award-Winning Short Story Writer

# THE DREAM OF THE TURQUOISE BEE

DIANNE AIGAKI

4.12
170

PUBLISHED BY DRY CREEK PUBLICATIONS



Dry Creek Publications
Attention: Permission Department
7128 Heather Tree Drive, Sacramento, California 95842

The Library of Congress has catalogued this edition as follows:

Aigaki, Dianne (1946-     )
The Dream of the Turquoise Bee – 1st ed./ Dianne Aigaki
p.cm.
1. Tibet-Fiction. 2. Dalai Lama-Fiction 3. Botanical Illustration-Fiction. 4. Exploration-Fiction. 5. Tibetan Nomads-Fiction.
6. Romance-Fiction. 7. Women Adventures-Fiction.
8. Historical Fiction. 9. China-Tibet-Fiction.
10. Women Explorers-Fiction.

Library of Congress Control Number: 2012947938

ISBN: 978-0-941941-00-6

First Edition: October 2012

Cover Design: Lander Rodriquez
Illustration of *Meconopsis horridula*: Dianne Aigaki

Primary Reference on Poems of the Sixth Dalai Lama:
*Songs of the Sixth Dalai Lama*
Library of Tibetan Works and Archives
Paljor Publications
K. Dhondhup (translator)

Printed in the United States of America

## Dedication

To all people who live as refugees
Dreaming of the return to their homeland
And to their families left behind
Who dream of the day when they will see
Friends and relatives
Walking over the top of the rise
coming home

*He imagined himself to be the reincarnation of the Sixth Dalai Lama,*
*A renegade who called himself the Turquoise Bee*

*This mysterious Dalai Lama*
*Left behind a seductive world of love songs*
*That even 300 years after his death,*
*Every Tibetan knows by heart*

*It is not for the Turquoise Bee to mourn*
*For the flowers that fade in the fall. . .*

# PART I

# CHAPTER 1

## *Until Death Do Us Part*

| | |
|---|---|
| *Ha chang sem la song nay* | *We are so much in love* |
| *Drok tree ae yong tree pay* | *I asked if she would be mine* |
| *Chee trel che na meen pa* | *Until death do us part* |
| *Son trel mee che soong choong* | *She whispered, Nothing can separate us* |

*- Sixth Dalai Lama*

## Erzebet's Story

### Paris, France: May 1959

"Maman," Lilia, my seven-year-old daughter, ran down the hallway and launched herself into my arms. "Who are those people in our front garden?"

"What do you mean, Lilia? What people?"

"Look out the window—I saw them from my room. There are a lot of men out there."

The doorbell rang. "Stay away from the windows." I hustled her back down the hall. "Go to your room and play. I'll see what's going on." Lilia hesitated, looking between the door and me, and then walked slowly down the length of the hallway.

The bell rang again. While unlocking the door, I pulled back the lace curtain to see who had arrived at such an early hour. A mass of reporters stared back in through the window, their cameras pressed against the glass. I cried out. My coffee cup flew from my hand and crashed to the floor. The strangers shoved the door open, but the chain stopped it short. Grappling at the opening, a hand forced the morning newspaper through the crack as flash bulbs blazed at the window, obscuring the distorted faces on the other side.

Yanking the curtain shut, I slammed the door. The disembodied hand pulled back just in time. When I looked down at the headline on the paper drowning in the pool of coffee, it seared a path straight into my unspoken fears.

### Le Monde: May 23, 1959 Girard Pelletier Missing in Tibet

I grabbed the newspaper and stumbled to my studio. My cheek pressed against the panes of the ivy-framed window, I soaked up the coolness of the glass, staring blindly into the garden. Seconds later, the phone pulled me out of my stupor, jangling the white noise of my mind.

"Have you seen the paper?" It was Arnaud, my eldest brother.

"I just got it. Haven't had time to get past the headline. I was just coming to call you."

"God, what a nightmare," Arnaud said. "I'll be right over." Ten minutes later I peeked through the curtain and saw him push through the shoving crowd. He struck out at a reporter who thrust a microphone into his face and the group moved back toward the fence, everyone shouting in our usually quiet street of Montmartre. I unlocked the door, lifting the chain.

"Madame Pelletier," the reporters yelled as Arnaud slipped inside. "Can we have just a few comments about your husband's disappearance?" Arnaud chained the door behind him, hugged me to his chest and pulled the blinds.

"What's going on, Uncle Arnaud?" Lilia stood in the hallway in a tulle ballerina skirt, cradling her doll. "Why are those people yelling and trampling our flowers?"

Arnaud glanced at me and I shook my head. "Give your Maman and me a few minutes alone. We'll tell you later." He swung her up into the air, ruffled her brown hair, and sent her back to her room to play.

With Lilia safely away from the confusion, my outer calm broke down and I pushed my face into Arnaud's shoulder.

"Let's see what the news has to say," he said softly as he reached past me and switched on the television.

We watched the same drama unfold over and over. I had seen Girard on television countless times before. Now it was as if I watched through a veil of disbelief. Expected to be out of Tibet and crossing back into Mainland China in early May, he had disappeared without a trace. Reporters on the streets of Paris held microphones up to strangers. Had they heard the news about Girard Pelletier? Yes, yes, just read the morning paper. How terrible this is, a man as respected and compassionate in his reporting as Monsieur Pelletier. They thought of him as a family member. They were saying prayers for his safe return. Their hearts went out to his family. To us.

Girard was a media hero in France. His natural charisma and boyish good looks had made him as fascinating and famous as the subjects he reported on. Night after night, he had spoken to millions in Europe telling the story of how the Dalai Lama in disguise had ridden a horse over the Himalayas, fleeing to exile in India with his family, and how the Chinese People's Liberation Army battled Khampa warriors on the Tibetan border. It was a tale of mythic proportions—a people's army of millions clashing with the forces of a man revered as a God-King by his people. More than fodder for conversation over afternoon tea, Girard's reporting had ignited debate among Asian scholars and China-watchers about whether the reality was "liberation" or "occupation" of the Tibetan Plateau.

Today's breaking story eclipsed the usual news on demonstrations in Johannesburg; the ongoing coverage of Fidel Castro who had recently been sworn in as Cuba's president; and the spillover news and analysis of the opening of the St. Lawrence Seaway in North America.

"Everyone picked up on a change in the last weeks," Girard's long-time editor, Nicholas Munro, spoke to the camera. He looked haggard with dark eyes; his face shadowed with stubble. "Small details caught our attention. We all commented on it. Reports wired to Le Monde hinted at a convoluted mess of political intrigue, human rights abuses. He thought the international community was turning its back on the Tibetans' plight. This situation is especially distressing as Le Monde has recently received news that Monsieur Pelletier is being considered for the George Polk Memorial Award for significant achievements in journalism for his coverage from Tibet."

Stock footage of Girard fording a raging river in a coracle, a boat of yak skin hides, flashed on the screen. Among the several cameras slung around his neck, I caught a glimpse of the silver rabbit-shaped pendant Lilia had given him for Christmas the year before. In the film, my handsome husband, my best friend, was moving silently down the river, and I slid down that river with him.

Arnaud turned down the television volume and patted my hand. "You received no clues as to another assignment after Tibet?" he asked. "Another region where he planned to travel?"

"Girard was anxious to get back here and digest the story's complexities," I said, my fingers kneading my temples. "He'd already begun to weave his insights into a book describing the takeover. He planned to write from his vantage point as a Westerner who traveled to Tibetan villages and hid in monastery halls as they were ransacked and burned."

"A book?" Arnaud frowned. "I don't remember hearing this before."

"I received only one brief letter about it. Weeks ago." Arnaud, my devoted ally, brushed aside the hair sticking to the tears on my face. It occurred to me I was not only crying for Girard, but for myself. In those first hours, I didn't know if I could survive another heartbreak that included Girard.

"I was too anxious to discuss it with anyone, even you. It was volatile material. Turns out, when Girard took that assignment, he knew all along that the Chinese troops were taking over Tibet; that it was a peaceful country that had been independent for decades, if not centuries. I've got a terrible feeling about what happened to Girard and what is happening in Tibet. It seems like no one knows what is really going on over there."

A whimper behind us cut the conversation short. Lilia stood in the doorway staring at the television. "Is that you and PaPa? Where is he?"

On the screen was a photo of me dressed in a peacock blue evening gown, standing alongside Girard at the International Journalism Awards dinner, Even in his tuxedo, he looked like the explorer -- lanky, tanned skin, his sun bleached hair out of control. In the photo, my smile was playful, youthful. A huge sigh escaped when I saw that picture. I felt neither of those now. I folded Lilia into my arms and stroked her hair as she stared at my eyes. "Yes, it's me and it's PaPa. We aren't sure where he is now. On his way out of Tibet, but we might not hear from him for a few days. He wouldn't want you to worry."

Hours later, I got up from the chair and turned off the television. "Come with me and let me fix you dinner, Lilia. We're all starved." In the kitchen, she rode on my hip as I warmed leftover food and put dinner on the plates.

During the meal, the telephone rang, continuing the calls of alarm we had been receiving all day. It was the editor from Le Monde calling to apologize for the paper's rush to print before the family had been notified. Then Anja Schumann, my oldest friend, and next Morris Cline, a family friend since I was a child. My parents checked in, keeping vigil with my sister and other brothers. The callers asked questions for which there were no answers. The doorbell rang. Neighbors slipped in through the reporter blockade, bringing meals wrapped in foil, questions and condolences, as if Girard's fate was already known. We unplugged the phone, turned out the light in the foyer, and stopped going to the door.

Well after midnight, Arnaud gathered up the newspapers and retired to the guestroom. I went to the kitchen and mindlessly assembled the ingredients to fix Lilia a special dessert from my own mother's recipe: a combination of lemon and pastry with bits of lavender chocolate tossed in at the last minute. A generations-old remedy, right at the top of the hand-written recipe card it guaranteed "to calm an anxious heart." I wondered where the recipe was to calm the anxiety that I was at least partially responsible for his disappearance.

It was 1:00 in the morning when I set the biscuits on a lace doily on Lilia's bed stand and reached up to close her curtains against the chill night air. Reporters camped across the street huddled on the edge of the neighbor's giant clay flowerpots, ducking under the espaliered fruit trees. Tomorrow, I decided, Lilia would stay home from school. There was no reason for her to run the media gauntlet and I wanted to monitor her intake of the news.

Down the hall, I rummaged in my closet, choosing one of Girard's flannel shirts to sleep in that night. I buried my face in the collar, smelling his sweat and his cologne, remembering our final good-bye at the airport, and his assurances he would not be gone long.

The next day, I brought out blankets and sheets so Lilia could construct a tent in the living room, a flashlight propped inside next to her storybooks. She invited me into her tiny world. Lying in a diminutive doll's bed decorated with sparkling mirrors were three figures, a paper man with her father's blue eyes but no mouth and a paper woman with no eyes and a white streak in her hair. Between them a paper girl with a full smiling face carried a sign on her chest saying "Lilia."

"Where's your PaPa's mouth?" I asked. "Where are my eyes?"

"He can't tell us where he is," explained Lilia, rearranging the miniature sheets and blankets to tuck in the figures. "You can't see him. But I can see and hear everything."

Two days after the front-page story of Girard's disappearance, Lilia returned to school. When she walked out the door, I went to my room to get dressed and instead collapsed onto the sofa in tears. I spent the morning reading and re-reading Girard's final letter. It typically short-changed the dangers of his reporting mission and described, instead, a flower he had picked on the mountainside. 'I am going to try and bring a few petals of this rare beauty back to you,' the letter said. 'The blue is extraordinary, light shining through like a Tiffany window. There's a legend in Tibet that a turquoise bee pollinates this flower. Coincidentally, the turquoise bee is also the nickname of one of the earlier Dalai Lamas. I'm staring at the flower now, my dear Erzebet, and the stem reminds me of you in a bristly mood--a mood I take full responsibility for creating. Thank you for forgiving me.' He had reached out to me with an image he knew would captivate my senses—an exquisite flower protected by thorns; the symbol of the hurt when he had breached my trust in him.

I raised myself from the sofa, tucked the letter in my pocket and took a drink of tea, swallowing my solid lump of misery. There were decisions I had to make to help Lilia through this time of tamped down terror. Should I allow my daughter to float with hope for her father's return or present the full range of possibilities? And what were the possibilities? I shuddered, simultaneously fearing for Girard's safety and plunged into uncertainty about my and Lilia's futures. Was he lying somewhere injured or even murdered in Tibet when I had encouraged him to go half way around the world to meet this fate?

Ironically, there were moments, not so many years before, when I had wanted to murder him myself. I buried my face in the flowered cushions, my eyes shut, bursts of light exploding and then disintegrating against my eyelids. Murder? That wasn't nearly true. Nevertheless, I had wanted to make him suffer as he had made me suffer. That was true. For making me feel useless, ugly, less than a woman.

# CHAPTER 2

## *My Lover Who Waits in the Bed*

| | |
|---|---|
| *Sha jam mal sa nang gee* | *My soft lover who waits in my bed* |
| *Nying rhub dung sems tsan ma* | *You will give me your full passion* |
| *O loe gyu nor hrok pae* | *But, do you mean well for me?* |
| *Gyo gyu sha pa meen gro* | *Will you also take my wealth?* |

*- Sixth Dalai Lama*

### Erzebet's Story

A dinner with friends, over two years before, had given me the first clues. Girard and I had spent the day riding bicycles through the back lanes of Paris, stopping for coffee and darting inside antique stores. My God, how we'd laughed; we couldn't have had a more pleasant afternoon. I'd even contrasted our good fortune with that of friends who were divorcing after years of marriage. We had somehow managed to escape the nastiness that drifted into the corners of the lives of many young couples after the birth of a baby. We were golden.

After stowing the bicycles back home, and making a quick change of clothing, we arrived at a dinner to celebrate the work promotion of a dear friend. While our hosts passed the wine, I was a phantom observer to an unsettling interaction between Girard and another guest. Marie-Heléne Cartier, brilliant graduate student intern at Le Monde, teased Girard about a mismanaged interview he had conducted with a French politician. I held my breath waiting for his predictable response, defensiveness, at a suggested lack of professionalism. Instead, he laughed playfully, bantering back and forth with Marie-Hélene, even imitating his own ill-fated interview. I was stupefied by his nonchalance, his good humor, at what would ordinarily be seen as an attack on his expertise. Despite our happy afternoon, I had the feeling he was more alive and forgiving with this virtual stranger with the blonde hair and starling blue eyes than he would have been with me, his wife.

After that evening, I began to instinctively, and obsessively, check phone records. I teetered on the emotional fine line between anger and despair, casually calling his friends to verify there had, indeed, been a soccer game they had all attended. The confirmation was always hesitant, an undertone of pity in their voices. I counted the minutes from the time the press corps secretary said he had left Le Monde until he actually arrived at the house. The discrepancies I uncovered tossed me into a whirlpool of confusion.

The final indignity had come when I confronted Girard, and he admitted his love for both Marie-Heléne and me. Even in the midst of this humiliation, I knew how to take disappointment and adversity and turn it to my own ends. My mother had dedicated herself to guiding the family ship smoothly through the precarious waters of my father's long-term depression. We Pelletier children watched and learned. We were masters at developing a back-up plan.

Those many months ago, when the affair was out in the open, I had managed to mock my own state of affairs by making up satirical fables about Girard and Marie-Heléne to entertain Anja and force myself out of the gloom.

"So, you're coming back to humanity, are you?" teased Anja.

"I guess I have no choice, do I?" I replied. "You know it's time to move on when you annoy yourself with the bored drudgery of your own story."

Still, I needed a task to recapture hope for my future and threw myself into a career of botanical illustration. An abstract painter steeped in Asian influences, suddenly too much of my life was abstract. I relished the grounding in the structured world of botanical art—not floral art which graces living rooms, wallpaper or cheap dime store vases, but earthly beauty where science meets fine art.

Botanical illustration was a field that brought back soothing memories of childhood visits to the British Natural History Museum. There I had spent hours in the archives, inspecting the paintings of Sydney Parkinson who traveled with Captain Cook around the world in the late 1700's and illustrated thousands of plants never before seen by Europeans. As a child, these illustration skills seemed impossible to learn; they were only the purview of those who were truly gifted. As an adult in a marriage of deceit and needing solace, I chose the botanical illustration field precisely because it was so exacting there would be no room for sorrow or outrage.

Now, I once again sought emotional reprieve and went to my studio to paint. I scanned the shelves for the first sketchbooks filled with my drawings and color studies from my beginning days at the Ehret Botanical Institute. The lines were a testament to my state of mind at the time--tentative and then bolder, some overwrought and aggressively laid out on the page. I could remember every day in class and every evening alone, while I made those sketches.

One afternoon during those months, Girard had been away on a dubious assignment, and I was distracting myself from my convoluted relationship by painting the *Solandra*, commonly known as the Chalice of Gold. The plant, a relative of the poisonous Datura, has a thick woody stem and dramatic cream and yellow flowers, each petal streaked with a purple stripe. I admit I liked the excitement of handling a poisonous plant, it made me feel adventuresome and dangerous instead of grey and worn. As I shaded in the trumpet-shaped petals, an ink blob splashed onto the page, blending in with the yellows to create a greenish smear. I had expected to lift the ink gently off the page, as any serious illustrator would do in an attempt to save the piece. Instead, I gripped the pen with white knuckles and gouged the painting, ripping across the pale golden petals and the sketched-in anthers. In that one quick motion, my elbow caught the inkbottle, sending it crashing to the floor, destroying the tiles, my left shoe and my illusion of being a woman in control of her emotions.

Girard had fallen in love and out of love, and still I painted. He was often gone for days at a time, twisting in his decision, leaving to be with his lover and coming back again. Still I painted, the time alone perfectly suited to both my disappointment at this turn in my life and an unexpected awakening on a deep spiritual level. When Lilia was at school or sound asleep I no longer fought against the desire to curl up and wither. Instead I brought magnificent plants to life on a piece of watercolor paper. One painting became an exhibit of five and then ten and then solo shows with forty and more.

I built an awarded-studded career as a botanical artist, a career rooted in diligence and beauty. On a fragrant April evening, I was speaking with my guests at the Galerie Vingee reception which featured my recent work on rare and endangered plants, when Girard came through the Art Déco glass doors. I saw him pick up a glass of champagne from the waiter's tray and greet friends with kisses and embraces, his eyes distant, wandering the room, searching for me. He smiled to see me dressed in the gown he had surprised me with on our first anniversary. The look on his face told me he was back. There would be no more late nights at the paper, no more absent weekends when he ran in on Monday morning before Lilia woke, rushed to change his clothes, and left again just after she departed for school.

Girard, in his renewed role as father and husband, took Lilia to the playground at the park, brought me coffee and croissants in bed, and invited my parents to a night at the opera--coaxing me back to caring about him, about us. The bunting that had blanketed my insides and compassionately dulled my senses dissipated. I was not an automaton after all. I was once again vulnerable, open to Girard.

Only those closest to us, long-time friends like Morris and Althea Cline, could see the remaining ragged edges and give guidance for smoothing them. In the beginning years, when my father had thought Girard and me too much alike, too headstrong to be suitable for marriage, Mr. Cline, my father's oldest friend, had been our advocate. He believed we would be passionate companions—swimming out of the mainstream of everyday life. After the affair, he and his wife offered solace to both of us, urging us to reconcile and go back to the vision that had brought us together in the first place. We followed their advice, traveling to Italy, lying in the country fern glens that had been the site of romantic trysts in the first weeks after we met.

One fall night, having just returned from another weekend alone in the countryside, we settled in for a family evening at our Montmartre home. A fire roared behind the iron screen of the fireplace. Lilia played a game with her dolls on the table, helping them dance to Mozart on the stereo. My thick blood had been given another chance, replaced with a transfusion of a lighter golden liquid. I glanced over at Girard, talking on the telephone in a corner of the study, and noticed the sunburn marks on his neck, a reminder of how he had balanced over me, making love in a deserted. park the previous afternoon.

Now his voice rose excitedly and then lowered. He cupped his hand over the receiver, moving so his back was to the room. My arms chilled. I was instantly thrown back to a paranoia I thought had disappeared for good. I strained to hear the conversation.

"Don't do this to me," he was saying. "This isn't a good time for me, for my family." The rest of the conversation was lost, as the crackling of the fire drowned out my thoughts and jammed my ears. He hung up the phone and came back into the room, moving to stand next to the fire.

"What was that about, Girard?" I forced the words out through a pinhole of space in my throat, trying to keep my voice even, though it teetered on the edge of hysteria. "Who were you talking to?"

"Hmmm?" He looked over at me, seeming mystified at my question.

"Who were you taking to on the phone?"

"The paper. Word is that more Chinese troops are moving into Tibet. They want me to travel with the army and report on their advances. The Chinese say they're marching to liberate the Tibetan Plateau from feudalism."

His words replaced the split second of nauseating fear that it had been Marie-Heléne on the phone. "When would this be?" I shifted in my chair, keeping contact with his eyes.

"They want me to leave in a few days. As soon as my travel documents are in order."

"Are you going?"

"This isn't really the time to be going away, is it? Not when we've just gotten back on an even keel here with our family. . ."

I knew my husband. I could hear the hesitation in his voice. "It is the assignment of a lifetime. You're not thinking of turning it down?"

"Are you sure?" He nodded toward Lilia who, absorbed in her dolls, did not seem to be aware of the conversation and then he turned to face the fire again. Running his fingers through his hair, he looked at me, questioning. The glow of the flames caught the tense lines of his jaw. "It would only be for two or three months. . . "

"Girard, you have to go. You've worked for years to have an opportunity like this. No one understands that better than me."

He walked over and stood behind me, his hands grasping my arms, his chin resting on my shoulder, as he pressed his body against mine. I sank against his embrace, feeling the months of healing surge up through the soles of my feet.

This memory generated a raw groan that escaped from my throat and echoed in the small studio. I lifted my eyes from the *Solandra*, and glanced at the clock, checking to make sure the telephone was plugged in, still working.

I feared I would miss a call from Le Monde with an update about Girard or a call from Lilia's school, telling me she wasn't doing so well. When the clock hit 3:10, I took off Girard's shirt, splashed my face with warm water, and dressed. I was ready to greet Lilia at the door. My daughter drooped up the sidewalk, lugging her backpack of books. Arriving at the bottom steps, she arranged her face into a sweet smile. "How was your day, Lilia dear?"

"Maman," she said as she threw her arms around me. "You were crying?"

"Yes. I've been thinking about your PaPa. I miss him. I want him here with us."

"When I came in the classroom door," she said, "the teacher was telling the children not to ask me about PaPa. She had a box of tissues on the desk for me to use if I needed them."

"What did you say?"

"I told the teacher I wouldn't be needing those tissues."

"Lilia, there's nothing the matter with crying if you want to, and nothing the matter with your friends and the teacher seeing you cry. Do you know that?"

"I think I do. . ." She took off her sweater and went to her room, leaving me alone with my longing for Girard and my memories of our best and worst days together.

# CHAPTER 3

## *My Mind Slips Back to My Lover*

| | |
|---|---|
| *Gom pa'ee la ma'ee zhal ray* | *I have come to ask for spiritual guidance* |
| *Yee la char gyoo meen dook* | *My lama's face does not appear* |
| *Ma gom jam pa'ee zhal ray* | *My lover's face instead* |
| *Yee la yang yang shar joong* | *In my mind is very clear* |

*- Sixth Dalai Lama*

### Erzebet's Story

I forced myself to get dressed each morning, attend Lilia's school functions and work on my illustrations. But, I couldn't stop my mind from retracing the lines of Girard's face. A note of music could stiffen my mouth; a familiar object could turn a sunny occasion into a grey one and refuel my despair. What if he was still alive and didn't know we were thinking about him every minute?

"I know this is rough," said Anja one afternoon as we sat in the garden. "But I'm a little concerned about how you're doing. You're always on the thin side, but you seem to be losing weight—looking a bit peaked. No one's seen you out for weeks."

"I guess I just need more time."

Where was the resilience I had always counted on when things were tough? There was nothing in this story that could be turned into laughter or theater. I continued to refuse invitations from friends, unable to relax on the same terraces where Girard and I had sat as a couple, laughing and drinking before we returned to fall happily into bed in our own home. Instead, I sorted and stacked his papers, getting the desk ready for his return when he would write his book. I bought him new pens, replaced the bulb in his favorite lamp over the study chair and cleaned the windows that opened to his favorite view of the garden.

Two months after that first headline announcing his disappearance, a telegram arrived reporting, in broken French, the sequence of events. Girard's car had skidded off a flooded roadway. The car rolled down a ravine and was found half submerged in the river. The body was not found and presumed washed away. They assumed death was instant. A more palatable death to me than what I had feared, the notification was a mixed relief.

Three days later, the mail brought the official death certificate (Exhibit A) from the Government of the People's Republic of China. Also in the envelope was Exhibit B, a grainy, slightly out of focus black and white photo of the accident scene. It showed a narrow road, what appeared to be tire marks in the mud, a drop off with a car at the bottom lodged among the trees. It was impossible to tell what was on the hillside beyond, whether the marks were scratches, a defect in the photo itself, or actual markings on the land.

The French Embassy reported there was no reason to suspect foul play. We could go on with our fractured lives; our situation was no different from that of any family who had lost a loved one. As simple as that. For them.

I wanted Lilia to stay at home for several days; suggesting we could travel together to the beaches of Spain. Lilia, however, seemed to have known the truth all along. She emerged from her waiting cocoon of the last months and insisted on going back to classes the next day.

Now, there was nothing left to do to keep my future without Girard at bay.

My relief over finally knowing the "truth" converted to disbelief in the face of insistent inquiries by friends and colleagues. The telephone began to ring moments after Lilia left for school.

"An accident?" my friends and family exclaimed. "Just when Girard was about to expose the Chinese occupation of Tibet for what it really was?"

I was dismayed at how easily I had taken the salve offered by the French officials. No one could be sure the photo sent by the Chinese Government had anything at all to do with Girard. That photo could have been taken anywhere.

Sitting alone in the study, I forced myself to make the requisite phone calls. I worked my way down the first tier list of influential people Girard and I knew, the ones I could call by their first names. These friends commiserated with me, promised to contact politicians and media colleagues, and called back, sometimes only an hour later, to say they had made no progress.

"Erzebet, we're so sorry," they said, hearing the strain in my voice and the choked tears I tried to keep from spilling onto the phone. "If there is anything we can do. . ."

Rifling through the desk drawers, I found a pack of stale cigarettes and matches. It had been years since I had been tempted to smoke. Stepping out to the terrace, I took a deep drag, letting the harsh smoke filter out into the afternoon light.

Lilia came home from school and climbed up on my lap, twirling the phone cord through her fingers, while I fixed her barrette with one hand and held the receiver with the other. She sniffed my hair, wrinkling her nose at the lurking scent of cigarettes, and went out to play with her friends in the garden.

Hours later, in the gathering dusk, I realized I had not fed Lilia or myself. I organized the notes that showed nothing but exasperating phone conversations and had turned up no guarantees of assistance, and went to find her curled up asleep at the foot of my bed, well before the moon had arisen over Paris. I fixed dinner, bathed my daughter and we snuggled together under the blankets, reading fairy tales about children lost in the forest and princesses asleep for ten thousand years. We fell into an anesthetized sleep ourselves long before the ice blue glow of televisions extinguished in the homes along our street.

Over breakfast the next morning, Lilia asked, "Did PaPa call last night when I was sleeping?"

"Not yet." The school counselor had said that asking if I had heard from him was Lilia's way of delaying the news until she was emotionally ready to face it and advised me to let her work through the news of Girard's death at her own pace.

The first call of the day was from a representative of the Foreign Journalist Association. "We're here to do anything we can, Madame Pelletier," the man said. "We're donating our offices for meetings to discuss the best method to sustain international attention and the next approach to solicit support from the French Government. We won't give up until we have the truth."

Their newly formed committees penned letters to the press in the evenings and during the day stood on street corners with photos of Girard and clipboards, passing petitions. Thousands of signatures filled the pages. Common citizens wrote letters to the editor of Le Monde expressing their concern and members of the Association of European Journalists petitioned their own governments to intercede. A forensic team volunteered their services to enlarge the photograph, examining it for clues that might tell something different from the official story. The ravine with the car at the bottom, trees with limbs sheared off or half-dangling from their trunks, the strange marks on the photo, almost like Chinese characters written on the hillside beyond: it all imprinted on my consciousness, but provided no answers.

Days turned into weeks. One night, after too many cups of coffee, eyes burning from the haze of cigarette smoke in the Foreign Journalist Association conference suite, I looked up to whispers just as Marie-Heléne Cartier walked into the room. Dressed in a black sweater dress and red jacket, she looked more like a high fashion model than a journalism student. She paused at my chair, leaned over and spoke in a low voice. She wanted to be helpful. She was so sorry she had caused such grief in my marriage. Was there anything she could do?

The others in the room looked furtively up from their work, perhaps anticipating an outburst. A wave of panic and then anger swept over me and receded. I wasn't going to give anyone reason to pity me. I stood up and shook her hand and then went slowly to the restroom on another floor, where I sat in a stall, my head in my hands, choking back bitter tears of grief and resignation. When I returned to the conference room, she had, with the unalienable hubris of the young and the beautiful, begun organizing the scraps of notes floating on the table, questioning each of the assembled friends and colleagues about the progress of their arm of the investigation. By the time she left, hours later, she had created a wall chart with all of the pertinent information and contact people, with assigned duties for everyone. I had been the first one to volunteer to have my name put up on the chart. Marie-Heléne Cartier wrote my name with her languid long fingers and sophisticated silver bracelet shining in the light.

Two days later, I arrived at a meeting of the foreign press, greeted Girard's colleagues and took a seat on one of the metal folding chairs in the front row. I still hadn't gotten used to seeing the poster size photos of my husband taped to the walls, his serious face just below the Le Monde banner head. I was staring at his blue eyes, conjuring up our last days together before he left for Tibet, when Marie-Heléne glided in, a stack of documents in her arms. She bustled straight to the podium, ready to call the meeting to order.

I quickly stood, went toward the podium and said as calmly as I could, "Thank you for the help, Marie-Heléne. I'll be conducting this meeting for the press. Feel free to take my chair with the rest of the audience."

She looked around for confirmation that she was being assigned to a minor role. Thankfully, my friends averted their eyes, letting me handle it. I read from my notes of conversations I had had with various functionaries, giving the report on the progress with the Chinese Government (none) and the French Government officials (little). I took questions from the audience, recapped for the national evening news and moved off the stage, surrounded by a cadre of assistants. I had taken charge of the meeting, but my mind was dead. All I could focus on were Marie-Heléne's slim legs in the black nylons and spike heels.

It was as if we competed for whom had the greatest desire to find Girard and resolve this mystery, yet I needed her energy, her focus, as she pursued the investigation into the disappearance of the man she had also loved. When I wanted to give up, and there were entire days when I did not believe I could go on, Marie-Heléne forged ahead. If I called five dignitaries, she met with ten. I fought to not feel relegated to the role of lesser player.

One night, exhausted by the daily trials of the investigation and my responsibility to keep Lilia's life on an even keel, I poured out my confusion and resentment to my parents.

"I can't think about Girard or how best to proceed without Marie-Heléne intercepting my thoughts. If I ask her to step to the side, I'm seen as ungrateful. If I choose to work directly with her, I'm reminded every second of my husband's hands and lips on this woman, someone who happily tried to wreck my marriage."

"Erzebet," said my father, as he slowly turned the scotch in his glass, watching the warm gold through the study light, "We need all the help we can get. Marie-Heléne is doing a fine job for Girard—and for you. Can't you put your jealousy about their affair to the side during this critical time? Do you have the strength to do that?"

"Well, I couldn't!" said my mother. Her face flushed through her tan, newly sunburnt from hours in the garden. "And I doubt you could do it, either."

I was stunned. He had no idea how difficult it had been for me to get past the affair; and I had gotten past it. But I never expected to have to work side by side with a person who had had sex with my husband. It was all I could do to force my face into a plastic smile, gather my things, and avoid another round of humiliation as a scorned lover and petty wife.

"Don't listen to your father, Erzebet," my mother consoled as I got into my car. "That was nonsense. I'm going back in there to give him a piece of my mind."

Every few weeks, someone called with an update that was merely a reiteration of no news. Eventually, more journalists were lost in the world, their causes more immediate and superseding Girard's. I had expected this. Perhaps I had been as accepting as Lilia without knowing it.

On the six-month anniversary of his disappearance, I filed a second official request for an investigation with the French Government and was told in private, "Madame Pelletier, we have great sympathy for your predicament. Nevertheless, we do not think it is useful or kind to give you unrealistic hope. An investigation will get nowhere. Diplomatic ties are all but non-existent. China is closing down by the hour."

The dutiful wife who will not give up in the face of depression, lack of progress or mortification, began to protest. Then I looked over at Lilia, playing with her dolls in the garden room. She was rocking back and forth, her hands clamped over her ears, a frown on her small forehead. I placed the phone back in the set with a distracted, "Thank you," in the middle of my sentence.

"Maman, are we ever going to play again?" asked Lilia peering at me through her doll's hair.

"Of course, we are—haven't we been playing?"

"Sort of. . ." Her voice trailed off. "But not like when PaPa was here."

In that second, I forced myself to rally through the heart and mind-numbing sadness my life had become. I had a lifetime to obsess over what had happened to Girard; a lifetime to magnetize the opportunity to do something about it. Now was the hour to reassure and care for our daughter. Now was the time to bring my own shrouded personality back to life. Lilia sensed the unwillingness, the inability, to leave our lives hostage any longer. She propped her dolls against the dollhouse, slid onto my lap, and immediately fell asleep. When she woke an hour later, she shook herself off like a puppy coming in from the rain and hopped on one foot to her room. She dusted her toys and arranged her books on the shelves, from the tallest to the shortest.

I followed suit. I roamed through the house, opening blinds and windows. Light spilled in. I called Anja and she arrived within the hour with three of my closest friends from university. They carried a basket with fine wine, cheese, and baguettes. We laid out the picnic in the unkempt garden, where I pantomimed rubbing like a cat against the tangy bark of the persimmon tree. My friends joined me to dig into the soil and crumble dirt clods. We let the pungent earth sift through our fingers. At dusk, with green light drifting among the cypress, we sat in the garden talking and laughing, having finished planting a hundred daffodil bulbs and iris corms that should have gone into the ground weeks before.

# CHAPTER 4

## *Promise Me Time Like the Full Moon*

| | |
|---|---|
| *She sum da wa gar pa* | *The moon is bright for three days* |
| *Gar goe nang nae chod song* | *It is completely clothed in white* |
| *Tso ngae nam dang nyam pae* | *Promise me* |
| *Zhal shay tsik gyang nang zhu* | *Time like that of the full moon* |

*- Sixth Dalai Lama*

## Erzebet's Story

### Paris, France: January 1964

"Erzebet, turn on the radio!" It was Arnaud on the telephone, his voice loud and excited. "France has established diplomatic relations with China—this is the opportunity we've waited for. The time to re-open the investigation into Girard's death!"

I called the Foreign Relations desk of the French Government immediately. "Erzebet," said Claudine Trigère, the senior receptionist who had long ago become a friend on a first name basis, "I'm not sure what this will mean for you—it's too early to tell. The President is going to address the media on Friday. Come by the office and I'll arrange for a press pass so you can hear this first hand."

"Don't get your hopes up too far," cautioned Anja later in the day, responding to my nearly manic enthusiasm about what was about to unfold. "This is a damn complicated scenario."

"I know, I know," I said, "but this feels like a sign. Every part of my being feels like this is a turning point." I felt almost giddy with relief that my life's background despair over Girard's disappearance was now moving toward resolution. I absorbed the news and debate about the diplomatic decision, making sure I was informed on every angle. Even the London Observer commented that 'Charles de Gaulle has entered the Asian stage like a diplomatic ice-breaker.'

Friday morning I was there in the packed room at the Elysée Palace as hundreds of journalists jockeyed for position to be near the speaker's podium.

"The great Chinese people," DeGaulle began, "are the largest population on earth, inhabiting a vast country that spans from Asia Minor and Europe's marchlands to the immense Pacific coast, and from the freezing Siberia to the tropical regions of India and Tonkin."

Evidence and reason, de Gaulle explained, demanded that he work with the Chinese leadership. Long-lasting solutions to any serious problem in Asia or even in the world would depend on China's active and constructive participation.

Nervously shredding a tissue in my hand, I inched forward, waiting for the right moment. I summoned up the courage to ask when France would be re-opening investigations into the disappearance of foreign journalists on the Tibetan Plateau, specifically Girard Pelletier.

Before I could speak out, a man from the back of the room called out. "President de Gaulle, it was only two years ago that Mao ZeDong proclaimed in his poem, *White Clouds*, that 'Only heroes can quell tigers and leopards; wild bears never daunt the brave.' He was referring to foreign powers as being hostile to China and a danger to its growth and future. How is it that you are now placing France directly in the path of China's wrath?"

While the crowd buzzed and craned their necks to see who had broached that topic in a press conference that was designed to smooth over differences with China, not highlight them; security personnel shuffled the journalist out the side door. The President, his red face radiating his annoyance at this disruption, continued his speech, speaking of China's great civilization and the opportunity for France to be associated with such a great power and people.

I stepped back into the crowd. This was not the time for me to ask a question that would call embarrassing attention to a subject that had long ago been placed on a back shelf due to France's reluctance to challenge China. I decided to wait until I had time in private to discuss Girard's disappearance with the President's staff. Three weeks later, I had my chance. Claudine arranged an appointment for me with Prime Minister Edgar Faure's assistant, Jacques Dumont. Faure and his wife had just traveled to China and Inner Mongolia with Chinese officials and he was negotiating details of the French-China agreement in relation to the Taiwan issue.

Monsieur Dumont greeted me with a kind smile and a warm handshake, inquiring about Lilia. His niece attended the same school as Lilia and we had met at a school function in the fall. His receptionist brought in tea and biscuits on fine china. My optimism grew. He had the files about Girard's disappearance in a folder on his desk, and as he shuffled the papers, I saw he also had copies of the death certificate and the black and white photo of the accident scene.

"Of course, I am willing to help in any way possible, Monsieur Dumont," I said. "I was very involved in the first stages of the investigation and have all of the notes and documents from that time period. You probably are aware that the Association of European Journalists. . ." My voice trailed off as Dumont's eyes shifted to the door, which had quietly opened. Standing inside, with a tense smile, was Prime Minister Edgar Faure.

"Madame Pelletier," he said, "Thank you for coming. I hope Monsieur Dumont has been able to help you understand our position."

"I was just getting to that Prime Minister," said Dumont, coughing over his last words and staring at me with concern. "Perhaps you will stay to help me explain to Madame Pelletier?"

I looked between the two men. My throat tightened. It took only a few minutes for the Prime Minister, in short brittle phrases, to present France's reality in dealing with China. There would be nothing said about any issue that might inflame the Chinese and derail France's fragile position. France had even capitulated on the issue of recognizing Taiwan, one of their primary negotiating points. There would be no investigation of Girard's disappearance. The French Government was requesting that I consider the good of the French people and the benefits that would derive from France having obtained a unique position with China on the world stage and not make a public statement or display.

My government overflowed with cowards. I picked up my purse and walked stiffly to the door, continuing in a daze down the hall and out to the plaza. Pigeons lifting into the air all around me, I fought the desire to create a scene and yell back at the blank windows of the complex. I had been a fool, allowing my hopes to soar once again, thinking this government would finally help me. But, surely there would be another time and I would be ready.

# CHAPTER 5

## *The White Moon Rises Anew*

| | |
|---|---|
| *Da wa dee nae phar dro* | *The moon goes away from here* |
| *Ting mai da wae tsur yong* | *Next month it will return* |
| *Tra shee da wae gar po* | *When the white moon rises anew* |
| *Da do chok la jhel yong* | *My beloved and I will meet again* |

*- Sixth Dalai Lama*

## Erzebet's Story

### Paris, France: January 1978

The veins of the rare fig I was sketching, just brought from the Polynesian Islands, had deep scallops like the border on a young girl's Easter dress. Leaning back in my office chair at the Sorbonne, I pushed aside the beginning drawings and finished reading the morning paper. Anwar Sadat's historic visit to Israel two months before was still front-page headlines—signaling possible peace between Egypt and Israel. He had arrived in Israel for a meeting with Prime Minister Begin wearing a gray suit and a polka dot tie. Continued warfare in Ethiopia. Spain was drafting its Constitution to replace the laws of General Franco.

Reaching for the pile of mail accumulated over the holiday break, I opened late Christmas cards and lined up the photos of my loved ones on the bookcase. Everyone brought a smile to my face; how fortunate I was to have known these people for so many years. Then I got to the anonymous white envelopes, with what I was sure was anonymous mail inside. I tossed one after another into the wooden trash bin without opening them.

The last envelope in the pile, however, caught my full attention. I looked at the calligraphy in the envelope's return address and the colorful stamp showing the Great Wall. Coincidentally, I had recently read an article about the United States diplomatic missions to China. They followed on Henry Kissinger's travel there in 1971. Only six months before, the Chinese Government had made a statement that the Dalai Lama would be welcome to return to Tibet if he accepted Communist rule and gave up his role as political and spiritual leader of his people. This was a proposition clearly untenable to the Tibetans who stated they had been an independent country before the takeover. There was also renewed discussion about international press reports that as many as a million Tibetans had been killed during the last three decades and the rest of the world had not known. China had responded to these accusations with anger and increased press censorship. These news reports had rekindled my interest in Asia.

I slid my fingernail under the envelope flap and extracted an official-looking document, an invitation to join a cross-hemisphere research project, a partnership between the Sorbonne and Peking University. It carried a round red seal of approval from the Chinese Government. I scanned the announcement for details. My venue would be botanical research; other scholars would study the Chinese prison system and sanitation projects. My role would be to complete twenty scientific botanical illustrations of wildflowers growing between 11,000 and 17,000 feet elevation on the Tibetan Plateau, an area that so far had had scant documentation of the flora. Of the plants to be documented, many were common the world-over, some grew only in the Himalayas.

The invitation spelled out why I had been chosen: my illustrations of rare and endangered flora of Borneo; my journeys to the Indian Himalayas over three summers to paint orchids growing in the Sikkim and Darjeeling regions.

My eyes skipped down the page, savoring the details, and then landed on the location for this expedition--*Sichuan Province, China*—the area that had been known as Kham, Tibet before the Chinese takeover. My hand jerked back from the announcement. The Sichuan Province--where Girard had disappeared almost twenty years before.

I crumpled the invitation and jammed it in the trash and went back to work inking and stippling the fig. My mind kept returning to 1964 and the humiliating meeting with Prime Minister Faure. After a few seconds, I laid the pen down. My hands flitted like bird wings with a life of their own. I stared at them with a certain fascination; I could not remember ever having my hands move in such a bizarre fashion. They stopped their erratic flutter. I picked up my pen, dipped it in the ink, and began the figs again. I was relieved that a letter with a coincidence related to Girard and the memory of my long ago pleas for help from the French Government had only the power to cause my hands to take flight, but could no longer devastate my life.

A week later, I received a copy of the first invitation, a note from Alain Bordelle, head of the Botany Department, stapled to the corner. "Interested? Erzebet, please respond. This could be a wonderful opportunity for you."

Something about it was unsettling. I walked down the hall to meet with my colleagues from the Botany Department. "What about this invitation," I asked. "Are you going, too?"

They looked at the invitation and shook their heads. "I wish I was going," remarked Claude. "I'd love to have an opportunity to be in the medicinal plant fields in western China. It's the next great frontier in terms of plant exploration. By the way, is Sichuan in China or is that area Tibet?"

He reached for an atlas on his shelf and flipped the pages until he came to China. On the map, the word CHINA stretched across a huge area, with Tibetan Autonomous Region written in small letters to the west. "Hmm, looks like revisionist cartography to me, but China wouldn't be the first one to remake the map of the world in its own image," he said. "If you pass on this Erzebet, let me know. I'd like to be considered to go in your place."

I left my colleagues' office and continued down the hall to see Monsieur Bordelle. I sat across from him as he lit his pipe and rocked back in his chair, one foot resting in an open drawer.

"Why now?" I asked. "Why is the Sorbonne being invited to go to China now?"

"We had administrative meetings about this—before you received your invitation," he said, rifling through several pages of notes on his desk. "We're guessing China is looking to shine up its image a bit. I'm sure you've been reading the news about atrocities during the Cultural Revolution—events the rest of the world is only now learning about. Since Mao died, they're emerging from what appears like quite a mess, trying to partner with various countries for foreign investment. That sort of thing. Looks like they're trying to create some cultural exchange bridges and see us as a high profile partner. Not a bad thing for the Sorbonne—to be on the leading edge of research and cultural exchange with China."

"What about the language? Would I have a translator?"

"My understanding is that Peking University will provide a translator, but the department also has a lead on a woman right here in Paris who could teach you the rudiments of the Tibetan language. The department will pay for the classes if you want to work with her."

Back in my office, my eyes once again glued on the words Sichuan Province in the invitation. Girard's disappearance had clambered for attention in the background of my life for two decades. How could it not? Lilia was his moral and intellectual doppelgänger, on the edge of every cause, fighting for recognition of the underdog. But while my brilliant daughter with her father's eyes had grown to adulthood, I had refused to be emotionally tied to the past, though I never failed to question my own courage on the anniversary of his disappearance. This was a chance to heal myself in the mountain meadows and among the people he found so fascinating, a chance to come to truly peace with his death.

A ladder of honey sunlight shifted through the wooden blinds and fell squarely across a photo of Girard's smiling face—the day we first met in Paris. I had stopped to use the phone at a local club, in a hurry to reach an appointment across the city. He was sandwiched in a booth with a group of raucous friends, already drunk at 3:00 in the afternoon, toasting the publication of his first article in Le Monde. Complete with photos. Complete with a hefty check. Heady on success, he had deserted his friends at their table and introduced himself while I stood laughing at the phone. Two hours later, we were holding hands, walking along the Seine. The next morning he moved his small bag of clothes and cartons of books, cameras and film to my flat on Graumelde Lane and never left.

I reached across the desk to gather up the silver-framed photos, the figures as vibrant and alive as when they were taken years before. Girard running on the beach in Greece. Girard holding newborn Lilia wrapped in a flowered blanket, her tiny mouth curled in a smile although she was only a few days old. Lilia and Girard laughing in the garden as they pursued the chickens who pursued the snails who were intent on devouring the new green tomato plants. My throat tightened. He hadn't lived to see Lilia grow to be a woman.

Flipping the invitation over in my hands, I stared at the words in the light of the reading lamp, willing a decision from my gut rather than my mind. A primary concern was my father's health. He had been ill for several months. A second stroke followed a first; bleaching the color out of him and giving my humble father an angry edge. He had called his friends and colleagues less and less frequently and finally most had drifted away. His captivating smile had dissolved into tentative, purposeful attempts to lift the corners of his mouth. When we hugged him, we embraced a pine tree. His team of doctors advised the family to prepare for the worst, while we siblings strategized on a daily basis about how best to support our mother and father in the final days of his life. It was a tender and complicated emotional scenario. What if he died while I was in Tibet? Would it be possible to return home for the funeral or would I be mourning alone in a foreign country?

The weekend after the conversation with my department head, I was at the family home in Paris. My brothers had arrived that morning from the Spanish beaches. My sister had recently re-married. I was pouring tea for my parents and siblings, preparing to tell them all about the invitation to go to Tibet. It was spring and the chirps of children playing in the street bounced over the brick wall at the rear of the garden. We were celebrating life when my father's voice cracked the pastel ambience.

"What happened to that nice young boy you used to spend time with, Erzebet?" My father's mouth sagged slightly at the corner, a bit of spittle caught in the deep wrinkle like the joinery used on a wooden puppet. I leaned over and handed him a handkerchief, which he clumsily used to dab at his mouth.

"Who?" I replied. I had an uneasy feeling in the pit of my stomach. "Are you talking about Girard?"

"Girard? That doesn't sound right. The one who had all the cameras, you know who I mean. The one who traveled and took all the photographs for the newspaper."

"I think you're talking about Erzebet's husband, Girard," said Arnaud.

"No, not him. That's the man who died in Tibet and my daughter refused to look for the people who killed him." His skin was ashen, his eyes watery, his face stricken. "A sweet young woman, quite beautiful girl she was, was working day and night on the case, while my daughter, I can't remember which daughter right now. . ."

"PaPa," yelled out a Greek chorus of my siblings. They weren't going to let him offer me up again on the altar of callous spouses.

"My God, PaPa. . ." I stood up and gathered my things, grabbing at my purse strap, which hooked over the arm of the bench and tangled, pulling me back.

"Henri, what did I miss?" My mother stepped onto the patio laden down with treats for those lounging in the sun. "What happened to your laughing voices?"

"PaPa got a bit confused," broke in Arnaud. "It's nothing to be concerned about."

"Nothing?" my father refused to let the moment go by undamaged. He sputtered as he wrenched the syllables from his crooked mouth, a spray of spit riding the words into the alarmed atmosphere. "When my own daughter's husband is killed and she just gives up trying to find out what happened. In fact, she goes on without a second thought, never spending a minute trying to find out who killed him. You think that is nothing?"

"What could you be thinking by saying that again? We've talked about this, Henri." My mother's strained voice threatened my father to cut this conversation short, if he could.

Again? The word revolved slowly in my mind, a top seeking equilibrium, threatening to totter and clatter to the floor. So this was a recurring conversation that I had fortunately managed to avoid. Is that what he had really meant years before when he dismissed my jealousy of Marie-Heléne as having no relevance next to the search for information about Girard? I had focused on the accusation of jealous wife, but he had really intended to let me know he thought I was derelict in my duty to pursue my husband's murderers.

As if I hadn't written hundreds of letters and talked to scores of people trying to get information after Girard's disappearance. Does one hunt for the murderers of a husband forever? When does one get to stop? And if one is allowed to stop, then when is it appropriate to do so, and for what reasons. Is a grieving child reason enough? Who decides this? The analysis was not a natural, animal response to a tragedy, but a survival strategy. It had been almost two decades since Girard's death. The sheer despair over never seeing him again had muted many years ago and left me with a grave appreciation and respect for people who have family members who disappear. But one is never immune to the judgment of one's parents.

"Henri, for just this afternoon, couldn't we . . ." Tears slipped down my mother's cheeks. I felt sorry for her, but sought anesthesia for myself. In one brief conversation, my father had scraped the awful scab off a wound. For a moment, I wanted to retaliate, say something equally as calculated to destroy my father's fragile grip on happiness. But his remark was not calculated at all. It was the jangled warbling of a man going mad. It was a feeble gasp at organizing his mind and I was caught in the web being blown to pieces by the slightest breeze.

Arnaud groped for my hand. I could see he was sorting a mental thesaurus for the vocabulary of consolation for everyone present. There was none. My father looked at our group shifting on the edge of the filigree lawn chairs, tea growing cold in our cups, half-eaten biscuits reduced to nervous crumbs between our fingers. We stared back, waiting for a recant or for our mother to lead us back to a festive afternoon. It felt as if we would be waiting all the rest of our lives.

Four hours later, I was back in my own home in Paris, escaping to my journal, sorting through the thoughts and motivations that would encourage me to go to Tibet, or dictate that I not. Had I stopped hounding the French Government for information for Lilia's sake, or because I couldn't handle the grief I felt at having encouraged him to go to Tibet? The dull ache in my chest questioned if I had been a loving wife at all, or merely an angry, jealous woman. Girard's death, and my retreat from the pursuit of information that would explain it, resurfaced as brittle guilt.

The first mauve light of dawn filtered through the trees. I closed the notebook and put down my pen, massaging my neck and shoulders. Suddenly, the exhaustion was gone and I sat up in my chair, clear-headed for the first time in days. My shame at my father's words transmuted into straightforward resolution. I owed Girard this last effort as much as I owed it to Lilia and myself. Under the guise of participating in the scholar exchange, I would go to Tibet, find out who was responsible for Girard's death, and have them brought to justice. My whole body pulsed with a resurgence of light and energy I hadn't felt in years.

I dragged file boxes out of the cabinet in the study, sorting through until I found the folders from the months after Girard's disappearance. The thickest folder, labeled Marie-Heléne Cartier in precise script, had been sent to me sometime after the official investigation had closed. Inside were charts of contacts and responses, a veritable roadmap of the investigation—all tidily signed and completed three years after the fact. There was the original snapshot of the car, barely visible at the bottom of the ravine, and the enlarged photo that had been sent to the investigative team by the forensic specialist. Someone had drawn a red circle around the strange marks on the hillside beyond, a question mark next to the circle. There was a chart of locations, with distance from Chengdu, China to various towns on the Tibetan Plateau jotted into the margins. Some were checked off; some had question marks next to them. *Meniganggo* was underlined. Seeing Marie-Heléne's name and notes, I felt only a blunted heaviness, not the acute pain of past years. This was progress.

I started at the beginning and read until it was all virtually committed to memory. This material had been Phase One in the investigation. Phase Two, I would be on my own. I made a list of materials and contacts I would need, but possibly would not be able to attain until I was in Tibet—maps, names of government officials who had been in the area in 1958-1959, and local people Girard might have encountered.

I imagined walking into the Chinese Government offices and requesting the records from that period—death certificates, names of authorities who had investigated the scene of the accident. The officials would go through their files and give me documents pinpointing where Girard had travelled and died. From that start I would research the people who had controlled the region during that period of time. The new bureaucrats would have no stake in preventing me from finding out about Girard's death. It was all so long ago. My request would have no effect on officials now.

Tucked to the side in the box, was a packet of personal letters from Girard. In a letter dated March 1959, I saw a brief comment about the book he was writing and his visits to decimated monasteries. Adding monasteries to my list, I recalled that recent news reports suggested that thousands of Tibetan monasteries had been destroyed over the past twenty years. The last letter was a thin folded paper. Without even seeing the words I knew what it was. My hand hesitated. It was the final letter with the description of the prickly blue flower that had reminded Girard of me.

I reached for the phone and dialed Anja. "Anja, can you come over? I need to talk to you."

An hour later, we sat at the breakfast nook, a gray sky over the garden promising rain later in the afternoon. "Don't you find it strange the Chinese would give you a visa out of the blue?" said Anja, sipping her coffee as she scanned the invitation on the table. "What about Girard's work? Aren't they making that connection?"

"I'm sure I'd never have been invited if the Chinese Government connected me with Girard and his reporting."

"How could they not?" Anja arched her eyebrows. "The petitions we all signed, the letters to the newspapers, pushing the embassy to make some headway. I don't believe Girard's name, or yours, is so easily forgotten."

"If my name came up red-flagged, I wouldn't have received this invitation. There are plenty of people to invite besides me." I tried to sound nonchalant, but Anja had touched on a question I had myself. How had anyone with a modicum of research skills missed this? I followed her eyes to my fingernails, which beat out a staccato rhythm on the table edge. If I upset Anja, she would send the alarm to friends and family who would try to convince me to abandon my mission.

"What about Lilia?" said Anja. "Won't this journey open old wounds for her? Thinking of her mother in Asia where her father disappeared."

"Lilia's an adult now," I said, "not a seven-year-old child, but if she's distraught over my leaving for Tibet, I won't be on that flight."

When Anja left the house, I caught a taxi to the family home. I would be able to say good-bye to my siblings who were leaving to return to their own homes and tell my father about the trip to Tibet. I hoped it would be a lucid day, that he would be pleased I had been chosen, and he could show it. Only with my father would I share my plan to avenge Girard, to honor Girard. I didn't care if his recent accusation had been from the mouth of a dying man whose eyes grew blank when faced with the dilemma of what to do when he held a tea bag in one hand and a cup of hot water in the other. Even as a grown woman, I yearned for his absolution, a signal that despite illness and depression, he could find it in his heart to reach out to me.

My mother met me halfway up the stone walkway, walking as if asleep.

"He's gone." She reached out for my arm to steady herself and seemed to shrink by several inches right before my eyes.

"Why didn't someone call me?" I heard my voice devolve into the plea of a little girl.

"It was another stroke. It happened so quickly. . ."

My father had taken his last breath just minutes before, with my sister and three brothers at his side. We gathered in the sunroom and my sister recounted the morning events.

"At the moment of his death," she reported like an impartial journalist, filling me in on the smallest details I had missed. "He was confused about what he believed, why he lived, afraid to let go. He stared at the bedroom ceiling, his eyes hollow and glazed." Despite final hour coaching from those in the family who were Christian and those who were Buddhist and those who wished they believed anything at all, he died with no prayer on his lips.

I sat next to the bed and gazed at his thinning white hair in disarray, damp with sweat, a crop of grey bristles sticking out of his ears. I placed my hand on his chest and felt for the slightest movement that would indicate a last remnant of breath escaping from his lungs. His body was still.

There would be no absolution for me.

The Tibet invitation temporarily migrated to the bottom of a pile that now held wills, newspaper obituaries, names of caterers, photos, and lists of friends and family to be informed about the funeral arrangements.

An hour before the memorial service at the Church of Saint Germaine-des-Pres, mother, Lilia, and I pushed open the metal doors. A wispy cloud of incense traveled in the vestibule, rising and falling in sunlight, which streamed through the red and ultramarine stained glass windows. Sweet frankincense cloaked the air. Ponderous and familiar, "Requiem for A Beloved Man," cascaded down from the organ hidden in the balcony. Arnaud met us as we entered the rear of the church and put his arm around my shoulders. I knew he guessed what was on my mind. We were doing everything we could to say a perfect farewell to our father, but I had had no such chance for completion with Girard. I buried my face in Arnaud's jacket as we greeted the next group of arriving mourners and went to sit in the first pews.

Morris Cline delivered the eulogy. Taking off his glasses to wipe his eyes, he wove a story of how he and my father had been classmates in the south of France. The two boys studied together until my father, at the age of fourteen, was forced to leave school to support his family.

"It has been more than seventy years since we met," finished Mr. Cline. "Seventy years without a moment of anger or mistrust between us. There is a saying that all things are connected like the blood that flows through a family, but I could not ask for a better brother, even though we did not share the same blood."

Two hours later, mourners said their good-byes, taking home photos from the memorial table to remind them of their relative, friend and colleague. The last of my father's friends to leave were the Clines.

"You know, dear," said Mrs. Cline, hugging me. She turned me so I could not avoid looking straight into her eyes. "You seem so stoic. . . I know things weren't going so well with your father, but. . ."

"I can't hide from you, can I?" I said, my mouth did the tense pucker it used to betray me when I wanted to hide my feelings. My eyes brimmed with tears. "I've been numb for some time. It's the suddenness. Isn't it always the suddenness of death, even if you've been expecting it for years?"

"Take care of yourself, Erzebet. It may take some time," she said, squeezing my hand. "Let Morris and me know if you need us. We're always happy for the opportunity to spend more time with you." She looked for her husband and crossed the hall to be by his side.

I was in the nearly empty reception hall, idly pushing bits of half-eaten cookies and sandwiches around on a plate when Anja approached.

"Mr. Cline's eulogy was lovely, Erzebet. Your father was lucky to have such devoted friends and family. Now it makes sense to take some time and sort out your own future. How does Tibet fit into that picture?"

I couldn't believe she would bring this up again. The night before she had questioned the wisdom of going to Tibet so soon after my father's death and I had changed the subject as quickly as possible. Now, I methodically stacked plates on the table, saucers into one pile, and dessert plates into another.

"Erzebet, look at me, my friend." I cringed. My own resolve had gotten shaky in the last days. The last thing I needed was for someone to throw me back into the muddled state of mind I had been forcing to the side.

"You seem strangely detached, which doesn't surprise me. It is your father's funeral," Anja said. "But there's something else going on. Will you still go to Tibet?"

"Yes, I'm going ahead with my plans." I averted my eyes again and reached for the cups and saucers, pushing them toward the center of the table. "I want to paint in the mountains while I sort things out in my life."

"Won't it be upsetting to be in Asia?" Anja stumbled through her concerns. "Do you really think it's wise to go?"

"I don't know what's wise anymore," I said. "When I saw the invitation, my first thought was, 'This is it. This is my true farewell to Girard.' PaPa's death has added another stratum of sadness to my life. I need an experience outside myself to tug me out of my emotional lethargy."

"You think traveling to Tibet is going to give you peace in terms of Girard?"

"Going to Tibet to work on my issues with Girard seems easy somehow, although it might seem radical to someone else."

"Anyone else would be more aptly put," said Anja, shaking her head. "I sense you've got more on your mind than you're telling me. You are going to the land where Girard died to paint flowers? Nice try, my friend, but it doesn't all fit to me. You aren't thinking of pursuing an investigation into Girard's death? You know how crazy that would be. You don't talk about it anymore, but I know you still carry guilt over not driving yourself harder to find out what happened to him."

"It was a long time ago," I said. Luckily, Lilia approached carrying a tray of cookies and I held out my hand to her. My daughter brushed the white lock of hair off my forehead and cocked her head with a puzzled frown at the conversation's last strings.

"We're talking about your mother's trip to Tibet, Lilia," said Anja.

"You're not thinking about putting it off are you, Maman? I've already told you I think it will be good for you to go and paint in the mountains. It's right for you to take some time for yourself after all the months worrying about GrandPaPa." She kissed me and crossed the room to visit with her uncles.

"Her mother's daughter," said Anja. "You two are quite the pair. However, I'm a harder sell. Tell me the truth, are you thinking about resurrecting the investigation into Girard's death?"

"I'm sure it would be impossible to surface information now," I turned slightly to Anja, trying to make my words casual, my face open and composed. "You know me, don't worry."

"Don't shortchange my intelligence or our years of friendship, Erzebet," said Anja. "It's precisely because I do know you that I am worrying."

# CHAPTER 6

## *From the Depths of the Ocean*

| | |
|---|---|
| *Rang sem song pa'ae mee te* | *The one I love* |
| *Den gyi tun mar jung na* | *If I could only wed her* |
| *Gya tso'e deeng nam nor bu* | *From the ocean depths would come the jewel* |
| *Tab nga rang che chok* | *To me, the choicest gem of all* |

*-Sixth Dalai Lama*

## Erzebet's Story

### Paris, France: April 1978

The unmistakable fruity fragrance of Fantin-Latour roses greeted me as soon as I unlocked my office door on the crisp April morning. My eyes darted around the room, landing on my writing table. The flowers had been placed in a crystal vase filled with water, probably put there early in the morning by the Botany Department receptionist. Named after the 19th century French impressionist who was famous for his floral still-lifes, the blush pink roses could only have come from true plant enthusiasts. An envelope was attached with a green ribbon to the stem of one of the roses. I slipped out an ivory card. 'Erzebet, please come to London and join us for dinner at our home next Tuesday evening. You leave soon on the Chinese expedition and it's been too long since we've seen you.' The card was signed by Morris and Althea Cline.

The phone rang.

"Hello, Erzebet? It's Marie-Heléne Cartier. We haven't seen each other in years, but I heard you will be going to Tibet to paint and I wanted to wish you well…"

Laying the receiver on the desk, I walked out of the office, and down the corridor to the staff kitchen. I poured myself a cup of coffee and read the morning news, pushing Marie-Heléne's voice as far into the background of my life as I could. After several minutes, I went back to my office, put the insistently droning receiver back in the phone cradle and went on with my work.

Tuesday morning I took an early flight to London from Paris, spent the day at the British Museum and was on the Tube to Kew Gardens Station by late afternoon. In The Economist on the plane, I read that the Chinese were negotiating for a $1.2 billion loan with the British Government. The loan would help them build much-needed infrastructure in their country, which had been depleted of resources during the Mao years.

The Clines lived only a half block from the Royal Botanic Gardens at Kew. Dinner with them was always an experience from another era and this evening was no exception; tea while perched on velvet chairs in the sitting room, dinner of game hens glazed with a light brandied sauce and perfectly-sautéed imported white asparagus. Mr. Cline had been with the British Foreign Service in Asia during the 1930's and 1940's—a period of time in his life that was always hastily brushed over if a reference came up in a social conversation. But their home reflected his exciting past. It glowed with original Tiffany lamps, each segment of the glass exuding flower petals of warm golds and oranges, leaves of quivering greens and blues. There were framed Chinese imperial robes, exquisite Persian carpets and bronze statues of the long-horned African kudu.

The dinner conversation focused on everyone's speculations about why the Chinese Government would be issuing educational exchange invitations now. Mr. Cline guessed that the scholarly exchange could smooth the way for the loan I'd read about—demonstrating to the finance titans that they were, indeed, global citizens again and capable of doing business on a world-wide scale.

After dinner, the three of us walked through the Clines' maze of manicured gardens, a wonderland of rare plants—30-foot high trees, magnificent flowering bushes, all grown from seed brought out of Asia over a forty year period. As children, we had loved to pretend we were Mr. Cline in his cloak and dagger role with the Foreign Service, running off after chasing spies to collect seeds in the hill country, smuggling them back to England to be planted in the special greenhouses.

As the final light disappeared in the garden, we entered the family art gallery through the beveled glass doors. The 20-foot high walls were covered with 17th and 18th century scientific botanical illustrations, echoing their fascination with Asian flora. Many had been purchased from estate sales and museums. A blank space on the wall was reserved for the one painting they craved--an original illustration of the Tibetan blue poppy.

"Might you be willing to illustrate this fabulous plant if you find it in Tibet? We can go to the archives at Kew and show you photos, sketches of the blue poppy and watercolor studies completed years ago in the Himalayas."

"It's late, Morris," Mrs. Cline admonished. "Shouldn't Erzebet be getting back to her hotel? She probably has to leave early in the morning for work in Paris."

"We can run over to Kew right now, if she's willing," said Mr. Cline. "I'm sure Gerald will let us through the gate."

"I'd love to do that," I said, remembering the weekend when I was eight and the Clines taught me to roller skate on the Broad Walk between the Palm House and the Pagoda. "I'm always fascinated at what you can dig up in the archives—that no one else ever seems to get to see."

Mr. Cline brought a shawl and gently wrapped it around his wife's shoulders. We walked the short distance down the street to the main gate, where, indeed, Gerald was on duty and waved us through with a nod and a smile. "Have a lovely time Mr. and Mrs. Cline. And enjoy the fragrance of the night blooming jasmine as you walk under the last archway."

In the archives, Mr. Cline went directly to the section with the journals of explorers who had seen the blue poppy in Tibet, some books dating back to the late 1800's. The browning pages had rough pencil sketches, but in the archive drawers were watercolors completed in Nepal over 100 years before. There was also a tray of photos of the plant, taken by Chinese botanists in the early 1950's.

"No one even knows if the *Meconopsis horridula* can grow below 16,000 feet," Mr. Cline said, taking off his bifocals to better examine the blue flower with the magnifying glass. I balanced on a stool next to him, a prickly sensation crawling at the base of my neck as I stared at the photo. Words from Girard's letter floated into my consciousness.

'It reminds me of you when you're in a bristly mood…'

My head spun. This was the flower Girard had teased me about. Mr. Cline had inadvertently helped me make a critical connection and opened a door to my quest. The Tibetan blue poppy grew in the same area where Girard had disappeared. If I could find the flower, I would have narrowed the search for where he had spent his final days—perhaps where he had actually been killed.

". . .the *Meconopsis betanicifolia*, a related poppy, was discovered by a missionary, Pere Delavay, in 1886," Mr. Cline continued as he thumbed through the pages of antique journals. "Then nearly forty years later, Kingdon-Ward sent seeds from Tibet. However, what I consider the true Tibetan blue poppy, the *Meconopsis horridula*, I do not believe seeds have ever been brought out of Chinese-Occupied Tibet. Partly because the timing is critical, the best seeds would be gathered in the late summer."

"Seeds?" I picked up my pen and sketched from the photos. It would be impossible to forget the almost lurid blue of the petals, the thorns or the placement of the blossoms, several flowers on one stalk instead of the familiar *Papaveraceae* display of one blossom per stem. "What would the seeds look like?"

"Quite small and black, like those of other poppies," he said. "But we don't need to talk about seeds. You're going to Tibet to paint, not collect seeds. The best time to complete your botanical illustration in the wild will be during the earlier summer months, if the rains have started early enough."

"I'll do my best, Mr. Cline. It's the least I can do for you. You know, you're family to me." Watching the fragile elderly couple holding hands at the archive table, a pang of melancholy overtook me as I remembered Mr. Cline referring to his wife as the most precious jewel in his life. For me, embracing love again after Girard had been difficult. Yes, I had lovers, men who were devoted to me and adored Lilia. But love had been elusive and over time these romantic liaisons evaporated.

As we walked back along the sculpted pathways, past the ponds of Kew, Mrs. Cline slowed down and patted my arm. She looked up at me and whispered, "Don't let Morris know I told you this, but it's been his life-long regret to have never grown the blue poppy from seed. If you were able to bring back seeds…I know it's against the law. . . perhaps hidden in your luggage. . .," she faltered.

"Mrs. Cline," I lowered my voice so her husband had no chance to hear the conversation. "Are you asking me to smuggle seeds out of Tibet?"

"It sounds almost dastardly when you say it that way, Erzebet," Mrs. Cline leaned in so close I smelled the powder in her blue-tinted hair. "But if Morris could grow this poppy in the West, to its full glory as in Tibet, he would be the envy of Asian plant enthusiasts and members of the Blue Flower Guild the world over."

We walked arm in arm over to Mr. Cline who absent-mindedly plucked at a clump of grass along the path. I imagined him walking with my father along the roads of southern France, two friends coming from vastly different circumstances. It was Mr. Cline who first gave me clues about one possible source of my father's depression: regrets for a life he viewed as compromised because he was an uneducated man. Now, catching the twinkle in his eye, I made my second major decision related to Tibet. I would add the search for the Tibetan blue poppy seeds to my investigation into Girard's death. It would be a gift to my father as well as Mr. Cline. Searching for blue poppy seeds could not be nearly as daunting as hunting for Girard's killers.

"One more thing, Erzebet," Mr. Cline said. The domed greenhouse rose as a Chinese lantern above the trees behind him. "You might find it interesting to know the legend of the turquoise bee and the blue poppy. The insect is camouflaged as a golden bee, but during a full moon night, it becomes enamored with the blue poppy and searches the meadows and the mountains to pollinate this seductive flower."

"Morris, dear," Mrs. Cline kissed her husband on the cheek. "You are an incurable romantic. You'll have our adventurous Erzebet searching for turquoise bees as well as blue poppies if you keep this up."

"That's a lovely fairy tale," I said, laughing, as Mrs. Cline wandered off down the walkway. "I've heard a bit about it before, and I'd love to hear more. Don't stop."

"Alright then, here's the rest of the myth. As the bee's ardor heightens, his body gradually transforms to turquoise blue. His nights and days infuse with the dream of the blue poppy until he buries himself in the flower and is sated."

He stopped as a man suddenly appeared from beyond the stately palm trees and nodded at the Clines, tipping his hat to me. He looked familiar. With a shock, I realized it was the former editor of Le Monde, Nicholas Munro. He was dressed in a rumpled suit, stooped over and his hair was completely white, his face a map of rivulets. After Girard's disappearance, Munro, under fire for having sent Girard in to China on what had been determined was a spying mission, had stepped down as editor at Le Monde, and retired to his place in the country. I hadn't thought about him in years.

"Nicholas," I said, "what a surprise to see you. What are you doing here at Kew at this hour?"

Mr. Cline said in a low voice, "I asked Nicholas to come tonight, Erzebet."

He gripped my arm. "Don't let Althea know I suggested this, but we wonder if you might engage in a little skullduggery and find out what happened to Girard while you're in Tibet. You've got the Chinese Government's permission to be there, it may be the chance…"

"The investigation into Girard's death can be resuscitated," Nicholas said. "It's never too late to bring new information forward."

"I heard that," Mrs. Cline called from where she had been inspecting the bark of the palm trees. "Find out about Girard? Don't you two be encouraging Erzebet to do any such thing. Have you taken leave of your senses?"

"Althea's got the ears of a puma," Mr. Cline muttered, grazing his hand over the top of the sculpted hedge.

"It's okay, Mrs. Cline, don't worry about me," I said, as she came close, shaking her head in displeasure at the conversation. "Please continue. Your advice will be invaluable. . . "

Nicholas remained in the shadow of the palms. "Erzebet, if you have the chance to find out anything about Girard's notes he kept while he was in Tibet. . ."

"It's been nearly twenty years," I said. "It's hard to imagine those notes would still be around. Surely if they existed they would have surfaced by now."

"The information he died for would still be of great benefit to the Tibetan cause," continued Nicholas. "You may not be aware, but I've continued to stay apprised of the Tibetan situation. It's never too late to confront an oppressor for their brutal deeds."

"Don't think you'll just walk into the government offices and request records," added Mr. Cline. "These days they aren't used to having foreigners in their midst. You'll have to be more covert than that. Just focus on your painting documentation, but also you're your eyes and ears open to getting information from the nomads and villagers who surround you. The best information always comes from people who trust you and have reason to care about your mission."

"That's the best advice these decrepit old agents can give you," said Nicholas. "I know you're wise about politics over there, but do be careful, the Chinese authorities will have someone watching you at all times."

Baffled about the direction the night had taken, I turned to Mr. Cline for more information, and when I looked back the editor had disappeared.

"Mr. Cline, how do you know Nicholas Munro?"

"Nicholas and I were in INTERPOL together—in Asia. He was just a young chap, but even then, he had a taste for living on the edge. Nicholas had met the Dalai Lama when he was a child and did everything he could to stop the takeover of Tibet, but it wasn't enough. I don't have to tell you how roundly he was bashed by the journalistic community after Girard's death—people felt he had put Girard in grave danger, and turns out they were right. It broke him personally and professionally."

So, Nicholas and I had something in common—we had both encouraged Girard to go to Tibet—and we both felt remorse for having done so.

"Be safe on your journey, dear, these old spies sometimes get carried away," said Mrs. Cline, winking at me as we arrived back at the main gate and she hugged me good-bye.

I walked to the Tube, watching the couple stroll down the tree-covered lane to their home. Raising my arm to brush the hair out of my eyes, the lingering scent of cologne on my coat sleeve remained a reminder of Mrs. Cline's poignant request for the blue poppy seeds.

# CHAPTER 7

## *The Sun and the Moon Revolve*

| | |
|---|---|
| *U gyu ree gyel lhun po* | *The king of the central mountain* |
| *Mee gyur den par shook thang* | *Stands steadfast and unswerving* |
| *Nyee ma da wa'ee gor chok* | *The sun and the moon revolve* |
| *Nor yong sem pa meen dook* | *And no one thinks this is an error* |

*- Sixth Dalai Lama*

## Erzebet's Story

### Chengdu, China: May 1978

Chengdu was the Western Chinese entry point for the few travelers who received permission to enter the Tibetan Plateau. Waiting for my final permits, I spent my time there gazing out the window at the charcoal horizon, a brew of acrid smoke. People in the streets wore cloth facemasks as if heading to the surgery theater, protecting others from their illnesses and protecting themselves from inhaling the smoggy air. Mornings at my hotel were a disturbing concert of hacking and coughing as the city cleared its lungs and prepared for the day.

Then one afternoon, I received a notice saying my permits were ready and I should be packed and ready to leave for the Tibetan nomad territory the next morning. An hour later, a man in a khaki uniform appeared at my hotel door. He notified me that the next morning, instead, I must appear for interviews with the Public Security Bureau, the PSB. At first I was bewildered. It might be that one department had created this scholar exchange, and the others knew nothing of it, and my papers had gotten caught in the middle. Then a dull fear crept in. The PSB had a reputation for enforcement of the "social order" in China—arrests, beatings and public humiliation of people during the Cultural Revolution. They were the department that had sent the official notification letter after Girard's death. I steadied myself for the possibility of my visa being withdrawn at the last minute. If the connection with Girard were to be made, this would be the time.

I telephoned the French Embassy.

"I need a translator." It wasn't until I heard my own ragged words riding on a surge of panic that I recognized the level of my anxiety. I set the phone down, while I took a deep breath.

"Madame," the voice on the telephone said after a few seconds of silence. "Madame, are you still there?"

"I'm a French citizen. I need help."

I was passed from one perplexed department to another, each one asking me to repeat what I was doing in China and what exactly the PSB had requested in terms of an interview. With each conversation, my voice took on a more nervous edge.

Finally, I was connected with Monsieur Gaston Lavonte, main translator for the French Embassy.

"So sorry for the inconvenience Madame Pelletier. We've had a change of staff recently and they aren't all up to speed. Of course, we know of the work you'll be doing on the Tibetan Plateau, and I am available to accompany you to the PSB offices for your appointment. Nothing to worry about, is there?"

"I don't think so. . ." My voice trailed off.

"How about if I come by your hotel in a bit and we go over your documents just to make sure? Would that be convenient for you?"

I thanked him and hung up the phone, trying to quell the chatter of my mind. Had the Chinese officials discovered that, before I left France, I had contacted people who had long ago been key in the investigation into Girard's death?

Within the hour, Lavonte arrived at my hotel room.

"It all seems to be in order," he said as he looked at my passport and visa and reviewed the original invitation letter. "This request for an interview is from the PSB division that deals with foreigner travel. They're new—a bit overzealous at times, but this kind of questioning is routine. Your credentials are faultless. You were first on the list of candidates suggested by the Chinese Government and Peking University. I'll be with you during the interview. I'm sure you'll be able to leave for the countryside within the next few days."

I woke at dawn to tinny loudspeakers blaring the Chinese national anthem and exhorting the population to get out and do their exercises.

Lavonte picked me up at my hotel at 7:45am and we drove through the hordes of bicycles and human-drawn carts to the PSB offices. Two women at the site of an overturned vegetable cart yelled at each other, drawing a crowd, which tried to separate them. The enormous red cabbages and carrots like orange batons were scattered in the street. School children in blue uniforms and caps with a red star skirted the confrontation, marching by in military precision lines. People stared in the car windows and withdrew to the edges of the street as we passed; they clustered in groups watching the official car's progress down the boulevard.

At the PSB offices, we were shown into a cement block room with a long green metal table where five men sat waiting. They had identical black-rimmed glasses and haircuts like mushroom caps. The man on the end wore a dark blue shirt and pants; the others all dressed in khaki uniforms, the same except for name badges I couldn't translate.

"Please take a seat," the man in the center said to Monsieur Lavonte and me, indicating chairs directly across the table from the five men.

"Your name, Madame?" said the lead interrogator reading the document in front of him.

"Erzebet Pelletier." He checked off the information as correct on his paper.

"Your age, Madame?" The questioner had the tiniest twitch in his right cheekbone. It did not seem to influence any other parts of his face to behave in a similar fashion. A keyhole pupil in the chestnut-brown eye of the man next to him threatened to run into the white sclera.

"Forty-eight." I adjusted my face into an agreeable half-smile.

The PSB team took turns asking questions. A few categories came up repeatedly, yet they scrutinized my responses each time as if I might say something contradictory.

"What do you think about the Government of the People's Republic of China, Madame? About Communism? Do you follow the Dalai Lama?" I tried to keep my mind off the recently reported atrocities of Buddhist monks and nuns being beaten and killed for daring to raise a Tibetan flag at their monasteries.

At 10:15, an astonishingly beautiful woman in a khaki uniform entered the room, carrying a tray. She poured a choice of Nescafe coffee, tea or hot water and offered salt or sweet biscuits. During the break, the police smoked cigarettes in a corner of the room and received messages delivered by men I guessed were government clerks. From time to time, they looked over at me, nodded and scribbled notes.

Sipping tea, I reminded myself I had not sought out this expedition. They had invited me. Obviously, these men had missed this crucial bit of information. Back in the interview room, I fought to stay alert, devising a game that consisted of taking note of subtle differences in my interrogators. The man in the middle had a large mole on his neck that peeked out from underneath his starched collar as he talked. It appeared and then disappeared, riding with the movement of his Adam's apple. Three black hairs curved out of the center and waved when he spoke. On his right, the officer mopped at a trickle of sweat starting just behind his right ear and running down to soak his shirt collar, a dark oval stain. The man at the end of the table was impeccable, with clear skin and long eyelashes. His back was rod straight. When he opened his mouth, however, his stained teeth were just a few shades lighter than his caramel skin. He did not interact with his fellow interrogators and from time to time; I thought I heard a soft clicking sound coming from inside his cheek.

The next round of questions focused on whom I might know in Tibet. It took two hours to convince them, if I did indeed convince them, that I knew no one.

"Are you doing alright?" asked Monsieur Lavonte during the lunch break as we sat on benches at the edge of an empty plaza.

Pigeons strutted by, heads bobbing for grain, and flew up in a grey cloud to roost in the eaves of the complex. "Why are they asking me the same questions over and over again?"

"It's designed to break you down--see if you won't eventually tell them something different, something incriminating."

"Incriminating?" The hair stood up on my arms. "A woman going to Tibet to paint wildflowers? How devious can I be?"

"Well, that's what they want to know," he said, "How devious can you be?" He let out a short chuckle and then cut it short as we both noticed the interrogator in the blue shirt standing nearby, leaning against a pole. He was staring at a newspaper.

After lunch, the questioning started anew, with similar queries. "What books are you carrying? Do you speak Tibetan?"

I had been told I would have a translator on the Plateau, and it suddenly occurred to me that I should not tell them I had been studying Tibetan during the last months.

"No, only German, French and English," I said.

Maybe this was also the time to get a sense of how long I might be detained in Chengdu—to suggest the questioning was going nowhere. "Pardon me, Sir, but I have answered the same questions over and over again. I'm an artist. My intention is solely to complete this plant documentation as part of the education exchange."

I planned to say this with a straightforward, professional demeanor, but my own emotions betrayed me. My voice broke and two cool spots of tears gathered at the corner of my eyes. The man at the end of the table reached behind him without taking his eyes off me and picked up a box of tissues from a ledge, sliding it toward me. I pulled a tissue out and dabbed at my eyes.

Monsieur Lavonte quickly said, "Just answer the questions. Don't make any expression and certainly don't question them. And don't cry. Do you have your invitation with you? Show them that."

I took the invitation from the packet of papers in my purse and handed it to the lead questioner who then conferred with his colleagues. They passed the document back and forth as if they had never seen it before, each man inspecting it, holding it up to the light, and looking puzzled. Only the man on the end did not look surprised. He took a perfunctory glance and handed it back to the main interviewer. My back ached and I felt a migraine headache sparking at the base of my skull. The smell of the lingering cigarette smoke from the police smoking during the break went straight to my brain. I rubbed my lower back with my hand, and pulled my shoulders up to release the stiffness from sitting for hours on the hard wooden chair. My neck and spine cracked with a rhythmic popping.

"Can't Madame Pelletier be excused for the day?" said the translator. "She is tired. Not feeling well." Abruptly, the interview was over and we were sent out into the humid, grey air of Chengdu.

That evening I walked along the canal accompanied by my assigned guide, a Chinese police officer named Xiao Ping. She was a formal young woman with shiny black braids and spoke only a few words of French. We sat at a café along the tree-lined canal and smiled at each other. Xiao Ping watched me like an exotic creature or perhaps, I thought, as one would watch a small animal trying to squeeze through the bars of its cage. Families stopped to joke with men hunched over board games, the men's pants legs rolled up to their thighs to keep cool in the evening heat. With Xiao Ping observing everything that was going on, I sensed I shouldn't be too friendly to the women or their children along the canal. Men poled narrow boats hung with lanterns up and down the waterway. They delivered squawking ducks and chickens to buyers crowded at the foot of steps leading down into the water.

I drank green tea, the steam rising through my fingers, mingling with the pungent odor of fish flopping in rattan baskets on the ground next to us. The dank, muddy smell of the river and the fish took me back to the years of buying fishing lures as gifts for both Girard and my father--the brass June bug spinners with the red bead, the turquoise feathered Sardeena flies, and the olive iridescent damselfly. I felt hopeful that I was near tying up loose ends from an entire segment of my life.

The second day began the same as the one preceding: a breakfast of dry toast, weak tea and hard-boiled eggs in the hotel dining room. The only guest, I sat at a banquet table with a cloth that did not even try to mask dried food scraps stuck in the creases. My colleagues, working on their own educational exchange projects, had started their assignments days before, and I saw them only in passing in the hallways. The same official car picked me up for the short drive to the PSB office.

Before we got into the vehicle, Monsieur Lavonte looked at me quizzically. "I thought this was a routine interview, but it seems unlikely they would put so much sleuthing effort into the journey of a botanical illustrator. Any idea what they're getting at with these questions?"

"I really don't know." I shook my head. His eyes followed my sweating hands as I wiped them on my skirt.

By the middle of the morning's questioning, my projected nonchalance evaporated. I lapsed back into a childhood habit of twirling my hair around my middle finger, creating a corkscrew that quickly straightened when left to its own devices. I jiggled my foot and kicked the table leg creating a thud that caused everyone to look under the table for the source.

Taking a deep breath, I caught the eye of the handsome interrogator. He gazed at me, his chin cupped in his hand, his fingers curled over his mouth. I had erred outright by not saying Girard Pelletier was my husband. It was obvious the French Embassy had not caught the omission on the visa application, and now there was suspicion here. They knew there was something amiss, although they weren't quite sure what. There would be repercussions for the Sorbonne University and my career if they decided I had purposely misled the expedition coordinators.

I excused myself and walked down the dark corridor to the bathroom where I splashed cold water on my face and attempted to pull myself together. Staring in the chunk of broken mirror glued to the wall, I smoothed my hair. I needed to knock this bureaucratic morass off center. I decided I would tell the investigators I intended to focus my research efforts on not only painting, but collecting the *Meconopsis horridula* poppy seeds. I guessed they would never allow this, as I had not applied for the documents necessary to export plant materials from Asia. Back in France, it had seemed like one more layer that might call unnecessary attention to my time in Tibet. My admission now, however, would give the investigators something to take back to their superiors—something to say, "We did the job. She broke under questioning and revealed her true travel intentions." They might then allow me to go ahead. There was nothing to lose.

Seated once again in the cement room, I was ready to inform Monsieur Lavonte I had something to tell the investigative team. Before I could speak up, a man in a uniform with ribboned badges and gold stars walked in and handed the team a sheaf of papers in a folder. There ensued a spate of hushed conversations between the questioners and the team leader stepped out into the hall with the man in the uniform. The window in the door rattled as the two men in the corridor yelled at each other. When the leader came back into the room, his face was a worrisome purple. He quickly stamped my travel papers, scribbled his signature on each page with a trembling hand, and mumbled what had the tone of a placating apology to Monsieur Lavonte.

"They're ready to let you leave, but you need to agree to certain conditions before you are given the final permits," Monsieur Lavonte said evenly. "I'm sure you'll be happy to do that, won't you?"

The lead questioner took the list of rules for the journey out of the final folder and passed them across the table. Each page had a line for my signature at the bottom. Jumping off the page was the restriction I was not allowed to take plant material (defined as flowers, stems, roots, seedpods and the like) out of Tibet and I must not travel beyond a forty-kilometer radius from Manigango in Western Sichuan Province. Manigango? Was that the same as Meniganggo—the location underlined in Marie-Heléne's notes? An attached map defined the area designated for the botanical research. It neared the border of the Tibetan Autonomous Region where demonstrations by Tibetan villagers against the Chinese occupation occurred on a regular basis.

I signed and dated the papers.

The team leader held out a clammy hand to me. "Good luck, Madame Pelletier. We sincerely hope you have a successful journey. We look forward to seeing your illustrations of the wildflowers. You may leave tomorrow, if you wish. Tea?"

Just as Monsieur Lavonte and I gathered our things to leave, one of the interrogators stepped forward from behind the desk. He was the attractive man who had never spoken; the one with the long eyelashes and tarnished teeth.

"Madame," he said, staring straight at me, and speaking in flawless French. "Let me present myself. My name is Zhang Kai Lun. My government has assigned me to be your guide and translator. I will make all travel arrangements and accompany you for the summer."

While speaking, he had the odd habit of tracing the contour of his face with his forefinger--from the forehead, down the bridge of the nose, outlining the lips and chin, as if he were a blind man committing his own profile to tactile memory.

"Mr. Zhang will be most useful to you, Madame Pelletier," said the main interrogator who had been standing to the side. "Let him know anything you need for a pleasant journey." He nodded at the translator once again, appearing to give him permission to continue speaking.

Mr. Zhang consulted a paper he took from his pocket and gave me instructions about when to be ready to leave for the Tibetan Plateau. He had an extraordinary vocabulary. I guessed he must have acquired his foreign language skills before the Cultural Revolution halted those anti-patriotic intellectual pursuits. Though he was deferential and soft-spoken, he stared unblinking into my eyes, not dropping his gaze until I finally looked away.

"What happened?" I whispered to Monsieur Lavonte as we walked down the hall and out of the building, just past 5:00. "What was the big change in the questioning?"

"I'm not sure. Something about a mistake. This department didn't realize your papers were already in order. Enthusiastic bureaucrats. I think they've been called on the carpet by their supervisors for putting you through this. Let's get out of here before someone changes their mind."

"What about that man, Mr. Zhang, who will go with me to Tibet?" I said as we stood on the step of the PSB building, the official car just pulling up in front. "He gives me the chills. He was listening to all of our conversations. I didn't even know he could understand French." I turned around to look at Mr. Zhang again as we walked down the steps. Tall and thin, he dressed like every man on the street in China with his standard issue glasses, navy blue shirt and matching pants that ended just above his anklebone. He wore spit-shined black shoes and white socks. His left foot splayed as if he was about to plié.

"I agree with you. There's something strange about all of this. . ."

Monsieur Lavonte began to speak and then halted mid-sentence as Xiao Ping, her pigtails swinging, appeared and climbed into the back seat of the car. There was no more talking as we maneuvered our way through the bicyclists and rickshaw pullers, driving across the city.

"You'll be alright?" Monsieur Lavonte asked me when we arrived at the hotel, inclining his head toward Xiao Ping, who had already gotten out of the car and was holding the door open for me. He reached in his wallet and handed me a card with his personal number on it. "Don't hesitate to call me at home if you need me."

"I'm fine," I said, not feeling so sure. "I don't know what else could happen today. I feel a bit sick, to tell you the truth. I think I just need to rest."

Xiao Ping followed me into the lobby and up to my room. She sat down in a chair next to the bed, her face an expressionless mask. I fell into a threadbare armchair, focusing my eyes beyond the yellow and brown streaks on the window. Cement buildings across the boulevard vied with the permanently overcast sky for the right to depress.

"Fut massagey?"

"I'm sorry," I said, trying to understand her French, or English, whichever it was she had spoken. "What did you say?"

"I know fut massagey," said Xiao Ping, reaching over to remove my shoes. She took my foot into her hand and massaged methodically, pressing her fingers deep into the tissue along the arch, into the recesses above my heel.

I awoke as out of a coma. I had no idea how long I had slept. Xiao Ping sat on the edge of the bed, my clothes for the trip stacked around her, and my art supplies arranged in small piles. This woman had intentionally put me to sleep so she could search through my luggage. I had a momentary sense of panic and mentally reviewed what I carried. Nothing of consequence.

"Madame trade clothes?" said Xiao Ping.

"Trade clothes? What clothes?"

Out of her own bag, Xiao Ping brought out two lovely dresses, both with Mandarin collars and slits up the side. One was a harvest orange with a contrasting brocade pattern; the other was green with hummingbirds. She held them out and I went into the bathroom to try them on. They fit perfectly. I could wear them over pants. They were just loose enough to allow for silk long underwear if I needed it in the mountains. I came out smiling and hugged Xiao Ping, who stood stiffly, then bowed.

"They're lovely. What would you like in exchange?" I surveyed my pile of sweaters and rugged trousers for the journey.

"That." Xiao Ping pointed at a new pair of lace underwear, still in the cellophane package.

"They're yours." I opened the package and laid out on the bed the peach-colored panties and bra with the embroidered roses. Xiao Ping held them up in front of her, then stuck them in the pocket of her khaki police uniform, and left. I returned to the bathroom, balancing on the bathtub edge to admire myself in the mirror. The woman in the hummingbird dress had dark circles under her eyes and a drawn look around the mouth. The relentless questioning had gotten to me more than I wanted to admit.

I woke in the middle of the night, to the strangled sound of someone nearby calling for help. My heart pounding, I sat up and listened more closely. The only sounds from the street were muffled conversations of people running by, pulling creaking carts. The way I was breathing, I guessed I had called out in my sleep and woken myself up. Then I remembered the photos of the Dalai Lama I had hidden in an interior pocket of my art supply bag. The few European travelers who had come to Tibet told me these would be a most treasured possession for Tibetans. They also gave the warning that the Chinese Government forbade photos of the Dalai Lama so I must be cautious if I carried them.

The pocket inside the bag was unzipped. It had been opened, but the photos remained.

# CHAPTER 8

## *Afraid of the Devil's Horns*

| | |
|---|---|
| *Gyab gyi lu dun tsen po* | *The devil's horns in back are fierce* |
| *Jik tang mee jeek meen duk* | *I am afraid of them* |
| *Dun gyi gar a gu shu* | *The apples in front of me are ripe* |
| *Thok su dak pa che song* | *I have decided to go for them instead* |

*- Sixth Dalai Lama*

### Kai Lun's Story

Six months before I sat on the interrogation panel facing Madame Erzebet Pelletier, I had been an unremarkable employee of the local Chengdu Public Security Bureau. Then one day, Comrade Wang slid a message on to the corner of the desk, and said, "The Director came to the office while you were out. He asked if you spoke French or English. I said I didn't know." Comrade Wang did not meet my eyes. Had he reported me for interjecting a foreign word into a sentence without even realizing it? Lesser infractions had brought down others before me.

My foreign language literature books and language texts were sitting on the shelves and propped against the baseboard of my home. I had to get home immediately. I looked around the office at my colleagues, heads down, pens pushing out tedious reports no one would read. "My son isn't well, I have to take him to the doctor and will be back in an hour," I announced to no one at all.

I walked slowly down the hall, and then rushed from the building to my bicycle, my shirt plastered to the cold sweat pouring from my armpits. Straining over the chrome handlebars, I rapidly pedaled through the back lanes of the city, dropped the bicycle at the side of the apartment complex, and sprinted to the stairwell. Two of my PSB colleagues were already ascending the three flights of stairs to my apartment, their arms loaded with empty boxes. I opened the door to my apartment for them, relieved my wife and son were not at home to see my fear and degradation.

Their eyes scanned the small living room and they scooped up the rows of texts into the cartons, asking me to help carry a box down the stairs to the car. I had treasured these books since I was a child, yet it was necessary to act as if it was no concern. I cried out in my mind. No! Please, leave them. I'll sign a paper saying I'll never read them again. Just let them stay here, in my home! One box fell and the flaps ripped open, my precious books tumbling out one after another, gouged by the jagged concrete steps of the stairwell. My God, be careful! The neighbors clustered on their tiny balconies and watched the procession. We had known each other for more than ten years, but now they treated me as a stranger.

My colleagues loaded the cartons into the trunk of the car, carelessly placing them on top of a dark oily stain, butted against rusted metal pieces that could easily pierce the cardboard.

That night I couldn't sleep. I lay in bed and calculated every move I could make at work to win over those who questioned me, who doubted my sincerity. I would become a superior organizer—doing the menial tasks that others left to the next generation of minions.

I left the apartment before Mei Ling and Jin Quon were awake and was at the door of the PSB office before dawn, knocking to wake up the guard who was slumped in his chair leaning against the cement wall.

"Why are you here so early, Comrade Zhang?" the guard asked as he unlocked the door. "Trouble sleeping?"

"Just wanted to organize some papers in the archives room. It's a mess in there," I said, happy that he had seen me come in to work at such an early hour.

The archives room was filled to the ceiling with mold-dappled boxes of police files, papers pock-marked from hungry silverfish hanging out the sides. Coughing in the musty air, I stacked and restacked files no one had looked at in decades. I was sweeping up piles of mouse droppings and powdered paper debris when my colleague came to the door.

"I was looking for you," he stared down at his feet. "The Director wants to meet with you at 9:30am. Is everything okay?"

"Yes, yes." Smoothing the lines between my eyebrows, dropping my forefinger and tapping the bridge of my nose, I pretended to be calm. "Just a routine meeting, I'm sure." The colleague looked at me sadly. There was no such thing as a routine meeting with the Director of the PSB.

At 9:20am, I went to the lavatory, thoroughly washed my hands and cleaned my fingernails, inspected my hair, and adjusted my shirt. At 9:27, I walked down the long corridor to the Director's door. My footsteps echoed against the cement walls and I slowed down to muffle the sound, stopping at the office door that was as old and splintered as my own. Comrade Liu showed me into the main room. She looked at me as a nurse seeking to assure a patient with a terminal illness. A bare bulb draped with cobwebs hung from the ceiling casting a chilling glow on the Director. A charcoal brazier threw off a hint of warmth along with its toxic fumes. Under my padded jacket, I shivered and wished to briskly rub my arms, but instead I stood at attention. The Director, seated behind his desk, wore a quilted jacket much like mine and a standard cap with fur flaps covering his ears.

"Comrade Zhang," the Director did not stand up, just continued smoking a cigarette, and sipping a steaming liquid from his metal cup. "I understand you speak French, and also English. Is this true?"

A nauseating sense of dread rooted itself just below my lungs. I alone was responsible for mismanaging my life to arrive at this dangerous place. I stood there mute.

"Speak to me in French," continued the Director, "I would like to hear some French words."

"My French is very old, from when I was a child." My mind jumbled, not recalling a word of either French or English. "I don't think I can remember any. Maybe a silly phrase or two."

"Please don't be modest." The deceitful stack of cartons was piled in the corner of the room. The faded indigo binding of my French poetry book pushed against the cardboard flap. "It is rare nowadays to find a man who can speak something other than Chinese. I insist that you tell me some French words. Now. I'm a busy man."

My face burning, I blurted out, "Resplendissant com rubis d'Oriant."

"It means?"

"It is a line from a very old French poem. It speaks of the jewels of the Orient." I stumbled trying to determine the source of the frown on the Director's face. "Not the jewels of wealthy people," I continued hurriedly. "Not the jewels of those who made their fortunes off the backs of the peasants, but cultural jewels."

"Oh, I see. It refers to the wealth of the common man. Is that what it means?"

"Yes, that's how I understand it."

The Director gestured for me to take a chair and then lifted the telephone, speaking to his secretary. He picked up some papers on his desk and began reading, all the while blowing streams of bitter tobacco smoke into the air. I waited, unsure whether I had been forgotten. A splinter from the wooden seat pricked my thigh. I slid my hand under my leg and probed the hairless skin through the small angled tear in my uniform. I would ask Mei Ling to repair it when I got home. It would not do to have a report in my folder saying I had ruined government property.

After several minutes, the door opened and two PSB officials entered, carrying thick folders of papers. The young woman from the front office brought in biscuits and more cups of tea on a tray and the men began to discuss the case of a European woman who was coming to China and then traveling on to the Tibetan Plateau. I sat quietly, listening. I was afraid to ask what this meeting was about and what it had to do with me. The next hour passed in a blur of perplexing information.

*Erzebet Pelletier is a French botanical illustrator. Daughter, Lilia, 25 years old. The husband was freelance journalist Girard Pelletier. He was covering the advance of the People's Liberation Army past Ganzi, Sichuan Province when he went underground--switched sides. A Tibetan sympathizer, capitalist dog tricked by the Tibetans into presenting the Great Liberation as an attack against Tibet.*

The PSB officials unfolded maps and spread them on the table. Markings identified the region as Sichuan, China, formerly Kham, Tibet. They traced the rivers with a red pen and drew circles around areas that seemed far from towns or roads. I examined the maps, too, acting as if it was quite clear why I should be involved in this at all.

*News reports in France (1959) that supported the Tibetans came from Pelletier. The PSB was given the very important work of stopping these lies about the Motherland. Completed. Pelletier killed in accident near Manigango. No papers on his body. His assistant, Marie-Heléne Cartier, tried to get information about his work in Tibet some years ago. She researched missing documents, apparently trying to secure them for the family. Her inquiries were stalled and dismissed.*

France, I thought. This was the connection to my language skills. They were going to have me translate some French documents, possibly French texts, for them. That was not such a bad outcome. I hadn't needed to be so paranoid. I reached for a biscuit on the tray and warmed my hands on the metal cup of tea.

They delved back into the maps, following a road from Kangding ("the Tibetans call it Dartsedo") westward to a series of peaked lines representing a mountain range and placed an "X" next to a river.

*Support in the West is growing for the Tibetan cause. Groups in several countries are meddling in our internal affairs, petitioning their leaders to pressure the People's Government. If Pelletier's documents appear, referring to monks being killed and monasteries destroyed, it will re-ignite the Tibetan independence debate. Papers may be in a red folder (reports from Lhasa, but not likely after all of these years).*

"But why do our leaders care about this?" I asked. I was part of the team. I had the right to ask reasonable questions. "We are the most powerful country in the world. What do we care about what the world says about our internal affairs?"

"Comrade Zhang," the Director sighed and reached for another cigarette. "Are you ignorant of the fact that the Great Motherland is part of the world again?" He turned to another member of the group. "Could you please educate Comrade Zhang about the glorious strides his country is making?"

The man, in a bored monotone, lectured me as if I were a child, while the Director went back to reading.

"Our Ten Year Plan to improve the lives of all Chinese is linked to foreign investment. We are negotiating for $1.2 billion from a consortium of British banks—a delicate operation. Imagine how complicated those negotiations would be if ignorant foreigners started questioning our internal policies—if the Pelletier papers surface, tell lies about our liberation of the Tibetan Plateau, and the Dalai Lama is able to get international attention for his splittist agenda."

*Lies about what?* I wondered. *What did Pelletier lie about?*

"Thank you for this excellent education," I said, still bewildered. "I just didn't know, but now I understand clearly."

The PSB Director picked up the thread of the conversation. "This is the time for the Dalai Lama to act. Although he is in India, his eyes and hands are everywhere. But so are ours. We heard from our informers that there will soon be an attempt to take the Pelletier papers out of Tibet and publish them in the West. We must get to the papers before the Dalai Lama's traitorous followers do. They'll be able to use Pelletier's lies to bolster their campaign."

"And his wife?" I said. "She is looking for the papers, too?"

"No Comrade Zhang," he rolled his eyes and let out a derisive laugh. "Pelletier's wife is a simple artist. She doesn't know about the papers. She'll be the bait. If the nomads or the monks have the documents, they'll try to pass them to her."

"Is it really possible that people would still have documents now, after so many years?" The chatter at the table stopped mid-sentence and the three men faced me, their mouths twisted into smirks. My voice trailed off. "I was just. . ."

"Comrade Zhang, you are so good with the donkey's lips on the horse's mouth. We will decide what is possible here," said the Director going back to the maps. "Two months ago, a man from Manigango appeared in Lhasa inquiring about sending documents out of the area. He was a giant of a man, a Khampa warrior. We believe it was Tashi Choegyal, the leader of a nomad camp at Yi-Lhun Latso Lake, near Manigango. We think he was talking about the Pelletier papers."

Picking up my tea again, I stared through the liquid into the bottom of the cup, imagining reaching out with both hands and grabbing him by the neck. I would squeeze until he apologized for his demeaning tone of voice, insulting me by suggesting that what I had said was irrelevant. I did nothing. If you are patient in a moment of anger, you will escape a hundred days of sorrow.

"You will accompany the woman to the Tibetan Plateau, find and bring back the documents. She will think you are just there as her translator. While you are there, you must also prepare a report on the monks at the local monasteries. Let us know what those parasites are doing to oppress the peasants who live near them. They'll be punished for working against the government and continuing to follow the Dalai Lama."

It was after 5:00 when the Director finished the briefing and I hurried home and told Mei Ling of our great fortune. "I'll travel with the foreign woman to Tibet and bring back the documents hidden there by her husband."

"Does the woman speak Tibetan?" Mei Ling asked. "How will she communicate?"

"I'll be her translator. The department is even going to send me to language school. This is a lucky assignment."

We bought special moon cakes to celebrate and talked about how the assignment would improve our lives through small rewards. Perhaps a better school for Jin Quon was in our future. A school where children learned to write poetry, spoke other languages and studied the geography of the entire world, not only China. My wife was happy for me, to see me advance in the workplace, gaining a position as a valuable member of the PSB.

I calculated everything I did in the days that followed so I would do well on the assignment without antagonizing others or seeming too ambitious. A good cadre should never be too ambitious. The tables could easily turn and I could become a suspect—derided and demeaned for owning foreign books, for learning foreign languages. I was removed from my normal desk job and sent to a training course, ten hours each day, learning to speak and write a new language--Tibetan.

When my instructor commended me for my dedication and quick acquisition of the language, the Director heard about it and reacted with pleasure and surprise. "Ah, Comrade Zhang, you do have the needs of the people at heart. Obviously, you are the best person to go and report on the foreign woman and the barbarian Tibetans. Moreover with your family connection to this assignment this is an important step for your career. To show you are loyal to the party and to the government."

I was too intimidated to inquire what this had to do with my family. The Director acted as if I should know more. Know what?

That night I told Mei Ling of the strange reference to the foreign woman and my family. Her eyes darkened and she grasped my arm, her small hand cold, like river water. "Kai Lun," she said, "he is talking about your brother. That is the family connection. This is not good. Be very careful what you do and say at work. Do not stand out like the crane that raises its head in the flock of chickens."

I had been almost 25 years old when I first arrived in Chengdu to work for the PSB. Everyone was talking about a man living among the bushes at Du Fu's thatched cottage, a man who spent his days looking into the waters of Huanhua Xi, the Flower Rinsing Creek. Curiosity and intuition took me there on a moonless night to see what sort of creature had gone out of his head so far that he would live in the deserted park and speak against the People's Government. There, hiding in the shadows of Du Fu's cottage was my own brother, his hair clumped together with twigs and leaves; his clothes tattered and smelling like urine.

"My brother," I had said, "what happened to you? Why are you living here like a rat among the garbage?"

My brother looked at me with glazed eyes and recited a poem of Du Fu, a poem familiar to all Chinese who had attended school and knew the poetry of the T'ang Dynasty.

*Red clouds tower in the west*
*The sun is sinking on the plain*
*A sparrow chirps on the wicker gate*
*I have returned from a thousand li away*
*My wife and children are shocked to see me*
*She calms herself and wipes her tears*

*I floated through that disordered life*
*And by chance have been allowed to come back toward my goal*
*The neighbors lean over the wall*
*They are sighing and sobbing*
*Late at night we hold a candle*
*And face each other as in a dream*

"I am a broken man. I am worthless," my brother said to me. "My life is now meaningless." He wept into my shirt as he remembered how our parents had died refusing to denounce their colleagues during a purge of intellectuals.

"But there is more," he whispered. "Something so ugly. Please forgive me, my brother, for what I am about to tell you."

With his head slumped to the side, he confided how he had caved in to pressure from fellow soldiers, and raped a Tibetan woman when he loved his own wife. The woman he raped was not a barbarian at all, as he had been led to believe. She was a frightened nomad whose husband was in prison for refusing to turn against the Dalai Lama. During the weeks he stayed at her tent, she cooked for my brother and prayed. She refused to speak, and developed a spastic motion, that would uncontrollably roll over her body until she fell on the floor writhing. After several minutes she would fall into a deep sleep, a near coma. Each day my brother descended into greater despair. When it was time to leave the camp, when the military moved on, he left with them. The woman's belly was already distended, his child conceived in violence living inside the body of a woman he had terrorized into seizures.

Back in Chengdu, he had deserted his army post and wandered in the gardens of Du Fu, the great Chinese poet of the 6th century. Hiding among the plum trees and the bamboo in spring and the chrysanthemum in winter, he approached strangers walking in the gardens and told them about the people he had met past Chengdu, the Tibetans who were supposed to be slaves to the monks. He told how the Tibetan villagers and nomads fed the monks, but relied on them for blessings and healings. He had seen it with his own eyes. They revered their leader, the Dalai Lama. They did not fear him. They were not enslaved. When he told the strangers of his own heinous acts in the village near the lake with the colored fish, they gathered their children and their parcels and ran away, never once looking back.

That day I saw him cowering at Du Fu's cottage, I begged him to come home and be cared for by our family. He refused. My brother would not return to the apartment with me. Not long after, the police arrived and searched the bushes, luring him out and throwing him to the ground where he was beaten, handcuffed and carted away to prison.

Remembering my brother's story cast a pall over our happiness, but I had no choice except to forge ahead with my preparations to leave for Tibet. Once you have mounted the tiger, a wise man fears to climb down. I continued the masquerade at the office, arriving early and spending hours studying Tibetan, researching and making lists of items I would need during the summer. I conferred with the senior officers about the best strategies to force the nomads into compliance with my requests—I would need the nomads' help to find the documents. My new colleagues chain smoked cigarettes, drank tea and gave me ideas, such as aligning with weak, poor people who would turn in their friends and family for a few Yuan. I was one of the PSB team. I didn't need to be afraid for my future with this goodwill.

One night after work, an officer from my unit invited me to his home for tea. He was a man, who had been denounced in many struggle sessions for his bad attitude, but I liked him, and he had always been kind to me at work. He lived in a 15-story cement housing project identical to my own. Not long after I arrived, a man who looked much like my colleague appeared from behind the curtain that separated the living room from the kitchen. The brother was shy, speaking from behind his hand. He was a geologist, before the Cultural Revolution.

"After the Cultural Revolution began. . .?" I asked.

"I don't want to talk about that, if you don't mind my rudeness." The brother dropped his hand from his face. He had been shielding a wicked scar that gave him a permanent smile. "Surely, Comrade Zhang, you understand my reticence?"

"My brother wrote an important academic paper about his research, but the government destroyed it long ago," said my colleague pounding his fist on the small coffee table. The metal cups of tea bounced up and down, sending a cascade of liquid onto the flowered oilcloth table covering.

I was alarmed he would speak this way in front of me, a person he worked with, but didn't know if he could trust. My colleague was not a prudent man. The colleague's wife came in with a sponge and mopped the table, saying under her breath, "My husband, watch what you say here. Haven't we had enough trouble?" She nodded at me as she left the room.

"I know, I know," the colleague said to his wife's retreating back. "I just think Comrade Zhang would have found it interesting."

Interesting? I was used to such guarded conversations. Who wasn't? It was always necessary to watch for a slight smile, a frown, a broken sentence to determine what was really being said, and the intention behind it.

"My brother told me you'll be traveling to the area of Yi-Lhun Latso, the most beautiful lake in all of Tibet," the geologist said. It was disconcerting watching his clown's face with the immovable smile, while his voice was so grave. "Comrade Zhang, the beauty of this lake is not a fairytale made up by children. I traveled to Tibet with the army. I saw this lake. I examined the landforms and the silt. They reflected sunlight and created a celadon glow, reaching to color the sky above the water. Even several kilometers away, this otherworldly color greened the Dri-Chu River that flowed past the town of Manigango."

The colleague's wife abruptly appeared next to us, gathering up the cups and plates from the table. "The neighbors are down below looking up at our windows. It's time to say good-night, Comrade Zhang." I hurriedly grabbed my jacket.

At the door, the geologist grasped my arm and said, "There was an old man at the lake, a hermit who lived in a hut. He knew everything that happened around there." The man's eyes filled with water and he reached in his pocket for a grey handkerchief. "You will want to see the carvings he made on the boulders in the lake."

"But why? Is there more I should know?" Had my colleague risked bringing me to his apartment just so I could hear his brother talk about the beauty of a lake in Tibet?

"Comrade Zhang, my brother didn't tell you? This was 1959 when your own brother was in Tibet."

He knew my brother in Tibet? I was alarmed. I had never told anyone the story of the insane man at Du Fu's cottage who was my brother. My grandfather's words entered my mind: Often one finds one's destiny just where one hides to avoid it.

"We both met the hermit at the lake," the geologist continued, breaking into my tragic memories. "Those were terrible times. The army wanted me to write a document that supported their plan to drain the lake and force the nomads to plant wheat in the lakebed. The glacier above the lake is the water source for thousands of kilometers of land and millions of people. It's a sacred lake. Draining it would have been an environmental disaster and a cruel act against the Tibetan people. They are simple religious people—they did not deserve that. Do not repeat my words, Comrade Zhang, I have suffered enough for refusing to write that report and allow the draining of that lake."

I wanted to ask more, but the geologist's wife was wringing her hands and pleading with me to leave. I ran down the back steps, pushed my bicycle out of the shadows and pedaled home along the river. After several blocks, the sound of the night birds warbling in the trees helped me shake off the anxiety of my colleague's home and I sang under my breath in the crisp air. My brother's story was not my story. The geologist's story was not my story. I had nothing to fear.

As I rounded the corner, happily greeted my neighbors and pedaled up to the government housing block, I had a chill. A black official car was parked in front of our sector. My wife and son were being pushed into the back seat. The officers handed in our small plaid suitcase with the brown leather straps. Jin Quon clutched a lifelike leather elephant given to me years ago by a professor visiting from an Indian university. I threw down the bike and ran alongside the car as it drove away. Splattered with mud thrown from under the tires, I was panting hard when the driver stopped and rolled down the window.

"Comrade Zhang," the uniformed man in the passenger seat leaned across the driver and smiled. "How kind of you to make such an effort to see your family off."

"Where are they going?" My alarmed voice rattled my own ears and my wife's eyebrows rose like the slight lifting of a bird's wing.

"They're going to be safe in Shanghai until you return," the officer said. "Surely you don't want to worry about them while you are in Tibet. When you return with your mission completed, they'll be so happy to see you again."

My beautiful wife slowly shook her head. Go. Do not make a scene here in the street. I reached through the window and grasped at her hand as the car sped off.

# PART II

# CHAPTER 9

## *Charms of a New Lover*

| | |
|---|---|
| *Sa day kha shoo teeng khyak* | *Over the slippery surface of the frozen earth* |
| *Ta pho tong sa ma ray* | *Don't let your stallion trot* |
| *Sar drok jam pa'ee chok soo* | *Toward the charms of a new lover* |
| *Nyeeng tam sho sa ma ray* | *Don't let your secrets be scattered* |

*- Sixth Dalai Lama*

### Kai Lun's Story

The ten-day journey to the Tibetan Plateau was startling in its beauty. Horrifying in its confusion. I was a hunter encased in the shell of an amiable translator—a role I wouldn't have created for myself in my worst nightmare. To describe the landscape would be senseless. Of course, my eyes registered the intense blue of the sky, the giant birds flying overhead, possibly eagles, the wildflowers and the clear rushing rivers. But my mind was focused on casual conversation with Madame Erzebet; conversation I hoped would cajole her into trusting me. It seemed impossible she wouldn't have guessed the sham of her painting mission. But she gave no sign. Hawk and sparrow, we crossed the pasturelands without incident. Without incident between us, I mean.

The estimate of arrival time in the Manigango nomad camp disintegrated before we even left the city. I had contracted for a brand new Jeep to carry us from Chengdu onto the Tibetan Plateau. The car's arrival three hours late collapsed the fantasy I had been harboring that I was doing crucial work for the government so would be treated as a high-level official--given everything I needed to work efficiently on my assignment. Two cracked windows were barely seated in the frames and the oily smell of a gas leak filled the vehicle. Broken seats, wires and stuffing held in by electrical tape all added to the message that I was a man who did not deserve respect, despite my mission.

"Comrade, this is unacceptable, I represent the People's Government," I said to the driver exerting my power as I waved my hand at the dilapidated Jeep.

The driver looked at me with disdain and went back to spraying water on the splintered windshield. I stepped back from the cool drops splattering my face and arms. They made dark circles on my blue shirt, but disappeared as quickly in the heat of the morning sun.

"Did you hear me? I said this is not acceptable."

The driver shrugged. "Only car available. Take it or not."

I had never been in a position of authority and was not good at telling people what to do. I looked over at Madame Erzebet, seated on the side of the road, engrossed in a European magazine. Her hair pulled back behind her ears, she languidly flicked at insects landing on her ankles and arms, glanced up to see if the status of the journey had changed, and went back to reading.

"Look at this," I turned back to the driver, jabbing my finger at the signatures of high-ranking officials on our travel documents. "See these names?" The driver examined the signatures, following the letters with his pencil as I shuffled the red-stamped official forms between folders. The man's eyes traveled around the pages from spot to spot. The poor fool had been given a pressed khaki uniform for the journey to the barren wastelands, but was not even literate.

Now the sun was almost directly overhead. If this charade continued, it would set the start of the trip back an additional day when we had only planned for six.

"We'll go ahead with the car," I said, "But I'll be filing a report about this." I grabbed the folders back from the man and gestured to Madame Erzebet to get ready.

Standing at the side of the Jeep as the driver tied down the boxes and bags, my memorized briefing at PSB Headquarters stewed in my mind. My mouth had a sharp metallic taste as if it leaked acid. If I failed at this assignment, if I did not find the Pelletier papers, I would go to prison and never see Mei Ling and Jin Quon again.

I frowned considering what would happen if this woman found the documents and brought them out unobserved. This would be impossible. I would search her possessions on a regular basis. My insurance for success was in my pocket, folded neatly into an envelope. My superiors had given me 500 Yuan to use as bribes if I needed it. It wouldn't go far in the city, but among the nomads it would be a fortune. I just needed to find the poorest, the weakest, of the village and my search results would be assured. If you have money, you can make even ghosts and devils turn your grindstone.

We climbed into the car. The engine turned over with an ominous clank and then a steady rumble and we raced down the road, scattering children and mangy dogs. Madame Erzebet shouted from the backseat as a stack of packages and bags slid forward and banged into her head.

"Mr. Zhang, if I may ask, how are we going to travel in this cramped car for six days?" she said. "I appreciate all you are doing for me, but am wondering a bit about the lack of space in the car."

The driver glanced in the rearview mirror and shrugged. I rubbed my own knees, cramped against the dashboard and looked back at Madame Erzebet. Six days? I snorted to myself. We are both deluded if we think we are only traveling for six days.

"Madame Erzebet, try to get comfortable. This is not an optimal situation, I know." I propped my legs back up against the dashboard and settled into my seat.

"Mr. Zhang," she said an hour later, hanging an arm over the back of the seat. "I had no idea the scenery would be so beautiful here. It's so green! Corn growing in the gardens along the roadsides, the magnificent stands of bamboo. Really this is a wonderful drive."

I took this opportunity to begin a friendly conversation. A friendship that would benefit me later. "Do you know about Chao Ch'ang a painter who lived at the beginning of the Sung Dynasty, a thousand years ago? I read he was a master of laying down light layers of color, attempting to achieve the most subtle rendition of the flowers."

"I don't know about him, but it's true," she said. "A thick coat of pigment, a rush to manifest the color in one broad sweep, is the death of an excellent botanical illustration. Are you an artist yourself?"

"Oh no. I have no such talent at all. But my father was a painter." I felt almost happy. I had never imagined I would ever have the opportunity to speak French with a foreigner—right out in the open, on official business even. I was a lucky man to have this assignment.

"Your father? Is he still alive?"

"No, he's been gone for many years." My father—he had tried to provide us with a life filled with culture and happiness, and he had been brought to his knees by the convoluted events in China over the last decades. Talking to Madame Erzebet about my father now caused my chest to constrict. It was better not to say too much to her, not to expose too much of my personal life. It was dangerous territory.

"Perhaps when we're in Tibet," she continued, "you can practice painting while I am working on the botanicals. I bet you have talent you don't even know you have."

We drove on, and I was quiet. Just before Kangding, a stronger smell of gasoline wafted in through the broken window. I started to ask the driver about the source and then decided to ignore it. An explanation could lead to a repair station, days of waiting for needed parts, putting us even further behind schedule. Over the next hour, there was a constant shifting in the backseat as Madame Erzebet raised and lowered windows, moved from one side of the seat to the other and leaned to the front of the car. The fumes were stronger when we slowed down and I imagined the consequences if she died, if she was asphyxiated while in my care.

"Please stop," Madame Erzebet's voice drifted out of the back. I turned around. She was lying on the seat, curled in like a seashell. Her head rested on a box of watercolor paper and paints, a jacket folded on top for a pillow. Her skin had begun the journey like the soft pink of tropical fruits imported before the Cultural Revolution. Now it had mutated into a translucent institutional green. The driver handed a steel bucket over his shoulder just in time. For hours, she gagged and vomited

"Comrade Zhang," the driver said, guiding the steering wheel with jerky motions to correct our movement as we half-floated through a muddy lake covering the road and the adjacent field. He looked nervously in the rearview mirror at the back seat. "Madame doesn't look good. I believe we should turn back."

He could easily report me and say I had insisted we drive on when it was obvious she needed a doctor. I glanced in the back seat again, averting my nose from the putrid pail. "Keep going."

Thinking it might not be the gas fumes that were making her ill; I pulled a medical book from my bag and ran my finger up and down the index columns, turning to the paragraphs on altitude sickness. Some of the symptoms matched Madame Erzebet's: headache, vomiting. I watched her closely over the next few hours for additional signs of trouble: a bluish tinge to her skin and shallow breathing.

"Comrade Zhang, Sir," repeated the driver tentatively. "If Madame's headache continues and she has trouble breathing, we must return to a lower elevation."

Madame Erzebet appeared to be dozing against the boxes, her neck bent forward at an odd angle. The car dodged sheep and drove up the sides of hills to avoid water buffalo, carts and stooped farmers carrying loads of sticks and furs on their backs. She dug her knuckles into her eye sockets and her thumbs into her temples, whimpering with each jolt. The PSB would not care about her comfort or her health, but they would demand to know why I had not done everything possible to continue the journey, to complete the assignment. They would hold me liable for not trying hard enough to find a hospital so she could be treated and we could move on. I had already been told this was a critical time period for finding the documents—my superiors would be outraged to have me delay this mission by several weeks because they had to develop another plan.

"Turn around," I ordered the driver. A wave of relief flowed through my body. I had to be careful on this trip to be decisive, not just let events unfold that might jeopardize my future. I would know better next time. "We will go back to Chengdu to get a doctor's authorization to continue."

"What's happening?" Madame Erzebet whispered from the back seat. "Where are we going?"

"Chengdu."

"Stop. Don't go back. Find me a hotel room."

"You must go to a lower altitude."

"I'm not going back." She lifted herself, only to sag against the car door. Her deathwatch skin was the color of my wife's when she was in labor with our son. Mei Ling had also vomited for hours. I had been terrified she would die right there in the hospital room with the stained green walls and the sputtering fluorescent tubes that cast ghoulish shadows on her lovely face. We had named the son Jin Quon, Bright Gold, because we were so happy she had survived and the boy had lived to see the light of day.

The driver pulled through the gravel to the side of the road, an area with small shops, broken down decrepit buildings and a meadow on the other side. While we sat in the car, he sprinted through town banging on doors and disappearing through archways into hotel lobbies. Each time he emerged shaking his head.

"No one taking chance on having foreigner in their building," he said. "They don't have permits for foreigners."

"Find out what they want," I said. "Offer them extra money,"

"I did. All afraid."

Another half hour passed and he came back nodding yes, waving his arm toward a narrow lane. We followed him down the alleyway, holding a cloth to our noses as we passed open pit toilets. Entering a sunny courtyard, we followed him to a cinder block dormitory room, paint peeling off the walls. It reeked of urine and the dull musty smell of mouse droppings. Madame Erzebet was the sole guest. She didn't seem to notice the smell. She climbed into the bed with her clothes on and, like a mole warding off the afternoon light, tunneled under the blanket layers. I retrieved the only pillow from another bed. Hard and lumpy as a sack of walnuts, she twisted it into a mound against the base of her skull. I slipped from the room and handed the owner five Yuan, ten times the normal price for the room.

By dawn, after a restless night in the Jeep, I was fully awake, going every few hours to peer in the guesthouse window to see if Madame Erzebet was stirring. I watched her as I had watched Jin Quon when he was a baby, staring until I was sure the blankets were moving and the figure underneath was actually alive. Now I peeked through the flyspecked window curtain and saw Madame Erzebet stretch and run her fingers through her hair. Rapping on the glass, I pointed at the sun, already a flat disk in the sky.

We had been in the town for fourteen hours.

"Do we go on or do we go back?" I spoke through the window. "How are you feeling?" Madame Erzebet got up from the bed, insisting her stomach was settled and the headache was gone. I admired her guts. She didn't look that well. As she regained her strength during the day, she apologized for being so much trouble. The poor woman had no idea that we were not traveling to assist her on her mission. She was traveling to assist us with ours.

After Kangding, the road ascended sharply to Zhedou Shankou Pass, 13,162 feet and the mountain panorama unfolded like a pop-up greeting card. Pine trees covered the hillsides and stands of airy birch and poplar clustered along the rivers. Granite sheets thrust out of the forested mountainside. Razor thin and 100 feet high, they shone metallic-grey in the sunlight, arranged like the remnants of a medieval city long since brought to ruins. The Jeep skirted red gashes of earth, ripped from the mountain by landslides. Boulders blocked the road and forced us to drive at a precarious angle along drop-offs to the canyons below. Ravaged trees pointed the way down to the final resting spot of vehicles slammed against rock outcroppings, tires long since stripped off the wheel hubs.

I heard a low whistling gasp from the backseat, and when I looked back, Madame Erzebet was staring out the window.

"What are you looking at?" I followed her eyes to the bottom of the ravine.

"Someone I know was killed in a car accident many years ago," she said, her voice trance-like. "A family member."

I looked quickly back to the front. She was certainly talking about her husband. My mind twisted around everything I had heard in the last months. The geologist and my brother were in Tibet at the same time, the same year Pelletier was there. When the Director said this mission was related to my family, surely he had not been inferring that my brother was involved in Pelletier's reporting. Is this why he was later branded as a traitor?

The cold, pure air shocked me as we ascended the mountain. My confused nose had spent forty years taking in the thick, warm pollution of cities. At the top of the pass, snow blew through the sky, creating a shifting whiteout. We slid through a sheen of ice and pulled over to the roadside. An old man dressed in a tattered cloth jacket with stuffing coming out of the seams climbed out from a small wooden hut to greet us. He reached in through the Jeep window holding a thermos of tea in one hand and three bowls in the other.

Bits of cloth printed with Tibetan calligraphy and pictures of flying horses clung to the sharp-branched bushes and littered the ground. "Prayer flags," said the old man. "When they blow in the wind, the windhorses carry prayers of blessings out into the universe."

Before we could get back on the road, Madame Erzebet threw on another sweater and scrambled out of the Jeep and up and down the hillsides, using a stick to poke and prod snow-covered mosses. I followed her. We had come too far to have her injured on this mountainside. Sleet blew against the rocks and froze the few plants foolhardy enough to grow at the 13,000 foot summit. She slipped and fell on the icy hillside, limping along as she rubbed her bruised shin.

Wielding a fork and a screwdriver from the Jeep, she carved frost off a hillock and uncovered a greenish-brown flower. "Look at this," she said. "Hundreds of pointed seeds like miniature black teeth fill the centers and the pods have heart-shaped leaves."

I looked. The flowers extended out from the base on long stems like a carnival ride that spins its passengers into the air. Jin Quon and I bought tickets for such a ride at the New Year's fair just the year before and rode until we were so dizzy our eyes crossed.

"Let's go." I stamped my feet against the cold and rubbed my hands together. "It's late. We've hours left to drive." She carefully wrapped the plants in wet towels and placed them in plastic bags she brought out of her suitcase.

We descended toward the valley floor. Two hours below the pass, the snow vanished and it was spring again. A dust cloud gathered on the horizon, screening the purple peaks. The source appeared--a rolling tide of sheep and yaks migrating to the mountains for the early summer grazing. Madame Erzebet called out for the Jeep to halt and before I could stop her, she bolted out of the car again.

"Madame Erzebet," I yelled after her as she darted into the field next to the road and stood fearlessly in the midst of the nomads. "I'm in charge of where we stop and who we speak to." She let out a high-pitched laugh, combined with a guffaw that I found unnerving.

One by one, the riders waved their hats in the air and whooped in a yodel, galloping to within a few feet of where she stood in the tall grasses. They wore sheepskin coats and leather boots with painted designs. Swords strapped to their waists and rifles slung over their shoulders, they trotted their stout ponies alongside the yaks. The yaks thundered by loaded with tent poles, fur blankets, pots, pans, and baskets of food with raggedy children cinched on top of the loads. Even from the side of the Jeep where I leaned, I could smell the animals' musky stench. I tried to imagine my own shy son looking like that with hair matted like a bird's nest, dressed in a stinking sheepskin and strapped to a yak running through a field. The ground vibrated up through my shoes, creating an erotic humming sensation in my legs. An old woman with turquoise in her hair sang a catchy melody and it merged with the pounding of hooves. I could just make out the words of a folksong about the Tibetan nomad pony:

*Your good horse is like the swiftest bird*
*The golden saddle is its feathers*
*When the bird and the feathers are together*
*Crossing the highland plains will be no problem for you.*

When the animals lumbered on, Madame Erzebet jumped back into the car, chattering excitedly and hanging out the window as we bumped along the road.

For eight days, the country mutated from pasture to mountainside and back again. Lonely nomad tents peppered the acres of buttercups and tall lavender stalks. Behind them, peaks stretched out in a brutal, jagged line on the horizon. Waterfall veils flooded from ravines and melded with torrents of muddy water churning between the canyon walls.

Each village we passed through was smaller and the buildings more dilapidated. When we stopped to buy biscuits, there were none. The stores had empty shelves, with cobwebs laced from door to the ceiling. Staring blankly at the Jeep and its passengers, the village people appeared beyond fear or surprise, continually moving prayer beads through their brown fingers.

Late in the morning on the tenth day, we rounded a bend in the road, a rainbow aura shimmering ahead. I shaded my eyes to see the source: the glacier resting above Yi-Lhun Lhatso Lake. The closer we got, the farther the glacier seemed to retreat. But by early afternoon, we entered the diorama of nomad pastures at Yi-Lhun Lhatso, banged through a rocky field and stopped. Yak, sheep, and goats grazed on the surrounding hills. Children rode horses with colored scarves braided in the animals' tails and manes. The tents in the camp were giant tarantulas hunkered down, ropes extended like hairy legs.

As we unfolded ourselves from the Jeep, stretching and kneading our cramped legs and stiff necks, a monk in red robes walked across the field, meandered through the gathering crowd of nomads and then approached Madame Erzebet. He handed her a folded piece of paper. She looked at it quizzically, rubbing the grit from the road out of her eyes, as he said to her, "I am Lobsang Phuntsok, from TriSong Monastery. My monastery rests in a gully on the hills above Manigango village."

I translated for her and then held out my hand. She dropped the paper saturated with the smell of incense into my palm and I unfolded it. An invitation held simple characters reading: *Madame, Please come to visit our monastery during your stay. We will arrange a room if you wish to stay for several days.*

I looked at the note, translating for Madame Erzebet as I read the characters. An informer from Chengdu must have told the monastery Madame Erzebet was coming, or perhaps someone saw the Jeep as it went through the village of Manigango. That didn't make sense. The monk would not have been able to get to Yi-Lhun Latso so fast walking. What if my own superiors slipped the information to TriSong Monastery, just to lure the monk to come and meet Madame Erzebet? This could be the first part of a trap that would catch her and the monks when they exchanged the Pelletier papers. If this was the plan, shouldn't I have been told?

I wasn't trained for deception. My style, which I had crushed into submission like we all had since the start of the Cultural Revolution, was more that of a man who would take this woman into his confidence, explain his ugly predicament, and then plead for cooperation so we could both complete our missions.

I watched as the monk slung his bag over his shoulder and backtracked following the course of the river. After unloading our bags in a pile at the roadside, the driver poured a bucket of water over his head, drank a cup of tea, and with a honk of the horn headed out for the return trip.

We were stranded.

# CHAPTER 10

## *You Are Like a Fool*

| | |
|---|---|
| *Kye gro mee ta chee ba* | *You say you don't take mind* |
| *Nying nae ma dran zer na* | *Of change or death* |
| *Chang rung zom do kha yang* | *You may seem smart and wise* |
| *Don la lyk pa dra chung* | *But you are like a fool* |

*- Sixth Dalai Lama*

## The Twins' Story as Told by Lhamo Sangye

I am Lhamo Sangye, nomad woman. My husband work hard and grow our yak herd to 100 animals. We have chests filled with barley grains and warm tents in winter. But do not praise my good fortune until vultures take me away. The army kill my husband six winters ago when my children were babies. But others have had it much harder than me.

I was young woman when yellow-haired foreigner man first appear in camp. He sit with our parents while they tell their grief after Chinese army came to villages. He write down our stories. Say he will tell world what happen here when army take our land. When army killed and sent precious teachers to prison. Soldiers murdered this foreigner man but not get papers where he kept our stories.

Listen closely. This not my tale. Twin girls, born of nomad woman and Chinese soldier asked me to speak for them. Birth problems gave girls short bodies with funny-looking arms. Twins not talk so well and those not in family not understand their words. But this no reason for them to not be heard. They want their story told about when foreigner woman came to the camp to paint flowers. I am their voice.

Three Chinese officers come to camp. Bring news that foreigner woman will arrive. They make all people in camp stop work and listen.

"Someone has to watch out for foreigner woman. Make sure she doesn't get hurt," main officer say. "Who will that be?"

Everyone shift from foot to foot. Look at ground.

"We herd animals. Plant crops," Tashi Choegyal, camp leader, say. "No one to take care of foreigner woman."

Chinese officer look around. Point at us. "What about them? They don't work in fields do they?" I sit on rock next to meeting. Play with cloth doll. Sister dig earth with sharp stick.

Officer walk over. Crouch down. Stare at our faces. Drool come from corner of Sister's mouth.

"What you two do in camp?" He stand in front of us. Talk loud. "Herd animals? Plant crops?"

I try to tell him. With stout heart, mouse can lift elephant. He not understand.

"Speak so I can understand you! Speak!" He grab my arm. Yank me to my feet. "What's wrong with you? Answer."

"They can't speak," say Tashi Choegyal. "Look at them. Not normal."

Chinese man turn and talk to other officers. "Perfect. They're useless. They can take care of Madame Pelletier. Won't be able to speak to her." Officers nod head and laugh.

"It's settled," officer say turning to Tashi Choegyal. "Those girls take care of foreigner woman. Make sure they do good job."

When officers gone, Tashi Choegyal come to our tent. Talk in low voice to Ama-la, mother. Tashi Choegyal and wife always kind to our family. When he leave, Ama-la tell us what he said.

"Make sure yellow-haired woman safe and happy here," Ama-la say. She drag body closer to fire. Ama-la had problem on one side of body. She look like lopsided creature instead of woman. "Tashi Choegyal say this your chance. Show people you more than silly girls. Maybe good work bring husbands. Taking care of foreigner woman important for people in camp."

"How is it important?" we ask. "What do we care about foreigner woman coming here?"

"Her karma tied to ours." Ama-la's lazy eye bulge from face. "No one come clear from other side of world without reason. Tell me if she talk with Chinese man and they act like friends. Do not tell foreigner woman too much."

We look at each other. What do we know we could tell her? People often yell at us for saying wrong thing. One time we told Jampa his wife having fun with Tsering at night when Jampa in mountains. Everyone shout at us for that.

Our family has much trouble. Bad karma piling up like load of yak dung drying for winter fires. Now we have chance to burn our bad karma and bring good fortune to the family.

Grief years in family start long, long ago. We not born when it happen. But we know story. Ama-la's first husband raise Tibetan flag at border of Kham and China. They beat and arrest him. Took him away. Fourteen years in prison. Even friends afraid to be seen with family.

Not long after, Chinese army come to village. Soldiers like stick people from long trek into mountains with no food. Most only boys. Homesick for families. They eat so much food in one month. Enough for nomads for year. Take over even poorest tents. Force our poor Ama-la to bed with army man. She say he kind. She say he poor man caught in fear. Just like nomads. Neighbors afraid he make Ama-la spy. She no longer able to speak of Dalai

Lama. Forbidden to say prayers. Other soldiers burn photos of her teacher. Break prayer beads in front of tent. Chinese soldier man go away. Never come back. We born later.

Then Older Brother disappear. Neighbors say he go to India to be near Dalai Lama. Police come next day. Force way into tent.

"Tell us where son has gone," they yell at Ama-la. "No answer?" They lunge for us. Swing clubs. Sister's short arms whirl in air to cover her head. Crack of her skull like sound of log split open with ax. Eyes roll back in head. Sister collapse like empty sack of *tsampa* onto floor. Blood spout from cut above eye. Ama-la fall to knees begging. She cry into man's shoes. He kick her away. Spit tobacco onto floor right next to her face. I stare at sticky juice on earth. It stay long, long time.

"Where is Older Brother?" man bark at me. "Talk or we beat your mother." I try to comfort Ama-la and sister with one arm. He shove us onto bed like pile of dirty chuba robes. "We'll be back. I'm sure one of you will remember where Older Brother went. If not, we bring large truck for journey to snowy mountains. You stupid animals will remember there for sure."

When car gone, neighbors bring bundles of herbs. Cool water for Sister. Sister's head had bruise like breathing black field mouse. Neighbors put things back in order while Ama-la cry. She not know where Older Brother went. By next morning, band around Ama-la's stomach and chest explode into hot, wet blisters. We pick plants growing on mountain. Soak leaves in boiling water. Fix paste to stop itching. When sores nearly gone, disease move to her arms and start all over. Afterwards, Ama-la not same Ama-la any more. She look at neighbors and strangers with narrow eyes. Ama-la trust no one. Her hands crept under chuba to scratch bleeding skin on her arms.

Men never return, but fear stay with us everyday. When we buy soap in Manigango, shopkeeper tell us police come. They ask about Older Brother. Anyone know where he went? Anyone see him leave? He go over mountains or leave by road? He follower of Dalai Lama? Older Brother keep papers with foreigner writing hidden in tent? Shopkeeper tell us stay away. He not need trouble with police.

When Jeep go back down road to Chengdu, we run up with other greeters. We want to see Chinese man and foreigner woman up close.

"Where is yellow hair?" Sister say to me. "This woman not have yellow hair. This woman have hair like skunk. Wrong woman."

"Once we get her to tent, carry Ama-la here to look. Right now we help her. Even if she wrong one."

We put her bags on our backs. Chinese man and foreigner woman hurry behind us. Walking through field, we show her white flowers along path. She here to study plants. Helping her find plants help our family. Using stick, we dig grey stems out of ground. Pull apart big, fat roots.

"Monks at Derge Parkhang Monastery cut paper into strips. Use paper to print sacred teachings," we say. We show how we pound roots with chopping motion. Mix roots with water. Spread onto boards using wooden paddles. We have to speak slowly. Chinese man tell us start over many times. He not understand about how boards set in sun to dry. Or how we lift thin sheets of paper off boards and stack in monastery for future use.

We smart. Not tell foreigner woman that Chinese Government try to close monastery printing press not so long ago. Head of printing press lock door and not open for three days. By then officials decide monastery should stay as it is. Ama-la say they want to show backward nature of nomads. Using old method for new problem. Making paper and books by hand when big machines can do faster and better. We guess Chinese man be angry with us for saying it, so we not make mistake with that.

"If water coming from your behind, use this plant as medicine." We squat down in weeds. Move our hand to show foreigner woman how liquid might rush from her bottom. "Plant get rid of worms. Maybe you make painting of plant." We smile at each other. Sun barely move in sky and already we big help to this woman.

Norbu come across field. He stand at side, listening. We proud to talk to foreigner woman. Then he take over. Talk about bees. Tashi Choegyal say this our job, not Norbu's. She not know who to depend on. Who to ignore. Norbu's friends are trouble. Especially Dhondhup. He bully. Pushing Norbu to side, we pick up woman's bags and cross pasture to tent. Nice tent. Little purple and yellow flowers grow front and back. At tent, we unload bags. Unfold silk *khatas*. Stretch up to put them around her neck. Neck very white. Like white stones at edge of big pit in next village. Foreigner woman need sun. One day we take her on picnic so she can brown sick skin.

We poke at tent panels. "Feel how thick is yak hair. Keep out cold. Let in light."

We pry driest yak dung patties off stonewall at pasture edge. Knock them against stones and black insects shake loose and fall to ground. Foreigner woman does same. She jump away from little skittering bugs. Stuffing straw into bottom of iron brazier, we stack dung on top of pile. Ready to light on cool night. Will warm tent when winds fill valley. When wind make white waves on Yi-Lhun Latso Lake.

"You stay all winter. We dig hole under bed. Fill with yak dung. Cover with fur blankets." We show how we carve out deep opening. "Heat from yak dung keep you warm."

Old Kalsang come into tent, rolling from side to side on unsteady legs. His pants hang in folds against flat leg. He move around platform to pile sheepskin blankets on foreigner woman bed. Kind man. Full of wisdom for us children. We rush over to take his arm. Lead him to foreigner woman. She look at ragged scar on his cheek. Big scar go past nose and into hair. Her eyes get narrow and she breath big sigh when she see scar.

"She is the flower painter?" Old Kalsang ask Chinese man. Fat tassel of red yarn in his hair bob next to cheek as he talk. He take woman's art brushes from boxes and put them on chests. He hold her papers up to light. Flick papers with finger. Funny to see, he put ear right next to papers.

"What you doing?" we ask. "Why you listen to paper? Paper talking to you"

"Listen to plink or thunk. It tells if paper fine quality," he say. "This fine paper. I never hold such paper before." He squint to read characters on brush handles. Almost blind. Eyes covered with milk.

"He famous painter," we say about Old Kalsang. "Work for biggest monasteries. Use finest gold. No one match way he shade clouds. His animals live on page." We not tell Chinese man or foreigner woman that police arrest Old Kalsang. He refuse deny faith in Dalai Lama. Ama-la told us they smash Old Kalsang's leg under truck wheel. Send him to prison for seven years. Still, he refuse to sign papers saying he guilty.

Chinese man go outside and walk in fields. I see Sister return carrying Ama-la on back.

"Where is your yellow hair?" Ama-la ask foreigner woman.

"Ama-la, she not understand. This woman not speak our language," I say.

But then foreigner woman speak. "*Nga la da sepo meh.* I don't have yellow hair." Face scrunch up. She look confuse, but we confuse, too. How she start speaking our language so fast? "Why do you think I should have yellow hair?" foreigner woman continued. "Maybe I am not understanding you."

Ama-la look at her closely, get up next to her face and reach out hand to touch the hair. Finally, Ama-la tell Sister under her breath, "Hair not like her husband's. But I believe is right woman. Why else a foreigner woman come here to Yi-Lhun Latso?"

Sister whisper to me, "What Ama-la talk about? Her husband? Who is foreigner woman's husband?"

She lift Ama-la onto her back again and I tie cloth straps tight to carry her across meadow. Then Chinese man come back. Big problem. Ama-la look up and make big loud scream. She wriggle on Sister's back and try to use useless legs to run away. Sister almost drop Ama-la to ground. She hurry out of tent. Take Ama-la home to put her back into bed.

I look at Chinese man to see if he angry at Ama-la. He grunt like bear from deep in throat, hand cover nose. That dead smell makes me sick," he say.

Why he say that? It is only delicious smell of yak cooking over the fire. Foreigner woman shake her head at him. She speak. I not understand her words. When Chinese man there she stop speaking our language. Chinese man move to side so Little Girl Chi-Tso, running by, not touch him. When Sister return he still brushing off jacket and pants where girl's sheepskin robe touch him.

Sister whisper again in my ear, "No good. This man hate children. Man who hate children not be kind to us with arms too short and heads too big."

"Ama-la and Tashi Choegyal wrong about what we twins should do," I say to Sister. "Tashi Choegyal not here. Ama-la back in tent. They not see ugly look on face of Chinese man. They not hear mouth click like insect. Chinese man hate people in camp. We look strange. But we not fools. Forget taking care of foreigner woman. Smarter to make this man like us. Ama-la not need to know. She scared when she saw his face. But she old woman. All Chinese people look same to her. We help Chinese man. Care for him like daughter care for father. Everyone know wise fox follow own mind. Stupid rabbit follow thoughts of others."

# CHAPTER 11

## *Last Year's Green Shoots*

| | |
|---|---|
| *Na neeng tab pa'ee jang zhon* | *Last year the green shoots we replanted* |
| *Da lo sok ma'ee phon chok* | *This year they are stacked like straw* |
| *Pho zhon gay pa'ee loo po* | *The young man's body grows* |
| *Lha zhoo lay gyong ba* | *Firmer than a bow made of horn* |

*- Sixth Dalai Lama*

## Norbu's Story

I buried my face in the grass on the mountainside. Breathing warm, green smells, I sang songs and poems of the Sixth Dalai Lama under my breath. I practiced using beautiful words the way he did—to tell a story. It was my favorite way to pass the time in the hills while the sheep grazed. Trying out words I learned from reading and the radio. Words that made my lips buzz and my nose tickle. I used at least five new words every day. Nuzzle. Beautiful. Curious. Itch. Invisible. I would find a way to use these words today.

"Hey yak boy, stop reading and thinking you're Sixth Dalai Lama. Look down there at tents, by the road. What's happening?" said my best friend, Dhondhup. He looked in my pack and took out my book from the village library. Pictures of strange animals living in other countries. We laughed as he pointed at the elephants. Elephants we'd heard of. The animal with the long spotted neck, we never heard about. Dhondhup rolled over in the grass and shaded his eyes to see the camp better. We stretched out and stared at the tents circling the lake. Nearby us, sheep chomped their way through spring leaves and plopped into a post-lunch dream.

"That's the foreign woman arriving from Chengdu. I heard about it in town last month. She makes paintings of wildflowers," I said, chewing on a piece of grass. The sun prickled the back of my neck. Breeze drifted off the glacier.

"What are you talking about? You're making it all up."

"You were in the mountains when the County Magistrate came to the camp," I told Dhondhup. "He said the foreign woman will stay all summer. See the Chinese man with her? He's a PSB officer who will be her translator. Didn't anyone tell you?"

"I never heard any of this," said Dhondhup. He looked up at the vultures flying in lazy circles above the sky burial site on the next hill. The birds were now diving and then lifting back into the sky. Old Man Jampa Kalsang had died yesterday after a long illness and already the body had been cut apart and laid out for the giant birds to come and take their fill.

"The rules, didn't you see the rules?" My mind went back to the night of fear when local officials came to the camp. On that night, rain slid out of the sky. The Magistrate told us a foreign woman was arriving from Chengdu. If she got sick or hurt, we would be punished. The Magistrate is Tibetan, but still he worked his way to the top of the heap, and got to be spokesperson for the Chinese Government. Sometimes he arrested nomads who did not follow directions and beat them. His snake-tongued son told the villagers he only did this to spare their lives. He could actually get in trouble for not being harder with wrongdoers. He had the power to send people to prison where they might be tortured. He was doing the camp a favor with his easy treatment. Couldn't they see that?

The Magistrate had unrolled a long paper and signed the bottom with black characters. Stamping it with a round red seal, he then nailed the paper to the wooden door of the grain hut. Everyone stood around and stared as the Magistrate read the words one by one. Few could read the list, but they listened. No one wanted to be trapped on the wrong side of this unheard of event--a foreigner in the village.

When my father was out with the sheep, I returned to read the rules. I didn't have much chance to read printed words right out in the open. My reading angered my parents. Some bigger words--jacket, travel, dangerous--I knew from the dictionary hidden at the village school.

ATTENTION
About Mrs. Erebtze Peltere

1. She must not become ill from the cold. If she is not wearing a jacket, give her one.
2. She must not be out late at night. Don't allow her to walk alone after dark.
3. She must not engage in dangerous activities.
4. She is to live by herself, not with local families.
5. She must eat to remain healthy. Make sure she is eating enough.
6. She will be easily bored. Make sure she is not alone so she is not bored.
7. Be helpful and get her the things she asks for.
8. Do not talk about politics or religious matters with her.
9. Do not talk about personal matters or answer personal questions.
10. She is not to travel to Derge.
11. Person(s) responsible for causing her harm will be punished.
12. Address all questions and concerns to her translator, Comrade Zhang Kai Lun

When I read the rules at the grain hut, my nose stung and I fought to keep from sobbing like a newborn baby. I was drowning in the quicksand of an old world. A foreign woman would come from a big life where she had the freedom to think many things. I would be an insect next to her. Just that morning, my parents had yelled at me again. They were upset about my "reading habit." They wanted me to stop. Afraid it would make me leave the camp and move far away.

Every day I crept back to read the sign. Then I lay in bed at night, imagining my brain shrinking. Soon it would become shriveled and small. Only able to hold one thought in a day. That thought would be about the mountain weather or how to best tan a yak hide. Sinking in my own pity made me feel important. I had bigger things to think about than braiding yak tail ropes.

"She's here to paint wildflowers?" Dhondhup pulled himself up on his elbows and strained again to see from the hillside. "Where is she from?"

"I don't know, but I wonder what language she will speak."

"Language?" Dhondhup met my eyes and laughed out loud. "Strange question, fake Dalai Lama. Your head always filled with strange questions."

"I'm going to see that foreign woman." I gathered my books and put them in the pack. "Coming with me?"

"I'm busy," said Dhondhup. "What do I care about foreigner woman?"

"Hah! You're afraid of the Chinese man."

"And you aren't? Reading making you stupider, not smarter, yak-headed Dalai Lama. Your mouth filled with too big words that talk nonsense."

I sprinted down the mountainside, joining the group greeting the new arrivals. Lotse and Dolma, Lhamo Sangye's children, dragged a lamb forward on a leash. The foreign woman leaned down and picked up the lamb. Nuzzling the body with her face, she kissed it on the nose. The white streak in her hair caught my eyes. It mixed with the pearly white of the lamb's fleece. The woman and lamb joined like a fairy tale animal. The villagers gathered around and brought her tea. Usually shy, now everyone was curious. Then I remembered the instructions on the grain hut wall. They were acting. They welcomed her on their faces, but their blood crawled with fear underneath.

The otter-faced twin girls lifted the foreign woman's bags. They led her and the Chinese man across the pasture, babbling in their garbled language. The rest of us trailed behind. The twins were not much younger than me, but they had children's bodies, strange-shaped children with barrel chests and large heads. The foreign woman spoke a mixture of English and another soft, slurring language I couldn't understand. When she spoke, the Chinese man told everyone what she was saying. The strange words bounced in the air next to my ears and an idea began a slow itch at the back of my mind. Maybe this woman could teach me English. The months of sneaking time to listen to the radio begin to have new meaning.

It all started when I had traveled to the big city with Grandfather. While

Grandfather looked at horse blankets, I ran down a cobble-stoned alley and slipped under a door curtain into a small shop. Two men huddled in the dark, cigarettes glowing. Between them was a wooden box, buzzing with sounds of music and strange words I never heard before. My body felt like the mountain nights when lightning cracks and my hair quivers and stands on end. I sneaked in and stood behind the men, listening. How had these men made the horns, drums, and people fit inside this tiny box? I leaned in closer, brushing against the shoulder of one of the men. The man spun around and saw me looking. He jumped up so fast I fell backwards over a wooden bench. The men grabbed the sound box and hid it under the table. They hung a cloth over the table edges.

"Get out!" they shouted.

"What is that?" I asked, darting behind the counter where they couldn't capture me so easily. "How is the box making those sounds?"

"It's a radio, you simple yak-headed boy."

"But what is that sound the people inside are making?" I said. The shorter man lunged for me. He seized the tender skin of my ear and dragged me toward the door.

"English."

"What do you mean? What is English?"

They slapped each other on the back and laughed at me. "English is another language. People on the other side of the world speak English," they said as they pushed me out into the street.

Two years later a neighbor who had gone to live in the big city returned to the village. He carried the same type box. This one spoke our nomad language. It played our happy music. The neighbor said I could borrow it. When I turned the knobs on the front, my heart jumped. There was also English. I listened whenever I could, my ear right up next to the cloth. I practiced until I thought I could say the sounds just as they came from the radio. After many weeks, bellows, shrieks and grunts began to make sense. Words stood out. Some I heard over and over—BBC World Service. Not long after, a trader came from Chengdu. He brought silk fabric, spices, and books no one could read. One was a children's book with dirty, torn pages. Each page had an animal dressed in foreign clothes. There were strange markings next to the pictures. I guessed right away. It was English.

The trader gave me the book for a bag of dried dri cheese. Every day, I studied the pages while I sat with the sheep in the hills, listening to the radio. Finally, after many months, I guessed the meaning of the marks. I stared at those marks until they gave up their secret and matched the sounds from the radio.

Grandfather once told me, "When you don't know the meaning of the alphabet, the pen is longer than an arrow." That was no longer me. I was the only person in the camp who knew any English words. Now, out of nowhere, there was someone to speak with. The foreign woman could tell me how to make questions. She could answer my confusion about "was" and "is." Did they mean the same thing or not? She could tell me when to use the words that mean something is happening now or happened many days ago.

I trailed alongside as the twins led the Chinese man and the woman through the meadow. The twins pointed out flowers and talked in their half-language about plant medicines.

"Do you know a plant that has flowers that are thin, like paper," the woman spoke first to the Chinese man. Then he told us what she wanted to know. "Flowers blue like the sky with needles to pierce your skin?"

"*Sher Ngon,* the blue poppy," the twins giggled. "Grow in higher mountains. Follow turquoise bee's trail. It crosses meadows and heads to highlands. Turquoise bee in love with blue poppy."

"I can help her find the poppy," I butted in, trying to get the woman's attention. I wanted her to notice me.

The Chinese man looked at me like he hadn't seen me tagging along. The twins tried to get rid of me with a wave of the hand. They acted like I was a small boy who could be sent back to its mother. "We'll help her," they said. "On your way."

"What about in this meadow?" the woman turned and smiled at me. She had white skin like the rice bowls the trader brought from Shanghai. Her eyes were circled like a raccoon. She looked ill, perhaps from the long journey. "Are the bees here?"

"If you're lucky, you'll see them," the twins said. "They fly for three nights under full moon. When poppy is bluest. Tonight in sky such a moon."

"At night I see the bees in the pasture," I forced myself into the conversation again. "And I've seen bees and poppies when I herd the sheep on the mountainside."

The twins snarled and hustled the woman into her tent. They were still angry for the night of the last full moon party. My friends rigged a rope outside their tent entrance. The twins fell on their faces into the mud. I wasn't even there, but my parents yelled at me and said we were unkind boys. We should be ashamed for teasing girls who had the unfortunate karma to be daughters of a Chinese army officer.

The Chinese man followed the woman inside, explaining words the twins and the woman could not understand. I didn't know if it was allowed for me to enter the tent. I was afraid of the man, just like Dhondhup was. He might strike me or even send me to prison for not knowing my place. I crouched behind the tent and rocked back on my heels. Foreign words drifted through the tent walls and shooshed in my ears. Then there was silence. I peeked around the side to see if they were leaving.

"Hey, you!" A hand dug into my shoulder. The Chinese man. Strange how much the twins looked like this man. Maybe it was the eyes. Maybe the way they walked. "What do you think you're doing out here?"

I leapt to my feet and ran across the field, hoping he wouldn't remember what I look like. Maybe I would have to hide in the hills for weeks until he left the camp.

"Stop!" The man yelled after me. I ran until I was invisible among the trunks of the pine trees at the lake edge. My chest heaving, I waited in the pines scratching at the tree bark, taking apart and smelling the oily resin of the needle bundles. That curious Chinese man hadn't followed me. I kept one eye on the tent until I saw him move away and a group of nomads gathered. Everyone carried a load strapped to their back. Carpets, pots and pans all went into the tent.

I could not stop thinking about the beautiful foreign woman. My monkey mind leapt from idea to idea. The new thoughts mixed with the English words I was trying to remember. My mind flooded with visions of the Sixth Dalai Lama. Famous for his laughter and his lovers--he was not afraid of anyone in his society and refused to be a monk. Invaders kidnapped and murdered him when he was only twenty-three, one year older than I am now.

*"Was Sixth Dalai Lama the son of the Fifth Dalai Lama?" I had asked Grandfather. A bold question for a five-year old boy.*

*"The Sixth Dalai Lama was reincarnation of Great Fifth Dalai Lama," Grandfather said. "He was captured by Mongols and taken away. Some people said they killed him at the sacred lake. Others said he escaped and lived to be an old man."*

*"Why did he call himself Turquoise Bee?"*

*"His way of saying he was free. He was free to be his people's leader. Also free to love as he wanted, do as he wanted. He even drank beer and wrote poems to women he met in streets. He had big mind and big heart."*

*"Am I reincarnated? Will people come to take me away, too?"*

*"Yes, you are reincarnated. But don't worry, no one take you away unless you want them to."*

Since that talk with Grandfather when I was a child, I always imagined myself to be another Sixth Dalai Lama. Not a reincarnation, as Grandfather had explained. Simply a modern version of the Sixth. Sometimes I draped a goldenrod cloth over my chuba as a royal robe. I made up simple poems in my mind and tried them out on my proud parents. Whenever I quaked in the stormy mountains, clinging to the cliff while I guarded the sheep from predators, I pretended I was not a lowly shepherd at all. Instead, I was the powerful leader surrounded by my own protector deities.

These thoughts gave me courage to approach the foreign woman's tent again. I crossed the meadow and wandered in behind my neighbors. The Chinese man looked up as soon as I crept in. When my parents saw Chinese officials in the big village, they lowered their eyes to the ground. They tried to be as invisible as the mud walls. They would beat me if I stood out and made myself a target for abuse and suspicion by the authorities.

Yet, this foreign woman looked straight at the Chinese man when she spoke, not afraid to meet his eyes. He stared unblinking back at her as his foot tapped in a jerking rhythm on the tent floor. What kind of woman looked a Chinese official straight in the eye?

# CHAPTER 12

## Out of the Corner of Her Eyes

| | |
|---|---|
| *So gar pak pa'ee tsoom dhang* | *She looked at the people sitting in rows* |
| *Shook trel chee la tae nay* | *Her beautiful shining smile* |
| *Mik zoor thra mo'ee tril tsham* | *But out of the corner of her eyes* |
| *Zhon ba'ee tong la dae joong* | *She slyly looked at my youthful face* |

*-The Sixth Dalai Lama*

### Erzebet's Story

Not long after we arrived in the camp after that arduous journey from Chengdu, a dust flurry spun into the air from the field's edge, and a massive man rode in on a sorrel horse that pranced and whinnied in the afternoon heat.

I stared at the man's rifle, braided hair and gold earring and felt my face flush with embarrassment at the patronizing stereotype that came to mind: the Old World explorer's view of the exotic tribesman. He was as handsome as a movie star.

"Who is that?" I asked. Kai Lun passed my question on to the twins.

"Tashi Choegyal, camp leader," the twins said. "Can beat anyone who fools with him."

"Can wrestle bear. Take down charging snow lion with one rifle shot," said a woman standing near as she shuttled small children off to the side, out of the path of the horse and its rider.

Tashi Choegyal dismounted and strode over to the group, leaping over the guide ropes from the tents. He towered over the rest of the nomads. Planting himself in front of Kai Lun and me, he took a paper out of his pocket and read it for a few minutes to himself, his finger following the lines of print.

"Mr. Zhang? Welcome to this village." Kai Lun was like a skinny schoolboy next to the imposing Tashi Choegyal. He pulled himself up straight, just beginning to answer when Tashi Choegyal turned his back and instead turned toward me. He looked straight at me, his eyes like hazel gems in his mahogany face and his breath smelling of meat and beer. He reached out to take my hand, clasping it for what seemed several minutes more than necessary. "Tashi Delek, Madame Pelletier, I am happy to have you in this camp. These girls will help with everything you need." He put his arm around the twins who had carried my pack. So this was their official role.

Forgetting my decision to not let Kai Lun know I could speak some of the language, I was just about to respond to Tashi Choegyal when Kai Lun began to translate for me. I could make his job easier by admitting I could understand, but something told me I should keep it to myself.

"She happy to be here," the indomitable twins said, clinging to my side.

"So you already know what Madame Pelletier is thinking?" Tashi Choegyal said releasing my hand. "Be careful you don't get in trouble." Without addressing Kai Lun again, he led his horse back across the meadow, an entourage of laughing children and backslapping men following in his wake. Dismissed, Kai Lun mumbled to himself and inspected the view across the meadow to the mountains. I felt sorry for him. He was a considerate man. He had been kind to me during the long journey from Chengdu, making it possible for me to continue on to Tibet when he surely wanted to turn back.

In the midst of the commotion, I tried to imagine any one of these people taking me to the proper authorities to approach about Girard's disappearance. The twins' mother? The old man who was a painter? Two of many who had been damaged by life circumstances. It was unlikely any of these nomads had ventured more than a few kilometers from the camp in their entire lives. It was hard to imagine that those who were young would know anything about a photojournalist coming to this area almost twenty years ago. The twins themselves were an enigma. They had told me they were twenty years old, but they looked like twelve-year olds. Wherever I went that day, they were there, carrying my pack, guessing what I wanted or needed—often wrong.

I looked for the tall young man who said he knew about the poppies—before the twins had cut him off and stopped him talking. He wandered in and out of the tent with the rest of the neighbors, lifting up my books, and examining my pens and pencils.

"I want to know everyone's name," I said. "Tell me your names." They intoned their names as I gestured toward each of the group. During my briefing in France, I had been told that many people were named Tenzin, either the first or the second name, named after Tenzin Gyatso, the Fourteenth Dalai Lama. Eventually, I reached the young man who had caught my attention.

"*Nga Norbu Tenzin yin*," the young man said. I am Norbu Tenzin. His eyelids curved over his pupils like a sea wave. Coming close, innocent as a child, he leaned against me, his forearm pressing against my shoulder. He had a striking appearance--smooth skin, with the signature pattern of cheeks with broken red veins telling of years in the mountains, herding animals in brutal wind and snowstorms.

The laughing crowd escorted Kai Lun and me on a tour of the other tents, the mud and stone buildings, and the boundary walls along the pathway. Metal chests, carpets and sheepskin blankets filled the living spaces. Most items looked they had been in the family for generations, probably hauled from location to location on the back of yaks, like we had seen on the

drive on the way from Chengdu.

"She can have altar in tent, Mr. Kai Lun?" the neighbors asked. He seemed to consider whether this was a good idea or not, but then nodded his permission. It was obvious they gave him more power than I thought he deserved—he was just my translator after all.

My neighbors assembled a bag of altar items, returning to my tent carrying all the implements. They set up the altar on a table at one end of the tent and filled seven silver bowls: two with water, one each of rice, incense, flowers, an apple and an orange. Packages of biscuits were stacked in a pyramid alongside pillars of orange soda bottles, photos of religious teachers, bells, butter lamps and offerings to Buddha.

"Arrange bowls in straight line," they began their meticulous guidance. "Empty them at night. Wipe bowls out. Turn upside down. Balance one on other and re-fill in morning. Must sit no farther apart than space it takes to place grain of rice between." The cinnamon-musk smell of the incense filled the air, mingling with the sweet fragrance of the flowers.

Once my home was set, they made *momos* filled with yak meat, crackling in fat at the outdoor fire, and then dipped them in chili sauce. When I finished eating these dough pastries, they took away my plate and gestured for Kai Lun to speak with me.

"They want you to paint a flower," he said. "I told them you're too tired."

I didn't like him speaking for me, and I suddenly remembered how I had told Monsieur Lavonte, the French translator in Chengdu, that Kai Lun gave me the chills. He was here only for me, but something of that first impression still lingered.

"Painting? Already?" Kai Lun was right. I was exhausted, forcing enthusiasm into my words. I felt overwhelmed by the last three weeks, starting with the interrogation in Chengdu. Now my head fogged from the effort of channeling all of my communication through Kai Lun and trying to remember the new faces and names. "Are you sure?" I asked the group.

"Yes! Yes! Begin now while children awake," they said. "We get grandparents." The men rushed out, returning moments later with wrinkled, stooped relatives hanging on their arms.

I took out the brushes, paints and paper, unwrapped the wet towels, and revealed the *Parnassia*, collected on the mountaintop. Carefully, I unfolded leaves bent over roots and flowers that twisted and overlapped and laid the plant on a piece of white cardboard. It was intact, close to the condition on Zhedou Shankou Pass when I first scraped away the snow from around its petals and roots. Using a caliper, I measured the dimensions of the flowers, heart-shaped leaves, stem and roots, and made notes. I sketched. A child broke away from his mother, reached out and touched the graphite lines, erupting into giggles. Norbu Tenzin was there. He leaned across the drawing; his face just inches from my own. A mixture of meadow and forest smells rose from his body.

"Could someone light a lamp for me?" I asked Kai Lun, focusing back on the painting. "It's getting too dark to see the lines or mix accurate colors."

Both the twins and Norbu responded to Kai Lun's inquiry and jumped up and grabbed at the oil lamp. The girls lit it and placed the lamp on the small table, but Norbu moved it and held it close to the painting, adjusting the light to cast no interfering shadows. I looked up and saw Kai Lun's eyes riveted on the boy. The tendons in his neck stood out like pulsing electrical cords. The clicking sound was back, beating inside his cheek. I looked back and forth between the two of them, wondering if something had happened earlier in the day that I had missed.

I went back to mixing colors, shades of green: pea-green, lime-green, dull forest green. With my brush, I soaked up tint for the first thin layer of color, barely visible in the pool of clear water in the porcelain dish. The hour went from 9:00 to 10:00 and then 11:00. Still I painted and still they watched. Midnight came and went before I completed the *Parnassia*, with its hundreds of seeds and minute color variations of the fresh and dying leaves and petals. In the half-light of candles and the oil lamp, I reached for the now-wilted flower, but grasped the painting by mistake. It was real.

"Aah, *mehto ngu ney re.* Flower is real," the guests agreed. They reached out and lightly touched the painting and it was time to go. Parents bundled their sleeping children into their arms and lifted them in slings onto their backs. Like a troop of circus performers, they slipped out of the tent.

I cleaned the brushes, put away the pigments and settled for the night. Just as I pulled the blankets over my shoulders, there was laughter at the tent entrance. They were back.

"Come outside," they yelled, gesturing toward the meadow.

I pulled on my clothes and ran out after them. The meadow was a shadow play of tents, animals and trees, with the backdrop of a buzzing symphony. Swarms of golden bees. Their wings reflected the white of the moon, and the nomads played among them in the meadow. Both men and women wrestled, jumped rope and chased each over the ropes. My exhaustion was gone, and I joined in, laughing more than I had in years. Hours later, as we headed back to our tents, I caught a glint of blue within the thinning swarm; turquoise bees rising and falling, heading out over the pasture.

Back in my tent, I took out my diary to record the events of the day. My eyes followed the wavering aurora from the butter lamp and the shadow of my hand poised above the pages. I wanted to be free of Kai Lun's interpretation of my conversations with the nomads. During the day, I had found myself monitoring my words and interest according to his reactions, something I shouldn't have to worry about with a translator. If he continued to stick to me so closely, I would never be able to directly ask questions about

Girard. Questions I had imagined would be perfunctory entrees to information now seemed unwise.

I set myself the task to learn one hundred new words everyday. When I had the opportunity to speak to the Tibetans, I would be ready. Shivering in the night air, I put the diary aside, dug in my bag for a sweater and socks, took out my Tibetan-English dictionary and started on page one with the first character, "Ka." After a few minutes of taking notes and writing down new words, I flipped to the middle of the book and searched for "Norbu," the name of the tall nomad boy who had held the lamp for me while I painted.

*Norbu.* Precious jewel.

# CHAPTER 13

## *Measuring the Stars in the Sky*

| | |
|---|---|
| *Sha jam lu po tree gyang* | *Her body can be caressed* |
| *Jam pa'ee teng tso mee lon* | *But her longing cannot be fathomed* |
| *Sa la ree mo tree pa'ee* | *Drawing plans upon the earth* |
| *Nam khai gar tso thook joong* | *I can measure the stars in the sky* |

*- Sixth Dalai Lama*

### Kai-Lun's Story

Luminous meteors trailed across the sky. I felt pure and alive, knowing my brother had gazed at these same stars when he was in Tibet. It had been more than ten years since anyone in our family had been allowed into the prison to see him, but I felt him with me now, in this meadow. I strolled the long way home, circling the pasture edge to my tent near the river. Kicking yak horns aside, I picked up clumps of satiny sheep wool stuck in the grass, stuffing them deep in my pocket. The paper plants' sweet fragrance saturated the air.

The tiny bones deep inside my ears buzzed, as if activated by a tuning fork. Then I saw the gold and blue river of shimmering light, coursing through the meadow. Bees flew low in the pasture, catching moonbeams on their wings. I had thought bees only flew in the daytime when it was warm, although I couldn't remember ever having seen an actual bee in the city. Just as I reached my tent, I heard laughter behind me, and saw Madame Erzebet with a group of the nomads running in the meadow.

My chest heaved with a deep sigh. She was unlike any woman I had ever met. She had begun more friendships in this one afternoon that I had had in ten years. And she was intelligent—she would be speaking Tibetan in no time and then it would mean trouble. The Tibetans would be able to arrange to get the papers to her and I wouldn't even know.

My eyes locked on the panoramic view in front of me. I had the strangest sensation I had been here before and slowly I realized why it was so familiar. At home in Chengdu, hidden in the chest under moth-eaten sweaters was a framed photo of me, Mei Ling and Jin Quon seated in front of an antique painted backdrop. I had wanted to surprise them with a special magical photo and asked around until I found an old man who would be willing to take our picture, as long as we told no one. Hours after curfew in our neighborhood, I had led my wife and son down an empty alleyway. We skirted piles of garbage and half-starved dogs with ribs like wooden barrel staves, eventually arriving at a rough-hewn doorframe, a curtain hanging lopsided in the opening. Holding up a match, I had verified the nearly obliterated address. The eye-stinging smell of photo chemicals greeted us as we ducked under the cloth and entered the damp studio. In the room, the photographer gave us the choice of a background scene with a windmill and bridge, a pagoda surrounded by cherry blossoms or a hillside with farm animals next to a stream. To risk arrest to stand in front of a tired windmill? It didn't make sense.

Then I had spotted a cracked canvas rolled on a rod hanging high above the studio. Unfurled, it was a landscape of a shining glacier, snowy peaks in the background, a lake too green to be real. Wildflowers too bright yellow and too bright crimson carpeted the hills. Out of the photographer's costume closet, I selected an orange ceremonial robe trimmed with gold braid and embroidered dragons. I was shocked at my own choice. I was an intellectual, never drawn to the trappings or myths of the royal emperors, but now I wanted to wear this robe, just once. My wife timidly chose a lovely amethyst flowered dress with a high collar and red and gold long-tailed birds flying around the border. Jin Quon, it was his fifth birthday, picked goldenrod silk pants and jacket and a striped tiger cap with pointed ears. My family had posed in the midst of the mountain scene on wooden chairs that from the front were regal and from the back were scuffed and barely painted.

I pulled aside the opening flap of my tent in the meadow. A cool mushroomy odor greeted me; the smell that usually means the rain is past. In the dark, my eyes focused on the space, less than half the size of Madame Erzebet's. A dirt floor, table with chairs, small bed covered with fur blankets, oil lamp, and iron brazier. There was one plate, spoon, bowl and cup. The furniture loomed like shadowy animals asleep in the corners. I tried out the creaking chair and pulled it up to the child's size table. My knees just fit under the edge, my pant leg snagging on a protruding splinter. It brought back a wash of fear at the memory of the day I met with the Director in Chengdu and he insisted I speak French. The blood drained from my face even though it had been months ago.

I moved to the bed and lay down. Hands clasped behind my head, I stared at the open smoke vent at the top of the tent, an opening to the universe where the stars winked back at me.

In the midst of my despair and loneliness, I felt a certain comfort. In fact, I'd never imagined anything so perfect. I was forty years old and had never had my own room, my own bed, or my own table where I could read and think in peace. I lit the oil lamp, removed my precious books from the suitcase and arranged them on the table, next to my pen. Opening my notebook to a clean page, I recorded my impressions of the nomads I had met that day. While translating, I had watched for clues. Some of them seemed simple and would be of no concern; others had left an unpleasant taste in my mouth. None struck me as likely candidates for having the missing Pelletier papers.

I tried to remember exactly what Tashi Choegyal had said to the twins. That they should be careful and not get in trouble. What was he talking about? What kind of trouble? The twins looked feeble, not like troublemakers. I felt a gnawing familiarity. They reminded me of nephews and nieces in my family—not the eyes, not the mouth, but something was familiar.

My briefings back in Chengdu had led me to expect the nomads would be rough and crude. True enough, but they had also been disarming in their welcome. It charmed me, though I kept my distance. I wished the camp children made me feel as happy as my own treasured Jin Quon. These ragged urchins smelled like feral animals born under trees in the forest. I liked to dress my son in a fresh white, ironed shirt and dark blue pants when guests arrived. No matted hair, no river of snot running from his nose, sliming toward his upper lip. Mei-Ling was always ready to wipe away signs of a cold before it crept over to repel or infect others.

As I continued to make my notes, the afternoon and evening's events blurred--too many people with gold teeth. I shined the barrel of the pen on my sleeve. In the light of the butter lamp, I grimaced into the silver strip, examining the reflection of my stretched smile, running my tongue over my teeth. I had never noticed how yellow my teeth are. They protrude at the top, push my lip out slightly, and one of the front teeth crosses over the other at an odd angle.

Tashi Choegyal. This was the man my superiors had told me had gone to Lhasa with the documents. Since that day, I had rehearsed in my mind how I would stride right up to him; make sure he knew I would be watching him. I hadn't expected a giant who rode in on a horse straight out of a fable. Pan Gu. In stories my parents read me when I was a child, Pan Gu slept within an egg. One day he awoke and stretched and the egg cracked open. Pan Gu climbed out. The light parts of the broken egg became the sky. The dark, heavy parts formed the earth. This separation of the earth and sky was the beginning of yin and yang, the two opposing forces of the universe. Me and Pan Gu. Me and Tashi Choegyal. Aaah, I am thinking about the way Tashi Choegyal fixated on Madame Erzebet's face and hair. She lowered her eyes and stuttered when she spoke, blushing at his obvious interest. I am blushing at the memory.

But now, as I remember. . . was it my imagination, or did Norbu Tenzin, the nomad boy, scrutinize Madame Erzebet's reaction to Tashi Choegyal? He touched her arm. At the time it had occurred to me he might be signaling her. She should trust him; speak to him later about something important. The papers. Perhaps the camp leaders thought sending a boy to make the first contact with her would be something unexpected and I would miss it.

I didn't miss it, but now I remember more. Norbu had stared at her back for several minutes before she turned and looked straight at him. That was when she blushed, looking at the boy, not at Tashi Choegyal.

# CHAPTER 14

## *The Willow Loves the Sparrow*

| | |
|---|---|
| *Chang ma chee'oor sem shor* | *The willow loves the sparrow* |
| *Chee'oo chang mar sem shor* | *The sparrow loves the willow* |
| *Sem shor thoon pa choong na* | *If they are suitable for each other* |
| *Gya thra hor pay mee thoob* | *Then hawk cannot enchant the sparrow* |

*- Sixth Dalai Lama*

## Erzebet's Story

The second day in camp, I slept for twenty-four hours, waking only for moments when the tent flap was pulled back by a Tibetan nomad woman, a glass of hot water was set on the table next to me, and the woman slipped away again. By the third day, I was renewed, ready to implement my plan: Find a land form that matches the one in the Chinese Government photograph sent after Girard's death. Locate the poppies that he spoke of in his letter. I needed to accurately label the maps so I could refine the search and identify what villages or nomad campsites were within walking range. I figured I would need a week to get settled, before I could start to ask questions of the nomads and people from the surrounding villages. I would walk in the meadows, sketch and paint and do nothing that would cause Kai Lun to be suspicious or spend even more time watching me.

Dew silvered my boots as I skirted the clumps of papermaking plants. These I had located in my botanical identification book and now knew were *Stellera chamaejasme.* I settled on a flat stone in the middle of the pasture, a lookout point resting on top of the second hill and took out binoculars, pencils, erasers, magnifying glasses, calipers, and maps.

One day at a time. One area at a time. Patience had never been one of my strong points. Now it was critical to have the patience to get to know the people in the camp and develop trust, and take the time to accurately evaluate the terrain and determine where the most likely location would have been for Girard to have disappeared. I needed patience to proceed at a pace that did not arouse suspicion—suspicion in whom I wasn't sure.

Unfolding the biggest map, I began to identify landforms focusing on what appeared to be gorges and ravines—areas where Girard's car could have gone off the road—if indeed, the photo from the government had had anything at all to do with his disappearance. I sketched them in on the maps and named the roads and villages near Yi-Lhun Latso Lake, calculating how long it would take to walk, ride a horse or take a bus between various points. When people came near, I slipped the maps between layers of watercolor paper and brought out the sketches of the wildflowers.

When I finished with the maps, I moved on to sketching the wildflowers. Near the *Stellera*, flowers similar to purple lupine from home sported a "hood" and palmate leaves. This was *Laminaceae scutellaria*, commonly known as the skullcap. Black filaments and amber anthers sprang like a tiny fireworks display from their wine-colored throats. This plant would be interesting to researchers at the Sorbonne—it had relatives worldwide and was being used in the treatment of a wide range of nervous conditions including epilepsy, insomnia, hysteria, anxiety, and delirium tremors. I interpreted the skullcap from three angles, slicing the flower down the center and taping it down to examine the floral mechanism. Enlarging details of the seeds, stamen, and root system, I created color studies, holding the leaves and the blossoms up close to the paper to get a perfect color match.

The sun heated the meadow, setting in motion the whirr of the grasslands. Red dragonflies with gold shimmering wings sped by to river pools and bees worked diligently from flower to flower. Two nomad boys approached, carrying slingshots. They drew back the bands and shot pebbles at straying sheep, plunked down on the grass, and pestered each other while they talked. One boy was Norbu.

"*Khye rang gi tsen la gare ser gi yor*? What is your name? " I asked the second boy. I didn't recall seeing him before, and I took this opportunity to start practicing my Tibetan with Kai Lun nowhere in sight.

"*Nga Dhondhup yin.* I am Dhondhup." Liverish stains marked his teeth, possibly signaling a high fever or malnutrition in childhood. His hair was short, ragged at the edges as if cut with pinking shears. He wore a shirt with a military-type panel crossing the chest, fastened with fancy gold buttons at the neck and down the sides. I looked at the faint shadow of a mustache on Dhondhup's upper lip. He was not a boy after all. Maybe in their twenties, both young men were childlike, poking and mocking each other's stories.

"Remember me?" Norbu surprised me by speaking in English with a slight British accent. He was quite handsome: a fine nose, straight white teeth, and prominent cheekbones.

"*Yin da yin.* Of course." I hadn't noticed how tall he was—well over six feet, typical of the warrior Khampas. Thick, shiny hair hung past his shoulders. He wore a chuba, black pants and blue-striped tennis shoes. I took a deep breath to see if I could smell again the fragrance of the meadow and the forest that came from his skin and hair that first night I had arrived in the camp.

"You speak Tibetan!" Norbu and Dhondhup said at the same time. "Why is the Chinese man talking for you?"

"And you speak English," I said to Norbu, ignoring their question about Kai Lun's translation. "Are you studying so you can go to the West?"

"Why would I want go to West?" he said in a mixture of Tibetan sprinkled with a few words of English. "Have all I need right here. This is the perfect place for me to be. What would I do if I traveled to West? I'm a nomad."

"Then why are you learning English? How did you get that English accent?"

"Listen to Radio Free Europe on radio. Listen to British scholars. Try to sound like them. And I want to learn everything. Not just English."

Girard. He reminded me of a young Girard.

Norbu looked at me intently and his face changed from pride to alarm. He jumped up and gathered his things to leave. "You're laughing at me because I'm a nomad and saying silly things."

"Oh no!" I exclaimed, realizing I had a broad smile on my face at the memory of Girard. "Not at all. It made me happy to hear you say that. I'm laughing out loud because it reminded me of a young man I once knew who was filled with bravado and curiosity. He also announced, 'Me, I want to know everything!'"

"Okay, " Norbu said hesitantly, as he settled back down in the meadow. "Ask me a question. I tell you if I know about that."

"Dinosaurs, what are they?"

"Hah! I know that. I'm not like my dummy friend Dhondhup here," he said with a laugh. "Dinosaurs are big reptiles. Little brains. Lived on earth millions years ago. Most ate only plants."

"*Nyima, thang dawa, sa. Trel ba, gar re ray*? What is the connection between the sun and the moon and the earth?"

"I know that too. You can't trick me by asking these questions. Moon goes around earth. Both go around sun."

"How do you know that?" A goat clomped over and nuzzled my shoulder, chewing on a piece of my hair. Devil's pupils were set in amber eyes, yet its mouth curved in a cupid's smile. It let out a guttural bleat as I laughed and pushed it away. The goat wandered over to Norbu, and he cradled its neck in his arm, winding his fingers in the silky fur.

"I read it in a book village teacher gave me."

Dhondhup snorted and jumped up, "Better be careful the wind doesn't carry your words back to camp. Your father will beat you if he hears you say that." The goat slid out from under Norbu's arm. He thumped it on the rump and the animal sashayed down the hillside, the tinkling of bells fading into the distance. Norbu lunged for Dhondhup. They wrestled through the flowers and rolled through the grass, pushing each other around until they tired. When I was in school, I had been curious about wrestling--the hand in the crotch, the tension of thigh upon thigh. A mysterious erotic activity now played out among nomads on a Tibetan mountainside.

As the boys lay panting and laughing in the grass, they reached for the magnifying glasses, held them closer and then further away, peering at the flowers and at each other. While they assessed all life forms on the hillside, I quizzed them about their lives and families, using the dictionary I kept in my bag. Each tended a flock of over 200 sheep. Norbu's family lived in the main camp, but he traveled back and forth with the flock to the mountains above the lake during the summer months.

"Do you like your life as a shepherd?"

"Like it?" Norbu considered the question, as he examined the lines in his palm with the magnifying glass. "I don't know. It's my life. No thinking about liking it or not."

"Why not?"

"Crazy questions," snorted Dhondhup. "Who's interested in these things?" His gaze followed the sheep as they wandered across the meadow. He stood up to follow them, gathering a hand full of small stones to toss in their direction, and then paused, obviously waiting for Norbu to go with him.

"I like these questions," said Norbu. "Ask me more."

I rummaged in my bag for a piece of dark chocolate I'd toted from Europe, knowing I would relish the opportunity to eat it far from home. They each took a section, smelled it, licked it, and then bit into it.

"Isn't it delicious?" I asked. "Do you like it?"

Norbu howled with laughter, hanging over the book as I went back to thumbing the pages of the dictionary. "Why you bring this all way from your country? Tastes like mud with sugar. Maybe we just graze in meadow and eat dirt."

I thought it was funny, but I must have looked dismayed, because he poked me in the side and said, "*Nga tso nye gur gi du.* We just tease you." He rested his hand next to mine on the easel. A rush of electricity spiked up my arms. I was attracted to this handsome young man. Had he touched my arm and hand on purpose that first day in the tent when I painted?

Suddenly, my lightheartedness disappeared. I felt uneasy. Where was Kai Lun who was ordinarily right at my shoulder? I looked around. He was propped against a boulder, not twenty meters away, calmly looking in our direction through binoculars. He didn't flinch when I looked at him, never shifted the gaze of the lenses. It was time to leave.

"The first day in the meadow," I said, turning to face Norbu, as I gathered all of my supplies. "You told me you knew how to find the blue poppies. Will you take me to where they grow?"

He stood up and shuffled from foot to foot. "I can take you. But I herd sheep everyday. I'll ask my parents when I can go."

"I'll be waiting."

# CHAPTER 15

## *Taming a Wild Dog*

| | |
|---|---|
| *Khyee tay dak khyee zeek khyee* | *Tiger-hunting dog, leopard dog, any dog* |
| *Da kha der nay tree song* | *Will follow the arrow toward food* |
| *Nang gee dak mo ray tzom* | *But the indoor tigress, when tamed* |
| *Dree nay thoor doo lang song* | *Will rise up again* |

*- Sixth Dalai Lama*

### Kai Lun's Story

The weather. I'll just dispense with it right up front. In Chengdu we talked endlessly about the weather: the heat, the rain, the smog, the chill, how it was last year, how it was ten, twenty years ago, and how it will be in fifty years. Here we merely absorbed it—living in the midst of yellow days, cooling afternoon showers, crisp nights that led to deep, satisfied sleep. And what more is there to say about the landscape? A magnificent mountain at the end of the valley that sometimes was blue-white, sometimes colored rose from the sunset, sometimes appeared as a haunting grey-blue in the distance. Every time I looked at it, it woke me, made me feel more human and alive.

It had been a week since we arrived at the lake. Erzebet, my charge, spent her days in the pastures and along the river, going out further each day to look for flowers in new locations. The lamp in her tent was often burning late in the night, and she emerged in the morning with completed paintings to show the appreciative nomads. I was impressed—she was very strong physically, worked long hours, and the paintings were startlingly accurate and beautiful at the same time. I had women in my life I was close to—four sisters. But I somehow had been pedestrian in my ignorance that a European woman could be hard-working. I just hadn't known.

I had begun to hang back and watch from a distance. It didn't make sense to hang over her shoulder every minute; in fact my presence was probably preventing the nomads from approaching her—something that was counter to my strategy for surfacing the documents. Patience is power; with time and patience the mulberry becomes silk.

Now I watched Madame Erzebet leave her tent and head toward the small village down river from Yi-Lhun Latso. She walked purposely toward the five mud houses scattered in a semi-circle at the far edge of the field. Her expedition ended abruptly. She seemed to have tripped on a rock and she pitched to the side. She was right next to a big hole in the ground. Even from across the field, I could hear frenzied snarling and barking exploding from the pit and see the top of what appeared to be a dog's head as it hurled itself up to the edge. I ran. Before I could get to her, the animal pitched back into the darkness and Madame Erzebet yanked her foot from the abyss onto the flat of the meadow. Struggling, she lurched to her feet, wobbling to the edge of the field. She cowered to the side, spitting on her fingers to wipe away the bright blood tracks on her ankle.

"Why this woman walk alone beyond your camp?" yelled a man running up just as I got there. "Dogs in other villages tear you both apart." He pulled a hunk of meat out of a sack and tossed it into the pit, and wiped his bloody fingers in the grass. The man's face was scarlet, a contorted mass of anger. "Stupid foreigner woman. Stupid Chinese man. Not even carrying stones to throw."

"I didn't know," Erzebet said, turning to me. "No one told me about the dogs." In the hole the barking had ceased, replaced by a glugging, slurping sound.

"Your foreigner woman almost killed. . .," the man yelled at me. "Make sure she know how to walk in fields. Not my job to keep her safe. This dog trained to protect us from predators. Only trusts us."

"I didn't know to warn her about the dogs," I was still panting from my dash across the field. "Why are these animals so vicious?"

The man explained. All nomad families kept two or three dogs. They acquired puppies, dug yak-sized holes, then lowered the dog into the hole and left it there for many months. Only the family fed it. When brought out of the pit, it was paranoid and ferocious. It would maul anyone except people in the family. My stomach roiled at his matter of fact description of such cruelty to a living creature, and Madame Erzebet looked like hers was doing the same.

"But what about visitors to the camp," she asked. "How can anyone get near without being attacked?"

He continued to explain: when visitors arrived, they hollered at the tent from a distance to alert the family that a friend was near. Strangers knew to give the camps a wide berth as they traveled through the nomad territory. During festivals, the dogs were tied up so they wouldn't attack the guests.

When the man was finished talking, we left. Madame Erzebet was very pensive not saying a word as we walked through the grasses, and she was obviously traumatized by the day's events. I carried her bag of paints back to the tent for her. If she were my wife, I would hold her, fix her broth and then sit next to her while she lie in bed sleeping. I pitied Madame Erzebet, but pitied myself more. The situation with the dog in the hole would never have happened if she hadn't gone out walking by herself—how did she think she would communicate with the people she met along the way?

I settled down to read a book in the meadow, watching to make sure she didn't leave the tent without me being with her. Still, she slipped out while I had dozed off in the sun and when I woke, I saw she had already come out and was sitting on some rocks, so I walked over to be near her.

As I approached Madame Erzebet, I spied a shiny mica-like object lying in the grass. A lifeless dragonfly, its glassine wings extended straight out from the velvet-segmented body. I placed it in a small metal box that also contained a bee I had found in the grass the day before.

"Have you seen an insect like this?" I called over as I slipped a flat twig under the bee and lifted it from the box. "It's a strange color."

She had a large paper on her lap, which she quickly folded like a map and slid into her pack. There was no reason for a map in these fields. While I gently prodded the insect with a stick, I tried to make sense of the image of Madame Erzebet with a map.

She left her pack of papers behind on the rocks and came closer. She stared at the insect, exclaiming, "Aha! It's the turquoise bee."

"So you've seen one. I guess I don't know much about nature. I thought it might be rare. I'm going to mount this bee on a board and put it in a glass frame for my son, Jin Quon." I tentatively put the box back in my pocket, wondering if I was being rude by not offering it to Madame Erzebet. Rude? Why was I worried about courtesy—I wasn't sent here to make life lovely for this French woman. Better to wonder if such a gift might ingratiate me to her, a situation that would be useful later. No, I would save it for Jin Quon.

She sat down on a large flat rock and began to sketch a daisy-type flower with elongated tangerine-yellow petals. There were fine white hairs all along the thin stem.

As she sketched, a burly man marched through the field, pulling a brown mastiff on a leash. The powerful animal, white markings above each eye, strained at its chain, pulling itself over backwards in an attempt to sink its teeth into passers-by. The man kicked it in the side and it crawled placating along the ground, until he reached down and scratched it behind the ears. The dog yipped with pleasure. A few seconds later, the chain clanked and it bolted back up to its challenging stance. The man headed straight for us, the dog pulling against the chain. My back tensed and my mind whirled again with the terror of having seen Madame Erzebet nearly mauled just hours before. There was no way the man could stop this dog from attacking us. We both ran.

"Come back. I am Nyima Rabten," the man called after us. "I brought guard dog for Madame Erzebet."

"Guard dog? I didn't ask for a dog," Madame Erzebet said. She stood at a distance, and I picked up rocks to throw if the dog broke loose and lunged for us. With one tentative step at a time, she made her way to the tent and slipped inside, listening and talking through the tent panels. "I don't want a dog. I'm afraid of these dogs."

"Must have dog," Nyima Rabten said. "Too dangerous here without guard dog. Dog will prowl area at night. Guard tent while you sleep, scare away bandits, wolves and leopards. During day you chain dog near tent to warn you of strangers."

Nyima Rabten looped the chain to a stake near the tent and left a shank of meat for me to feed the animal. When he walked away, Madame Erzebet peeked out of the tent and I threw the meat toward the dog, watching as it got up and stretched its paws to reach it. The meat was a few inches too far away. The dog strained at the chain, dug its claws into the earth and tried to crawl to the pulpy offering. Blue bottle flies lifted off the meat and then set down again, unperturbed by the dog stretching closer. I grabbed a long tree limb near the tent, but was afraid to get close enough to shove the food to the bear-like animal.

I was relieved to see a woman, braids looping to her waist, walking across the field with her children. She would know what to do.

"Be careful," were her first words to Madame Erzebet. She went over to the meat, picked it up and tossed it close to the dog's head. "Dog can kill you."

I moved closer to the children.

"Stay away until dog know you." Lifting the sleeve on her robe, the woman showed us a nasty scar and pantomimed a dog biting her arm. "*Kyi gyab gi du.* Dog bite."

Madame Erzebet had a daily ritual--bringing water to the tent, heating it on the brazier with a yak dung fire, and maybe pouring it over her head while she stood in a large metal tub. She would emerge from the tent with wet hair hanging down to her shoulders. A black hair clasp shaped like an iris held it behind her ears.

The next morning, after Nyima Rabten brought the dog, she left her tent just after dawn, carrying the bucket to the river. Swinging the metal bucket, she moved in a wide circle past the dog. I saw her nervously pick up a large rock as the dog followed each step, its eyes locked on her as she backed to the river. I picked up a rock myself mentally rehearsing how I would throw it at the head. Calculating how fast I could run to safety if attacked.

She filled the bucket at the river, and started back. She was still ten feet away when the dog sprang to its feet, thrashing and jerking its head to squeeze out of the chain and collar. The fur bristled stiff in a ridge on its back and it charged at her legs. As I ran over, she screamed, dropped the rock and threw the bucket at the dog. It thunked off the ground and she fled to the tent, tearing at the entrance flap ties. Rushing to see what happened, Lhamo Sangye and two neighbor women yelled to the men who raced behind them. They yanked the dog by the collar and pulled it to the ground. The dog, its chest heaving like a car motor trying to turn over in the winter, lie flattened in the earth and the women roughly looped the chain closer to the stake.

"This animal is a nightmare," Madame Erzebet sobbed, looking back and forth from the dog to the tent. She wiped her nose on her sleeve as the women clustered next to her and stroked her hair.

I felt like a frightened woman myself, standing there with a rock in my hand, a nervous clacking coming from my mouth. What had been a sporadic bad habit in my earlier years at school when I was anxious was now turning into a constant occurrence. I had to save face, so I lashed out at the nomads, accusing them of giving her a wild dog that couldn't possibly be tamed. They responded with raised voices, rapid explanation, waving their hands and arms.

"I'm not going to hide from this beast," Madame Erzebet said in a quivering voice. "Your government issued me this invitation. If it's so dangerous here, you have to make it safe. Arrange for me to stay with a family."

The nomads shrank back and huddled together. Their eyes darted between Madame Erzebet and me, and I felt my face heat up to a boil. My fear of the dog diminished next to my alarm at having been humiliated in front of these nomads--by a woman, no less. This woman had laughed at me when I told her to stay in the car on our way into this forsaken land. Now she was making me, a PSB officer, look like a peon. She would find that to be a big mistake.

"Madame Erzebet," I croaked. It took a huge effort to keep my clicking cheek under control. Her demands undermined my position and the nomads were watching to see how I handled it. "You accepted the invitation from my government. You chose to come to a barbarian land, and you know what the restrictions are. The government will never allow you to move in with a family. That is impossible."

"I'm going to the river to write." She grabbed her notebook and pens. "I want to be alone." She hustled with stiff legs like a scared schoolgirl as she walked across the field, her head down, clutching her book.

My careening mind jumped from event to event on the treacherous path that led me to this no-man's-land where people wore leopard skin robes and poked holes through their ears to hang gold tubes. Zig zagging through the field, I tried to track down Nyima Rabten, the dog owner. He wasn't in sight. He must have heard about the situation by now, and he was afraid of being punished for giving Madame Erzebet a dangerous beast—under the guise of protecting her.

Slipping into my tent, I stared at the blank walls. I was exhausted. I dropped my head to the desktop, pushing into the wood until my spine ached. It diverted my attention from the creeping despair over the inevitable: my wife would meet another man who was not a political target and fall in love. My son would forget me. I would be old when I returned, if I returned. Then I remembered what my grandfather said to me when I was a young boy: the man who removes a mountain begins by carrying away small stones. I must keep moving forward, no matter how small my progress appeared.

I woke after midnight, listening. An animal scuffled near my bed. Something chewing, breaking into my boxes. I lay quietly waiting to hear it start up again so I could slip out of bed, and find a trap or a weapon. The man, who years ago had dreamed of having a small family pet to enjoy, now imagined snapping the neck of a living creature and throwing it out of the tent, as far across the field as the night air would carry it.

As I drifted back to sleep, the grinding noise started again. The creature would have to be spared. The sound was my own teeth attacking each other.

In the morning, a husky, familiar voice called from the pasture. Nyima Rabten. He made no acknowledgement of his wrongdoing by bringing the vicious dog to Madame Erzebet. Instead, he talked as if the day was all going according to plan.

"Next two days," Nyima Rabten said, taking a piece of raw meat and a big bone out of a sack he had slung over his shoulder. "We bring dog at night when Madame Erzebet safely inside. Take dog back in morning. After that, nephew come from mountain and help." He threw the meat to the dog. The dog pounced on it, shredded the bloody flesh in an instant, and then broke into the bone with a series of sickening cracks. One paw held the splintered bone steady, while his tongue slurped the pink-grey marrow; his face digging into the juice until it was stuck glistening in his whiskers and fur. I glanced at Madame Erzebet. Her mouth hung open in a horrified expression I was sure matched my own.

"If you don't like this arrangement," I bluffed to Madame Erzebet, "you're welcome to forgo your expedition and return to Chengdu--that is your prerogative." My calculation was that a woman who could not be dissuaded from a journey while deathly ill from altitude sickness would not be dissuaded by a nomad dog--even a vicious one. If I was wrong, my own mission would be decimated.

"I'm not going back to Chengdu," she said after several seconds, echoing her resolve on the drive into Tibet. "Leave the dog at my tent."

That's what I thought. She was either remarkably dedicated to making these paintings, or something else was on her mind. And that's what I was beginning to wonder—was there something else on her mind?

"The nephew is willing to sleep in the tent at night so the dog can see a familiar person coming and going," I said. " If you agree, they'll send a blanket and mat for the boy."

She sighed. "Do whatever you think is best. I have to be alone. I need to sleep."

I walked across the meadow with Nyima Rabten. "She not bad person," he said. "She deserve kindness. Like members of your own family." My face got hot. Who did he think he was, judging me?

I wanted to lash out at him—after all, he created this conundrum. In the end, I had no will to challenge anyone. "Of course," was all I could utter.

"Then agreed," said Nyima Rabten, "Norbu Tenzin come in two days."

I drew back, startled. Norbu Tenzin? The obnoxious nomad who insinuated himself into Madame Erzebet's life the first day in the camp.

"He's not acceptable. Choose another person."

"Only person we have," said Nyima Rabten, sounding puzzled. "Dog attack anyone not from family. No one else can come here. We're herders. Not caretakers for foreigner. Only so much we can do. My nephew acceptable or not?"

I had no choice. "The nephew can come, but make sure he knows his boundaries."

"He good boy," said Nyima Rabten. "Quiet. Like to study. No trouble for her."

I was being pulled down into a fetid bog. Every time I extracted a foot from the sucking ooze, a hand came out and grabbed my ankle, pulling me back in. If the Director found out she had a Tibetan staying in her tent, someone she might receive the documents from or be able to plot they might harm my Mei Ling and Jin Quon, and I wouldn't even know it had happened until I returned.

# CHAPTER 16

## *Please Take Me to the Temple*

| | |
|---|---|
| *Tong den ha lo'ee me tok* | *If hollyhock blossoms* |
| *Cho pa'ee dzay la pheb na* | *Are given in worship* |
| *Yu drang zhon noo nga yang* | *Take me, too, the young Turquoise Bee* |
| *Lha khang nang la tree dang* | *Take me to the temple* |

*- Sixth Dalai Lama*

## Erzebet's Story

Despite my display of bravado in front of Kai Lun, the attack by the dog threw me into a dark spiral. I was not only afraid of the dog, I felt like a fool--a woman who believes she can challenge police and survive in a desolate foreign land. I felt very small and unprepared in relation to the enormity of the task I had taken on.

I turned to my art to both calm me and move me forward in my quest. One morning before dawn, I sat at my table and concentrated on sketching and painting an exquisite purple poppy I collected in the foothills above the camp meadow. Long in limb, it was the *Meconopsis quintuplinervia*, a relative of the blue poppy. Wearing a miner's headlamp for light, I took the plant out of the wet towels and plastic wrap, measured the length of the stem, the long taproot, the pods and the petals. Then I dabbed a mixture of French ultramarine and cadmium red on the smooth white surface of the porcelain dish. I added water. It pooled lighter in the moat and smeared deep and rich on the mound in the middle.

I carefully swiped the razor blade, splitting the hairy green flower pods in two. Inside, the purple petals wove back and forth like a luminous velvet curtain at the opera, captured in the oval boundaries of the pod. White anthers scattered amongst the folded petals, their filaments hidden in the drapery of the still-to-be-exposed flower. A second dissection disclosed a pod already finished with its flower, the belly filled with white crystalline eggs.

Tapping my forehead with the end of the brush, I considered how best to do the shading of the eggs, how to achieve the depth that would show they were clustered together by the thousands in the small space, one on top of the other, crowded to the edges.

The brush made a light feathery swoop across my face, reminding me of the small river grasses brushing against my cheeks when I had ducked my head into the Dri-Chu River to look for fish.

Completing the pod studies, I set the painting aside to dry and got dressed. Within the hour I was headed to the fields to sit on a pile of flat stones and opened my diary to sketch the mountain at the valley's end. It stood out in dramatic dark relief against the sky. Deep ravines of grey and black were streaked with snow. There were no lateral lines to indicate roads anywhere near the ravines--they were sheer cliffs with thick vegetation. In some areas, huge pillow-like bowls of snow came down almost to the bottle green water's edge. A breeze blew along the river, rippling the water, and now I could smell the pink scent of *Stellera* on the afternoon air.

Lhamo Sangye and her children came across the field carrying a thermos of tea and wooden bowls. She sat down next to me while the children lingered at the river.

"You not afraid to be here alone?" she said. It seemed like now everyone in the camp knew I could speak their language. Everyone but Kai Lun. As soon as he showed up the nomads turned away and spoke among themselves, asking him to translate for me.

"Alone? By the river?"

"No. In this country, Madame Erzebet. Where you have no one."

"I'm not alone. Kai Lun is with me."

"He is not here for you. Not like husband watching out for you." She poured salted dri butter tea into the bowls and passed one to me. Lhamo Sangye turned the bowl in her hands, blowing the butter to the side and sipping the hot liquid. "Where is husband?"

"He's dead. He died a long time ago."

"But new husband," Lhamo Sangye looked at me. "You got new husband after accident?"

"No, I never felt like marrying again," I said slowly. My mind scrambled to make sense of her question. I was treading water on two levels—had I felt like marrying again? What happened to me over those years since Girard disappeared? But, competing with these thoughts was the way this nomad woman had asked the question. Why did she assume my husband had died in an accident?

"Not marry again? Then you not know how to be kind to yourself," she said simply.

There's nothing like having a nomad give you the same life lesson that your friends had hinted at for years. I didn't have the vocabulary or the will to try and explain my marital decisions to Lhamo Sangye. Instead, I decided to use this opportunity to finally ask a direct question of the nomads.

"You used the word accident when you asked about my husband—why did you say that?"

"I not say that," said Lhamo Sangye. She continued walking to the river without looking at me. "You not understand me."

"My husband was somewhere in Tibet when he died. I don't know exactly where. I want to find someone who knows what happened to him."

"If husband die," Lhamo Sangye said, "what more do you need to know?"

"Where he died. Why he died."

"These are questions that go nowhere," she said. "Better to go on with life now, not thinking about things you cannot change that happen long ago."

The children had run down the path far ahead of us, and Lhamo Sangye abruptly looked around and said in a low voice. "Dalai Lama photo for me?"

Why was Lhamo Sangye asking me this now? Maybe I should have told her nothing at all about Girard. And yes, she had said accident. I know I didn't misunderstand. I was becoming paranoid. Giving her a photo would probably make no difference at all at this point. I searched through the side pocket of the supply bag and slipped out the packet concealed in the narrow compartment. I selected a photo of the Dalai Lama in a yellow teaching robe and handed it to her.

"Madame Erzebet," Lhamo Sangye touched the photo to the top of her head and slid it inside her chuba. "Do not leave Dalai Lama photos where Mr. Kai Lun can find. He is cold sneak."

"He's been helpful to me so far. He's doing what he can to help me with my work here."

Lhamo Sangye glanced down the hillside, and looked across the mountain meadows. "Will not always be kind to you. His job is more than just speak Tibetan for you. You know that. Don't you?"

"What do you mean?"

"He search your tent. When you in fields. Looking for flowers."

"I have nothing to hide." I zipped up my bag and we left to catch up with the children. Crows squawked in their pine tree perches and vultures flew like giant mobiles, searching for rotting animals in the ravines.

"Really?" Lhamo Sangye hurried along by my side. "Then why he risk being eaten by dog. Just want to see how foreigner woman live? Why you don't show him you speak our language? You don't trust him."

"No, you're right. I don't trust him."

"I also lose husband, Madame Erzebet," Lhamo Sangye continued. "We not so different."

We finished walking in silence as I turned this new information over in my mind. I hugged my maps and photos closer to my chest. Far away from Chengdu and the government headquarters, Kai Lun's presence had evolved in my mind from frightening to annoying, but benign. If Lhamo Sangye was right, then I was naïve.

Back at the camp, I went into my tent and leafed through my portfolio retrieving photos, letters and mementos from home, searching for anything that would reveal my intentions to Kai Lun. The maps I always kept with me. Kai Lun was smart—if he found them, he would realize I was doing more than painting flowers. He might not know what, but he would be suspicious.

In late afternoon, the light scudded gold across the fields and I took my diary and paints and crossed through the pasture, watching the small curls of dust I kicked up as I walked. A cluster of sunlight-dappled grasses along the riverbank caught my eye. Opening to a blank page of the diary, I sketched the slim leaves, checkered green and yellow right down to the loamy earth. Reaching out my hand, I collected a bunch of the fresh green blades from the riverbank with one sweep. They rested lightly on my fingers and rode a breeze back to earth as I let them fall. Behind me, the wind vibrated nervously down the gulch and fluttered the tree branches.

"Madame Erzebet! Madame Erzebet!"

I looked up from the young shoots. In the distance, three people stood outside my tent. One was Kai Lun. One was Nyima Rabten, the dog owner, who faced in my direction, with his hand against his mouth like a megaphone. The third person was the ubiquitous Norbu. He reminded me of Lilia's university boyfriends--open and even a bit flirtatious with me at times. As I watched, he leaned down to pet the dog, lying at his feet.

I quickly packed my bag and ran across the field.

"This is nephew, Norbu," said Nyima Rabten as I came toward the tent. "Good boy. Responsible. He stay at your tent and help with dog. Shy. Won't bother you."

Norbu kept his eyes downcast and didn't utter a word. He helped Nyima Rabten carry in a heavy plaid blanket and a red and turquoise carpet with a lotus design. They placed them in the corner of the tent farthest from my bed.

"Today, we talk and eat together," Nyima Rabten said. "Dog see us being family. Dog has name. *Nyika.* Means danger," The four of us brought wooden boxes into a circle around the outside fire. I forced myself to greet the dog with a smile. It responded with a growl and a chilling stare. I shrank back.

"Don't show dog teeth," said Nyima Rabten. "He think you fight with him. When he know you, then smile." Norbu said nothing.

Darkness fell. The wind picked up and dried brush and scraps of paper blew around the encampment. The dog was unchained and left to patrol. Kai Lun and Nyima Rabten went home. Norbu stood up to go into the tent and I edged behind him, watching the dog to make sure it didn't ambush me before I got through the tent flap. Safely inside, Norbu lit a kerosene lamp for me, lay down on the blankets in the corner, and muttered a few words, "*Nyi sa duk*. Good night," and fell asleep.

I was disappointed. I had hoped he would want to stay awake and talk to me. I was craving companionship. My brave smile was wearing thin. I took out my Tibetan history book. Page after page referred to the Sixth Dalai Lama's poems. I whispered them to myself, practicing my Tibetan, memorizing, seeking to infuse my dreams with the passion of the renegade leader.

| | |
|---|---|
| *Tong den ha lo'ee me tok* | *If hollyhock blossoms* |
| *Cho pa'ee dzay la pheb na* | *Are given in worship* |
| *Yu drang zhon noo nga yang* | *Take me, too, the young Turquoise Bee* |
| *Lha khang nang la tree dang* | *Take me to the temple* |

Before I extinguished the lamp, I took a last look at Norbu sleeping. A ribbon of soft snoring floated across the tent and mingled with the snuffling of the dog outside. Norbu's full lips, slightly parted, quivered as the breath flowed in and out. His eyelids flickered. I crept over, standing a few feet away, controlling my breathing as I looked at the light pooling on his earlobes. He rolled over on the bed, his arm flung out to the side, grazing my leg. Slowly he turned his head and opened his eyes. The corners of his mouth lifted into a smile.

I blew out the lamp and crossed the tent to slide under my own blankets.

# CHAPTER 17

## Do Not Trap the Mind

| | |
|---|---|
| *Tong den ha lo'ee me tok* | *First, best not to see* |
| *Cho pa'ee dzay la pheb na* | *Then mind won't be captivated* |
| *Yu drang zhon noo nga yang* | *Second, best not to become intimate* |
| *Lha khang nang la tree dang* | *Then the mind will not be trapped* |

*- Sixth Dalai Lama*

### Kai Lun's Story

The day after Norbu moved in with Madame Erzebet, I began anew to organize my search for the documents—my priority was to search all of the tents. First on the list was Palden—a man with welder forearms and coral and amber chunks braided in his hair. He speared yak meat *momos* using a silver saber from a brocade holster, stuck the *momos* in red chili sauce and then popped them into his mouth. He chewed tobacco, spit it in glistening brown streams into the grass, and laughed so hard he fell off the log at the fire after drinking too many bowls of *chang*, a beer made from barley. Palden lived with two sons and was somewhere between 40 to 60 years old. He could have befriended Girard Pelletier.

Sharp whistles, clanging bells and calls of "Eh, eh, eh" filled the air as Palden and his sons crossed the field, moving their sheep closer to the river. On the undulating hills opposite the camp, a single sheep balanced on the hillside, grazing in a patch of pear-yellow light. I circled behind the camp, out of sight of the herders. , I scanned the fields. No dogs in sight. I moved to enter Palden's tent.

Just as I reached for the tent flap ties, a dog roared out of nowhere, sinking its teeth deep into my calf. I shook my leg in a frenzy, dragging the dog back and forth across the ground, but still the jaws locked on my leg. A sickly white sinew wrapped around the dog's teeth. Bloody saliva spewed in every direction. A branch whirled past my head and there was a crack like gunfire. The dog slackened its grip as Palden's club struck squarely on its arched spine. It crawled away, whimpering. I heaved myself in the other direction, my gory calf soaking the tatters of my pant leg. Dragging myself across the field to my tent, I guessed if I turned to look, both Palden and the dog would be laughing behind my back.

The twins saw me just as I came along the river path and helped me to my tent. My mind was thrashing with pain and confusion and I wasn't sure I knew who these people were. My entire body was convulsing. Cold sweat ran down my face, my hands were clammy, and I could hardly breathe. They propped me on the bed and then rushed to gather plants in the meadow. I lay on the bed sobbing, as they peeled the outer fiber off the plants and pounded the stems and leaves and mixed the mash with water. While one sister soaked the leaves, the other lifted her child-size hand and stroked my brow, murmuring *Om Mani Padme Hung*.

"Mr. Zhang," the twins said, slowly rolling up the shredded pant leg and patting the wet mash on the wound, pressing it in and around the ripped tissue. It absorbed the blood and became a pale pink pillow against my white skin. "Why you go into Mr. Palden's tent?" I passed out.

I have no idea how long it was before I regained consciousness, but when I opened my eyes, the girls were still there, staring at me.

"Why you go into Mr. Palden's tent?" I had to ask them to repeat what they said three times before I could understand. They had an unfortunate condition. Their lives could not be easy in a nomad camp.

"I'm missing some papers and thought Palden might have them." If they believed this, I would continue.

"Not good for you to go into Mr. Palden's tent. We help you." The twins' chatter brought me out of my thoughts. "What papers look like?"

"I'm not sure—they have foreign writing. Maybe a red book, with loose papers inside."

"Stay," they continued to wet and press the mash against the cooling leg. "You sleep. We look." They seemed delighted, almost as if they had hoped for such an assignment.

"Don't let Palden know," I cautioned as they left the tent. "I don't want to disturb him."

"We quiet as hawk circling mouse!" they clapped their doll-sized hands together. "We help!"

By nighttime, the pain had been reduced to a dull throbbing that felt like an extra heart beating in my leg. The twins returned, thrilled with the adventure of snooping in their neighbor's tent.

"No papers," they reported. "Not in boxes. Not under blankets. Not in rice bags. Nowhere."

In the morning they were back and began anew to change the compresses. I decided to formally enlist their services. "Is it possible you can also look in other tents? Just in case I left them somewhere else? We don't want to bother people, do we? So perhaps it is best to go when your neighbors are in the mountains with the animals."

"We won't bother anyone," they giggled.

"In exchange for your help, I would. . . Perhaps I could do something for your mother. . ."

They looked at me with blank expressions. I wasn't sure they could understand. It seemed they expected nothing in return.

With the twins working for me, I was able to take my strategy beyond searching tents. While I talked to the nomads, the twins rummaged in feedbags, crawled under beds, and rifled through their neighbor's belongings.

I concentrated on projecting a benign presence to every dog and human I encountered. I drank tea with the nomads in the afternoon, and ate dinner with them at the fire at night. Turquoise-handled knives sliced meat from yak and sheep legs. They ate right off the knife blades, a thin sheen of grease glistening on everyone's lips. A swipe of a chuba sleeve wiped it away.

The sight of the bloody meat and the burning smell no longer caused an urge to vomit. I chewed the tough meat until my jaws ached. Coming through the spare years with Chairman Mao as our guide, we had all learned well that anything that walks, swims, crawls, or flies with its back to heaven is edible.

Since I'd arrived in the camp, I'd been judicious in my meals, picking and choosing among the sparse offerings. Now my belt was on the last hole and when I took off my pants at night, I could see my hipbones jutting out. Few vegetables grew at the high altitudes and yak and sheep meat were a mainstay. From time to time, a trader rode through with fruit from Ganzi or vegetables from the valleys south of Manigango. When this happened, I rushed from my tent to the road to buy apples, oranges, kale or other leafy vegetables--the same foods the Tibetans disdained and referred to as rabbit food and grasses.

One morning, I gingerly pulled on my trousers. Simple movements like taking off my pants or bathing still exacerbated the puffy, festering wound, but the skin had closed and I could no longer see the gleaming white ligament I had pushed back into its hiding place among the shredded muscle. Once dressed, I limped out to start my day as an astute politician, currying favor with my neighbors.

I learned to mix butter, sugar and tea with my *tsampa* and drank *chang*, until my tongue loosened and I told the nomads about my days fishing with Jin Quon on the river passing through Chengdu. When they went home, I walked with them, past their tents, right past their dogs. Not to say I was part of the affable group. Nevertheless, there were times I thought it might be possible to find the documents without anyone being harmed.

After one such evening, the twins came by with their usual report of "nothing found" but wanting to extend their search to Madame Erzebet's tent.

"Will be easy for us. We take care of Madame Erzebet. Tashi Choegyal and Ama-la told us to do that. We go her tent everyday. She not mind. We can ask her if she saw your papers."

"That wouldn't work—I would have to be with you. She can't speak your language."

"Yes, she can. We heard her."

"Heard her say what?"

"Yellow hair—she talk to Ama-la about yellow hair. First day. When you come to camp." Apparently the ignorant twins didn't recognize that Erzebet had lapsed into French without knowing it.

"She speak like us," they chattered on. "Sometime she make joke and make people laugh. She talk to everyone."

It didn't make sense, but my clicking jaw told me it was true. She couldn't have learned this quickly. She had lied to the PSB team in Chengdu and had studied the language before she ever came to China. This meant the Tibetans had been communicating with her all along.

# CHAPTER 18

## *Do I Tempt You?*

| | |
|---|---|
| *Zum dang so gar ton chok* | *You smile with beautiful white teeth* |
| *Zhon pa'ee lo hrid yeen dook* | *Leading on this youth* |
| *Nyeeng nay sha tsha yod med* | *Swear to me* |
| *Boo na zhay rok nang dang* | *Please, do I tempt you or not?* |

*- Sixth Dalai Lama*

## Norbu's Story

Earthquake. I printed the new word in my notebook.

"Eerth-quaaake," I spoke it one sound at a time. "How would I use this word? Verb or noun?"

"Where do you hear these things?" Erzebet asked. She had told me not to call her Madame Erzebet. Too formal she said. I had to look that word up in the dictionary. Formal—having to do with stated conventions of behavior. I didn't know what that meant. But now I called her Erzebet. I'm a friend with a foreign woman.

"On the radio everyone is using this word. Many people died in earthquake in a country called Greece."

Just as she started to tell me about earthquake, light washed into the tent. My father and mother marched in through the open tent flap. Mother swung a prayer wheel and mumbled mantras under her breath.

"Madame Erzebet, you have many books." Father picked up her books scattered on the bed. He stacked them in a pile. "Not for Norbu. He shepherd. Not scholar. Have important jobs to do for family. He is here for many days. Now carrying books when go into fields. Do not let him do that."

"We are just talking, not reading," Erzebet said.

"Norbu pray. You read. He is good boy. Kind to parents. Take good care of sheep. But we more happy if he stop reading." My father acted like I was a small child who needed to be scolded. In front of a foreign woman. For reading, no less.

"Be careful what you tell our son," Mother said. Her hair was pulled back in a shiny braid. She wore her best gold and turquoise earrings. "Norbu my favorite child. Very good worker. Only son. If he leave family, it will kill me. Do not allow him to read."

"We never let Norbu move from camp," Father mirrored Mother's words. "Would destroy family."

"I don't think Norbu's going anywhere," Erzebet said. She slowly brushed paint onto her wildflower drawing. "I don't think you need to worry."

"Madame Erzebet, you old woman from West," my mother said. "You come and go as you want. Impossible for him. Don't let him leave and make our lives miserable."

My parents thought she looked like an old woman from the West. I thought she was beautiful.

My parents left and a copper-red butterfly used their exit to fly in. The butterfly landed on the corner of the painting. Erzebet picked up the magnifying glass and held it just above the insect's body. "Look," she said. There was a narrow gap where the parts of the butterfly's body joined together.

"Hear that?" I said. "Parents think I have no brain of my own to decide what is good for me." The bulging eyes of the butterfly stared into space. I moved forward and backward with the magnifying glass, wondering if the insect saw me staring. "Parents watch me. Like I watch this insect."

I threw myself on the bed, hanging my arm over the edge. With Erzebet, I saw how different I was from my own people. I was a mutant member of a species. I had heard this word on BBC. Looked it up in the dictionary. Mutant. The one born with the pointed ears when others had round. The duck-webbed feet. The one thinking of reading rather than yaks.

"How can your parents stop you from reading? Why would they want to?" She laid out new paints and brushes and taped a plant right next to her paper and began to paint again. The thin paper soaked up the paint and crinkled. She tossed it to the side and lifted a thicker piece from her bundle.

I told Erzebet how Grandfather and Uncle Nyima Rabten taught me to read one summer, while my parents herded animals in the mountains. I showed her how, as a young boy, I hid books under my chuba. Held them tight in my armpit. When my friends saw me they poked my arms and chest and teased, "I feel a book in there! You better be careful your father doesn't feel that!"

"My parents believe reading can ruin my life. Reading makes me think about odd things. Things that have nothing to do with life here. I might get confused." I leaned over to examine her sketch. It was exactly like the plant, oval leaves lined up like emerald feathers.

"Confused about what? What are you talking about?"

"You come from a rich country. Everyone goes to school. On BBC, they say it is the law. Woman like you can never understand. You don't know how it feels to be ignorant. Forbidden to read. To have a mind decaying in a human head."

"I understand more than you know," she said. "My own father lived such a life. Not because he was forbidden to go to school but because he had to quit school to support his mother and sisters. Our family lived his regrets with him." She peered at the edges of the leaves through the magnifying glass.

Very slowly she painted a thin line of green. Her voice sounded like she was angry with her father.

"You don't respect your father because he is a man with no education?"

"My God, no. I loved him."

"Loved him? He is gone? What happened to your father?"

"He died in the spring, just before I came to Tibet. He said some things to me before he died that made me sad." She was doing the funny thing with her mouth I had seen before. She pressed her lips together into a tight line. That face made deep wrinkles all around her mouth.

"That's what parents do," I said. "Still we still have to listen to them. They are much older and wiser than us. We must try to understand."

"Well, aren't you angry at your parents for trying to keep you from reading?"

"No. Parents are saying what they think will help me. Just like your father did. Everyone knows the job of the snow lion is to teach the cub."

"Indeed," she said softly, "who doesn't know that."

She gathered up her painting and brushes. We went out in the sunshine. Talking to Erzebet made me feel strong, but it also made me uneasy. She understood me. In some ways she was more like me than my own family.

"And your husband? Where is he? He is an educated man, right? Then why did he let his wife go so far away without him?"

"My husband died a long time ago."

She had no husband? I started to sweat in the heat of the day. I was ashamed as I imagined Erzebet's naked body next to mine. She had no husband. I wanted to have her love me. My eyes skipped over the meadows. Past the pine trees. I stared at the mountains beyond the lake. A grey cloud hung over the highest peak, trailing off the wind. I imagined the mountain was a volcano. It exploded with a blast that deafened my ears. The cloud was the smoke the volcano blew into the air. I made myself look away.

"What's the matter? What happened?" Erzebet looked at me with a curious expression.

"Nothing."

"You seemed. . ."

"Nothing happened," I said, shaking off my crazy thoughts. The way she watched me, I felt my chest split open. Like the carved mani stones around the lake. She could see inside my mind and my body. I was consumed by my desire for her and my wish to have her take me away from Tibet. *Take me away from Tibet?* Until that moment, I didn't know I was thinking these things. This was what I meant when I told her I might get confused.

I changed the subject. "What's the best way to learn your language?"

"We're through talking about my husband and my father? Just like that?" She looked at me strangely. "Okay, if that's what you want. Do you mean the best way to learn my language or the best way to learn any language?"

"Any language."

"I'd say the best way to learn any language is to learn words that have to do with your own interests."

"Me, I'm interested in kissing," I blurted out. I could have hit myself in the head with a rock. My mouth talked while my brain was asleep.

She laughed a startling animal bark. "Kissing?"

I looked at her out of the corner of my eye. "How do you know when you're kissing that the other person feels the same thing? What if you're kissing and they don't feel anything for you?"

Erzebet smiled. "You're approaching this backwards. It's likely no one will be kissing you who doesn't already like you. Kissing will be the result of them liking you."

"Of course that is right. I never thought of it that way before. This makes me happy." I grabbed my jacket. It was time to help Nyima Rabten with the animals.

She smiled and went back to painting, putting the darker paint on the petal edges to show a downward curve. With the last stroke, she placed the painting in a clear envelope and moved to her shelf in the tent corner to get more watercolor paper. I followed her. When she turned to see what I wanted, I kissed her on the cheek and then ran out into the meadow. Like a child. Like a fool. I bounced straight up into the air like spring lambs that graze in the pasture.

That night, I pounded and flattened a dough ball. Soon it was a long fat coil. "Stand at the flap. Make sure no one sees me cooking," I said. I tore the dough into small sections and dropped them into the meat broth with vegetables. "Father doesn't like me doing women's work. But I like to cook. I like to wash the pots and pans. He yells at Mother if she lets me do these things. Here in this tent I am a free man. Even free to do women's work if I want."

"You're not allowed to read and you can't cook, either?" Erzebet teased me. "What else are Tibetan men forbidden to do?"

My courage rose in my body like a white fire. "This is something they're not forbidden to do." I put down the ladle and slowly walked toward Erzebet. I grabbed at her waist. She laughed and ran away across the tent. We jumped over the bed and the small cabinet. Burning incense fell from the tabletop onto the mud floor. My nose tickled as the smoky air filled with the smells of cinnamon, sandalwood and cloves. Erzebet cracked her knee on the table. She yelled out, laughing and hopping around the room.

We dived at each other's ankles. I struggled to pin down her arms and legs. I snarled like a snow lion. She snorted and growled like a bear cub. We howled at our own animal natures. I scrambled to get away, dragging her along as she clung to my ankle. She laughed until tears raced down her cheeks. I had never had such a wrestle with a grown woman. I let her win. We crawled, circling each other on the carpet. Then we collapsed against the chest painted with tigers running through a field of purple poppies. I was so excited blood flew through my veins. Hair tingled at the back of my neck. Then just when I was ready to touch her breast, she jumped up and ran out of the tent laughing. She looked back over her shoulder at me as I stumbled after her.

Right outside the tent, she stopped and pulled her sweater around her. The laugh was gone. I looked up. Uncle Nyima Rabten and Kai Lun stood at the edge of the tent boundary. They stared with dark eyes and angry mouths.

"What's going on? Madame Erzebet, are you alright?" Uncle said. "Norbu, there's work to be done. Go check on the flock."

Erzebet picked straw out of her sweater and pants, smothering a laugh.. Like a child caught doing something wrong. She shrugged and went back into the tent. I ran past Kai Lun and Uncle to the hills.

Night came. I waited until everyone would be asleep. Then I returned to the tent. Inside, Erzebet read by the light of the butter lamp. She looked up at me and nodded. Without a word, she put aside her book. She blew out the lamp. I sat down next her and she took my hand and held it over her heart. Over her soft breast. I kissed her on the lips—not like in the morning when I hardly dared to touch her face.

"Was your husband nice to you?" I whispered, my face pressing into her neck. I had been thinking about this during the day, while gathering the flock. "Did he care about how you felt?"

"Most of the time, yes," she said. I smoothed her hair. She took off her sweater and shirt. Moonlight from the tent top made the outline of her face glow in the darkness. Her shoulders shone white. My fingers were shaking as I touched the small bones in her back.

"But your husband went away."

"Sssh," she said putting her finger against my lips. "This isn't the time to talk about my husband. He went away, but he meant to come back. He died before he could return to me."

Nyika barked. A shuffled scraping sounded outside the tent. Picking up a stick, I crept to the tent flap.

"Who's there?"

Untying the ropes, I burst out into the night air. Speeding across the field was a figure in blue pants and jacket. The man tripped over the tent ropes. Kai Lun. He dodged the barking dogs, heading to his tent next to the river.

I watched until he disappeared into the pine trees. Then I came back into the tent. We needed to be careful. Kai Lun might be her translator, but everyone could tell he was keeping track of where she was at all times. The police might decide Kai Lun wasn't watching Erzebet closely enough. Then they would send in someone who was much brighter. Much smarter and much crueler.

## CHAPTER 19

### *Wild Horses Flee Over the Hills*

| | |
|---|---|
| *Da go ree yar gyeb pa* | *Wild horses flee over the hills* |
| *Nyee thang zhak pay zeem gyu* | *Neither traps nor lassoes can capture them* |
| *Jam pa ngo lok gyeb pa* | *The lover who rebels* |
| *Thook ngo zeem pa meen dook* | *Even charms cannot hold back* |
| | *- Sixth Dalai Lama* |

### Lhamo Sangye's Story

Chinese Government bring Erzebet to Yi-Lhun Latso. But why? Why government go to so much trouble to bring woman from other country to paint our flowers? Or did they send her to find husband's papers? Maybe she even work for Chinese. Maybe she not know what police and army do to nomads. Maybe she think they help us. Maybe she think Dalai Lama bad leader. Maybe she different than her husband. Not a kind person.

Over the days, we watch and wait for her to show true self. We all know if inner mind not deluded, outer actions will not be wrong. But time running out. Not many days before she leave Tibet with her paintings. One night camp leaders meet at fire pit to talk about Erzebet.

"Good man like Pelletier never marry woman who not kind," Tashi Choegyal say, "How can that happen?"

"He here long time ago," argue Tsering. "His wife live many years without him. In that time, even most beautiful bird can lose its feathers."

"Has Norbu found out why she is here?" I ask.

"Too soon to tell," say Norbu's parents. "He young. Will need time. We not tell him story of Erzebet's husband. Afraid he do or say something stupid with information. Then Kai Lun be on alert. Then our son in big trouble."

"Norbu will gain her trust," say Tashi Choegyal. "Already friendly. Before long, he find out if she will take husband's papers to West."

"I don't believe she really Pelletier's wife. How we know Chinese Government not trick us? How she come here and already speak our language? Who teach her?" spoke Yangdon.

I think we should take her to hermit at lake. He is wise man. He can tell if she real wife or fake wife. But I am not camp leader and this is not my decision to make.

"What about King Gesar Festival in Manigango?" ask Old Kalsang. "Hundreds of people from other villages come to festival. Many people know husband when he stay after Chinese army move on. They can help."

Everyone nod and agree. Tashi Choegyal decide we will send rider to three villages. Rider find someone who knew husband who can speak to Erzebet at festival. Then we watch to see how she act when someone talk of her husband. Her face and words tell if she can be trusted. Until we know this, too dangerous to talk about her husband in Tibet.

The week of the festival comes. Erzebet watch families wash horse blankets. Pull finest clothing out of metal trunks. Scrape mud off children's shoes and tie coral beads in their braids. "What's going on?" Erzebet ask me. "Why is everyone so excited and busy?"

"Festival in Manigango to celebrate our hero. Compassion warrior, King Gesar of Ling. Born near Derge. Actors come from Derge and Dartsedo. They dress in fine costumes. Sing songs that honor Gesar."

While we herd sheep and yaks, we practice festival songs. Erzebet sing with us. One person start, then others join in and voices carry across meadow.

*This bowl of wine in my hand,*
*Is not made by ordinary means*
*In the blue sky of the far heaven,*
*Thunder roars are the Green Dragon.*
*Lightning flashes are glowing fire,*
*Fine raindrops are sweet dew.*
*With this essence of the pure sweet dew,*
*People on earth make tasty wine.*

"Many people from camp will enter horse races," I say when Erzebet ask me more about the festival.

"I rode as a child," she say, "I want to ride, too." She sad over last days. Eyes stare straight ahead and mouth pulled down. Now, talking about the horse festival brought her to life. "I'm going to practice riding and compete in the horse races."

Norbu find me in the fields. "Erzebet said she will ride in the horse races. I never heard of a woman riding at the festival. She was teasing me?"

"You'll see."

"Tashi Choegyal will never let her be in the race," Norbu say. "She might get hurt."

"I already told her this not good idea," I say. "She laugh. Say she saw notice on grain hut wall. No dangerous activities Number 3 on official list."

I tell Mr. Kai Lun we all go to festival. He say he ill, his head hurt. He stay behind. I tell him I watch out for Erzebet. I have surprise when he agree so easy.

I leave with children and Erzebet early morning day of festival. Norbu take sheep to hills. He come to Manigango later in day. Mist still burning off fields. Road crowded, people lug heavy baskets of food and carpets on their backs, but their feet are light because of this happy day. Everyone dress in finest silk chubas. All year they save money to buy fabric from traders who travel from China, India and Mongolia. Purple trimmed in orange brocade. Royal blue and bright red. Even children wear fancy clothes and shoes.

New prayer flags stretch along road. They dangle from trees, snap back and forth in wind. Cheers and laughter reach our ears before we come to pasture. Air smell of mutton cooking over fires. Dust kicked up by horses' hooves hang over field. Glass bottles, gum wrappers, yak and sheep bones already finished off cover ground.

We get good seats at Manigango fairgrounds. Lie down on carpets. Around us are pots of *tsampa* and rice and yogurt. Containers of hot water and salted butter tea. I point out people from other villages to Erzebet. Teach her about their different clothing. I look for person who will talk to her about husband. Every village have story about him—how he come to hear about their lives before and after Chinese army come to Tibet. But no strangers come near. Few hours later, Norbu walk through fairground gate. Erzebet's eyes follow him as he run to be with Dhondhup and his friends. I see them laughing, smoking cigarettes. They drink *chang* out of large pot. Boys stand up on drunken legs and wobble by, teasing Erzebet.

"We are princes today," they say. They stand with shoulders thrust back, as if they wore brocade capes and crowns. "Norbu sit with us not you. We think he forgot all about you."

Norbu punch his teasing friends. Wrestle at field edge. Brushing dirt off their clothes, they twist each other's arms behind their backs and cry out with fake pain. Everyone laugh. Erzebet laugh, too, but her cheeks red. She uncomfortable. Norbu had told his friends he like her. I wonder what else he know he had told them? Something they might say to wrong person. Big mistake with his parents. Should have told him why he stay in Erzebet's tent. He intelligent, handsome young man. Erzebet educated, beautiful woman. Not impossible they like each other.

Horns blare. Loud shouts. Everyone turn toward center of pasture. Races begin. Men in first race shoot at targets. They speed down field on best horses. Rifles straight out from their shoulders. Field all dust and flying hooves, while crowd whoop and holler for men from their village. Parents put children on colorful saddle blankets on backs of winning horses. Trader bring out old camera to take their picture. He deliver photo next time he come through Manigango. Next, men with white headbands, ties blowing in breeze, ride forward with bows and arrows. They gallop down pasture. Aim at figures nailed to straw bales. People on side of field talk, drink *chang* and laugh. Along edge of field, traders had set up small tents and sold knives and *gau*, shrines, to be worn around neck on leather cord. Men and women squat down inspecting piles of coral, amber, and turquoise, and bargain with seller. Packages of tobacco with pictures of snow lions hang on long strings.

Race watchers drink barley wine and sing in competitions. Two men from one family challenge two men from another. Whole villages stand up and sing to competitors who follow them. Sky fill with hawks and turkey vultures screeching and circling above fairgrounds. Riders line up and race again. This time, they try to grab gold ring hanging from pole.

In fourth race, men lean out of saddle backwards, arms nearly touch earth as they stretch for white scarves waving from sticks pounded into ground. People yell out funny jokes about riders, make bets on who will win. Favorite is man from Derge in gold shirt, trimmed in blue and red. Erzebet watch him closely. He gallop down field, leaning over backward to grab scarf. His legs grip horse. Hair and red yarn braid drag on ground.

Erzebet get up from her seat. Forehead have big wrinkle and mouth doing funny thing that pretend to be smile.

"Are you ready," I ask. "Are you sure you want to do this?"

"Yes, I'm ready," she say. I am thinking she *De-tse de-tse ngonpa re.* Little bit crazy in head.

We slip behind watchers to end of field. Tashi Choegyal wait there, holding reins to his favorite sorrel horse. Tail and mane braided with yellow and green scarves.

"You know you don't have to go ahead," he say. "No one knows you plan to ride but us and Norbu."

"I'm ready," say Erzebet reaching for reins.

"Just leave toe in stirrup." He help her into saddle. "Don't want foot caught if you get in trouble out there."

She ride onto pasture bouncing on saddle. Head thrown back. Borrowed cowboy hat held on by string under neck. Crowd silent. Then they let loose with wild yelling and cheers. She laugh and wave at neighbors from Yi-Lhun Latso camp. She get into position to race to stake.

"*Su re? Su re?* Who is it?" Calls circle the field from watchers from faraway villages and camps.

"Our foreigner," nomads from Yi-Lhun Latso yell back.

With a jolt, horse take off at full speed. Erzebet's legs fly out and then bang against horse's sides. Why she hold saddle and reins with two hands? Grip rope tied to saddle, then loop it around her wrist. She hug horse's foaming neck. Her lips tight against teeth, like mask. She lean over backward to snatch scarf as she see other riders do. Oh no! She jerk too hard on reins and horse whinny and rear up! Horse twist to left! Her body fall and she hang to side. She cannot bring herself upright. The ground race by just beneath her chin. Stones kicked up by horse's hooves hit her face!

Stick in ground just miss her head, as horse gallop down field. People run out to stop horse, waving arms and yelling. They grab reins and Erzebet pull herself back up on saddle. Horse slow to trot. No scarf in hand, she ride past judges, slumped over in saddle. One hand rub her back. Face has little spots of blood where stones hit. She slip off panting animal. Her foot tangle in stirrup and she hanging in mid-air, then try to stand on her own. Released, her legs collapse and she fall to ground in heap. Main judge himself run out. He grab her by elbow to help her stand up. A rush of friends and scared onlookers follow him.

"Madame Erzebet," crowd wait. "Are you hurt?"

With judge's hand still holding her elbow, Erzebet stand up raise arm in air like rag doll's limb. Crowd roar. Hundred more people rise from seats at field boundary. Run onto pasture.

"Madame Erzebet," yell Tsering, "You not like any village woman who ever came to Manigango!"

People standing nearby laugh. Then, man with large amber and bone earring and leopard-skin chuba come out of crowd. His boots have blue band at the top, with red circle above white stripe. He speak in low, gruff voice to me. "This wife of foreigner man who come here many years ago."

"Yes, it is her," I say. "You come to talk to her?"

He nod his head. "I knew husband. He show me photo of wife and little girl. Now she look different, but this same person from photo."

"Not much time to talk," I say. "Be careful."

Just then, voice call out. "Who is foreigner woman riding horse in races?"

"Wife of long ago yellow-haired foreigner," say man with leopard chuba. Words rise above noise of crowd. "saved. . . Abbot. . . TriSong Monastery. He. . .martyr. . .our country."

"What did that man say?" Erzebet whip head around, looking. She hold my arm. "My ears are buzzing. I think I'm going to vomit." I place my cool hand on her forehead. Crowd press forward. Someone hold ladle of water to her lips. Strange smacking sound as she lap water like parched dog. I see man in leopard-skin chuba come toward her through crowd.

"Lhamo Sangye, who said that about the monastery?" Erzebet ask again. "Who said that about a foreigner here?" Then man next to her, his hands raised in prayer greeting, holding white *khata*.

Suddenly, voices buzz like insects during drought year. Chinese officers in green uniform come through crowd, pushing people aside. People cover their faces and hang heads, stare at ground. Parents put children onto their backs and hurry back toward the tents. As Erzebet turn to see police approach, man in leopard-skin chuba quickly hang *khata* on her neck, run back through crowd and disappear.

Looking frantically back and forth, Erzebet say, "Lhamo Sangye, that man? Where is he from?"

"Sssh. Police," I whisper. "His boots and chuba—man from over mountains. Near Derge." Erzebet grab at my arm, just as officer approach.

Officer wave big wooden club and tell people go back to their tents and blankets. Roughly ask to see Erzebet's papers. She take folder from her bag.

He look at it, hold photo next to her face. Slowly he hand it back, look out over the heads of crowd, and walk away. When officer gone, Erzebet run between families, asking everyone where man from Derge go. They shake their heads. No one know or no one feel safe talking to her. Much later, she return. *Khata* wrapped around her throat, silk tassles hanging down.

"You found man who spoke?" I ask.

"No," she say. "I looked everywhere." She rub back with her hand and her shoulders slump over. This only reminder that less than hour ago she was riding in the race down the field on Tashi Choegyal's best horse.

"Why does it matter to you?" I ask, touching her shoulder. Her body feel thin under her dress, not tough like nomad woman who ride horse all day long. "Why important what person said?"

"Lhamo Sangye, My husband was lost near here," she say. "I must find out what happened to him. There is important work he was doing. Work that would help all Tibetans. Now, it is my responsibility to complete his work, if I can."

"If husband here and his work important for Tibetans, why Chinese Government bring you here? They not know who you are?"

"I don't know the answer to that," she shake her head. "It doesn't make sense to me, either."

I say nothing, but now we know. We can trust her. We can make plan. Erzebet help us get her husband's documents out of Tibet to West.

Hours later, we walk home, follow carts and horses back to lake. Parents haul sleeping children on their backs. Erzebet, Norbu and I walk with Lotse and Dolma in moonlight.

As we walk, Norbu lag behind. "What will happen to me when you leave?" he say to Erzebet.

I pull Lotse and Dolma to my side. I listen.

"I don't know what I'll do when you're gone."

"What did you do before I came here?" she ask. She have love feelings for Norbu. Tender voice tell me that. I guess love for learning make them care about each other.

"My future looks like the same color as grey mountains ahead of us now," he say. "Before you came. . . I can't remember that life anymore."

"Then I'll remember for you. I'll never forget any of your stories. A boy wanting to be a shepherd. The lake and your Grandfather. All the strange and wonderful ways you see the world. Your life will go on when I am gone."

"You are same, but I am different now."

"You don't know this,' she say. "But, I am different too."

We come home to moaning dogs. Tents ripped open. Wooden chests broken. Giant bags of *tsampa* emptied onto tent floor. Dry *tsampa* scatter on every surface and rise in wisps into air on slightest breeze. Jewelry and chubas flung into corners. Beds overturned. Dried yak meat dumped from boxes. Bottles of hot water and tea drained onto ground.

Ama-la, twins' mother, tell us story. After last person leave camp for festival, cars with police from Derge arrive at Yi-Lhun Latso. Ama-la drag herself to tent flap. She see Mr. Kai Lun wave cars on through pasture. Men have sticks and guns. They wear pads on legs to protect against dogs. Put medicine in chunks of meat and toss to dogs. Animals gulp meat and fall to ground.

When men get to Ama-la's tent, she cower under blankets; sure they will rape or kill her if they find her there. Outside the flap, she hear Mr. Kai Lun argue with officers and tell them ignore this tent. It belong to sick, old woman with nothing of value. He guarantee she not have hidden papers. The men go away and she left alone, listening to whine of stricken dogs and crack of furniture being broken apart in the fields.

# CHAPTER 20

## The Swan Yearns to Stay Longer

| | |
|---|---|
| *Ngang pa tsho la chak nay* | *The swan is in love with the lake* |
| *Ray zheek ta goe sam gyang* | *It yearns to stay longer* |
| *Tsho mo tar kha dreek nay* | *But ice covers the lake* |
| *Rang sem kho thak cho song* | *And the swan is filled with despair* |
| | *- Sixth Dalai Lama* |

### Norbu's Story

Erzebet no longer looked at her maps. When she slept I couldn't wake her. Not even to see the full moon shining on turquoise bees in the meadow. This morning, I wanted her to laugh. Be happy with me. First thing when she woke, before she even dressed, she asked about the Chinese Government. I didn't bring it up. She did. I looked out the tent flap to make sure Kai Lun was not listening outside. This was talk that should be spoken in a low voice.

She asked me the names of people who headed the government in our area. I had no business with them. I saw them drive by in their fancy cars. Men with gold stars on their uniforms. Know their names? How would I know these important people? I was just a shepherd.

"What about your parents? Do they know the officials who run this area?"

She was always asking questions. And my parents were always asking questions about her. What did we talk about when we were in the tent together? I told my parents nothing. If they knew she asked about the government, they might make me leave the tent.

"My parents know the officials," I said. I glanced at my paper with the words I would practice using today: control, amphibian, random, mimic, massive. She laughed when I used big words. I would try to use some in my answers to her. "It's not something they would tell you. Why do you want to know? Nothing to do with painting flowers."

"I need to know what happened when the army came years ago," she said. We went outside in the bright sunlight. Erzebet crept up behind a butterfly just as it landed on the petal of a daisy. She made her hands into a cup and caught the butterfly inside.

"They were all over the Tibet," I said, "From here to Lhasa and even to Mt. Kailash, the sacred mountain. Army sent soldiers to all nomad camps. They controlled everything, even where people lived. A Chinese soldier came to Yi-Lhun Latso to be our leader."

"A Chinese soldier? Here?"

"Yes, I was little. I don't know much about it. During that time Chinese

Government changed borders of Tibet. Their own ideas of how Tibet should be." I remembered some children in the next village sent away to Chinese schools, to get rid of bad Tibetan ideas and culture. Their parents never saw them again.

The butterfly left Erzebet's hand. It flew close to the meadow edge and then went away to the center of the wildflower field. "No one can control me," I said. "Like that butterfly, no one has the right to tell me where my border begins and ends."

Erzebet said I was a fast learner. I wanted her to admire my learning. I pulled out a tiny notebook from my bag. 123 pages. The book was written in my tiniest Tibetan script. I had named it GEOGRAPHY.

"At the beginning of this book, I wrote down my dreams. Learn names of all oceans, seas and longest rivers. Learn names of all mountain ranges in the world."

She leaned over the book filled with facts. Continents. Oceans. Races of people and where they lived. Major cities and how many people lived there. Erzebet flipped through the pages, looking at the charts, graphs, and my Table of Contents.

"I have thirty notebooks hidden in my trunks," I said. "All on different subjects. I study books I get from the school library. Copy only the best information. My books are so small I have to be careful. When I leave Tibet, I will take only the GEOGRAPHY book with me, because it will be the most useful."

"Are you leaving Tibet?"

My cheeks caught fire and she could see it. Why did I say that about leaving Tibet? Every conversation happened on two levels. What I was saying and what I was really thinking. Sometimes the two crossed in the middle. Then I felt like the amphibian that lives part in water and part on land. Did those creatures ever get confused? Stop on the edge of the sea and forget what direction they were going?

"I will never leave Tibet. I have everything I need here. Just talking."

"For someone who isn't thinking of leaving, you bring it up a lot."

"I do?" I was glad she couldn't read my mind. If she knew my true thoughts, she might tell my parents I wanted to run away from the camp. The conversation made my heart sick. There was no reason to think I would ever be more than a nomad. A nomad who had, by chance, learned to speak another language.

Erzebet picked up the GEOGRAPHY book again. "Some of this information is a bit old. Now the world is divided into different regions and you'd have trouble if you tried to use this map to visit India, Africa or even Europe. What's the farthest place you've ever been?"

"One day, just before you came here in the spring, I hitchhiked to the city. I traveled six hours by truck and then walked to the university area. I had heard on the radio that while Chairman Mao was alive—schools only taught what he wanted people to learn. Now some schools reopened for real learning. Many thousands of students were coming back to complete their education. I wanted to see if it was true.

"I didn't know what I would find at the university. I stood in my sheepskin chuba, with my red and black sunburned nomad face, smelling like a sheep from the dung fires. The students read in restaurants and on park benches, and argued at street corners about the day's lesson. They dressed in white shirts and Western pants and carried armloads of books. I heard how expensive those pants are. Worth a year's supply of food. I found this out in the city."

Now I lay on the grass, a dictionary open on my chest.

"Tell me more," Erzebet said. "I want to know what you saw there."

"The students I saw loved to learn. They held their books proudly. I carried some of the small notebooks with me, *BIOLOGY* and *WORLD HISTORY*, but I was afraid to bring them out for fear they would laugh at me. Me, a nomad with hand-written books. Those students looked so clean, so bright, and so happy. I felt like none of these things."

Inside my head I pleaded with Erzebet. *Take me to Europe so I can go to school. Help me become an educated person.*

"You're an intelligent man. If you were in the West you'd be in college, too," she said unexpectedly.

"If I were in the West? I'll never be in the West," I buried my nervousness over the conversation deep in my gut. "I'm a nomad."

She put her hand on my arm. "Norbu, do you want to go to another country where you can get an education?"

She could not read my mind. I forced the words out of my mouth. "Can you help me do that? If you could help me, you would, wouldn't you?"

"Of course, I would help you." She looked at me sadly. "But I have no idea how to do that. I think it's impossible for people to leave China without the government's permission, and I have no ability to get that." We sat there in the meadow, both of us staring at the clouds and floating in the current of our own thoughts.

"Let's make up a game. To practice English and Tibetan," I said after a long while. I had ruined the day with my talk about leaving Tibet.

"Okay," she said kindly. She patted my arm. I knew she was also sorry that we had said those impossible things out loud. "You look up a word in the dictionary and I'll use that word to tell you a story in Tibetan. Then you tell me if you can understand my Tibetan."

I turned the pages of the dictionary. My eyes closed, I randomly put my finger on a word. "The word is swaan."

"Swaan? Swaan? I don't know that word." She looked over my shoulder. "Let me see." I sat very still. The soft weight of her breast on my back. I was breathing very slowly.

"Oh, swan." I could smell perfume on her neck. It made me so dizzy I could barely breathe.

"Sw-ah-ah-n, with an 'a' like a cough in the throat, not with an 'a' like a whisper on the lips. Swan," she said.

"Okay swan," I mimicked. I pretended I was thinking about learning English words correctly, but my attention was on her breast pressing against my back. "What should I do now?"

"Nothing. Stay as you are in the grass. Keep your eyes closed and listen."

The story began.

"*Yong gi re.* It is coming," Erzebet said. "*Cha garpo chenpo yong gi re.* The giant white bird is coming. Can you feel it?"

The sun seemed especially close today. All I could think about was how it cooked my head and arms. I was a miniature person lying in the tall grasses. Then my mind grew to take in Erzebet's story. The bright light against my eyelids eased. A shadow made a cool dark place deep in my cells. A massive bird was flying over the fields and circling above me.

"I feel it now," I said. My body tingled like it was covered with tiny fern-like antennae like those I had seen on the moth under Erzebet's microscope. The breeze from the flapping of the swan's wings moved in a wave over my face. The wildflower smell traveled on the wind. Far away, I heard the sheep bleat as the ewes gathered their lambs near the rocky outcropping.

"*Cha jor song*! It's here! The bird is landing near you," Erzebet said. The swan's shadow grew larger and blocked the sun. My body shivered. The movement of the wings stirred up the dust and bent the grasses to the earth. The tip of the wing touched my face. I shivered again. "The bird is ready for us. It's time to get on the back and ride."

"But, how do we get on?" I asked. I lay with my eyes shut, the giant swan resting next to me in the field. I could smell the feathers. The grainy odor of the bird's breath. The heart beat fast. Like my own.

"Put your foot behind the wing. Feel that thick quill? Put your foot there," she said. "Then climb up holding onto the downy feathers at the neck. When you're on board, nestle among the largest feathers and I'll climb up next to you."

I brought my leg up and over the back. A rasp broke from the swan's throat. The swan arched its neck to the back and looked at its passenger. At me. I shrank back. Crouching down, I used a giant feather in front of me as a shield. From my hiding place, I looked closely at the feathers. Each slid against the other. Joined yet separate. Smooth and tough. They made a screen against the weather. Yet how easily they fanned out. Letting air flow over and through.

The golden eye stared, unblinking, at me again. I looked into the dark cave of the eye. Straight into the bird's mind. "Let's fly to Europe."

"I don't think it can fly that far," she said.

"It can. This bird is big as an airplane. Giant wings."

"Maybe it's never carried passengers before."

"That doesn't matter. This bird is not a prisoner. It can go anywhere in the world," I said. "It can cross any border. It follows no laws but its own."

"We need to go somewhere closer first. We should practice flying to where the blue poppies grow."

There were footsteps and then a scuffling in the grass. Erzebet's voice faded to nothing. Even nestled amongst the swan's feathers, I was chilled again.

"What are you doing?" A familiar voice pushed into my soft white dream. "What are you talking about? Bird? Prisoners?" A stick poked me in the side.

I forced my eyes open. Dhondhup. With a crazy grin on his face. "What are you two doing out here?" he said.

I was confused. As if I had been caught having sex with Erzebet. But we were just lying in the meadow telling stories, learning foreign words. Dhondhup laughed again and jabbed his stick into the soft skin under my ribs. I leapt to my feet and chased him down the hill. Looking back over my shoulder as I ran, Erzebet was picking up my books and her paints. She put them in the pack to carry back to camp.

We ran until we came to the lake and then threw ourselves down on the shore, laughing and panting from the run. Dhondhup took a wad of bread from his pocket and tossed the dough into the lake for the fish.

"How is it living with Madame Erzebet?" Dhondhup asked. "Heard you were wrestling in tent. That must have been fun!"

"Who told you that? She's fun to be with. My parents got mad at me, though."

"What does she do all the time? Only paint flowers?"

"She likes to look at maps. She's curious about how we live here. Wants to know about the government and the authorities in this area."

"Why does she care about that stuff?"

"I don't know. Ask her."

"No, she only likes talking to you," Dhondhup said. "You don't have to watch dog anymore. You should go back to parents' home. Stay away from her. Don't spend time with old woman like her."

"I'm having a good time."

"Don't be stupid. She's dangerous." The lake was a whirlpool of fish. Gaping mouths sucking in air.

"You're jealous. I'm having a good time with a foreigner. You aren't."

"I'm scared for you. You're idiot." Dhondhup wadded a chunk of bread into a ball and threw it at my chest. It thudded off and fell into the dirt. "I think you like her. But she not here to fool around with dummy like you. Looking for papers husband left behind. Husband wrote newspaper articles about Chinese invading Tibet. He kept notes. Talk to everyone in camp. Notes disappeared."

"What do you mean?" I reached down for the ball of bread. My head spun. Dhondhup was crazy—what he said made no sense. My ears refused to hear more. I picked the dirt off the bread, pushing my fingers into the center. I started to throw it back at Dhondhup. Instead, I just tossed it into the water.

"Who told you this? She's here to paint flowers."

"My father told me. Her husband was in Manigango. Long time ago. Chinese kill him near here. Your parents know. Everyone know. Only reason Tashi Choegyal let you stay with her because trying to find out if she can be trusted. Haven't you figured that out? She doesn't care about you. She's just using you to get information."

# CHAPTER 21

## *The Arrow Has Hit the Target*

| | |
|---|---|
| *Da mo pen la phok song* | *The arrow has hit the target* |
| *Da'ee sa la tsul song* | *Its point has cut into the earth* |
| *Choong tree jam pa thre joong* | *I have met my childhood beloved* |
| *Sem nyee jay la trang song* | *My heart follows her, all by itself* |

- *Sixth Dalai Lama*

## Erzebet's Story

Dhondhup snapped back the flap, poked his head around the corner and burst into the tent. His eyes darted between Norbu and me before he took a bowl of butter tea, ate a few biscuits and studied the flower paintings propped up on chests around the room.

"Hey Mr. Dalai Lama, let's go," he said sarcastically, throwing Norbu his jacket. "Sun is high. Sheep eating everything in front of their faces. We stay on mountain tonight. Good-bye, Mother."

Mother? Dhondhup looked for every opportunity to point out the difference in Norbu's and my ages. I pretended like I hadn't heard it. Norbu grabbed his slingshot and a bag of *tsampa*, but then before he got out the tent flap, he spun around and kissed me on the cheek. Startled, I turned my face to the side. The kiss grazed off and landed squarely on my lips. I dug in my bag of paints and papers, pretending not to see Dhondhup's eyebrows shoot to the top of his forehead. Norbu was showing off. It made me nervous.

The two shepherds headed out, Dhondhup walking backwards watching me with a frown, while Norbu trotted on ahead. My God, what was Norbu thinking with that kiss? If Dhondhup became jealous that Norbu no longer spent all day with him tending the sheep, he might cause trouble. He could concoct a story that would cause Kai Lun to expel me from the camp, convincing the Chinese Government I was incompetent as a scholar or a troublemaker. There was no question I had a problem—a problem I had created myself. I was excited by Norbu. His tough handsome face and body, his unusual way of seeing the world and his thirst for education were a tantalizing combination for me. I was lonely in the camp and Norbu's playfulness with me had sparked desire. Wrestling with a nomad. Undressing for a nomad. I was losing my mind.

As I was mulling over this dilemma, Lotse and Dolma arrived, followed by Kai Lun. He walked as if he were a stranger who'd just rescued two orphans from the street, the children gripping his hands and playing with the edge of his shirt. I didn't want to entertain there now—I needed time to get my thoughts under control and assess the situation with Norbu. There was no question I had been encouraging his attention, but I never imagined he could be so indiscrete. What did I expect—he was only 23 years old. I was too distracted to play with Lotse and Dolma and instead, gave them paper, brushes and paint, sitting them on the edge of the bed. A brief lesson on painting leaves, instructing them to be sure to follow the line of the main vein to create a realistic illustration, and they were happy. Kai Lun sat to the side, fiddling with a cord and beads. For hours he tied and retied the beads onto the cord in various combinations, keeping me under house arrest.

Late in the afternoon, the children finished mixing and applying ten shades of green to the leaves they had drawn and Kai Lun walked them home. I had been invited to Norbu's parents' tent for dinner. I hadn't forgotten they had called me an old woman when they confronted Norbu that day in the tent. An old woman? With Norbu acting so carelessly, it was probably better they saw me as old rather than as someone who could capture the attention of their son.

I arrived at their tent just as Dhondhup was scurrying out. I thought he was supposed to be on the mountain with Norbu. He shuffled past me, his hand raised in a half greeting, not meeting my eyes. Tashi Choegyal was inside and made a place for me on the platform covered with carpets. We talked about how many yaks the villagers owned and how many were lost in last year's biggest storm. How many lambs froze to death in the spring blizzard. What the TriSong lamas predicted for the weather this year, so they wouldn't lose more.

Tashi Choegyal used a curved knife to cut slices off the hunk of yak meat they kept in a bag in the tent. The knife conjured up images of marauding hordes crossing desert sands as he peeled the purple-black, eggplant-shiny yak skin away from the fresh vermilion meat.

"Picnicking?" Norbu's parents said. "Enjoying the flower hills? So many beautiful flowers after the spring rains."

"They're all wonderful," I said. "But *nga Sher Ngon ta gi yor.* I'm really looking for the blue poppy. I want to paint the flower, but also collect seeds for a friend of my father's." I had been going out at dawn and again at dusk with Norbu and Lhamo Sangye under the pretense of looking for the flowers that just opened in the dawning or fading light. We wandered down trails which might have been full-scale roads two decades before. They scanned the fields for blue poppies, while I looked for hillsides with a river running alongside a road. I was coming to the conclusion that looking for a landform from a photo that might have been doctored or even taken in a completely different part of the world was an ill-conceived strategy. I was losing time and needed to get real information from people who would know what happened to Girard.

"Best stay close to camp. We send someone to high mountains. Collect flowers for you." Tashi Choegyal said. The group had moved on to the round bread, dipping it into the yogurt bowls, scooping it under the thick yogurt cream on the top. "Problems with dog? You are comfortable having Norbu sleep in tent. Better to have different person there?"

"The dog doesn't attack me. Norbu helps." They went back to eating, licking the remaining curd from the bowls with large flat tongues like lions in the zoo. Tashi Choegyal and I smiled and nodded at each other. I could trust him.

"Tashi Choegyal," I took a chance. What I needed now was not more people to go with me on fraudulent searches for flowers; I needed an advocate to go with me to the regional government offices at Derge to ask questions. "I had a friend who was in this area many years ago. He was killed in a car accident." Norbu's mother stood up so fast her plate flew off her lap and clattered to the ground. She hastily retrieved the plate, swept away the food into a pail, and moved to the fire.

"His family wants to get more information about it," I continued. Norbu's mother watched me as she stirred the thukpa. Only a blind person would have missed the alarmed look she cast over her shoulder at her husband, giving a quick shake to her head.

"What information?" said Tashi Choegyal. "Why friend's family want to know about something happen long time ago?"

"His family isn't at peace. They don't really know how he died—or where. Can you help me talk to the authorities?"

"What authorities?"

"Anyone who might know about his death. So I can take information back to his family. The officials in Derge could have this information."

"Impossible," Tashi Choegyal said. The tendons in his neck stood out like white ropes. "You must tell friend's family China not like other countries. No way to find out these things. Curious snake pokes nose into hole of mongoose. Instead should be searching for field mice to feed its stomach."

"But it's just a car accident I'm talking about. Why would anyone keep that information from his family?"

"Don't know. But impossible questions."

"I'm on an official study exchange here, I guess I can go to Derge and ask myself."

"This about your friend's family," Norbu's father said. "Nothing to do with you. You ask too many questions Mr. Kai Lun send you away. Finish your painting project and give honor to your family and university. Think on that, instead."

They went back to eating and drinking tea. Norbu's mother put more yak dung into the brazier without making a sound. She held the spoon motionless above the pot of soup. A pool of liquid had gathered at the lip and slid, one glistening drop at a time, back into the pot. The conversation about a man who died in a car accident was over.

I gathered my jacket and said goodnight, suspicious about why they had been so troubled with my questions. It seemed like more than concern about Kai Lun sending me back to France prematurely. They were tough people. They challenged Kai Lun all the time and were not so willing to be pushed around by him. Then it struck me— Lhamo Sangye had told them about the man at the festival who tried to talk to me. She had reported what I said about looking for information about Girard. They all knew now. They would all be trying to protect me—to stop me.

"Think about this," said Norbu's mother, buttoning my jacket and pulling the collar up close to my face. "Butter never wins. Butter attacks knife, it loses. Knife attacks butter, the butter still the loser."

# CHAPTER 22

## *Perhaps We Will Meet Again*

| | |
|---|---|
| *Da tae she thung dee la* | *In this short life* |
| *De kha tsam zhik zhu nay* | *We have shared so much* |
| *Ting ma yu pa'ee lo la* | *Perhaps we will meet again* |
| *Jel zom e yong tay* | *In our next childhood years* |

*- Sixth Dalai Lama*

### Kai Lun's Story

After the PSB helped me search the tents the day of the festival and we found nothing, I began to wonder if Pelletier had even left papers in Tibet. There was the story in Chengdu of a man who had come to Lhasa trying to get someone to smuggle documents out of Tibet. My Director thought it was Tashi Choegyal. But were those even the same documents? Would he have waited almost twenty years to have Pelletier's notes revealed to the world? Isn't that what I had suggested to the Director when he and his comrades had laughed at me?

I had developed a system for keeping myself from sinking into depression. Whenever pessimistic thoughts surfaced, I thought about playing with Jin Quon on the carousel in the children's park in Chengdu and remembered the wonderful conversations with my grandparents when I was a child. I reminded myself to be thankful for being alive. In my best moments, I was overcome with the beauty of the mountains and the lake right outside of my tent. Unfortunately, this was often followed by a deep sadness that my wife and son could not enjoy it with me.

*Chik, chik, chik, chitter-ree, chitter-ree.* A drango called from its perch on the tent top. I sat in the sun, waiting for a sign Madame Erzebet was up and had moved out into the meadows so I could go into her tent and search her books and clothes. The twins had been working their way through the neighbor's tents, but Nyika, the dog, now allowed me into Madame Erzebet's without incident. Each time I was there I looked for the iris obsidian clip she wore in the evenings. I liked the smooth cool feel of the black glass as it rested in my hand, strands of her white and dark hair entwined in the clasp.

*Chik, chik, chik, chitter-ree, chitter-ree.* I waited outside Madame Erzebet's tent for almost two hours. I knew I couldn't be with her every minute, but the twins report that she was speaking Tibetan had unnerved me. She was usually up much earlier in the morning. Norbu was already gone with his friends, crossing the meadow, moving the sheep to the western side of the lake. She might stay inside all day.

I heard peals of laughter and looked to see Lhamo Sangye's children playing across the pasture. Lotse and Dolma, threw grass to the yaks, tied their dog to a metal ring near the water trough and chased each other to Madame Erzebet's tent. Cheeks smeared with thick black grease to block out the sun, they ran in a wide circle past the barking dogs, calling, "Madame Erzebettie, Madame Erzebettie." She must still be sleeping.

Back in my own tent, I reviewed my notes to see if there was something significant I had missed over the last weeks. The nomads were getting used to me. They were loosening up and soon I would catch a conversation I could report. So far, the notes did not capture anything worth passing on to Chengdu. I doodled in the margins of the notebook, a rudimentary sketch of the mountain and the pine trees. I would tear out these pages later and keep them separate.

Giggling and rustling at the tent flap preceded Lotse and Dolma crawling in on their hands and knees. They popped up next to me. Lotse strutted in black pants and a grey chuba tied at the waist. Dolma hung on to her brother's hand, her eyes downcast, dressed in a green brocade chuba and a flower-print blouse. Attached to her waist was a tiny cloth doll attired in the same clothing.

"Ama-la say you walk in meadow. Head down. No smile. You miss your family," they said. So, they were watching me like I was watching them. Children checked on my mental health. Nomads were concerned about my loneliness while I only cared about reporting them to the police, finding the missing documents and getting out of Tibet and back to my family as fast as possible. If they only knew. Well, I was sure they did know. Maybe the children were miniature spies.

"We stay and play?" they asked.

I didn't want them to stay and play. I was an intellectual, a man who liked to read and study, not play, and I had never been drawn to children other than my own son. They often smelled like urine and their noses ran with disgusting mucus. Whenever I left my friends' homes in Chengdu, I had to scrape off crusty smears of food and shiny saliva dried on my clean shirt. I continued to read, not making eye contact with the children.

Undaunted, Lotse and Dolma pulled off their shoes and climbed onto the bed. They snuggled under the blankets.

"Come. Play."

I went over, more curious about myself than them. It was a full-scale assault. They jumped on me, messed up my hair and tickled me. They poked their grubby fingers into my side and chest. I retaliated by poking them, probably harder than I should have, but they just laughed and squirmed under the covers. Dolma launched herself off the bed and slammed into my nose with her big head. My eyes stung with tears and I lifted my hand to see if blood trickled from my ballooning nose. The burnt smell of smoke from yak dung fires stuck in my nostrils. It was going just as I had imagined, but they would not stop.

"We got two new baby sheep," they chirped as they continued to bounce around and I pressed a wet cloth against my nose. "Have to be careful. Wolves sniff lambs. Come to tent for dinner."

I pantomimed being a wolf and pretending to eat them. We all giggled and when my nose stopped throbbing, I could see I was being unnecessarily cold with them. They were really lovely children, so full of life and fun. Beautiful reddish-brown skin and flashing black eyes.

I leaned over to my table, picked up a pen and paper, and drew a sheep with curly fur and a smile. I had never drawn an animal before. It was rather charming. I would give it to Jin Quon when I got home. If I got home. It was shameful the way I laughed and drew pictures with these children, while my own son spent his summer locked inside a cement building in a broiling, teeming city.

I idly smoothed the cloth in their chubas. I'd run out of things to say. What was the matter with their mother that she didn't warn them to stay away from me, a Chinese official, and instead encouraged them to come to my tent?

What was the matter? Why were they here? I jumped up and ran the short distance from my tent to Madame Erzebet's, tearing open the tent flap.

She was gone.

# CHAPTER 23

## *A Soul More Cunning Than A Human's*

| | |
|---|---|
| *Khyee gen gya oo zer wa* | *The old guard dog* |
| *Nam she mee lay chang wa* | *Has a soul more cunning than a human's* |
| *So la lang song ma zer* | *Don't tell who left at dusk* |
| *Tho rang lok joong ma zer* | *Don't tell who returned at dawn* |

*- Sixth Dalai Lama*

## Erzebet's Story

I awoke hours before dawn, disoriented, with Norbu's legs entwined around mine and his warm lips against my neck. I had had a disturbing dream in the middle of the night, a mix of bizarre images.

Men carrying a hive-shaped container tied to the end of a long bamboo pole had come into my garden. I saw them through the window. Inside the hive a squadron of blue bees flew from side to side, rising and falling, banging against the mesh. As the men parted the ferns in the garden, inspecting the earth underneath the elm trees, the bees buzzed languorously and a pool of blue light emanated from the cage. Then the interlopers discovered a sapphire blue flower with a ring of barbed wire around the stem. I watched, mesmerized, as they dug up the flower and cut the petals into precise pieces, as a master chef might do. They mashed the petals and mixed them with liquid from a large dusty bottle.

Rushing out of the house, I demanded to know what they were doing. They turned, startled, as I came across the lawn. Two men grabbed me and pinned me down. The intruders took out a vial and a rubber-tipped glass dropper filled with swirling liquid. They tried to put blue drops in my eyes. I shut my eyes, joggling my head back and forth in a panic to prevent the cobalt serum from entering. It laked against the corners of my eyes and spilled down my cheeks and neck, leaving trails of blue on my dress. As I twisted under the men's hands, a familiar fragrance traveled on the breeze in the yard. It was Girard's cologne. Why was he with these strangers?

"Give up," one of the men said to the others. He stood and ceremoniously brushed the grass off his trouser legs. "Only she can put the drops in her eyes. We can't do it for her."

They took the hive and left the garden. Girard's scent on the night air became fainter and fainter until I could not detect it at all.

Without getting up, I reached for my journal and wrote as much of the dream as I could remember and then checked my small calendar. Today was exactly nineteen years since we had received the official news of Girard's disappearance. Next to the calendar, I had taped a photo of Girard, my father, mother and Lilia. Smiling, bundled in wool coats and hats, they stood together on the bank of the Seine. Snowflakes fell, softening the air, creating ivory epaulettes on their shoulders. It seemed eons ago and when I turned the photo over, it was dated the month before Girard left for Tibet.

A second photo taped underneath showed the Clines at Kew Gardens, standing in front of the greenhouse. Mrs. Cline's request to bring back the seeds of the blue poppy for her husband kept being pushed to the bottom of my agenda, yet it was a potent symbol of everything left unsaid or undone in my marriage and in the confusing months after Girard's disappearance. A symbol of my own new life which would begin after this hazardous summer in Tibet.

A hand reached out and lightly touched my back. "What are you looking at?" said Norbu, pulling a blanket around my shoulders.

"It's a photo of my father's oldest friend. He loves Asian plants and I want to bring him seeds of the blue poppy from Tibet."

"I'll take you to find seeds," Norbu said. "Best to go up to Muri-La or Tro-La Pass. Millions of seeds for you to take back. We can haul seeds in giant bags. Like the men who collect salt at the great lake!"

I smiled at his exuberance. "I don't need bags full of them. I only need a small packet. That will do just fine."

Moments after Norbu left to go with the sheep, I forced myself to get out of the bed, dressed, grabbed my bag of art supplies as a charade, and headed from the tent. It was still dark in the pasture, only the hint of dawn providing the palest backdrop to the peaks. I had taken note of the approximate times when buses headed toward Derge. Dinner with Norbu's family had confirmed my sense there was no one in the camp to go with me—their lives were precarious enough as it was. I had no option other than to do exactly what Nicholas Munro and Mr. Cline had advised me not to do—go to the government offices and directly solicit information about Girard's disappearance.

I sneaked by Kai Lun's tent, giving it a wide berth. Lhamo Sangye was milking the yaks next to the stone wall. She looked up with a curious expression as I crossed the field.

"Where you go at this hour?" she said.

I had nothing to lose. "Lhamo Sangye, I told you I needed to find out what happened to my husband. I'm going to Derge to the government offices. Now. Before Kai Lun is awake. I am going to find out who was responsible for my husband's death."

"Sometimes when we are with you, we feel we stupid about many things in the world. But you, Erzebet, you are a lot stupid, a lot of the time. Not good idea go alone. I find someone to watch Lotse and Dolma. I go with you."

I sat down at the edge of the field, nervous about the possibility of Kai Lun waking early and seeing me out here near the road. Out of the corner of my eye, I saw Lhamo Sangye run, not to her tent, but in the direction of Tashi Choegyal's. They were going to stop me from going to Derge.

I picked up the pack and ran to the road just as a bus rattled around the hill coming from the direction of Manigango. Sticking out my hand, I waved for it to slow down. Brakes squealing, the bus fishtailed in the soft dirt and pulled over to the side. The door opened and the passengers leaned out of their windows to stare. Just as I lifted my pack ahead of me onto the steps, the driver, a cigarette hanging out of the corner of his mouth, shook his head no and started the engine. I grabbed the bag back just as the door closed, catching my arm. He opened the door again a few inches, I withdrew the arm and pack, and the bus drove off. Panicked, I looked back to the tents, just as Tashi Choegyal and Lhamo Sangye started running across the field, waving in my direction.

A truck barreled toward me, lights off, black smoke pouring from the exhaust. I waved it down, the driver ground to a stop, opened the door, moved a pile of papers and rags over on the seat, and I climbed in. He was going past Derge and on to Jomda. It didn't seem to register with him that I was a foreigner. Maybe he didn't care—maybe he never got the rules.

I slept most of the way, a slight headache signaling we were gaining altitude. My shoulder banged against the truck window as we rammed into potholes and over large rocks in the road, my neck crammed into a recession in the seat. I woke only once as we crossed Tro-La Pass, a heavy snow gradually obliterating the road. The mountain peaks appeared and disappeared through the snow. We rolled down our windows a crack to toss paper prayers into the sky. Through the colorful papers rising on the wind and then falling back to earth, I saw scattered clumps of bright blue against the rocky outcroppings and let out a muffled cry to ask the driver to slow down. I dug the altimeter from my bag. 4,916 meters. More than high enough for poppies to grow and seeds to be collected.

"Please stop!" I called out over the rattle of the wind coming through the jammed windows.

"Only for few minutes." He yanked the steering wheel and the truck flew into the gravel on the side of the road. "Behind schedule."

I got out of the cab hesitantly, afraid he might leave me behind on the mountain, but he just lit up a cigarette and closed his eyes, leaning against the window. I ran over to the clumps of blue, appearing and disappearing in the blowing snow. The colors were magnificent—sky blue and turquoise blue, some with lavender and traces of magenta shading. The spines covered the stem, as well as the flower pods and the underside of the leaves. I held my jacket sleeve against the thorns and snapped off several poppies near the ground. There were no seeds but the withering petals still held the intense blue color. I slipped them in a bag and climbed back into the cab of the truck. I had found the link to Girard—he had been right here. On this mountain pass. I was within hours of answering the primary questions of my life: what happened to Girard and who was involved.

"You freeze in snow just to get common flowers?" the driver said. "Save yourself trouble. Same flowers everywhere."

No, that was impossible. This man was wrong. They weren't everywhere—they were rare and only found in the area where Girard had disappeared. Girard's letter came back to me. '*I am going to try and bring a few petals of this rare beauty back to you. The blue is extraordinary, light shining through like a Tiffany window.*' I had plenty of time over the next few hours to contemplate that I had continuously, and obliviously, written in information into my mind about Girard, the blue poppies and Tibet, without a real basis for doing so. I had to consider that, despite thinking I was acting in a rational and intentional way, in reality in my desperation to find out what had happened to him, I had read more into the letter than he meant.

The driver cranked the engine and we headed down the side of the mountain again. Along the way, I examined the poppies, studying the thick stem and the fragile flowers as we bumped down the road. It was late morning when we drove through the valley into the town of Derge. The driver slowed at a corner and while people stared, I climbed down from the truck. He looked straight ahead and then drove over the bridge out of town.

I walked down the street, unsure of where to go, unsure of where I had thought I would be going. Passing a few buildings, I pulled out my dictionary to try to decipher the meaning of Chinese characters over the building entrances—characters that would lead me to the right office. Shop owners watched from their doorways and school children in tiny Chairman Mao outfits gawked. After I crossed the bridge over a rushing river, a man in the familiar PSB khaki uniform with the stars appeared and steered me toward a cement building with an official-looking sign above the entrance. An old man sat next to the steps, drinking tea and scratching his head. We went down a hallway and through a metal door into the first office.

Crowds came in after us and stared. More people gathered at the window, children standing on their parents' shoulders to get a better look. The musty smell of the building reminded me of the first day walking down the hallways to the Chengdu interrogation room, passing cubicles stacked to the ceiling with folders and bound ledgers. A few minutes later, the insistent honking of a horn signaled a Jeep pulling into the courtyard. There was a flurry of activity as the people who had squeezed into the doorway and pressed against the window scattered and ran away.

A tall man in a crisp uniform entered the office. "Why are you here?" was all he said, speaking Tibetan.

"I am a flower painter. From France. I am an official guest of the government." I shuffled through my bag for my visa and the letter of invitation I now kept with me at all times after the nerve-racking interrogation experience in Chengdu. I was queasy again, reliving how the interrogators had shaken me.

His face morphed into a smirk, all centered around the corners of his mouth, as if he'd seen an instructional movie of a smile and had been practicing in the mirror for days. "You came all the way to Derge over the mountains to paint flowers?"

How did he know I came from over the mountains? "Yes." I laid out my brushes and paints on the desk, sorting them to show the extent of my project—how much I planned to accomplish that day in Derge.

"And do you see flowers you will paint in this office?" His face hadn't altered from the brittle, brilliant smile.

"Not right here, of course." My stomach was doing more of its familiar twisting. No one knew where I was. I could be ushered out the back door and end up in the gorge at the head of the canyon, face down in the river.

"Then where?"

"On the hillsides, in just a bit I'll go to the hillsides to paint," I ventured. "In fact I have some flowers here I will paint." I took out the bag with the blue poppies and placed the flowers on the desk.

"Aaah, the *Sher Ngon*. Very beautiful, but you didn't come to my office just to show me this flower, did you?"

"No sir, I came for your help. Years ago a member of my friend's family came to Tibet and stayed near where the blue poppies grow. He died in Tibet and they asked me to find out where exactly, so they could have a memorial. . ." I continued, looking at his eyes, trying to read his face. He drummed his pen on the desktop and then called for tea.

"Tell your friend his family member did not die near here. This is a very big country and naturally, we do not know about incidents that happen far away. Sorry we can't help him."

"It must have been near here," I calmly protested. "I picked these flowers on the pass just above Derge."

"Madam," he laughed. "Someone has played an unfortunate joke on you. Especially if you came clear from France thinking you would find blue poppies in just one area. The flower you have picked grows everywhere in the mountains of Tibet. Common as a monkey picking lice from its mate's fur. Anyone can tell you that."

A dull throb began in my temple. I had placed all of my hopes on believing the blue poppy was so rare that its presence would be the signpost to information about Girard. The basic premise of my search was false.

"It would be too bad to go back without having found out anything for my friend and his family. Is there anyone else who might know?"

"Might know what, Madame?" A man brought in two smudged glasses filled with hot water, tea leaves floating on the surface. He slid one of the glasses across the table to me. It was too hot to pick up. The officer held his by the rim with two fingers, as he blew the steam away and sipped.

"Someone I could talk to who might have information about the death. I would like to see the files from that time period—the accident was in 1959, maybe in the winter."

"Madame, you are talking to someone about it—you are talking to me. Am I not an important enough person to talk to?" He had tired of my chatter and was ready to dispense with the pretense.

"Of course you are. I will tell my friend it is impossible to find out. Thank you."

"I'm sorry we have taken so much of your time," the officer was continuing. "A car is waiting to take you back across the mountains. It is not safe to drive with local people, you know. They are bad drivers and often have accidents on the mountainsides. An official guest of the government, such as you, should be careful with whom they travel. I'm sure you will be more prudent in the future."

As I walked out the door, the officer caught up with me. "Madam, would you like to ask the driver to stop for you so you can pick more of the lovely blue poppies? He could stop on any of the roads and you would find thousands. If you like, at the top of Tro-La Pass, he can point out all of the mountains beyond—every one of them will have your poppies growing there."

"That won't be necessary," I felt contaminated by the taunt in his voice. "I have all I need."

Back in the camp, the lamp burned down low, and Norbu reached up and gently ran his fingers through my hair. My body leaned into his and we lay back on the bed, holding each other in the cold pre-dawn air. I curled against him, wanting to be closer, to make love, to erase the strangeness of the day. He did not respond to my touch, but lay his face next to mine, breathing warm air into my ear.

"Erzebet," he said, "I told you my secrets. I told you my stories. You know everything about me. You haven't told me your secrets."

"Why are you saying this? I don't have any secrets."

"Dhondhup told me you keep a secret from me."

Dhondhup the troublemaker. There was no way Dhondhup could know

I was looking for the people who killed Girard. Norbu was testing me.

"Dhondhup said you don't care about painting flowers. You search for your husband's secret papers."

"That's ridiculous." My rough laugh sounded like the bark of a wild animal. "What kind of secret papers would there be in a nomad camp--or anywhere for that matter?"

He shrugged.

"Answer me," my voice was sharp. I had been through too much today to be questioned by Norbu. "What did Dhondhup mean by that?"

He took a deep breath. "Dhondhup said your husband was right here at Yi-Lhun Latso Lake. Everyone knows you and Kai Lun both looking for your husband's papers."

"What?" That question came out of my mouth as such a primal wail of disbelief that I had to lower my voice to not call attention to the tent. "My husband was here?" My mind raced--the man at the King Gesar festival. I guessed he had been talking about Girard. But Lhamo Sangye said he was from near Derge, not Manigango. None of this made sense. What had I been doing here for the past weeks spending time with people who knew about Girard, but no one had reached out to me? Or had they—the day Lhamo Sangye asked me about my husband and mentioned an accident—why had I let this comment slip by?

I was suddenly so exhausted I felt I would pass out. "Everyone knows? Even that idiot Dhondhup knows? You've known all along?"

"I didn't know," he said, "but when I found out. . ," he hesitated, staring up at the roof of the tent, examining the smoke hole and the sky beyond.

"When you found out what?"

"When I found out," he reached tentatively for my hand. "I wanted you to think of me. Not think of your husband here in Tibet." I looked at Norbu, shaking my head. I wanted to curse him, but no words came out.

Norbu wrapped the sheepskin blanket closer around me, holding me close to his chest. My body was stiff and then began to tremble uncontrollably. After a few minutes, as I moved to burrow deeper under the blankets, my eye caught the maroon binding of a text of Buddhist teachings I had always meant to read. I took it from the shelf and opened it, Norbu lying next to me staring at the top of the tent.

On the second page, the teacher talked about blue drops of space and consciousness that give clear insight and vision to the recipient. In my early morning dream of the bees in the hive, a dream that seemed like it had happened years ago, the men had been trying to put blue drops in my eyes and I had been fighting to keep my eyes closed. Had I known all along that Girard was here and refused to see it?

# CHAPTER 24

## *Clouds Bring Frost and Hail*

| | |
|---|---|
| *Prin pa kha ser teeng nag* | *Yellow skin, black within* |
| *Sa dang se rae zhi ma* | *The clouds bring frost and hail* |
| *Ban de kya meen ser meen* | *Sage, not grey nor gold* |
| *Sang gya stan pae gra bo* | *This is the foe of Buddhism.* |

*- Sixth Dalai Lama*

### Kai Lun's Story

By early afternoon, it was hot under a cloudless sky and the meadow reverberated with the dull hum of insects moving through the wildflowers. Lotse and Dolma had been gone for hours, and I still hadn't seen a sign of Madame Erzebet or Norbu. I wondered if they had gone somewhere together. What were they doing the other night chasing each other out of the tent, carrying on like children?

When Dhondhup came to the tent, I asked him what he thought. "They're having a romance," he said. "Norbu likes Erzebet even though she's an old woman."

This boy knew nothing. What an absurd thing to say. Impossible. Not something I had even considered happening with her age, European culture, and his barbarian ways, lack of education and immaturity. I thought they were playing like silly teenagers when Erzebet ran out of the tent that day. What in the world could they possibly talk about?

Oh yes, suddenly I knew it was possible.

"So, have you heard Madame Erzebet speak Tibetan?"

"Of course," he looked at me like I was a moron. This boy was nothing but an arrogant nuisance. "Who hasn't?"

A Jeep rumbled down the road and crossed the meadow, weaving between the sheep and the yaks, cutting the morning calm. The vehicle sliced tent ropes, collapsed shelters, and kept on coming. Dhondhup saw the cars, grabbed his slingshot, and quickly ran off to his flock.

I saw the familiar uniforms of the PSB officials before they stepped out of the car, their hands on truncheons swinging from their hips, shifting from leg to leg while the dogs barked. I sped across the meadow to greet them. The superior officer was all the way from Chengdu, his uniform covered with red stars. The others had come to help the day of the horse festival when we searched all of the tents. I led them to my tent, past the dogs and the sheep. They looked around at my home with the small bed, wobbly table and the single chair and smirked as they lit up their cigarettes. I hastily smoothed a place for them to sit on the corner of the mattress, defensive of the meager surroundings. They had no right to sneer at me and ridicule the place where I lived. They had sent me here, made my life impossible. I put river water on the brazier to boil for tea.

"Where is the foreign woman?" the senior officer said as he blew the steam off his tea and flicked ashes onto the earthen floor.

"Out painting," I said. "She goes out everyday to draw the plants."

"You imbecile," he yelled. "She's in Derge, trying to get information about her husband. Where are the Pelletier papers?" My jaw started moving so fast I was afraid my clicking teeth would break off into points.

I made an elaborate show of going through my papers, pretending the notebook with the inconsequential reports about the nomads wasn't lying right there on the table next to them. The officer tapped me on the shoulder. He held the notebook in his hand.

"What's this?" the officer said, with a plastic smile. "Your report?"

I picked up the sketchy notebook and turned the pages, looking for something meaty to show. "No. Well, yes."

"So is it, or isn't it? Comrade? Do you know your own report when you see it?"

"It's just the beginning of the report. I haven't assembled all of my notes." I caught myself tracing my forehead and nose, moving down to my lips with my index finger. A habit since I was a child, it was soothing, and gave me time to think. "I need more time. I'm just gaining the confidence of the people who are in charge."

The senior officer chopped his hand in the air. "Stop!" he yelled. His breath breezed past me, the slightly animal carcass smell of a man with bad teeth. He took the notebook back and leafed through the pages himself, looking up now and then with a frown. He tossed the notebook to the other men with a flip of his wrist. "Is this all?"

"The nomads and monks have been at a festival for many days and are only now returning." My forehead and neck danced with cold sweat. Images of Mei Ling and Jin Quon darted through my mind. Who was shopping for them? Who chose the best market vegetables and grains? Were they being given rotten leftovers from the street stalls?

"Monks are at the festivals?" the officer said. "Lazy monks are at the festivals?"

"Everyone goes. The monastery has been empty."

"Then you searched the monastery while they were gone?"

"Yes, yes, of course I searched the monastery." I refilled the teacups. "I spent hours searching the temple and the monks' quarters. I've found nothing so far, but I'm close. I'm working to get a monk to cooperate with me, help find the documents.

"A monk promised to help you? You're jesting, aren't you Comrade Zhang? A promise from a monk—how much is that worth? Have you gone daft in the head?"

"I didn't mean he promised." My fingers trembled, touching my damp pants, which stuck to my leg. The wound on my calf had reopened and was oozing pus. "I've already found out where his family lives. He won't let anything happen to them. He'll cooperate."

The officer scowled. "Demand results, Comrade Zhang, don't ask for them. We didn't expect to have to wait all summer for you to find the Pelletier papers." They stood and left the tent. When they started across the field, the dogs barked, running maniacally at the edge of the meadow, straining toward the men. The junior officer pulled his club out of its holster, jabbing it into the air.

"No! I'll get them out of the way," I yelled. From the meadow, I saw Lhamo Sangye and Jamyang rushing to pull the dogs back on their chains.

"Comrade Zhang," the officer with the stars turned to face me. "I almost forgot. Your wife and son send their greetings. They're doing very well in Shanghai. We've been fortunate to spend some lovely days with them. They hope you successfully complete your mission, so they can see you again soon." The officers climbed in the Jeep and headed back towards Manigango and Chengdu.

I watched until I could no longer see the dust on the road and was assured they had not changed their minds and would return for more questions. Then I moved on brick legs back to my tent, my heart thumping like the pile drivers used to place the posts for the PSB station in Chengdu. I lay down, wondering if it was possible for a man to die of fear just like a mouse with a weak heart. I stayed still until the bed stopped shaking. There would not be another time to use a weak excuse like a festival for lack of information.

# CHAPTER 25

## *Rabbit in the Moon*

| | |
|---|---|
| *Tsay chen cho nga'ee da wa* | *The moon tonight appears to be* |
| *Yeen pa dra wa duk day* | *A full moon* |
| *Da wa'ee gyeel gyee ree bong* | *Yet, the rabbit in the moon* |
| *Tsay sze tsar nee duk goe* | *Does not seem to be alive* |

*- Sixth Dalai Lama*

### Erzebet's Story

I awoke to the sound of water boiling in the kettle. Lhamo Sangye was in my tent, kneading *tsampa* together with butter and tea. Norbu was nowhere to be seen.

"Come for picnic in hills," she said, as I rolled over in the bed and rubbed my eyes.

"I don't think so. Today, I'm going to paint here."

"Better you go with us," Lhamo Sangye replied. "Warm day. Things to see on other side of lake. Flowers to paint you not see before. You find poppies you looked for? After rain they cover hillsides of higher mountains. We hike to find them."

More illusive poppies to find? I was suddenly exhausted at my masquerade. "Lhamo Sangye," I lowered my voice. "This isn't about the blue poppies anymore. You know that—maybe you have known all along. I believe my husband was murdered. He wrote to me about the poppies in a letter before he disappeared. That was the only clue I had. I thought finding the poppies would tell me where that was."

"Why you not tell me this before?" Lhamo Sangye asked. "I could have told you that poppies should not be trusted as way to find out about your husband."

She assembled a bag of *tsampa*, bread and thermos of butter tea, gathered up my art supplies and pack and waited for me to get dressed. "Your trip to Derge was bad idea, Erzebet. You not using your head. No need to foolishly go to authorities to ask questions about husband. Other ways to find out what you want to know. The man who gave you ride to Derge arrested and disappeared."

"What I did led to that man being arrested?" My actions were putting innocent people in jeopardy. How could I justify these poor people being sucked into my careless wake? "Believe me, I didn't know I wasn't supposed to travel with people on the road. I wouldn't have put him at risk."

Lhamo Sangye looked over. "But you knew not allowed to go Derge, right?"

"Yes, I knew that," I said. "Now I'm responsible for that man's misfortune."

"Because you from West, you think you are cause of everything. That you have power over all life. Not so. Karma of that man to see you on road. Pick you up. Just like your karma to come here and paint our flowers. Your karma to try to find out what happened to husband."

A crowd had gathered at the tent flap, all jockeying to carry my things and lead me to the lake. I headed out with the women and children, wading across the shallow neck of the river, our long underwear rolled to our knees. Kai Lun joined us as we followed a well-worn path along the lake and through the pines and then he sat down on the edge of the group, reading from his notebook.

After setting up a white tent, the picnickers lay down on carpets for afternoon naps or hunted for berries in the nearby bushes. They brought stained handfuls of the red-black globes to me, the remembered smell of berry tarts as a child reaching my nose before I popped the fruit in my mouth. Stones as large as one-room houses, others only as big as stepping-stones, stood as sentries at the lake shoreline. They had the Tibetan characters *Om Mani Padme Hung* carved in the sides, some outlined red, blue or yellow, others with no color at all. I spread out flat on a boulder, the sun blanketing my neck and arms. I needed an ally. I needed Lhamo Sangye to help me. She had told me weeks ago that I could trust her. So why hadn't she trusted me?

Large vats of barley beer, *chang*, appeared from the bundles people carried.

"Could you ask Lhamo Sangye if someone has my bag of art supplies?" I said to Kai Lun as I took a small cupful of *chang*.

"Why should I do that?" Kai Lun held out his bowl and was given a large ladleful to drink. The scornful tone of his voice was chilling. "You're perfectly capable of speaking Tibetan to her yourself, aren't you?"

"I guess I have learned enough by now to speak for myself," I murmured.

The sun was beating down and Kai Lun gulped the beer as if it was water. When he took off his jacket and folded it to place against the stones, the nomads filled his bowl again. He drank it down. Within minutes his face had changed from a grim mask and he was laughing, slurring his words, and teasing the children. Pant legs rolled up above his knees, he waded in the river with a group headed up by Lotse and Dolma. They made leaf boats with paper masts and sailed them along the green rivulets, the children laughing at his side and hanging on his sleeve. While we watched, they tickled him and he pretended to fall into the water and swim like a fish, grabbing their legs while they kicked and splashed around him. He returned to the adults smiling and they refilled his bowl. Before I knew it he was asleep curled against the warm stones, his head cradled on his jacket.

Through the haze of my own napping dream, a tinny noise creaked from the direction of the path. At first, I mistook it for the metallic chatter of a cicada. A man with a basket strapped to his back drew near, spinning a prayer wheel in his right hand. Clinging to his other hand, a small boy used a stick to root in the soil, finding earthworms and insects with polished bronze wings. He scooted the insects along, guiding them to a safer spot in the grasses.

"Hermit's grandson is good boy," Lhamo Sangye greeted them as she spoke to me. "He make sure people and animals not step on bugs and kill them."

The hump-backed man was breathing in short, labored puffs and stopped, leaning against the boulder where I sat. His clouded moonstone eyes focused not on me, but on the bush beside my head. "You are pilgrim?"

I considered the question. I was a pilgrim of sorts, too hard to explain. Lhamo Sangye looked over at Kai Lun, who was snoring, and spoke up. "Po-La, Old Man, this is flower painter I told you about."

"Come from Europe to paint flowers here?"

I nodded yes. "Grandfather, foreigner woman shake head to say yes," the boy said to the old man. He placed a large stone in his grandfather's palm, and the old man turned it repeatedly, probing the tiny crevices, traveling the surface with his fingers to feel the texture. His hand was my father's spotted hand, weathered, knuckles like knotted twigs. Blue veins bulged above the skin's surface like the tributaries of a river.

The old man motioned toward a narrow trail heading away from the water as he picked up his basket again and walked away. His soles hung off his shoes, slapping as he shuffled along. I looked over at Lhamo Sangye, wondering if I was meant to follow him. She waved her hand at me and nodded toward Kai Lun. "Go now," she mouthed silently. "Go quickly."

Without a word, I followed the old man and his grandson up the path to a windowless shelter on the hillside. A threadbare cloth was nailed to the doorframe and I hunched down to enter, grazing my spine against the wood as I passed through. Near the roofline, a knothole permitted a chink of light to enter through the tin, just enough to illuminate the altar. The light struck a piece of silver, creating a white-hot dart on the metal. My mind grappled to recover a memory I could not quite access.

I sat down on a splintered wooden bench, as the walls of plastic sheeting and odd-length broken boards rattled in the slight breeze. The old man deftly poured hot water into a dented tin cup and handed it to me and then pointed toward a photo of his teacher tacked to the newspaper-covered wall. Below it was the familiar stack of altar items--biscuits, a bottle of soda pop, bowls of water, and rice. The perfume of a *Stellera* resting in a water glass was a fresh contrast to the dank smell of the dark hovel.

"When I was child," the old man said, picking up a stone and guiding his fingers through the Tibetan characters carved into it. "Grandfather held me against his chest. Chanted *Om Mani Padme Hung*. Prayer flowed into my ears.

Entered my blood. Traveled to my heart. Now, when worried, my mind goes to Grandfather. I am at peace. I hold grandson same way after his father and mother died."

As the man recited his prayers, swinging his prayer wheel, the boy, cobwebs tangled in his hair, crouched in the corner and scratched pictures into the dirt floor. I sipped my cup of hot water and thought about Girard's death and how every day I was sidetracked by events in the camp and people herding me to and fro like they herded their animals. I felt drowsy in the heat of the shack and slipped out into the daylight. Behind me, a hammer and chisel struck stone, the sound of the tapping reverberating through my body.

Grey clouds fused with the blue of the sky, a transparent sheet of shimmering labradorite suspended above the mountains. Rain fell like needles, puckering the surface of the lake until it was the cratered surface of the moon.

"*Ta dro*? Time to go?" The picnickers called, as I approached. The rain had slowed to a drizzle. Mountain shadows invaded the valley and in the distance plumes of smoke rose from evening fires in the tents, calling us home.

"How does the man in the hut live?" I asked the women and children who ran to join me. On their backs, blankets bulged with the pots and pans from the picnic. They leapt from stone to stone down the rocky hillside. "How does he eat?"

"Pilgrim travel from all over Tibet to pray at lake. Donate food and money to hermit." In exchange, she explained, he chiseled *Om Mani Padme Hung* into stone, a self-appointed archetypal mission.

"What did hermit give you?" Lhamo Sangye asked me.

"A cup of hot water. And he prayed while I was there."

"That all? You give hermit offering?"

I blushed to realize I had given him nothing. Perhaps I should have given him money for a carved stone that would then be placed on one of the giant piles of mani stones near the lake. I ran back to the hut, extending my hand with a half-filled bag of biscuits and all of the coins I had in my pack. The boy took the offering, pressed it to his forehead, and then placed it on the altar under the photo of the teacher, rearranging the altar offerings.

As the Yuan notes shifted, the glint of the silver piece on the altar, half-hidden, caught my eye. My entire body was electrified. I moved the few steps back to the altar, as if I must sneak up on the metal object. There, exposed, was the silver rabbit pendant Lilia had given Girard, the necklace he never took off. I turned it over and read Lilia's distinctive, childlike scroll, PaPa, engraved into the back.

"Where did this come from?" My voice faded as I rubbed the cool metal against my cheek and remembered the day when Lilia bought this gift for Girard at the Paris flea market. The seller had allowed her to use the metal inscribing tool so it would be her own handwriting. "How did you get this?"

"Grandfather," the boy said, "foreigner woman hold necklace with *ri-bong*, the rabbit."

"This belonged to someone I knew," I whispered. It seemed impossible. The hermit or his grandson had found the necklace in a market or alongside the road.

"*Ri-bong* belonged to man who was your father in other life," the Grandfather said. "Soldier carry him here after accident on road. I hold man who wore *ri-bong* in my arms. Like Grandfather hold me. Like I hold this boy. I blow prayers of *Om Mani Padme Hung* into his heart. Not just for him. For all sentient beings who suffer."

"What soldier? Who carried him here?"

"All soldiers same. Many years ago."

I forced myself to ask the final questions. "Were you with him when he died?"

"No, not die here."

"Where was the accident?"

"What would you do with information about accident, if I knew?" he said. "No one can change past. Think of future."

"Can I take this with me?" I held out the pendant, afraid it would be taken back. The front of my dress was soaked from tears I didn't know I was crying. Girard had been here, only meters from where I had been walking all the past weeks.

"*Ri-bong* wait for you many years," the hermit's voice brought me back to the pendant in my hand and this hut on the mountainside. "Take with you to TriSong Monastery. Show Lama Lobsang Phuntsok."

# CHAPTER 26

## *Love Songs Washed Away by Tears*

| | |
|---|---|
| *Dee ba'ee yee ge nak joong* | *Love songs written in black ink* |
| *Chu thang theek pa'ee jeek song* | *Are washed away by tears* |
| *Ma tree sem gyi ree mo* | *But love, though unwritten* |
| *Soob gyang tsoob gyu meen dook* | *We cannot erase, even if we try* |

*- Sixth Dalai Lama*

## The Twin's Story as Told by Lhamo Sangye

Once again, I tell story told to me by twins. When Magistrate come to camp, he say twins should watch out for Erzebet. Better if I say, no. I was afraid. If I speak out then, twins with us today. My job is to tell their story so no one ever forget.

The twins tell me: We search Lhamo Sangye's tent. Look through her boxes. She come home. Catch us. Grab us by ears and drag us across meadow to our tent. We squeal like piglets. When Lhamo Sangye tell Ama-la hear we help Mr. Kai Lun, Ama-la face get purple and she yell. She say if she could, she get up and beat us. Throw us out of tent because we are stupid. We turn against own neighbors. We tell Ama-la we find nothing, so no one in trouble. Only look for papers Mr. Kai Lun forgot in someone's tent. Papers might be in red folder. Not make any difference to Ama-la.

Lhamo Sangye rub her eyes. "My fault." She put arm around Sister's shoulders. "Should never have allowed twins to take care of Erzebet."

"You carry on family tragedy," Ama-la cut in. Her face look like it melt in heat. Not good with hand that not lift and leg that drag behind. "My own children work for enemy."

"Enemy?" Sister whisper when we back out in meadow. Still rubbing ears to make sting go away. "Mr. Kai Lun enemy? Why someone not tell us sooner?"

That end of our job. Later that day, Mr. Kai Lun himself tell us we finish. We not find anything useful. He not need us anymore. Already have someone else to help him. Good. He scare us. Always staring. Look at our faces with big wrinkled frown on his.

But now we wonder. Mr. Kai Lun trick us? Maybe now he spy on us. He sit at edge of meetings and parties. Listen. Watch. Write what people say. Write who they spend time with. One man talk crazy when Mr. Kai Lun near. Try to fill Mr. Kai Lun's notebooks with nonsense. We laugh at what he say. How to tie down yak. How to make mountain shorter moving one boulder at a time. Another man say to anyone who listen, "I don't care what he write about me. I will live as free man." People at fire tell man to shut up. He ask for trouble.

We worry. What he write about us? Maybe he say we useless. Not helpful. We should be punished. Maybe he say we have Older Brother who disappear. Maybe he think we should go to prison for helping Older Brother.

"We have to do something. Everyday scared. We die like rabbit trapped by hawk in meadow," say Sister.

Next day, we watch Mr. Kai Lun from first sunlight to moonrise. He not carry notebook. No pack where it might be hidden. We stay near his tent. Wait for right time to sneak in and find notebook. Like standing on cliff edge. Trying to leap to other side. Teeter. Fall back. Creep forward. Sitting on rocks, we wait for nightfall, braid yak tail for ropes. We make long tight rope. Will hold up tent in even worst weather.

Many hours later, yellow light from oil lamp shine through holes in Mr. Kai Lun's tent. He not leave. I sleep. Sister watch tent. Ready to act when he visit another tent. Or walk to farthest end of pasture. Before midnight, we both fall asleep on logs. Bundle together in sheepskin chuba. At dawn, we wake. Cold. Stagger to our tent. In tent we eat *tsampa* and fill seven offering bowls on altar with fresh, clear water. Spicy smell from incense fill air. We each do 100 prostrations to Buddha. Pray for guidance. Ask for good fortune. Ask for forgiveness. All at same time. Afterward Sister run from tent. She throw up *tsampa* in reeds at riverside. I heat water on stove. Hold cup while Sister sip hot water. Everyone know hot water first medicine, best medicine for any illness.

In afternoon, we light butter lamps. Pray for Lama's long life. Cannot eat. Without speaking, we pack *tsampa*, dried meat, socks and gloves in yak skin bags. We might need to escape in night over mountains. Just after sunset, Sister run to tell me, "He leave tent. He walk with Dhondhup to other side of lake."

Red star blink in sky. Millions more sweep sky in dusty, glittering white band. We rush to Mr. Kai Lun's tent. We squat down at rear of tent. Sister, with big eyes, take my hand. She hold it over her chest. Her chuba puff in and out. Heart beat too hard. Lifting tent panel, we slide on stomachs through cool soft grass. Sharp rock dig into my arm. Bulky chubas jam against lower edge of tent. It hold my fat sister half inside and half out. I struggle. Sheepskin oven cook me in own sweat. I squirm and kick. Swim my way free. We surface inside.

Mr. Kai Lun tent darker than night outside. Inch by inch, we feel our way past iron stove. Past shoes. Over piece of tree trunk on tent floor. I crash into table, leaning to side. Groaning on its wobbly legs. Piles of papers fall to floor. We pat ground for paper, drag crumpled pieces from under our knees. We hear paper tear. Big problem. We widen out in circle to make sure none escape. Loose papers tell bad story later to man who live in tent. We stack pages quick and neat, then glide hands over tabletop. My shaking fingers find hard edges of textbooks. Fingers find ink brushes and pens. Finally, feel cold metal loops that hold notebook together. Sister put notebook inside chuba. We slip back under tent edge and run away.

In our tent, Ama-la grunt in sleep. Her useless arm hang out from under blanket. Like piece of dried yak meat from fall slaughter. We lean in close to light of single candle. Open book. Our eyes fly back and forth over pages.

"What you doing up so late?" Ama-la mutter. "Go to bed. Not cause enough trouble today?"

Blowing out candle, we sit still in dark until Ama-la breath like everyday. Like injured animal drag through forest, choking and sputtering in own blood.

Then we light candle again. Look at notebook. "Read like this." Sister grab book. Turn it around. "Upside down."

Other way, book still mystery. Marks like animal prints in soft dirt on day when no rain. Stealing book was plan. We didn't know we not know how to read it. Never try to read before. Were our names there? What he say about us? Did Mr. Kai Lun thank us for helping or say send us to prison? Neither of us know how to figure it out.

"Norbu," Sister say simply.

"He can read, but won't help us," I say.

"Our only chance. He not care what Mr. Kai Lun write about him or his friends. He already act in many wrong ways. He already in big trouble. Norbu have nothing to lose."

Sister once again stuff notebook inside her chuba. We run to Madame Erzebet's tent. Dog bark. We call out from distance.

"Norbu, it's us, twins."

He appear in tent flap. Wearing half chuba, tied at waist. "Why are you here at night?" Rushing out he chain dog. "Should be home with your Ama-la."

"Help us. Mr. Kai Lun watch us. Write about us. We have to know what he say. Ama-la say he is enemy. He send us to prison."

"Enemy? Well, maybe you two shouldn't have been helping him. Going into everybody's tents. Keep your voices down. Erzebet is sleeping."

We hold out notebook. Norbu jerk back as if notebook scorpion, not bunch of paper hold together by metal loops. "You broke into Chinese official's tent? You stole what belongs to Chinese Government," he whisper, and look back inside. "Now you bring this here causing trouble for me. Where are your brains?"

My grey-faced sister push notebook at Norbu. He go back inside. Come out with butter lamp. Tie tent flap closed and sit down on log at edge of tent boundary. He open book. His eyes move fast over pages.

"Can you read it?" we ask. He nod.

His finger slide down marks. He tell us what he see. Notes on nomads' conversations fill first part. Problem when dog attack Madame Erzebet. Talk about her trips to hills to collect flowers. Searching tents while we at horse races. Number of yaks in Damdul's herd. Arranged marriage of Tsetan's daughter and Gyalpo Tashi's son. Pages covered with marks. Many marks about missing papers.

*June 16: Madame Erzebet's tent-no documents.*

*June 17: Madame Erzebet's tent-no papers. Tents to left of meadow where Jigme lives-no documents*

*June 19: Tents at right of meadow, next to road-no documents found.*

*June 22-23: Nothing. Searched all tents from river to end of lower meadow.*

*June 28: No papers. Twins are searching tents. Don't know if they have any clue what is going on.*

*July 6: Searched all tents with team from Derge, while nomads at horse festival. There are no papers in this camp! I cannot find them here, if they exist at all.*

*July 7: Can barely get myself out of bed to continue this absurd and what will almost certainly be a disastrous plan. That's the problem—what should the plan be to find the papers-or are there papers? Were there ever papers? Did my Director at the PSB know there were no papers and they have actually sent me here for an entirely different reason?*

"So, Dhondhup was right. Kai Lun's been searching everywhere for the documents," Norbu said, "and you stupid girls helped him do that."

"Mr. Kai Lun lie to us. He say they his papers." I kick corner of log. "But we never find anything anyway. Why everyone mad at us? What he say about our family? Read to us what he write."

"He hasn't said anything much about you at all. He hasn't said much about anyone. There isn't anything important here."

"You sure you know how to read this book?"

"I know most of words, not all, most of them. Your names are here, but nothing to be afraid of. The twins are sneaky. They have to be watched more closely," Norbu said. "You are sneaky—that's no secret."

"Tell us truth. He write about Older Brother?"

"No. He doesn't mention your Older Brother."

Marks become less. Small drawing here and there. Flower in field. View of lake. Mani stones on shoreline, Eagle fly above hills.

Norbu trace his finger under group of words. "I don't know this poem," he say. "It's in Chinese, but I think I know what it says."

*Tonight my wife must watch alone*
*The eclipse of the moon over the river at Fuli*
*My heart breaks as I think of my son far away,*
*He was born in hope not knowing we would separate*
*When I travel many kilometers to Emei Shan*
*And stand at the foot of the sacred mountain*
*I see my wife appear in the shine of the waterfall*
*Her face is fresh and beckons to me*
*I weep*

"I not understand. What mean?" I say. "Not make sense,"

"Maybe this is his own poem," Norbu say. "It's what is called literature. You not understand. Don't worry, only people who go to school can understand."

As he read, Sister's face change from confuse to happy smile. She hold out short arms and take back book. "We go back while he still away. Return book to table," say my twin, younger than me by seconds, but always braver. "When he see notebook missing, bring police again. Even bigger trouble."

"*Tsub, tsub che ah.* Be careful," call Norbu as we rush out.

Nearing Mr. Kai Lun's tent, happiness turn to ice. Light burn inside. Juniper smoke pour from chimney. Good smell for meadow. Dogs from neighboring tents bark until pasture full of noise. Yelping, howling animals.

"Who's there?" Mr. Kai Lun call. "Who's out there?"

We run to side of field. Sister shake, bawl into my chuba. Sitting by river, we turn prayer beads in our hands. Chant *Om Mani Padme Hung* very loud. We stay at stream until only sound is whinny of horse and bleat of lamb snuggling next to its mother. Moon move from overhead to three finger's width above glacier. Icy wind blow off lake and whip chubas around our legs. It time.

Creeping back to meadow edge, we move like lions stalking lambs. We cross over tent lines anchored to ground with stones. Tiptoe to back panel, where we enter before. In damp cold grass, we lie down and listen. No sound. Take off sheepskin chubas. Pull off our boots. Lifting panel away from ground, we slide under tight yak hair felt. Pull ourselves forward like legless creatures. Dragging on elbows past edge of bed. Past chair. Bump again against table leg.

Gentle shushing sound rise and fall like sad wind. Chanting of a prayer? No. Murmur of man not asleep. My breath thunder in my ears. Louder than sounds come from bed. We afraid to go closer, afraid to leave.

Man's whisper come from darkness, "Leave book on table. Go back the way you came in."

I clamp hand over Sister's mouth. Breathing too loud. Too fast. Frozen on ground, our hearts pound and swell. Air stick in our chests.

"Leave notebook on table. Go back the way you came in."

Sister slide notebook onto table edge. We edge backward in dark toward rear of tent. Scrunch under panel into freezing night air. We grab our chubas and flee along riverbank. Safe in own tent, we squeeze into bed under bony arm of Ama-la and clutch each other. My twin take milk from long leathery breast of Ama-la. Breast look like eggplant trader bring from Chengdu. It dry up years ago, but still comfort in night.

I dream. I travel on long hike with strangers into mountains. I turn and look back to village. Trees, sheep, tents twinkle down in valley. Tents and trees appear, disappear in thick mist. I confuse. Which family tent?

Sister dream. In her dream, family own large yak with rope through ring in nose. She tie rope at night. In morning, yak break loose. She search for yak. She hear yak's sad call. Not find yak until she hunt for many hours.

That is story twins tell me in morning. They come to river where I wash clothes with other women. Clear day with gold sun in sky circled by rainbow. Storm coming. Twins just finish telling night's adventure with notebook when Mr. Kai Lun approach.

"You are stupid girls," he say. Usually he have soft voice. Now loud enough for all to hear. Twins hide behind my chuba, pulling themselves in close to my lags.. "Do not come into my tent again," he say even louder.

He walk away and head toward hills on other side of road.

"It is trick. He return for us later," twins say. "When no one watch he be mean to us." Their child bodies shook. They grab each others' hands and wail.

We women try to make them feel better. Mr. Kai Lun not evil man. He have child of his own. He not hurt them. Twins not believe us. They see too much in their short lives. In early afternoon, I spot twins on footpath heading toward Khowalangri Mountain. Packs on their backs. Going to look for sheep at rocky outcropping.

Later in day their Ama-la cry out asking where twins go. Only then, we know what happen. Search party leave right away. Storm coming in mountains. I sit with Ama-La and wait for news. Twins good girls. Before they leave, they light butter lamps and prepare food for their Ama-la to last many days. They sweep clean earthen floor of tent. Tiny photo of Dalai Lama, usually held by splintered wood in drawer of painted chest, gone. Searchers return two days later, faces weighed down with sadness. They find empty pack on mountainside, but no twins. I regret for rest of my life I let those girls go into mountains on day when sun circled by rainbow.

# CHAPTER 27

## *Destroy the Foes of the Dharma*

| | |
|---|---|
| *Sa tsoo'ee yeeng so zhuk pa'ee* | *The transcendent Dorje Chokyong* |
| *Dam chen Dorjee Chokyong* | *The oracle of the Tenth Spiritual Stage* |
| *Thu dang nu pa yo na* | *If you have supernatural powers* |
| *Den pa'ee dra po trol dang* | *Destroy the foes of the dharma* |

*- Sixth Dalai Lama*

## Erzebet's Story

I listened to Norbu outside the tent at night reading to the twins from Kai Lun's notebook. Just as Norbu had reported from Dhondhup, Kai Lun was scarching for the documents--the link to Girard. What advice would Mr. Cline, that old Foreign Service agent have for me now? After talking to the twins, Norbu came back into the tent and he went straight to sleep. I didn't tell him I had heard about the twins' exploits through the tent walls. We had enough complicated issues between us.

In the morning, as usual, I turned to painting as the calm where I could gather my thoughts. I walked to the wide part of the river and sketched some small purple flowers growing among the rocks. They looked like African violets. My identification guide told me it was *Scrophulariaceae Lancea tibetica Hook* I was immersed in capturing the deep grooves of the leaves, allowing my mind to work in the background of my painting task, figuring out what to do with the information that Girard had indeed been here. I was at a dead end in the camp. I sensed that even Lhamo Sangye was holding back information. After the horse festival when I told her I wanted to go to TriSong Monastery, she said it wasn't time. Time for what, she wouldn't say.

A shadow fell over my drawing. I looked up. It was Norbu's father with Tashi Choegyal standing beside him.

"Madame Erzebet," said Norbu's father. "I went to TriSong Monastery last night. Monks are doing ceremonies. Good time for you to visit." Tashi Choegyal reached out his hand and helped me to my feet.

As we walked to the tent, he handed me a piece of paper with the message: *Madame Erzebet, Please come visit. Please stay many days. Lobsang Phuntsok.*

Just as I was deciphering the words, Kai Lun appeared from behind the tent, took the note from my hand, read it and handed it back. Norbu's father and Tashi Choegyal exchanged a quick glance behind his back.

"I go on business to Sershul. You ride with me," said Tashi Choegyal. "We leave within the hour."

"I'll come later this afternoon," said Kai Lun. "I need to inspect the monastery to see that all is in order there."

My bag, with the silver rabbit pendant deep in the pocket, was packed by the time Tashi Choegyal returned on his stallion. Leaning over, he grabbed my wrist, pulling me into the air and I swung onto the back of his horse.

We rode along the dirt trail winding down to the river, from time to time, paralleling a bus that rattled down the road to Derge, Manigango or Ganzi. The sky was a cloudless powder blue. The whistle of boys herding sheep cut the air and yaks grazed in the wildflowers.

As we rode, I asked Tashi Choegyal about the houses we passed, hoping to glean information that would link the farmers and herders to Girard. My questions gained nothing.

"How long has that family lived there?"

"Generations."

"Did they fight the Chinese when the occupation started?"

"Everyone fight Chinese. Erzebet, you have many questions. It is time to wait for the answers to come to you. To set fire to the wood, you need the help of the wind."

Three hours later, we arrived at the monastery's lush setting between two sloping hills. Chanting rumbled from the temple. We rode up the final prominence passing pilgrims moving in a clockwise direction along the path that circled the buildings. The pilgrims journeyed like snails, extending their arms in front, prostrating full length in the dirt, and then pulling themselves back up to their feet. Protective pads from old tires, cotton and sheepskin were strapped to their knees. They traveled through mud, over stones, up hills and down the other side. Their faces were the black and red of steel just brought out of the furnace. Some had been on the pilgrimage for years.

I slid down off the horse and Tashi Choegyal handed me the pack. "Be careful, Madame Erzebet. Stay close to Lama Lobsang Phuntsok."

He wheeled in the return direction and rode away. As I walked toward a group of curious monks, a familiar face emerged from the crowd. It was Lobsang Phuntsok. I remembered his smile and big ears from the first day when I arrived at Yi-Lhun Latso—what felt like a century before. He greeted me with a white *khata* scarf and led me to a small cubicle down the hill from the main complex. When the door pushed open, my nostrils flared and quickly pinched shut at the dense moist smell of a Grimm's Brothers dungeon. Brown water spots stained the walls and mold spackled the corners.

"Kai Lun is coming later this afternoon," I said, sneezing and looking around at the table, hot water thermos and single bed. "To inspect the monastery."

"We've been told. Nothing to worry about."

In the main temple, the air was ripe with the smell of sandalwood and pulsed with chanting. Creeping behind rows of monks sitting cross-legged on red cushions, I settled in the dark along the back wall. A thirty-foot high gold Buddha rose like a mythical figure from the temple floor itself. The cobalt hair twisted into a topknot--a symbol of enlightenment.

Above us hung paintings with frightening devils—fire blazing around them, necklaces of skulls around their necks, and human bodies being ground under their bare feet.

"What are those?" I asked Lobsang. "Why does a monastery have pictures of devils and hell hanging near a Buddha?"

"Wrathful deities," he taught me. "Their job is to frighten away negativity. Bodies under their feet represent ignorance, greed, jealousy, and anger. The wrathful deity is overpowering negative emotions."

I thought of my father and his brusque statements during the time of the investigation into Girard's death. He had been my own wrathful deity, pushing me to conquer my own desire to stop searching for the truth about Girard's disappearance.

Now each monk chanted three or four bass notes simultaneously, their hands swaying back and forth like synchronized dancers in a Hindu temple. Lobsang leaned over and explained the symbolism. Left hands rang *tribu*, bells, each high-pitched clang signified wisdom. In their right hands, they rocked *dorjees*, metal objects in the shape of a thunderbolt, symbolizing compassion. It all signified that without wisdom, the action of compassion cannot happen. Without the action of compassion, your wisdom is worth little. The hands crossed and crisscrossed at the level of the monk's hearts.

*Rat-a-tat-tat. Rat-a-tat-tat.* A drum, similar to a child's toy with a ball swinging back and forth, beat out a staccato rhythm to bring pleasure to the wrathful deities.

The chanting moved into long stretches of hypnotic melody. I was dozing off when the mood in the temple abruptly changed. Young monks swooped into the room swinging large silver kettles. Robes flying out to the sides, they ran the length of the rows pouring steaming tea into the monks' wooden bowls and then scurried backwards out of the room.

We joined the monks for lunch, a clear soup with green vegetables and shell-shaped *ting-mo*, large puffy pieces of bread. Bread and tea in the morning, a single potato at lunch, or a handful of rice or noodles at night were the usual meals. Today they had the luxury of kale because I was visiting. My appetite was slight; my interest in anything other than uncovering information about Girard short-lived.

Finishing lunch, we climbed the temple steps to look out over the Dri-Chu River valley. Prayer flags snapped and fluttered in the breeze. Sheep and yak salt-and-peppered the hills sending low bellows in our direction.

"Lobsang-la," I said, using the respectful 'la' attached to his name. "Is your invitation to come here about more than a casual visit?"

"We need your help," he said over the tidal wave of chanting, which had started up again and flowed out the temple doors. "Chinese propaganda says there is no problem in monasteries. Monks can pray as they wish. They say monks live like royalty. Monks are parasites feeding on hard work of common people. I want you to see the truth of how monks live here."

My whole body felt depleted. My mind crashed once again into disappointment. This visit had nothing to do with Girard. The monks knew nothing. I had fallen into another trap of distraction. This monastery needed help and nothing more. Maybe Norbu's father had asked the monks to invite me merely to get me out of the camp, away from Norbu. The possibility of finding people who knew what happened to Girard when he was in Tibet now resided more solidly in the realm of fantasy than any daydream I had ever conjured up. I would stay only two days and go back to Yi-Lhun Latso.

We climbed a wooden ladder with steps that seemed too small for normal human feet and too steep for a normal ascent or descent. I could barely get myself to talk to this gracious monk or be interested in what he was showing me. In another time, I would have been eager to know more, eager to know how I could help, no matter how impossible it might seem. Now it merely added a layer of supreme exhaustion to my life.

We emerged into an ochre and orange-walled inner courtyard where murals depicted fanciful flowers and landscapes with jewel-laden trees, dominated by large images of the Buddha. The Auspicious Symbols, cues for the compassionate life, were sprinkled throughout the paintings. A monk awkwardly held a torch between two fingers of a deformed hand, while he lit hundreds of butter lamps in rows on tables. His other arm jutted out at an odd angle, dangling like a confused pendulum from the elbow.

"What happened to those monks?" I rallied my human emotions again, whispering to Lobsang as I inclined my head toward men who hobbled by on deformed legs and feet.

"Crippled while in prison. By Chinese. Tortured for refusing to denounce Dalai Lama as their leader. Beaten because they demonstrated against the Chinese occupation of their homeland. They have damaged arms and legs from days of standing in buckets of ice water. Many nights they were beaten with a hammer every time they refused to turn against Dalai Lama."

"They must hate the Chinese."

"No. They pray to forgive. Even their torturers. For a monk, loss of the compassionate mind is far worse than losing leg or eye."

We walked down a corridor to the monks' living quarters. Rats scurried along the hallway, pushing their noses into cracks in the walls and then disappearing into the gloom. Points of light came through the rusted tin ceiling. The smell of mold permeated every wall. The rooms contained little else than wooden plank beds doubling as meditation platforms with thin blankets folded neatly at the foot. I tried to imagine what these men did for warmth in the middle of a Tibetan winter.

The tour continued, each monk's story an echo of the one before, each room we entered more dilapidated than the others. By midnight, I had seen and heard enough. I was overwhelmed at the enormity of their suffering and had no idea how I could help. I couldn't even help myself. When I left in a few weeks, I was going back to Paris. It would be over. I had no power to influence the Chinese Government or my own. I questioned if I had the mental strength and will to even try. It brought back hints of my depression years ago trying to convince politicians to follow up Girard's disappearance with an investigation. And it reminded me of my recent conversation with Norbu, whose suffering was minor compared to these monks, but he was also desperate for me to help him, and my ability to do so seemed negligible.

Eyelids gritty and drooping, I tore myself away to trudge the short distance down the hill to the guest room. As I walked, it occurred to me that I hadn't seen Kai Lun since that morning in the camp. Had he arrived at the monastery without my having seen him?

The guesthouse was locked. Peering into the windows of the darkened rooms, I tapped on all the doors and then banged harder and harder. The knocking bounced back off the monastery walls, but no one came to see who was outside. I adjusted my sweater and jacket, buttoning both to my neck and put on a second pair of socks I dug out of my bag. Chilled, with no entry to my room in sight, I wended my way rapidly back up the hill, twisting from side to side to see what might be stalking me. Every shadow seemed to conceal a leopard or wolf terrorizing the monastery, sniffing my scent.

I was coming up the final step of the temple, trying to remember the exact location of Lobsang's room, when a movement next to a pillar caught my attention. I looked up and was staring straight into someone's eyes. Stifling a scream, I backed away. A tall monk with a bloated face and a deep scar across his cheek stepped out of the shadow.

"I can help you with something?" he asked.

"I forgot my bag during the day," I stammered. "I'm staying in the guesthouse." I didn't want to tell him the guesthouse was locked; that it was just him and me out here in the night, no one knowing where I was.

"Go back to the guesthouse," he said as he turned and went into the temple. "I'm sure your bag will be where you left it in morning."

I pretended to go toward the guesthouse, and then doubled back. Creeping up the steps as silently as possible, I ducked into the corridor scanning each door for clues as to which room held Lobsang. "Lobsang-la," I whispered as I tiptoed down the corridor, studying the doors, which now all seemed the same. "Lobsang-la." The third door on the left looked familiar. I lightly tapped and heard stirring and mumbling inside. I tapped again and the door next to it opened instead. Lobsang stood there dressed in a baggy yellow t-shirt and maroon skirt, his body slight as a child's.

"Who's there?" He peered into the darkened corridor holding a candle in one hand.

"It's Erzebet. The guesthouse is locked. I can't get in."

He opened the door wider and I could see his muscular arms from years of prostrations. A spiral-shaped birthmark stained his shoulder. "You sleep in my room." I frowned. "No bother," he continued. "You can sleep on floor."

I knew I had few options at this poor monastery. "Someone saw me coming here."

"A monk? Someone you met during day?"

"No. I would have remembered. He was tall. He had a big face, a fat face."

"Come in quickly. Go to sleep."

I lay down on the floor, squeezed between a chair and a grey metal cabinet. Lobsang leaned over and blew out the candle. Lying in the darkness, I listened to the wind blowing down the corridor and gentle snoring from the room next door. Girard's laughing face, a grin just like Lilia's, loomed before me.

"What is wrong?" Lobsang's voice reached me through the dark.

"I can't sleep. I have something to show you. I went to see the hermit at the lake, and he gave me this necklace with a rabbit." I took it out of my pocket and Lobsang held it in his hand. "He had it on his altar in his hut and told me to bring it to the monastery," I continued. "Do you know why?"

"Yes, I know. Go to sleep now. We talk about it in morning. Tomorrow will be a tiring day."

He handed the necklace, as smooth as liquid mercury, back to me. Then he rummaged around at the foot of his bed and dredged up his monk's robe, draped it over my body, and said goodnight.

# CHAPTER 28

## *The Face of My Mother*

| | |
|---|---|
| *Shar chok ree wa'ee tse nay* | *Over the eastern mountains* |
| *Gar sel da wa shar joong* | *Rises the clear shining moon* |
| *Ma gyay ah ma'ee zhel ray* | *The face of my mother* |
| *Yee la khor khor chay joong* | *Turns around and around in my mind* |

*- Sixth Dalai Lama*

### Lhamo Sangye's Story

Most people already leave for high meadow with herds. Only elders remain behind. Those too frail, too blind or too tired to make journey to mountain pastures. I stay to dry cheese and braid yak tail ropes. Want my children to paint with Erzebet when she return from monastery. I never think they can learn to do such a skillful activity. Just like in school.

Norbu's parents send him to mountains. They afraid Mr. Kai Lun cause trouble for him. Time for parents to see he can be trusted. Norbu not a child. He having sex and playing with grown woman. Erzebet desperate to find out about her husband. Much I can tell her. But monks must decide how much she should know about husband's death. Only they can say if she should take husband's papers. This not decision to be made by uneducated people in camp.

I slap wet clothes against rocks at river. From corner of my eye watch Lotse and Dolma crawl on hands and knees, looking for eagle feathers in grass. I tell them not to bother Mr. Kai Lun, but now they edge alongside his tent. There were rumors County Magistrate threatened to report Mr. Kai Lun to superiors in Peking for not doing his job. Better to stay away from him.

I hurry over to tell children to change place of play, just as they run toward me. "Ama-la, Mother," Dolma whimper. "Creature growl in Mr. Kai Lun's tent. Maybe leopard attack him. Maybe he sick or hurt. We're afraid to look."

As I near, a horrible moan come from tent, like winter wind when forces itself up ravine. Dolma scramble to run away, but I catch edge of her chuba and pull her back. We stay in grass. Listening. Strange sound begin again.

When I last see him? At least two days before. I think he follow Erzebet to monastery to report on monks, but maybe he in tent. Mr. Kai Lun kind to my children. Make them toys out of objects he find in meadow. He have gentle nature. But I afraid to go into tent alone. Too easy to forget he here to spy and make our lives miserable. Just like every other Chinese who come here since I am child.

Still, if I refuse to see what happening and he die, will be my fault. I will have caused suffering to another living being. I run back to anchor clothes in river with rocks. Return hand in hand with children to tent. I grab thick stick to use as club and children carry stones to beat animal that might even now be eating Kai Lun. Lapping up his blood. Gnawing on his leg bones.

"Mr. Kai Lun?"

From inside tent come strange voice. I not understand words.

"Mr. Kai Lun?"

Voice so low I can hardly hear, "Come in."

I slowly enter tent. Lotse and Dolma stay outside. Ready to run if I say to get away fast. Light flood in through open tent flap. Mr. Kai Lun's pale face and arms slick with sweat. My throat close up tight at smell like animals left in riverbank when spring flood recedes. Mr. Kai Lun burning. Heat rise from his body and roll across tent.

For next two days and nights, I drown in sick man's crazy talk.

"Mother! Mother!" he call out. He speak in language I never hear before.

I bring water and tea and cradle his head in my arms. Force water between his dry, cracked lips. Mucous clings to corners of his mouth like rubbery strings. I clutch cloth to my face as shield against rancid breath. When he sleep, I haul heavy soiled blankets to river and wash with yak fat soap. Send Lotse and Dolma to search fields for sticks and build roaring fire. Then boil blankets in large tub. Spread them in pasture to dry. At night I sleep on floor next to Mr. Kai Lun's bed. Children in sheepskin blankets next to me. Strangle noises slosh in his chest. Liquid making sound like waterfall in his throat. He string sounds together like story. Wave his hands and arms as if teaching children. He pull at his ears, moaning.

By third day, his skin color of ashes. His breath come out in short puffs like worn-out bellows used to start stubborn fire. No longer whisper stories that start and stop like fairy tales told to child on edge of sleep. No life force. Mr. Kai Lun carried on breezes.

Dark fear pool in my heart.

I try everything. I can't cure this man. Only doctor can say what is wrong and give proper medicine. Maybe I wait too long to call one. Someone must ride to Manigango for help. I can't go for doctor myself. Afraid to leave Lotse and Dolma alone with him. They tender children. If he die, their futures become nightmare. In world of Chinese Government, even children can be found guilty and cruelly punished. Even from events over which they have no control.

"Ride as fast as you can to Manigango." I saddle horse and lift Lotse and Dolma on. Brother in front. Sister behind. "Find old man who was monk and now doctor. Man with office at village crossroads. Where yak meat and beverages sold. Bring doctor back."

"Ama-la," Lotse cried out, "We only small children. We can't go alone to Manigango. Wild dogs and leopards track us on road between Manigango and camp. One time Tashi Choegyal carry me on his back, run around camp growling, pretending to be monster Migou, half-man, half-beast who look for little children to eat. Now it is no game and hairy Migou itself will be on the hunt for us."

"You are more powerful than the Migou," I say to him. "Take care of Sister, Lotse. After tonight, you will no longer be little children. You will be strong as Tashi Choegyal."

I whip horse's flanks. Horse take off running. My children hang on to reins, saddle and each other.

Full moon rise above the camp. Dogs bark. Stranger coming. Amchi Gyaltsen, doctor from Manigango, shout from pasture edge, "Quick! Where is Chinese officer's tent? Take me to the tent."

"Here! Come here!" I yell from open tent flap. My eyes dart from one end of meadow to other. I rush out into field. "Where are my children? What happened to Lotse and Dolma?"

"Asleep at monastery. They come in morning, starting before light," doctor say. "Monks will bring them."

He enter tent. Grab cloth to hold against his face. Smell so bad I almost faint. "Show me the blankets." I hold out latest soiled sheepskin. Stained with watery feces. Smears of dark blood.

"*Gya-mi jo-la,* Chinese older brother, open eyes. Can you open eyes?" Mr. Kai Lun's eyelids like heavy iron gates. Doctor use fingers to lift and close them. His body tremble. But when doctor touch his arms or feet, they like wooden logs. Not even twitch.

"*Jo-la,*" doctor say again, "Brother, can you hear me?" No response. He lift Mr. Kai Lun's wrist and press down with his three middle fingers. Listen to rhythms and messages traveling from all parts of body. Rock fingertips back and forth, he read layers of illness in the nearly lifeless man. When finished, Doctor unbuckle his bag. Take out blue silk package tied with red thread. Sealed with wax.

"What is that pill?" I ask. "Will it help this Mr. Kai Lun?"

"*Rinchen Mangjor Chenmo,* Great Precious Accumulation Pill," say Amchi Gyaltsen. "Will calm 404 ailments caused by blood disorders. Take away throat swelling. Fight fever. Stop bleeding from anus."

I know this medicine. As child, I watch Amchi Gyaltsen make these pills. He harvest medicine plants himself in Himalayas during summer and tell us the names. *Saussurea lappa, Strychnos nux-vomica, Eugenia caryophyllata, Areca catechu, Syzigium armoaticum and Myristica fragrans.* He dry plants. Grind them into powder. After he add purified gold, silver and iron. Mix with coral and turquoise, then cover mixture with liquid. Roll into tiny balls. Finally, TriSong high lamas bless pills in special ceremony.

"Put water on to boil," he say to me.

I grab pan and rush out to fill it with river water. I cross meadow in haze of blue and golden bees. Buzzing and swarming under full moon light. As I scoop up water with ladle, some creatures fall in. Wings weigh down by water and they struggle to fly out. I pick broad leaf from nearby plant and quickly lift them out. One by one, place them in grasses before I rush back to Mr. Kai Lun. Water boil. Amchi Gyaltsen take silk package, shining in light of lamp. He pound it with mortar and pestle. Peel off wrapping and pour contents into water. Powder swirl on surface.

Then he take second pill from bag: *Rinchen Ratna Samphel*, Precious Wish-Fulfilling Pill, for poisoning from plants, insects, animals, or chemicals. Stop problems from too much sunlight and cure deafness. Pill have bits from rare Zhi stone and lapis lazuli, the blue all-healing mineral, Medicine Buddha's symbol. Dying man will need both tonight.

Doctor strike *Rinchen Ratna Samphel* with heavy stone. He remove from orange silk wrapper. Powdered gold, silver, copper, iron, coral, turquoise, and pearls tumble into water in sparkling waterfall. Water churn purple as cloves, bamboo, mannu, nutmeg, and herbs *Terminalia chebula retz, Terminalia belerica roxb* and *Emblica officinalis* mix together with rest of brew.

Mixture boil down. We refill water and wait. Healing spirits enter liquid. Sweat pour off Mr. Kai Lun's brow, drip from bony cheeks, and soak blankets. Amchi Gyaltsen take out prayer beads. He recite Medicine Buddha's mantra: *Tadyatha Aum Bhaishiya Bhaishiya Maha Bhaishiya Raja Smud Ga Te Svaha.* Let this suffering be ended. Fill this doctor with compassion and healing energy.

2:00AM. Full moon traveling toward western mountain peaks. Doctor stir mixture. He put spoonful at a time through Mr. Kai Lun's barely open lips. Cup of hot water follows. I wrap Mr. Kai Lun in dry sheepskin blankets. Once again we sit back to wait.

Just before dawn, my children and two monks arrive. Lotse and Dolma rush to my side and excitedly tell me story of night ride to Manigango and how they searched in the town, going from shop to shop looking for doctor, and finally find him at monastery.

"We saw Migou's eyes shining where he hide in forest, but we rode faster than Migou can catch us," said Dolma. "The moon showed us the way."

"You are brave children," I tell them, as their eyes grow heavy with sleep and they huddle together under a sheepskin on the carpet. "You have saved a man's life tonight. Never forget, those who have saved one life, have saved the entire world."

The TriSong monks sit down at the bedside. Place hands around Mr. Kai Lun's head. Spit milk in fine spray over his face and body. Monks chant and toss rice grains into air. Take dry *tsampa* from cloth bag and knead it with tea to make stiff dough. Clutching dough in their hands, they leave behind marks of fingers and thumb. Then monks rub *tsampa* dough over Kai Lun's face, arms, body and legs. *Tsampa* absorb illness' dark energy.

Fever break within hour. Mr. Kai Lun open eyes.

"Where is my mother?" is first thing he ask. I sit on stool, prayer beads clicking. My children sleep at my feet. His eyes shift to monks sitting along edge of bed. Their fingers never stop moving their beads. "How did I get here?"

I put my finger to his lips, "Sssh, go back sleep. You've been ill. Alright now."

"*Thu chi je.* Thank you," he whisper. His fingers touch packet hanging on ribbon around his neck. He hold it up to light. Gold silk pouch tied with blue cord. "What is this?" he ask Doctor, as he slide ribbon back and forth between fingers.

"Amulet filled with healing prayers. Mandala inside will protect you from negativity. From all ten directions of universe. Will remove obstacles to your recovery. Will keep you safe."

"But I'm not Buddhist," Mr. Kai Lun move his head just a bit on pillow. "I am not a good man. It wasn't meant for people like me."

"Buddhist or not does not matter. Good man or bad man all the same," say Amchi Gyaltsen. "You are like all beings. Don't deserve to suffer."

## CHAPTER 29

### *Escaping Like a Wolf*

| | |
|---|---|
| *Bu mo choong dree jam pa* | *My childhood love* |
| *Chang gi'ee reek gyu meen nam* | *Seems to be wild like the wolf* |
| *Sha dree pak dree choong yang* | *She tries to escape* |
| *Ree la yar trab tse gyee* | *Like a wolf to the hills* |

*- Sixth Dalai Lama*

### Norbu's Story

As my father and Kai Lun dragged me from the meadow, I hurriedly took one last look at my list of five new words. Hoist. Prickle. Jealous. Intimidate. Permission. I quickly added one more word, Devour, then jammed the list in my pocket so Father couldn't see it.

Kai Lun had intimidated my Father. He was jealous of me. He wanted to be with Erzebet himself. His job might be to look for missing papers, but he spent more time sneaking around our tent than he needed to know Erzebet didn't have them. I wasn't scared of Kai Lun or my parents.

Erzebet had left the day before for the monastery and I was planning to spend the next days making her a present. Living with Erzebet made me excited about my life. I wasn't going to lose my opportunity to make love with her. Have her teach me English. Maybe help me go to the West.

My father walked only a few steps and stood waiting. "Time for you to return to family tent. Get back to your duties," Father said. Kai Lun followed slowly along as we went to Erzebet's tent to get my things. Father rolled up the extra bedding. He hoisted it onto my back before I knew what was happening. Father treated me as a small child who can be told what to do and led here and there.

"Boy, let's go. We have work to do." Father's comments attacked my brain. I wasn't a boy now. I was a man. Father snapped his fingers like you would call a dog and I followed him back to the family tent. Kai Lun came in right behind us.

Kai Lun didn't look so good. His cheeks had strange spots of bright red. Not like his usual white skin.

"Erzebet needs me to help," I said. I wasn't going to let Kai Lun intimidate her. "I'll go back to her tent when she returns from the monastery."

"Okay, that's it," my father rubbed his eyes like he had a headache. Then he turned to Kai Lun. "I'm sorry my son caused you trouble this summer. Won't happen again."

My strong father who fought bears and invaders was asking permission.

He was weak next to this skinny policeman. No wonder we had lost our land to the Chinese.

"Don't let him push us around," I said. Don't let him devour us, I thought.

"What's gotten into you?" Father said. "Get your things. Go up to mountains with Dhondhup's family and the flock."

"No, I'm not going," I unloaded my blankets in the tent. "I'm taking Erzebet to the mountains to look for blue poppies. I'll stay until she comes back from the monastery."

"She's not going anywhere with you," said Kai Lun.

Father grabbed my arm. "Get some brains in your head. Or you'll spend rest of summer in high mountains."

Within the hour, I left the camp. I traveled with Dhondhup, his father, and three other families. Kai Lun watched from the edge of the field. We herded 200 sheep in front of us. I took two horses and a yak packed with supplies: *tsampa*, rice, onions, garlic, chilies, oil, flour, potatoes, dried yak meat and cheese, salt, sugar, and apples just arrived from Ganzi. In saddlebags, I carried carpets and sheepskin blankets. Between us, we had iron kettles and pans, mugs, plates, bowls, soup ladles, flashlights, rain capes, soap and steel knives with curved blades and ivory and turquoise handles. Nyika and two herd dogs ran alongside. They yipped and danced. Glad to run free.

We climbed for two days into the mountains. Our family yak carried twenty books borrowed from the village school library. It was the seventh summer I took books to the mountains. When I was sixteen, I had visited the local school. Never told my parents. I asked teacher for permission to attend class. Alongside small children just beginning education.

"Impossible, Norbu," teacher said to me. "Your father furious if you come to school. Will cause big trouble for me." She looked around the barren schoolroom. Scarred blackboard. Stubs of pencils. Splintered benches. Broken window frame refused to give up final jagged piece of glass. Searching my face as I turned to leave, teacher thought again. "I will do this for you. You can choose 20 books to take to the mountains. But you must promise, don't show your father."

One day, not long after I visited the school, I overheard a conversation. "Don't know why you don't encourage that boy to study," Dhondhup's father said to mine. "If Dhondhup had half a brain in his head, next generation of our family might have a future beyond herding these animals up and down that mountain."

"This is our family business," said my Father, just barely raising his voice. "Watch what you say to our son or you will answer to me."

In past years, Dhondhup's family defied my father's wishes. They picked up the stack of books from the school library. Hauled them to pasture above the kidney-shaped lake. They deposited them in a slate cave, around the bend of the first switchback. I arrived a few days later. The books shone like waiting treasure. While the sheep grazed on the mountain, I read.

This year I could take my own books. It was not a secret anymore that I was a reader. Inside my pack was a Tibetan-English dictionary. Writing exercise books. Extra pencils. Paints and watercolor paper that belonged to Erzebet. I was going to try to paint a flower for her. A blue poppy. Every year I had seen them clustered beyond the third hill. They glowed blue in the strong summer light.

I saw around me with new eyes since Erzebet came to the camp. As we herded the animals higher and higher into the mountains, my eyes looked for beauty everywhere. Dove-grey clouds edged with rose floated above the peaks. Below the peaks, mountain shadows devoured the silk hills. Below the hills, flowed an ocean of wildflowers. And on that flower ocean was my family's primary grazing ground.

I cleared a space to stretch the felt tent. I uprooted shrubs and tossed sharp stones out of the way. I stood up the tent poles. The sheep nibbled their way through the wildflowers. I collected and stacked ovals of dried yak dung and sticks for the fire. My parents had sent me to the mountains. That made me angry. But I also felt relieved to be free of the fear in the camp. Against the boulders I made a space to read. My friends wrestled. Played archery. Pitched stones. I read.

"Tell us what you learned reading book," my neighbors said the first night on the mountain. We gathered around the fire drinking tea and *chang*. The sheep huddled near the rocky outcropping. The dogs searched for lions and wolves.

I taught my uneducated neighbors how the mountains were formed. "There are tectonic plates under the earth. When they shift, they rub up against each other. Earth rises up into mountains. It is still happening, slowly. Mountains getting taller and taller." I used two steel pan lids to show the motion of continents sliding over each other.

I proudly finished my long explanation. "Now, does anyone have any questions?"

"Good story," said Lhadon's father. Everyone laughed and nodded. "But book play trick on you. Giant fish that lives under earth formed mountains. We all know that. When fish arches back and thrashes tail, mountains lift in air. Be careful what you read in future. Don't get so confused."

The next day, Dhondhup and I followed the flock. We hadn't been in the high mountains for weeks. I had forgotten what it was like to spend time with him. Laughing. Wrestling in the hills.

I watched eagles fly beneath the huge white clouds. "I'm getting married," said Dhondhup. He didn't look at me as we walked along the rocky outcropping.

"What did you say?" I looked back to check lambs that lazed on the edge of the flock.

"I'm getting married. Parents found me wife. Getting married before first big snow."

We continued behind the sheep, neither looking at the other. "Where did you get the money to be married? How will you give her family presents?"

No answer. Maybe he hadn't heard me as he scrambled over the rocks.

"This is what you want to do?" I asked. I swung my slingshot over my head. The cord pulled and buzzed as it whistled through the air. "These are not medieval times. No one has to get married unless they want to, you know."

"I asked parents find me bride. I want wife and children. Children herd sheep. Wife cook dinner. Make yogurt in tent. At night I want to know wife has already warmed bed for me. You should get parents to find you wife."

*Zzzing. Zzzing.* A pebble from the slingshot pelted a sheep wandering away from the flock. The sheep slowly headed back, munching flowers along the way. "Maybe I won't get married at all," I said.

"You're learning strange things from books you're reading," Dhondhup said. "Maybe you can marry Madame Erzebet."

*Marry Erzebet? Are you crazy? She isn't going to marry me. She'll go back to her other life and leave me alone. Don't you know that you dumb ox?*

"How did this happen to you so fast?" I asked when I got my furious thoughts under control. "Is she the right person for you?"

"Parents visit lama. He throw sticks to make divination. He say, yes, she is right person."

I had a faint decaying feeling in my chest, a ragged memory. Yes. Now I remembered. Erzebet told me Dhondhup was leaving my parents' tent the night she went there for dinner. I saw him coming from Kai Lun's tent the day Erzebet went to Derge. That was the day the police came and there was all the trouble in the camp.

"And did your parents also visit Kai Lun? Did Kai Lun also say she is the right person?"

"What do you mean?" Dhondhup moved away. "I'm a man now. I make own decisions."

I picked up my slingshot, aiming it at Dhondhup's face. "Have you been spying on me? Did you tell Kai Lun about Erzebet and me? Is that why they dragged me out of her tent? Made me come to the mountains?"

"I didn't need to tell anybody anything," Dhondhup ducked and ran down the hill, "You think they're blind?"

I was on his heels. I scooped up rocks and fit one into the sling. Gaining on him, I caught him from behind. I pushed his face into the dirt. Wrapped the slingshot rubber around Dhondhup's jealous neck. It tangled in his hair and I twisted.

"What did he give you to report on me?" I yelled, twisting harder. Purple streaks lined up on Dhondhup's neck. "Did he give you money for your marriage?"

"You think you only one who get good things from Madame Erzebet being here?" Dhondhup struck out at my arms and legs. He wrenched himself away. My foot landed square in the middle of his spine. He fell over face first and then struggled to his feet. He stumbled down the hill with me clinging to his back.

On the following days in the mountains, I only wanted to see Erzebet. I wondered if she would return from the monastery and miss me. How long would my father make me stay with the sheep? I began the special present I had planned. I would send it to the camp for Erzebet when someone went back for more supplies.

In tiny writing, I copied fifty love songs and poems of Sixth Dalai Lama. The poems wandered in and out of a painted field of wildflowers. Grasses around the tent I sketched in black ink. I sewed the spine of the book together with hair from a horse's tail. I had wound the tail with hundreds of twists of orange thread. For centuries, Tibetan artists made cords this same way for cloth paintings. I painted the cover with mountains. Clouds. Yi-Lhun Latso Lake. Underneath the mountains, I wrote the title in both Tibetan characters and English letters. I hoped a person who comes from a country on other side of world would like such a simple gift.

As I painted, a howl came from the crags. Angry winds rumbled across the meadow. The tent became a giant lung breathing in the high pasture. The sides lifted, expanded and then collapsed. A faint bleating came from the flock. The sound of stirring as 200 sheep rose to their feet. They smelled danger in the meadow. I stopped painting. My ears stood up like the rat going home who hears the puma's padded step. The next gust swelled the tent panels again and the butter lamps blew out. Ropes loosened and then yanked tight. The dogs yowled. Metal clanked as dogs pulled on their chains trying to break free. A moan drifted from the meadow's edge. An animal scream followed soft, confused bleats.

I leapt to my feet. Grabbed my chuba, pulling a wooden club from earth next to the tent opening. Dashing to the flap, I released the frantic dogs. The smell of fear rolled in waves across the pasturelands. One moment the sheep were restless. The next moment frozen. They bolted in a mass, stumbling into each other. They fell, struggled to their feet and ran again. Two thin shadows ran along the rocky outcropping. The shadows kept easy pace with the confused flock, then gained speed. Racing to choose their victims, they darted in and out. Snapped at the feet of stragglers and searched for unsteady lambs. The flock leader took charge. He headed the sheep to the cliff, rising high above the river.

I bellowed, running toward the intruders, my club whipping the air over my head. The wolves glanced back without losing speed. They guessed their chances at gaining fresh meat or death and chased the flock with me only a bit behind. I ran in an arc to cut off the strike. I flew past a lamb, its head bent at a sickening angle. Dark red pumped from a triangle in its tender throat. Blood already soaked the earth. I threw the club. The wolf dodged to the right and the club grazed off its back.

Dhondhup's father appeared out of the dark. Club in one hand. Knife shining in the other. He raced between the second wolf and the sheep. Too late. The wolf lunged into the flock. Brought down one lamb, then another, and dragged the dying lambs before dropping them in the wildflowers. Nyika faced off with the wolf. Both creatures snarling and striking. Lunging forward. Falling back. Squeezed into a crack in the rocks, its eyes glittering, the wolf's breath steamed out in meaty haze. Then, it knew it would not eat these sheep in peace. It leapt out, straight toward us. Bounding from boulder to boulder until it stood above the camp, calmly licking the blood from its fur. The other wolf disappeared into the shadows of the palisades.

I slumped to the ground. My chest heaved. The muscles in my legs tightened into a thick band of cramps. I yelled out and pulled my foot toward my face. Beating my fist on the ground, I stomped my legs to release the piercing pain. I staggered to the flock. Dhondhup's father was leaning over the body of the sheep with the red scarf. The one chosen by the family to never be sacrificed for meat. To live out its days grazing in the wildflower meadows. I was the protector of this sheep. I had failed it.

As if they had already forgotten what just happened, the sheep went back to their interrupted sleep. I whistled, forcing the newborns and their mothers to their feet once again, coaxing them to a safe place near the tent. When they settled, I slung the carcasses over my back and hauled them to an area opposite where the flock rested. The stars like a scorpion had already traveled half the sky. But there was more to do.

"Norbu," Dhondhup's father said while he helped me butcher the lambs, "You not spend summer here. You needed back in camp."

I set aside the skin and wool, and carved up the limbs. "My father said I had to stay here on the mountain."

"Those words for Mr. Kai Lun's ears. Your parents afraid he use any excuse to have you arrested. You give him plenty."

"Kai Lun is jealous of me," I muttered, stuffing the steaming meat into bags. I hung it from the trees to be further dressed in the daylight. "He's a skinny police officer. A beautiful foreigner woman like Erzebet would never read love poems with him."

"That might be so," Dhondhup's father nodded, "But more to be worried about than Mr. Kai Lun's jealousy. You sent to stay in Madame Erzebet's tent for important reason. Never about help her with dog."

"I don't know what's going on. Erzebet told me her husband was here. Dhondhup said Kai Lun is looking for documents. Papers her husband wrote when he was in Tibet."

"I come to your tent," said Dhondhup's father, quietly. "Don't want Dhondhup hear us talk." So he knew his son was a sneak. Working for the enemy. At least my father would never have to carry that shame.

He followed me into the tent. We washed our hands with warm water from the kettle on the stove. The tiny book I was making for Erzebet lay near the kettle. Red droplets spattered the cover, creating strange patterns like a flower that exists somewhere between animal and plant. Dhondhup's father dried his hands on his chuba. He gently lifted the book. "What this say?"

"*Erzebet and Norbu, A Summer in the Meadow,*" I read the title to him, hoping he would not laugh at me.

"You were smart little boy. Now you strong, gentle man. Like grandfather," he said. "Your grandfather would be proud of you. Now time for you for to honor him. Mr. Kai Lun nervous. More crazy every day. Under great pressure from Peking to find papers. We need you to help Madame Erzebet get husband's papers. Papers must leave Tibet before Mr. Kai Lun do something that bring disaster to camp. Get your things ready to leave in morning. Dhondhup go down with you. Don't let him know you not return to mountain."

"I can go by myself. We had a fight."

"Forget fight with Dhondhup. You have fights before. This more important than your boyhood feelings about my son."

I dragged the carpets and blankets out of the tent to the pasture edge next to the sheep.

That night I dreamed I was in a restaurant in a village near my home. The food was good. It was a clean place. I sat inside at a table all by myself. Through the window I saw a person herding yaks up the street. I couldn't see his face, but through the lower part of the window I saw he wore leather and cloth boots just like the ones we wear in this area.

I thought, Oh, I must know him. I looked up to see who it was, but he was gone. I tried to go out the door into the street to follow him. The door was too small to get back through. I didn't remember it was that low when I entered the restaurant.

I got down on my hands and knees and crawled through the opening as it became smaller and smaller. I ran out into the street to call after him, but there was no one there. I turned to go back into the restaurant. The people inside put up a wooden barrier to stop me from entering. They said I'd changed when I went out. I could no longer fit through the door. I knew they just didn't want me to come back in. I could have fit if I tried, but they didn't want me to.

I woke in the morning still covered in blood from the sheep. Just one day before, I had sat in this same place. I had recited poems about a turquoise bee flying from village to village on a search for a lovely maiden. It was my fault the lambs were killed. When the wolves sneaked into the camp, I was inside. Thinking about Erzebet. Making her a present. I had forgotten I was a shepherd.

# CHAPTER 30

## I Have Met My Beloved

| | |
|---|---|
| *Khu chuk mon nae yong pay* | *The cuckoo returns from Tawang* |
| *Nam loe sa tchu phel song* | *Bringing rain for the dry fields* |
| *Nga thang jam pa thra nae* | *I have met my beloved* |
| *Lu sem lho por lang song* | *My mind and body relax in bliss* |

*- Sixth Dalai Lama*

### Erzebet's Story

By dawn I was wide-awake and ready to hear what Lobsang Phuntsok had to tell me. I wasn't going to spend another day in Tibet swallowed up by conversations about either yaks or flowers.

He wasn't in the room, so I gathered my things and climbed the steps above the first terrace. Monks in yellow hats stood at the edge of the roof. They held six-foot long horns, puffed up their cheeks and the moan of the horns careened off the monastery walls and down through the valley, like the call of wild elk mating in the mountains. I leaned on the parapet, taking in the spectacular view to the mountain range above Yi-Lhun Latso Lake. Buttercups, poppies and peonies dusted the layered green hills. Tents and small shelters were tucked into creases in the hillside. A picturesque scene, which on another day would have thrilled me. Now, I was too anxious to enjoy it.

When the monks stepped back from the railing and folded their hats under their arms, I climbed back down the stairs and headed to the guesthouse. The door was now unlocked and the manager and Lobsang were perched on a bench outside in the sun. Lobsang brought me butter tea and bread. As I ate, sitting in the one chair in the small room, he squatted on the floor and the guesthouse manager left.

"Why did the hermit tell me to bring you the rabbit necklace?" I asked him.

"The *Ri-bong* was final sign you could be trusted. The hermit is an oracle, but he was not the only one watching. We could not afford to be deceived."

"Deceived? How?"

"We weren't sure you were truly Pelletier's wife. Even if his wife, you might have been a spy for Chinese Government. Do not look so surprised—that would not be the strangest thing that has happened here. We need your help."

"Help to do what?"

"Madame Erzebet, your husband was here at the monastery."

"That was almost twenty years ago. Can you be sure it was him?"

"I was young when he came. Saw him first day he arrived. Tall man. Yellow hair. Blue eyes. We never saw such hair and eyes before. He wore jacket with many pockets. Carried cameras around his neck. He first came in army truck from Chengdu. Within short time, he saw how Chinese attacked monks and villagers alike. One night he came to monastery alone. He stayed. He talked to every monk. Took pages of notes. He promised to take these papers to the West and tell the world."

"I received a letter saying he intended to write a book upon his return to Europe."

"After that, you heard from him again? You received papers about problems here in Tibet?"

"A few details, not much. Just a letter to say he was coming home."

"Your husband was *sem sangpo*, a compassionate man. His karma was to help Tibetan people. Like your karma. That's why I wanted you to see how we live at monastery. What he saw and you saw are much the same. Twenty years of Chinese Government not improve our lives. Come." I walked in a liquid daydream, following him along the corridor.

He opened the door to his room. "You lay here on last visit and couldn't sleep. Because you felt your husband's presence."

"Here?" I whispered. "In this room?"

"He died here."

"I don't understand. The Chinese Government report said he died in a car crash. And the hermit at the lake said he had been carried there, and was still alive. Who took him to the hermit?"

"Earlier on the day he died, police broke into monastery. No time for monks to prepare. Monks praying in the temple and Dalai Lama's photo on small altar. Police beat them with rifles and pounded monks' heads on stone floor. Months before, Khampa men were trained to fight against Chinese. When Khampas forced back, they left behind weapons which were hidden at monastery. The monks ready to fire on police. But monks scared and easily overpowered. Police shot two monks right there. They clubbed others until they fell unconscious. Two monks fell over balcony and died. Heads smashed open on temple floor before statue of Buddha. I saw this with my own eyes.

"My teacher came out to stop fighting. Police grabbed him. Jerked his arms behind back. I could see arms bulging from shoulder sockets. They took stick and ropes. Twisted arms even tighter behind him. Then hung him on big hook used to dry meat in courtyard. A police officer laughed at him as my teacher cried in pain. Army officers sat and read newspapers. Drank tea. Smoked cigarettes. All the time laughing while my teacher hung like slab of yak meat. Flies buzzed around his wounds and landed on his eyes. Teacher never stopped praying *Om Mani Padme Hung*.

"I have great shame. I was in corridor. Frightened to get him down. On second day, your husband slipped out of his hiding room. He ran up next to police officer who laughed at my teacher. Smashed policeman in head with brick. Man fell to ground, unconscious. Blood poured out of hole in side of his head."

Lobsang Phuntsok looked at me. I was barely breathing.

"I don't understand. I can't imagine Girard hitting anyone with his hand, much less a brick--hard enough to knock a man unconscious? It seems impossible. I know he was trying to save your teacher's life, but. . ."

"Remember thangkas of wrathful deities in main temple? Flames that surround them burn away ignorance. Purify the mind. There are times when the most compassionate action is one that stops another from doing great harm. Stops another from earning negative karma that will condemn him to eons in hell realms."

"Do you mean when my husband struck that soldier, he saved that man from himself?"

Lobsang Phuntsok nodded yes. For the first time, I truly understood the depth of my husband's commitment to people who were treated unjustly. Girard was more than a journalist, a father and my husband. He was a hero.

"We took my teacher down from hook. He collapsed on floor," Lobsang Phuntsok continued. "Your husband had to escape before police caught up with him. He jumped in car, intending to head to Ganzi. Then back to Chengdu. Somehow, either in confusion or because he needed to see someone at lake, they drove back toward nomad camp. In the middle of night, he was brought to us at monastery. Badly injured. Broken leg. Broken collarbone. Bleeding from nose and mouth."

"What happened? Did the police intercept him?"

"Villagers heard honking from cars on hillside. Saw two sets of lights, one chasing other. They heard a gunshot and the grinding of two cars colliding. Husband's car went out of control. Slid off road in storm." He looked at me again, his frown questioned if he should continue.

"Go ahead," I said, my stomach a roiling pit. "I want to know everything."

"Later that night, soldier from Chinese army climbed down mountainside. He pried your husband from wreckage of car. Took him first to lake and then brought him to monastery."

"A Chinese soldier? I don't understand. We always thought it might have been the Chinese army who killed him."

"That is mysterious part of this tragedy. Soldier who brought husband here also part of his death. He was in car that ran him off road. Soldier had been living with woman at nomad camp for several months. During that time, he grew to have great respect for nomads. But soldier forced to be part of group who took life of your husband. Later, in great regret, he tried to save his life."

"What happened to that soldier?" I stood up, needing air, and opened the door of the room. I looked out over balcony of the monastery to the valley below. A flock of black birds rose and fell in the air like a fisherman's net cast over the sea.

"I don't know," said Lobsang Phuntsok standing behind me, gently bringing me back into the room. "We heard he was sent out of this area. I'm sure it was ugly."

"And Girard?"

"Monks did many hours of prayer pujas, but too late to save him. We prayed while his consciousness left to travel seeking positive rebirth. Then we took body back to car at base of ravine. Afraid the police would return and find out he had been taken away and it would start new trouble for the monastery and the nomads."

"Lobsang-la, how can I find out who killed my husband?"

"What will you know when you know their names?" he said. "What will you gain by seeing their faces, if they stand before you? Think hard on this. Must be worth your life and that of people who help you make this connection. Is worth it to you to identify murderers? Because I can guarantee you, in your lifetime, they will never be brought to justice."

"May I be here alone?" I felt as if I was about to faint and needed to lie down.

"Not for long. Abbot has said you must leave. At least one monk here is a spy helping Chinese."

"A spy? Here at the monastery?"

"Spies everywhere in Tibet. Even Tibetans have turned against own countrymen." Lobsang went to the door and opened it. "Do what you must now. Not possible for you to come here again." He paused before he entered the hallway. "It may help you to try for a big mind and realize that your husband's suffering small compared to many other beings in world."

I picked up the maroon robe at the foot of the bed and lay down on the floor, my head resting again on the earthy shoes. I emptied my lungs and took three deep breaths, concentrating on detecting and absorbing any particle of air that Girard might have breathed nineteen years before. A molecule that might remain, hidden in the corners, waiting for me to claim it. I inhaled, sucking in dark clouds of pain. The vapor drifted inside my lungs, working its way into my cells. Twisting on the floor, I struggled against the temptation to shut down my mind and flee. I held the breath until my thoughts quieted. When I exhaled, it swept into the room in a white stream, seeking other molecules that also lingered. I inhaled again, breathing in Girard. I was ready.

Lobsang tapped on the door and looked in. "No more time. Abbot is here. You must go."

"I'm still confused about how all of this is tied together. What does my husband's death have to do with my botanical illustration work here in Tibet, with Peking University, with the Sorbonne exchange program?"

"We believe whole botanical illustration project is tied to finding the notes. You were brought here to serve as bait to draw them out."

"But I came with several other scholars. We're all studying different issues."

"Smoke to hide government's real intention."

"Where are the documents?" I asked.

"Here at the monastery. Not time for them to surface."

"And if Kai Lun finds them?"

"Chinese Government will destroy them. It would be disaster for them if notes were released to world. All propaganda says People's Liberation Army saved Tibet. Your husband's reporting would tell truth."

"Why didn't Lhamo Sangye or Tashi Choegyal tell me this when I first came to the camp?"

"Not for them to decide. Monastery had to know you were to be trusted. Able to help. You're not only person whose life affected by knowing where documents are. Those papers are hope of millions of people. If destroyed because of negligence, your husband's courage and death worth nothing."

I heard shuffling in the hallway and went to the door just as the Abbot, bent over a cane, entered the room. It was the same man in the photo that the hermit had on his altar. He carried a rolled-up cloth tied with red strings.

Lobsang bowed deep at the waist as the old man entered. The Abbot spoke so softly that Lobsang leaned over with his ear right next to the man's mouth to hear.

"Abbot wants you to take present," Lobsang said. He untied the red strings and unrolled a hand-painted thangka with Buddha figures sitting in rows, each in a slightly different position. Around the sides were lavender clouds and trees garlanded with gold. The painting was framed in brocade silk, woven with stylized lotus blossoms.

"I can't take this," I said, choking back tears. "It's too beautiful."

Lobsang talked quietly to the Abbot, who held the painting so it hung full length in front of me. "You must. Abbot insists. Meditate in front of this thangka and you will receive great peace." Lobsang continued to translate, "When on your journey away from Tibet, look closely at thangka and questions will be answered. Concentrate on lessons of Buddha Families. Buddha helps us act mindfully, in a way that reflects the situation as clearly as looking in mirror."

"Thank you," I said wiping my eyes and nose with the sleeve of my dress.

"Thangka has Thirty-Five Buddhas of Forgiveness of Sins. They represent essence of compassion. It is thank you from monastery for husband's courage and kindness." I impulsively reached out and put my arms around the Abbot. His body was as fragile as a baby bird.

Hunched over, the Abbot grasped my hand again and then left the room.

"Was the Abbot at the monastery the day Girard saved your teacher's life?" I asked, watching the elderly man hobble painfully away down the corridor.

His eyebrows raised in surprise. "I thought you knew. The Abbot is my Venerable Teacher. This is the Lama your husband saved."

# CHAPTER 31

## My Love Stories Have Been Revealed

| | |
|---|---|
| *Nying tam pa mat ma she* | *Talk of the heart is not for parents* |
| *Chung dri cham par she pae* | *Instead it is to share with old friends* |
| *Cham pa shwa po mang nae* | *My love has many stories* |
| *Sang tam gra bos go song* | *They have been revealed* |

*- Sixth Dalai Lama*

### Norbu's Story

Dhondhup and I left the mountains before first light, heading for the camp. "After we get supplies, we come back to mountain together," he said. On that long day, I pretended as if our fight had never happened. Pretended I didn't see a problem with him spying for Kai Lun. Pretended I did not care about Erzebet. Pretended I was not dying to see her and hold her. When Dhondhup was napping in the sun in the late morning, I took out my book and wrote down words about flowers to remember and then tell Erzebet. Vein. Petal. Translucent. Words I was feeling: Concentrate. Desperate. Emerge. I would soon find a way to use all of these words. We slept on the mountainside under a blaze of stars.

Lhamo Sangye met us on the trail early morning the next day, as we came past the far side of the lake. She told us Kai Lun had almost died while Erzebet was at the monastery. The twins had disappeared from the camp. Trackers had gone out to look for them. There was no trace. A few days later, word had come back from traders. Twins were seen crossing one of the high passes. Heading in the direction of Lhasa.

Dhondhup ran off to his parents' tent and Lhamo Sangye walked with me. "Mr. Kai Lun leaves in mornings," she said. "Walks to houses and tents on hillsides. Questions nomads and villagers. Sometimes policeman from bigger town with him. Leaving trail of fear."

A man had come down from his pasturelands above the lake. He asked the nomads from Yi-Lhun Latso to keep Erzebet away from his grazing grounds. "Take foreigner woman somewhere else to find flowers in future," he said.

Kai Lun came to my parents' tent minutes after I arrived.

"Why is he here?"

"He came with Dhondhup for supplies," said my father. "They take care of Tsering Yongden's sheep here and go back up in few days."

"Make sure he does," said Kai Lun. His mouth was clicking like angry locust. My parents lit more butter lamps and began to pray as soon as he left tent.

I needed to talk to my parents. Hear their story about Erzebet's husband and the papers. But first, I only wanted to be close to her. Smell her hair. Make love with her.

I had been gone for several days. Is it possible she had forgotten me while I was gone in the mountains? She could have another man living in her tent. I was afraid she didn't want me to come back.

In the afternoon, I found Dhondhup in the meadow with Tsering Yongden's sheep. I saw Erzebet by the river. "Let's go feed the fish," I said to Dhondhup.

Dhondhup followed my eyes to where Erzebet sketched and painted. Near the largest mani stone. "Right. Let's go feed fish," he said with a snort.

We ran down the hillside, herding the flock in front of us. We both walked over, stopping to watch her paint. She was concentrating on the fine hairs that covered the buds. Tracing the thin reddish-purple veins. They streaked from the base to pointed tip of the petals. She glanced up.

"What's that flower?" Dhondhup asked.

"Muskmallow. *Moschata rosea.* Take a look." She handed him the magnifying glass. While he was looking through the glass, she stared right at me and I could not take my eyes away. I bit my lip to keep from moaning out loud and grabbing her.

Dhondhup handed the glass back after peering at the flower and ran off to the fish schooling at the lake edge.

"Well?" she looked up again from the deep pink shading along the muskmallow's main veins.

I cleared my throat, but no sound came out. I snapped off a muskmallow and rolled the stem in my hand, crushing it until the sticky juice ran out and covered my fingers. Pressing my thumb and forefinger together, I watched the shiny liquid make a bridge between my fingertips.

"Dhondhup is getting married," I said. "His parents arranged a marriage for him. They needed money. He went to Kai Lun and Kai Lun paid him. That's why my parents made me move from the tent."

"So Dhondhup is a rat. All this time you've been hanging out with him, he was getting money to report on you?"

"Doesn't matter now. I want to come and see you. Tonight."

"Do you think that's a good idea?" She nodded toward Dhondhup. She held the magnifying glass close to the base of the muskmallow petals. She took a ruler and measured the length of the stems as they emerged from the roots. "I don't want you to come to my tent."

"I don't believe you. I know you want to see me. I'll come after the moon has set behind the pine trees at the lake." I separated the light green, translucent fibers. Peeled them away one by one. Arranged them on my hand in rows. I flicked the stem in her direction and set off to feed the fish.

That night, as the moon disappeared behind the hill, my family huddled around the fire drinking tea. I stood up to leave. "Where you go at this hour?" my mother asked.

"Erzebet's tent." My father watched as I picked up my pack with the book I had made in the mountains.

"Wait, we need to talk to you."

"I'm not talking now. I come back later." There would be time tomorrow to find out how I would be part of finding her husband's papers. Now I wanted to make love with Erzebet.

"Madame Erzebet not want you there now. She smarter than that. You danger to family. Danger to village." Father called over to my mother and Uncle Nyima Rabten. "I knew this would happen. Better he stay in mountains all summer."

"Quiet," my mother said to my father. "You and Uncle arrange for him to stay at Madame Erzebet's tent with dog. You create this problem."

A cup of steaming water vibrated in my father's quaking hands. Water sloshed over the sides and splashed his shirt. "Mr. Kai Lun waiting for chance to have someone make wrong move. You not see enough bashed-in heads in this camp? Enough missing eyes and crippled limbs?"

"You sent me to her tent," I said. "Why did you send me there? Anyone could have helped Erzebet with the dog. You treat me like a child. I had to find out from that weasel Dhondhup and his father about her husband's papers."

"Are you crazy? This kind of talk worry us, son. This is why we not tell you about papers before," Father said.

He was right. I did feel crazy. I also felt alive, excited by my courage to go to her tent. I was like Sixth Dalai Lama. Doing what I wanted to do. I wasn't afraid of the people who could smash my body. I was afraid of the dead feeling in my heart when I thought of being away from Erzebet. The end of my dream. My dream was no longer just to learn a foreigner language. Now it was to help her find her husband's papers. So my Grandfather would be proud of me in this life. So Erzebet would know I loved her. It is better to live for one day as a tiger than to live for a thousand years as a sheep.

My mother carried in bowls of *tsampa* and a thermos of hot tea. The men squatted down. They took the bowls, poured tea and chunks of butter into a well in the middle of the *tsampa*, and kneaded the dough. They ate. No one spoke. The silence was sickening.

Then Father reached out and grabbed my arm. He dug his thick fingers into my flesh. "What thoughts you spin in your mind?" he said. I tried to wrench the hand aside. I saw that the arm in my father's grip was not a twig anymore, but a strong branch of a tree. I pulled hard and Father's hand fell away to the side. "You think you go with her when she leave Tibet?"

My eyes darted up to the tent corners. I wondered how much my father needed to know. "I'm not thinking that," I said, my voice louder than I ever spoke to my father before.

"All I need to know, my son. Goodness and truth speak in whisper. Lies and deceit yell to rooftops."

I looked toward Uncle, pleading for understanding. For protection. Uncle played with me when I was a small child and was proud when I learned to read a few words. Now he stood up shaking his head. He stared at me as if I were a stranger who wandered into the tent from the road. He tossed the water from his cup into the tent corner. The water splattered mud against the chest and then soaked slowly into the earth. Mother gathered Uncle's *tsampa* bowl and then went back to scraping the yak hides with the silver knife. She left me to face my father alone.

"She's going to help me go to Europe," I yelled. I wrenched my arm free from his grasp.

"Even Mr. Kai Lun couldn't leave China if he wanted," my father snorted. "What chance would you have? Who do you think she is? She can't do this for you."

Mother placed the yak hide aside. She hurried across the tent to stand between my father and me. Her hand flat against his chest.

I shifted from foot to foot. I wanted my Father to look up. "I can see problem out of our hands," he finally said. "You are man. You make own decisions no matter what we say." He turned his back to me, and started working again on the yak tail ropes. Twisting the black strands into long cords to hold the tent corners.

I picked up my pack. I was going through the tent flap when I turned and saw Father staring at me over his shoulder. I couldn't leave when he looked at me like that. He captured me with his eyes. I squirmed.

"You good boy, Norbu. I hope not capable of using woman to get only what you want."

My face burned as I blurted out. "You care more about her than you do about me." As I rushed from the tent, I heard my father say to Uncle, "I saw this coming, I made this happen."

"Life is more than one night of anger. The son has watched the father," Uncle said. "When time comes, he make right decision for family and his people."

"*Tashi Delek*," I said to Erzebet. I pushed aside the flap and looked around inside. There was no other man drinking tea and eating *tsampa* in my lover's tent. Sketches of flowers were on the floor. She was unrolling a thangka and hanging it from a string on one of the tent poles. When I looked at her I felt a tenderness I didn't know I had.

"Where did you get the painting?" I asked.

"The Abbot at TriSong gave it to me. Isn't it beautiful?"

"Yes, an old one for sure." I looked closely at the precious painted Buddhas. This was an old, old painting—finely done. It was a treasure the Abbot had given her. Everyone loved Erzebet, not just me. I was not so special to her.

"What do you have there?" She looked at my pack. She made no move to have me set it down.

"Some things. For the night. Can I stay?"

She got up and tied the tent flap, walking slowly back to me. I sat on the edge of the bed. She unbuttoned her sweater and her blouse. I saw the soft swell of her breasts and the curve of her stomach. She looked straight into my eyes, like she had in the afternoon. I untied my chuba.

She took off her shoes and pants, and slipped under the blankets. My clothes fell in a pile on the tent floor. I lifted the blankets, climbed into the bed next to her and pulled her close. Curving against her back, I pressed my face into her hair. "You smell like flowers on a hot day in the meadow. Just after the rain."

"I have on perfume."

"Perfume? That makes you smell that way?" I sucked in the flowery smells. My mind drifted in the beautiful air. "Where did you get it?"

"I brought it with me. I bought it years ago in India. And you smell like a bear coming in from a thunderstorm," she rolled over and wrapped her legs around me. "You smell wild."

"You smell like flowers and I stink like a wild animal?" A small river of anxiety seeped into my arms. A memory was nagging at the back of my mind. I was confused. Somewhere there was a photo of a tall man with yellow-white hair. He had leaned over to pat me on the head and hugged me when I was a child. We had been in the upper meadow the day the man picked *Sher Ngon*, the blue poppy. He took a photograph to send to his family. Not long after, he went away and never came back.

The man in the photo who gave me sweets.

The clean, flowery smell of his skin.

It was her husband.

She lay against my chest looking at me out of the corner of her eye. A quick puff of breath brushed my cheek. My body tensed. I slid my hand between her legs, touching her soft thighs. Her muscles tensed and then relaxed. She stretched and moved her legs slightly apart. The tip of her tongue traced the curve of my mouth. She followed the line of my lip. Hardly moving. Kissing. Sudden gasps of breath shook my body, and then drifted away. Her hands slid over my skin. She touched every bit until she reached my feet. My warm feet wrapped around hers.

"Your feet are so smooth. They have no calluses. You must spend your days being pampered by servants," she laughed. I felt her rough heels catching on the blankets. The sunbaked skin on her neck and arms mimicked alligator I had seen in a storybook. An animal living in rivers far away.

"Your skin is smooth like dri butter," I said. I wanted to say things that would make her happy to be with me. I turned over in the bed. Repeated her moves until her breath traveled into the air in soft gusts.

She whispered in my ear. "Norbu, it is night. We are on a brightly lit Ferris wheel spinning over the Seine, a river near where my family lives."

"What do you mean, Ferris wheel? What is that word?"

"It's a big, big wheel people build into the sky, and it turns around," she said. "Just listen to our story. We're sitting in wooden seats, carved with fantastic circus animals. People on the ground laugh and call back and forth to us, but their words are lost in the wind. Lights flash and mingle with the stars. The stars blur into a mass of colored mirrors. The wheel reaches the top, pauses and then swoops down the other side. It grinds and clacks, climbing once again to the heavens."

I could only understand some of the words. But my body throbbed as I entered her. My mind and heart spun like Ferris wheel.

"We whirl on through space," she whispered in my ear, "Faster and faster, free-falling. The seat tips us face to face with the earth and back again to the stars. We swing back and forth, raising our hands high over our heads and yell out to show our bravery to the people watching below."

Her body pulsed with mine. She gripped me inside of her. Tightening and loosening her body's hold on mine. After some time, the Ferris wheel slowed and stopped its night journey.

"Norbu," she sighed. My damp hair clung to her cheek. "You're a sweet lover."

"I want to know. Will you come back to me when you leave?"

"I'm only thinking about this summer. I'm scared about some things that are happening here. I don't know how I would ever come back."

"Erzebet, I like it here with you. I like me when you're here." I leaned over the edge of the bed, reached inside my pack and brought out the striped bag closed with a red silk drawstring. "I have something for you."

Opening the bag, she took out the book, *Erzebet and Norbu: A Summer in the Meadow*. She read the love poems of Sixth Dalai Lama aloud in Tibetan. She stopped every so often to kiss me.

"This is not an ordinary night and this is not an ordinary present," she said as she examined the precise stitching on the spine. "I love this book and I love you."

Those words made me feel like I had a man's heart. Open and pumping rich red blood through my veins. "When we're in bed at night and you're sleeping," I said, knowing the words to make her love me more. "I'll hold you. I'll whisper Dalai Lama's songs into your ears. The poems will travel into your dreams and heart. When you wake in morning, you'll be able to say the poems in perfect Tibetan."

"That's the best gift of all," she said. "I want to. . ." In the middle of her words she stopped. Her head cocked to the side as she listened. There was a faint rumble of a car far down the road. Coming from the direction of Manigango. Time to leave. First I had something to tell her.

"Erzebet, I think I saw your husband. I remember him patting me on the head. When I was a child."

She pulled up the blanket close to her face. I could only see her eyes, not believing me. "When? How can you be sure it was him?"

"Only white man I ever saw here. Must have been him." I reached out to touch her arm. "I'm sorry your husband died."

"Norbu, you need to go," she said after a long time. "But, I need your help. We need to make Dhondhup think we have turned against each other. That we hate each other."

"Then we look for your husband's papers? I will help you?"

"I'm not only looking for papers. I'm looking for the people who killed my husband. I want to find out who they are and have them brought to justice."

I left Erzebet's and came back to my parents' tent. Mother and Father sat next to the stove, sipping tea. Father brought his cup and sat down next to me. "What did Madame Erzebet say to you?"

"Dhondhup told me she was looking for her husband's missing papers," I told him. "Kai Lun is looking for them, too. Dhondhup was partly wrong. She's also trying to find out who killed her husband."

"Who's helping her?"

"I don't think she has anyone to help her. I think she's afraid people in the camp will become involved and get in trouble. Why is her husband so important? Why do you care about this man who was here years ago?"

Mother came and stood beside my Father. "Husband, tell him."

"Her husband held our dying children in his arms," Father began. "He cried with men whose wives were raped and murdered. He listened late into night, and then wrote their story on pages in his red folder. Her husband gave his life to tell our story. Saved our village. Saved Abbot of TriSong Monastery."

"Erzebet's husband did this for our people? Then why did Chinese Government let her come here?"

"At first we think she is part of government trick. Now we know that government also trick her"

I turned to see Uncle standing in the corner of the tent. He had come in without me seeing him. "Has taken many weeks to decide if she is to be trusted to take husband's papers to West. Just because husband man of courage does not mean wife is."

# CHAPTER 32

## *The Rocks and the Wind Have Been Cruel*

| | |
|---|---|
| *Dral thang lung po teh nay* | *The rocks and wind have been cruel* |
| *Go poe dro la sen joong* | *To the wings of the eagle* |
| *Yo chen tzsu pak chen gyee* | *The sly and scheming ones* |
| *Nga la tsen po che joong* | *They harass me without ceasing* |
| | *- Sixth Dalai Lama* |

### Erzebet's Story

"Chain your dogs!" Peering through a slit in the tent, I saw Tashi Choegyal and Kai Lun rushing to meet police officers. Their Jeep had crept silently into the nomad camp, after all the tents were dark. Footsteps pounded through the meadow and halted nearby, muffled questions seeping through my tent walls. There was a spate of yelling and I recognized Tashi Choegyal's voice and then Kai Lun's, conciliatory to the angry tone of the others'.

"Madame Erzebet," Tashi Choegyal's voice was strained. "Come out."

When I appeared in the tent entrance, Kai Lun was standing next to three police officers.

"These officers seek Tibetan young man," Tashi Choegyal said. My knees buckled and I pretended to have tripped on the thick carpet at the entrance. "They will search your tent."

"There's no one here." I held onto the tent flap, feigning an examination of my ankle.

Kai Lun and Tashi Choegyal spoke for several minutes to the officers and then they barged inside the tent. The police opened my books, fanning the pages. They pushed on the bed, got down on their hands and knees and shifted the bags and boxes, probing with a stick beneath the bed. One officer held the painting of the *Bistortoides* to the light. When he set it down it had a black thumbprint smudged right next to the flower. I would have to paint it all over again.

"This is the foreign artist living in the settlement," said Kai Lun.

"We know this, you imbecile." They spoke in a combination of Tibetan and Chinese. Scrutinizing my passport and travel documents, they tried to insert a knife between the face page and the cover, checking to see if the book had been altered, reassembled and reglued. Passing the book back and forth, they peered at my photo in the dim light, and then looked back at my face.

"This photo isn't you," they finally said. "Your skin darker than this photo."

"It is her," Tashi Choegyal said.

"Let her answer," the officer lifted his club and shook it in Tashi

Choegyal's face. Tashi backed up only a few inches, his face set in stone.

"It is me," my voice cracked like a dry day in summer.

"She paints outside. Her face is burned from the sun," said Kai Lun.

The police officer whipped his head around to glare at him and yelled at me again, "Where is the boy?"

"There's no one here," I said. It was Norbu's good fortune to have gone before they arrived. "What boy would be here?"

"Don't be impertinent to these men who represent the people," yelled Kai Lun. His hand flew out and cuffed me on the side of the head. I fell on the bed, the metallic taste of blood in my mouth. Out of the corner of my eye I saw Tashi Choegyal shift his weight toward Kai Lun, nearly pressing up against him. Kai Lun's shoulder came only up to Tashi's chest.

"Get over there," one of the officers poked his club at Tashi Choegyal and pushed him to the other side of the tent. "This woman is harboring a criminal. A parasite. Why are you protecting her?"

Kai Lun shifted his eyes away from the massive camp leader and backed up. "Now she'll cooperate. Ask her again."

"The boy. Where is he?" A muffled voice came through the ringing in my ears.

"There is no boy." The words came out distorted; the side of my mouth was numb and swelling. "I don't know who you're talking about."

"You know where he is."

I stepped to the side as Kai Lun rushed toward me again. His hand raised and my arm automatically flew up to fend him off.

"A boy has been staying in your tent."

I looked at Kai Lun. He gave an almost imperceptible slight shake to his head.

"You can see there's no one staying here." I scanned for telltale objects that might indicate Norbu's presence. There was nothing. The handmade book had already been slipped inside my bag. "What is his name?"

"Gyalpo Samdhup."

"Gyalpo Samdhup?" Bewildered, I looked at Kai Lun for confirmation of the name. The wrong name. He looked away. "I don't know who that is. I've never heard that name before."

The police lifted sheepskins and threw clothing in a heap on the floor. They took the small silver box from my jacket pocket and pried it open, staring at the dried blue poppy petals from the day on Tro-La Pass on the way to Derge. One of them took out a loose petal and rubbed it back and forth between his thumb and forefinger until it shredded and drifted in motes to the floor. They left as quickly as they came and Kai Lun avoided my eyes as he ran out after them.

Angry shouting in Chinese and subdued Tibetan replies sputtered across the field as they carried out tent-to-tent searches. I stayed inside with cool compresses on my mouth, stunned by the pandemonium outside. There were screams, the blunt thud of wood hitting a human and the yelp of animals. I brought Nyika inside and sat still on the bed, tracking the path of chaos through the camp.

Hours later, a happy bark from Nyika signaled Norbu's approach. Slipping into the tent, he whispered to me, "The police are looking for a Tibetan boy spreading rumors about Dalai Lama. They believe he's here to get documents he can smuggle out of Tibet to Dalai Lama in India. To cause trouble for Chinese Government. They're threatening Kai Lun. Come to my parents' tent if you don't feel safe."

"Is it my husband's papers he's looking for?" I asked.

"They must be." He drew back, peering at my face, turning me to the side so he could examine the bruise in the light of the butter lamp. "What happened?"

"You don't want to know," I said. "I'm okay. You should go." He hesitated at the tent entrance and came back, holding me for a few minutes before he left again.

At dawn, the police returned without Kai Lun. They marched in, kicked at my pile of clothing and looked at my passport again. Speaking rapidly to each other, they left as suddenly as they had arrived. They got into the Jeep and drove down the road.

"Police say they went to Derge and then Jomda," Lhamo Sangye said when she came to the tent. "Most people think this is lie." She gently touched my swollen cheek. "They think police say this so they can double back to catch leopard in yak tail snare."

Silence drenched the morning. I walked through the meadow in the dawn light and no one spoke to me. We now lived in a world where talking was a hazardous affair. Even a foreign woman was not immune to violence. People passed me in the fields and nodded, afraid to start a conversation that would reveal fear. I dragged myself back to the tent, isolated from my friends. A few hours later, Lhamo Sangye came and gave me a bowl of dark muskmallow salve to put on my face.

"Am I to blame for bringing the police to the camp and all the trouble that followed?" I asked. Looking in the mirror, I smoothed the sticky paste over the purple area. Immediately my skin cooled and the swelling in my lip began to lessen.

"This all happened long before you come," said Lhamo Sangye. "You not responsible for every bad thing that happens here. Since army come through many years ago, no one safe. Dogs killed before. Grandfathers beaten and made to crawl in dirt for chanting *Om Mani Padme Hung*. You collect trouble. But could have been anyone. The twins and Older Brother who disappeared. Even Norbu listening to radio could bring this trouble."

The nomads posted a lookout for the returning vehicle on the highest rocky ledge above the lake. By afternoon when no car rumbled back along the road, caution abated and they spilled out their fear of the Chinese, the nerve of the Chinese and the most essential subject of all--loyalty to the Dalai Lama.

Lhamo Sangye came to the tent every few hours to update me. "Big argument. Between those who believe Dalai Lama is alive and those who think Dalai Lama dead," she said. "Many think this trick by Chinese, to smoke out Dalai Lama followers. Others believe Gyalpo Samdhup sent by Dalai Lama himself and come here for your husband's papers. No one know anything for sure."

While the campfires showered sparks into the cold night air, I stayed in my tent and calmed myself by painting a thick, woody-stemmed plant I had discovered on the mountain among the rocks. It had pink delicate flowers, but was covered with three-inch long, raw umber spines. *Fabiaceae Astragalus.* The spines were sharp enough, but the real danger that could only be seen with close inspection was the barbs on the spines--protrusions that would snag and rip the skin if pulled out.

I fell asleep at the easel and woke with a start. Nyika's bark signaled the approach of a person he recognized.

"Madame Erzebet." It was Kai Lun's voice at the tent entrance. "Forgive me. There was no choice. One of them would have hurt you far worse than me."

"Get away from here," I said. "You're a monster."

"I'm not a monster. I'm a frightened man. "

"You're frightened? You actually helped me? Then I guess I should thank you. Get out of here."

"I have to talk to you."

I opened the tent flap. Kai Lun stayed outside, looking straight at me, but shifting from foot to foot like a child.

"There's only one thing you can talk to me about. What happened to my husband?"

"I don't know."

"But you can find out."

"I could never find out. I am nothing. My life is worth less than your husband's. I have no authority to find out anything from anyone."

"But you know he was murdered." I stood in the shadow and shifted so he could see the mottled, purple swelling on my cheek.

"Yes, I know that." He drew back from the ugly bruise. "He was shot. His car was run off the road."

"I want the people who did it to be found and imprisoned. International pressure can force the government to do an investigation."

"You're naïve. China doesn't care about international opinion."

"China is opening up to the world. That openness is what brought me here."

"That's not what brought you here--your husband's missing documents brought you here." It came out of his mouth just as if we were associates who had been discussing missing papers from the first day we met, back in Chengdu.

"What kind of man are you to come here and terrorize these poor nomads?"

"I'm here to save my family's life. They're being held hostage until I return with your husband's papers. Papers that lie about my government. These poor nomads, as you say, told outrageous, disgusting lies to your husband about my government."

"Save your family's life? Don't use melodrama on me. I sent a letter to the Ganzi Prefecture Magistrate, requesting his assistance in finding information about my husband's death."

"No you didn't. If you had, I wouldn't be speaking to you now. You'd have been the unfortunate heir of an accident or worse."

"What can I do?" I said in a near whisper, worn down with the weeks of turning up nothing. I sank to my knees in front of him, my head against his legs. "Help me."

"Here is my best advice to you. If you want to spend the rest of your life trying to find the people responsible for your husband's death, then so be it, but that's what it will be--the rest of your life. I can tell you right now, it was probably someone like me--someone trapped in an ugly world, with no choice except death. Either his own or that of his loved ones."

"Get out of here," I said wearily. "Leave me alone."

# CHAPTER 33

## *Talkative Bird*

| | |
|---|---|
| *Cha te ma khen net so* | *That talkative bird* |
| *Kha rok shook rok dzo thang* | *Please shut your mouth* |
| *Chang leeng ah che jol moe* | *The thrush in the willow grove* |
| *Soong nyan gyur goe che joong* | *Has promised to sing a song for me* |

*- Sixth Dalai Lama*

### Norbu's Story

Crows flew between the tent tops and the pine trees next to the lake. *Caw! Caw! Caw!* I dashed across the pasture to see what caused the noise. A man rode up the dirt path on a small roan horse. He appeared like a trader making a circuit between the villages and nomad camps, like traders had been doing for centuries. He carried fabrics, thread, beads, salt and biscuits to sell and trade, but as soon as I saw him, I knew who it really was. Gyalpo Samdhup. Trouble. The village leaders quickly agreed. Give him tea and food. Tell him to ride on. They sent the children to the pasture edge to play, so they could not eavesdrop and learn too much. They could endanger their families when the police returned.

"Where is Chinese man in camp?" asked Gyalpo Samdhup.

"Early morning, walking down road toward Derge," said Tsering.

Gyalpo Samdhup opened his saddlebag. He took out many papers printed with news about Dalai Lama and the Tibetan Exile Government in India.

"Dalai Lama alive. Dalai Lama live in Northern India," said Gyalpo Samdhup in a low voice. Those who'd been determined not to hear him speak came closer.

"This is truth," he continued. "I was there. I saw him. He live in freedom. Thousands of Tibetans live in town with mountains and trees like Tibet. Other people live in villages all over India and Nepal. Tibetan Exile Government help refugees. Dalai Lama work for freedom of Tibetan people."

Information gushed out of his mouth. Like Dri-Chu River after the first glacier melt of spring.

"Dalai Lama teach in India," Gyalpo Samdhup continued. "If you can get to Nepal, Exile Government help you find relatives who escaped to India many years ago. With enough money, guides even take children over the great mountains without parents. These children go to school. Learn to read and write Tibetan language. Cared for by Dalai Lama's sister."

Tashi Choegyal stared at Gyalpo Samdhup then stood up from the fire and walked toward the horses, shaking his head as he wandered in the pasture. A long time ago, when I was a small child, traders brought word that Lhasa was under attack by the Chinese army. In disguise, Dalai Lama escaped to India with his family in the middle of the night. People say Tashi Choegyal was one of the Khampas who guided Dalai Lama on the dangerous journey. They drifted in rivers in coracles, yak hide boats. Crossed over Che mountain pass into Nepal just a few days ahead of the Chinese military. Tashi Choegyal never said if any of this was true. The twins believed he fell into the hole of a dragon while he was out walking. He would have starved there. But he licked the precious jewel the dragon hides in his den. After many weeks, he came back, looking not so well, but alive. The elders sat and listened, trying to make sense of it all. Many wept.

The people at the fire asked question after question. "Is Dalai Lama coming back?"

"Not now. Too dangerous," Gyalpo Samdhup replied. He knew the answer to every question.

"Where monks go who escape from Tibet over mountains?" The answer was not good. They worked on roadcrews building roads in the mountains for the Indian Government. Waiting for monastery to be built for them. Many monks die in winter breaking up stones on roads.

"Do Tibetan leaders in India know about people who go to prison here? People tortured? Killed for speaking out against Chinese?" Once again, answers came quickly. Tibetan Exile Government interviews all those who have escaped. They write down the stories and contact governments of other nations to help. No one knows when there will be help from other countries. Dangerous for other countries to defy the Chinese. They're afraid of Chinese Government's power.

"If you have documents that tell of these crimes against Tibetan people, I will take them with me. Make sure world knows," he continued.

The people at the fire looked back and forth at each other. Too simple. Why now? After almost twenty years, why had this young man shown up asking for the hidden documents?

No one came forward to talk. Gyalpo Samdhup then asked those around the fire to take his papers about Dalai Lama. Spread them to neighboring villages. Kalsang Tenzin, who never spoke in public, jumped up, "Yes, yes, I'll do it."

His father glared at him, "Shut up and sit down, you yak-headed son." Kalsang looked around at the rest of the group. He stirred the burning embers in the fire ring with his boot until his father looked away. Everyone else was silent. Gyalpo Samdhup shrugged. He stuffed the papers back in his bag, mounted his horse and rode into the night.

We clustered at the fires reviewing the news. No one dared go back to his or her own tent for fear of missing details. Many didn't believe Gyalpo Samdhup could have come all the way from India. Still they wanted to know what the others thought.

"What about the papers? How would he know to ask about papers if he not come from Dalai Lama himself?"

"We don't know who he is. Came here to gain our confidence. Fast talking mean nothing."

"He talk about sending children to India. If children go, who take care of parents and grandparents?"

"Nyima Rabten, you sent your daughter to school in another village. Did it improve your family's life?"

I trembled at the subject of education. Education was a lightning bolt that struck in different years, different generations. Always threatening to split apart our family. I looked across the fire to Uncle. His mouth froze in a downward turning line. Prayer beads slipped over his rough fingers. For Uncle, this night must be a bad reminder of a time in his marriage that no one dared talk about for years.

Night after night, he and his wife, Sonam Dekyi, had argued about their daughter's future. Pema Mehto, the Lotus Blossom Girl, was then eight years old. Uncle wanted her to go away to boarding school. Learn about life beyond the nomad camp.

"If she go to school, who help me in tent? Who start fire and make bread?" Sonam Dekyi's weeping grew into horrible crying. "Who weave yak fur into felt for winter tent and churn dri milk into butter and set yogurt?" Plates broke. Curd spilled onto the carpets and spattered papers hanging on the walls.

"I never agree to this," his wife had said. "My daughter is my heart. My life. She go away to school, I die of loneliness. You cruel husband. Willing to cut out my beating heart." She wailed and beat him on the chest. "What kind of man suggest daughter be educated? For what? Who give you these crazy ideas?"

This storm blew chaos through his household, but Uncle Nyima Rabten did not back down. For two years, Pema Mehto studied. She learned to read and write Tibetan and Chinese. The teacher said she was the best student in the class. Pema Mehto played games called basketball and stick and hoop. She found friends. At night, she buried herself under yak wool blankets, her head on a cotton pillowcase embroidered with red Chinese peonies. And she cried and she cried and missed her family. While she cried at school, her mother cried in the tent. She cried in the village and at the evening fire. She sobbed while butchering the yak. She wailed while roasting the *tsampa*. Her tears salted the dri butter tea. She refused to sleep with Nyima Rabten.

Water can wear away stone faster than a bone-handled silver knife blade can cut through. Nyima Rabten gave up. He fetched his daughter from the school. She arrived singing on the back of the cinnamon stallion on a blue day. The stallion danced and reared as it entered the nomad camp. Before the dust settled, Pema Mehto jumped down from the saddle. Family and neighbors greeted her with laughter and hugs. She leapt over her bags on the ground and into their arms.

Uncle laid her schoolbooks to rest in a chest decorated with a jewel-eating mongoose and sunflowers with bright green leaves. Three years later on a misty spring morning, he slipped the thin books out of the trunk at dawn. He gave them to me. There was no need to say, 'Don't tell.'

I hid them in my chuba sleeve. I walked off with a big smile and a stiff arm right past my parents in the meadow. *Tashi Delek*, Ama-la! *Tashi Delek*, Pa-la! I strolled to the cottonwood tree along the Dri-Chu River. Underneath that tree, I buried the books in a metal box. It had a brass lock with the flaming sword of wisdom. I threw the last handfuls of dirt over the box and patted it down. I covered it with leaves, moss and dirt clods.

On days when my parents went to the mountains, Uncle took me to the cottonwood tree. We chose a book to read. Word by word my world beyond the camp grew. Stories of good and bad children and animals who dressed in people's clothes. I admired King Zari Ngo-Yung, the Mouse King, and his loyal Regents, Ambe and Rambe. They helped each other cross swollen rivers and won the war with cat enemies.

Pema Mehto's school adventure was not the end of the story. I was ten years old when I was jolted out of a deep sleep by loud voices. My parents and Uncle held cups of steaming, salted butter tea. Their voices rose and fell. They argued the value of school. Who should go? Who should stay home? Why was it important at all?

"Uncle, you live with us. We will take care of you when you old," Mother had said. "But you teach our boy to read. If he read and want education and the city, he go away. Who take care of sheep and yaks? Who care for us when we are old?"

Dishes clattered to the ground. Uncle sputtered in his tea. This was an old argument. Everyone knew their parts.

"Nyima Rabten, tell us," the chattering of the group clustered at the fire woke both Uncle and me out of our daydreams. "Did education help your family or ruin it?"

Nyia Rabten looked over at me. I met his gaze. "Too soon to tell," he said.

When the fire was out, and everyone had exhausted their questions, they stood and went back to their tents. I told Uncle I was going to check the sheep. I walked slowly back past Kai Lun's. Listening outside, I heard nothing. He had not come back from Derge. After several minutes I walked silently to Erzebet's tent and rustled the flap.

"Who's there?" she said.

"It's me," I whispered.

She untied the strings and held out her hand. I went inside and held her in the dark. She moved her hands down my back. Slowly I touched her hair and her breasts. We lay down on her bed in a dream.

Hours later, I stared into the darkness, remembering mysterious times with my Grandfather.

*I was a boy wearing wool leggings and a nightshirt, cuddled in Grandfather's lap next to my sleeping parents. It was a windless night with no moon, the fire in the pit reduced to glowing embers. Before bedtime, we had trudged through the snow banks along the river. A snow lion bounded over a rise pursuing a rabbit that zigged and zagged toward the safety of its burrow.*

*"Grandfather, tell me again about Sixth Dalai Lama," I had asked. "How could he go against his parents and teachers when they were so kind? I'd never do that."*

*Slowly nodding his head, Grandfather moved his prayer beads through his fingers, click, click, click, one bead at a time, murmuring under his breath. The plaintive howl of a wolf paused all life in the pasture, but the wolf was on the mountain and the dog had not even bothered to bark.*

*Grandfather's chin leaned into my hair, smelling me, a boy who played in the river and threw sticks for the dogs. "Boy, you can't say you never do these things. It is long life. You don't know what will seem like the right thing to do."*

*I pulled myself up to gaze into Grandfather's eyes, a translucent film grown over them from 80 years of sun in the hills and smoky fires in the tent. "Not me, I like to do what is right. I won't cause worry like Sixth Dalai Lama."*

*The beads continued their path, the thumb rolling one bead at a time toward the heart of the man. Grandfather's words rode on a breathing river of familiar prayers. "Fine intentions," he said. "But along journey between birth and death and birth again, people do many things they do not expect to do."*

# CHAPTER 34

## *Going Out As a Hermit*

| | |
|---|---|
| *Dzang ma'ee thook dang toon na* | *Suiting my bright one's heart* |
| *She dee cho kel cha gro* | *I lose life's religion* |
| *Ben pa'ee ree hrod reem na* | *Going out as a hermit* |
| *Bu mo'ee thook dang gal gro* | *I belie my girl's heart* |

*- Sixth Dalai Lama*

### Kai Lun's Story

The night smelled cold and the stars absorbed the blue-white of the glacier. Sudden outbursts of scratching and scurrying in the sedge and cobresia announced mice running to their burrows, hoping to escape the nighthawks pirouetting in the sky. A soft whoosh of air passed my face. A bat swooped in to gobble up a flying insect, a creature itself on the quest for a meal.

I neared my tent, homesickness percolating in my heart. I must find a way to go home to my family. Day by day, I had lost my grip on my mission, jeopardizing my future by not paying attention to details. Dhondhup was turning out to be a fool, yet he was the only person I could rely on—the only one willing to trade his friends for the little I had to offer. Every grain shed has a rat living in the wall, waiting for an opportunity.

I would go to the monastery the next day and complete my report about the monks. Madame Erzebet had slipped away again and Dhondhup said she had been at TriSong Monastery. In the beginning I thought their activities would certainly be tied to getting the Pelletier papers out of Tibet, but had turned up nothing to make this connection. I had only been to the monastery once. Everything was in order. It was as if they expected me, they were so welcoming and gracious.

Reaching inside my shirt, I stroked the silk amulet given to me by the monks to ward off sickness and misfortune. The prospect of returning to the monastery made me nauseous. I would travel to the home of the people who prayed for my health, the people who sent a doctor to my side to cure me. These men I hoped to expose as evil so I would be rewarded with a few extra food ration coupons when I returned to the city. Perhaps I would receive a certificate with a red and gold seal and a new bicycle to ride to work. My wife and son would sit with me at dinner in our one room home, eating delicious fresh bean curd and drinking tea. In exchange, the monks would be thrown out of their monastery, imprisoned and tortured because of my report. I didn't need to go to the monastery to write a report, I could do it out of my own head.

I entered the tent, lit the oil lamp and took out the notebook with the spiral binding, preparing my materials for the next day's reporting. Picking up my pen, I dipped it into the midnight black ink and precisely wrote, as if the pen traveled on its own, observations from a series of non-existent visits, going all the way back to June:

*June 14: There are 100 monks living at the monastery at Manigango. I searched all of the rooms and found no pictures of the Dalai Lama or the Pelletier papers. I searched all shelves and cabinets, went through the temple altars, looking behind and inside. I searched the kitchen and supply rooms, pouring out rice and flour and sifting through other grains. There is nothing. I believe the notes did not exist or were destroyed years ago.*

*June 18: The monks appear to be very poor. They live in rooms with holes in the walls and eat meager food. They give no indication of being involved in politics in the village. I interviewed 20 people in the nomad camp and in Manigango village with no reports that the monks work against government policies. I have found no reason to suspect they are currently a problem.*

*June 25: The monks at TriSong are obedient. They have stopped praying to the Dalai Lama. A middle of the night search of the rooms turned up no photos. There are no weapons. They are under control. The plans to have an officer make periodic checks at the monastery after I leave the area do not need to be implemented.*

The scream of a mountain lion woke me with a start in the middle of the night. I sat bolt upright, my forehead covered with sweat. I had been dreaming of my wife and son. They were being pushed into an official car. Was my wife or my son pushed in first? Did she stumble and look back at me? Did my son carry his leather elephant or was he holding a furry toy yak? I reached for my glasses and the papers I'd written early in the evening--written in my moment of weakness. My earlier dull thoughts of resignation now scared me. I tore the pages about the contrived visits to the monastery out of the notebook and threw them into the fire. I blanched thinking of how close I had come to trading my family for a group of pitiable monks and a foreign woman.

I made a new plan—one of the long series of new plans. I'd go to the monastery, but first I'd go the easy route and confront Tashi Choegyal. A man with his power didn't get there by adhering to high moral priniples. He was a landlord, a king, like the Dalai Lama—the common people were captivated by his charisma and were controlled. A man like him would be easily bribed.

Tashi Choegyal was saddling the sorrel horse when I approached in the morning. I plunged right in. There wasn't time or necessity to pretend this nomad and I were friends or colleagues and required pleasantries in conversation.

"I can offer you a large sum of money for the documents that Madame Erzebet's husband left in Tibet." I didn't know where I would get a large sum of money, or even a small sum. I had already paid that ignorant upstart, Dhondhup, most of the money I had with me. A waste of my precious resources. It had gained me absolutely nothing. Now I was running out of options. "Tell me who has the papers."

Tashi Choegyal sneered and spat into my face, with people watching from the meadow edge. The slime hit my check and dripped to the side before I could brush it off with my sleeve. "You are a damn menace, as well as a fool. I have nothing to lose. You have everything," he said. He smashed me in the chest with his huge fist, knocking the wind out of me. I fell over backwards and crawled into the grass, stuttering like a scared child.

"You are a coward. Snake," Tashi Choegyal yelled. "Two innocent girls lost in mountains because of you." He was talking about the twins, but what did their disappearance have to do with me? I had done nothing but allow them to go on their way, when I could have punished them severely for breaking into my tent.

"You lucky I not kill you for striking Madame Erzebet," he threatened. "You want to leave here alive, you want to see your wife and son again. . ." The horse's hooves came within inches of my face as Tashi Choegyal leapt on the sorrel and rode away.

I limped to the tent, wiped my face and scrubbed the dirt off my clothes. I wanted to climb under the blankets, shut out the light and sleep for the rest of my life. I forced myself to keep going.

The hermit. The day I drank too much *chang* and fell asleep in the meadow, I had woken up to see Madame Erzebet leaving the hermit's shack. He was the person who received and concealed the documents. No one would ever think to look in this old man's broken down tin hut. It would take only minutes to tear the place apart. There weren't many places the papers could be hidden, if rats hadn't eaten them all years ago.

Circling the lake, I hiked up the small hill until I reached the shelter. From inside the hut came the deep chanting of *Om Mani Padme Hung.* I lifted my hand to rap at the door. There were blood streaks on my palm and wrist where I'd ground my hand into the dirt, crawling away from Tashi Choegyal. I sucked on the bleeding scratches just as a small boy ran out of the hut. The boy threw himself at me and hugged my leg. I kicked my leg to shake him off, as if I were dislodging a dog or a monkey attached to me. The boy laughed and ran to the spring, carrying a jug to bring back water.

"Come in," said the hermit. I crouched down and went into the dark room. A single butter lamp burned in front of a picture of the Buddha taped to the wall. "You finally come back."

"What are you talking about? I've never been here before."

"You don't remember me? The night man with yellow hair died. I pray for his positive rebirth. You brought man to me. My eyes clouded, but I recognize your walk and voice."

I had nothing to say. My brother and I were specters, following each other through this lifetime.

"You come for papers?" the hermit said.

"Yes, the papers the foreigner left behind." My chest collapsed, a twinge of pain where Tashi Choegyal had struck me. The words "coward" and "snake" rang in my ears. I folded my arms over my chest to cushion my ribs, and felt an absolute relief. I didn't have the will to terrorize this old man. I didn't have to. He was ready to help me.

"Hot water?" The old man held out a cup.

"No, no," I brushed the steaming cup aside. "The papers. I only want the papers. I'm in a hurry, old man."

The hermit reached under the bench and pulled out a wooden box. The container was smaller than I had imagined. The papers must be folded into a small packet. The lid was stuck, swollen shut. The hermit rummaged in the corner of the hut, tossing tools to the right and left, finally surfacing a stone-carving knife. He pried at the corners, tapping the box, turning it upside down and knocking it against the bench. I had to restrain myself from grabbing the box and smashing it with the mallet hanging on the wall. I breathed slowly and forced myself to sit and watch. This man and the documents weren't going anywhere. The hermit dipped a rag in oil and rubbed the rusted metal, working the hinges with the metal tool. The lid creaked open. The man held the box up to the light of the butter lamp and extracted a small red booklet.

I closed my eyes and sucked in the air of my family's bright future. Why hadn't I come here weeks ago? I now remembered the geologist in Chengdu telling me the hermit knew everything that happened at the lake. I hadn't understood the significance. Strangely, Pelletier's notes were bound like a book. I took it out into the daylight. The cover was beaten up, the pages crisp from years of storage. It was handwritten in Tibetan, not the French I expected. There was a heading: *The Wheel of Sharp Weapons Effectively Striking the Heart of the Foe.* An obvious reference to the People's Liberation Army invading Kham and the use of guns and bayonets to subdue the Tibetans. I thumbed through the pages searching for the dates and names I assumed would be documented. Instead, I found nothing of the kind.

*When we lack all control over where we must travel*
*And always must wander like waifs with no home*
*This is the Wheel of Sharp Weapons returning*
*Full circle upon us from wrongs we have done*

*Til now we have disturbed holy teachers and others*
*Forcing them to move from their homelands*
*Hereafter, cease to cause grief to others*
*By evicting them cruelly from the homes that they love*

"What is this?" I cried out, causing a rupture of pain in my rib cage. My breathing deteriorated into staccato bursts of tortured air. "What is this? These aren't the documents."

"Yes, these the valuable documents." The hermit came out of his shack, turning his prayer beads, mumbling prayers, and peering at the yellowed pages. "Dharmarakshita, teacher from India wrote this centuries ago. Nothing more valuable."

"The other papers, old man. I want the papers from the foreigner who came here many years ago."

"Another foreigner came here?" the hermit scratched his head. "Not Dharmarakshita from India?"

I swallowed hard. I wanted to weep in front of this old man and have him hold me on his lap like my grandfather held me when I was a child.

"No, no," said the hermit as I tossed the book back in the box. "Take this with you. It is gift. I memorized it all long ago."

I stuffed the booklet in my pack and coughing like a near dead man ran back down the hill to the lake, avoiding my tent for fear I would enter and fall into such a basin of despair I would never have the energy to emerge again. At the road, I hitched a ride on a government truck and an hour later was let off at the base of the monastery hill. Clutching stones to throw at attacking dogs, I continued up by foot, steeling myself as I neared the complex. I passed by the pilgrims. Why do these damaged people keep prostrating around this monastery? Back home they would be slumped in wheel chairs, living in darkened, urine-saturated rooms, their exhausted relatives bringing trays of soft food to be picked at until it was all finally taken away and tossed in the garbage to be rummaged through by feral cats who would see it as a delicacy.

At the temple, monks bent in half to bow to me and shuffled away into the buildings. Within minutes, Lobsang Phuntsok appeared in the corridor.

"I'm here to make a deal with you," I said. A spasm of coughing hacked through my body. It took me several minutes until I could choke out my demands, and by then I had lost all authority to threaten anyone. "I want Pelletier's papers. I'm not leaving Manigango until I get them."

"Come into my room." We went down the corridor and Lobsang Phuntsok closed the door behind us. "What do you think I can do? This is a monastery, not a repository for missing documents."

"I'm not here to debate with you. I'll trade you Madame Erzebet Pelletier's life for the documents. If I don't get the papers, I'm prepared to engineer a situation where she'll never leave Tibet. It won't be hard to do."

I watched Lobsang Phuntsok's face for signs of anxiety, indications of alarm. None. The monk's training served him well.

"I don't believe you." He reached into his robe and extracted prayer beads, which he slowly turned through his fingers, bead by bead. "You're not the kind of man who would cause harm to an innocent woman."

"You don't know what kind of man I am. I'll do whatever is needed to get the papers." I concentrated on keeping my voice level and evil, just this side of insane. I had to convince the monk it was true, I was capable of doing anything to get the documents.

"You're talking about a woman who has already suffered greatly from the death of her husband. At the hands of your comrades," said Lobsang Phunstok.

"I'll make sure she suffers less here than if she were caught with the papers leaving Tibet and China." I jerked my hand down from my face. My fingers had started their telltale trace of the outline of my forehead and were creeping toward my nose and lips. "I don't care how you do it. Get me the documents. If they're not here, find them. Use your highly esteemed monk's training to save this woman's life."

# CHAPTER 35

## *Seeking a Fortune Teller*

| | |
|---|---|
| *Nying took gu la shor song* | *My love was stolen from me* |
| *Mo cha tsee bul ren song* | *I must seek a fortune teller* |
| *Bu mo dung sem chen ma* | *To search for that passionate girl* |
| *Mee lam nag la khor song* | *Who circles round and round in my dreams* |

*- Sixth Dalai Lama*

### Dhondhup's Story

News travel through camp like fire burning dry fall meadow. A while back, two boys who live in neighboring village escape to India. Now they return to visit. Will stay in village only one day. Even from hillside where I herd sheep, I see them come down the road from Manigango. Laughing, teasing each other. Falling off bicycles into meadow and rolling around.

All our friends run down to meet boys. They wear puffy jackets even though very hot day. Tennis shoes, blue foreigner pants, shirts with foreigner words. With big pride, boys say words aloud: "Chicago," and "Pro." No one know what they mean, but we laugh and nod our heads, congratulating boys on having these clothes. A watch with silver face flash on oldest boy's wrist. They listen to radios with small black covers on ears. Wires hang down to machines in their pockets. When I stand close, I hear music come out of machines. When they leave for India, boys had red cheeks burned by wind and sun. Now cheeks smooth and pink like people in magazines in nearby city. Don't look like nomads anymore.

"In India, red trucks with flowers painted on sides lumber down highways," they say. "They carry huge loads of goods. If you're behind them, it look like giant elephant strapped down! Billows of black smoke pour from factories and cover cities. Against law to eat cows. They are Hindu." Men, women and children squat to hear these stories. Rock back and forth. Poke each other in side, laughing. Some roll their eyes and shake their heads in disbelief. No, this all made up story. Impossible to be true. Prayer beads click through grandmothers' fingers. Grandfathers spin prayer wheels and nod off. Wake again to roar of laughter.

Evening come and we move next to fire. Women take turns serving butter tea. Carve off slices of roasted yak meat for boys. No one want them to stop talking. "In India, are lepers with no noses. Stumps of fingers wrapped with bloody rags. They beg in streets. Foreigners come from Canada and Europe to help Tibetan refugees. Most people attend school. Many Tibetans live in one-room houses or tents on mountain hillsides. Others start businesses and bring belts, turquoise and carpets from Nepal to sell to tourists."

"Where you get clothes?" Old Kalsang ask. "*De dra kong chenpo re.* They look expensive."

India boys wink at each other and laugh again. "Western women pay for our brand name clothes. It is called having sponsor. Even give us money to come to Tibet to visit. Now we live like kings. We don't have to go to fortune teller anymore to have our parents decide who we should marry." Some people believed them, others did not.

That night, away from camp, I meet Mr. Kai Lun at usual place. He hide in stone cave that hold mani stones. Even before twins disappear, he come and ask me to help him watch people in camp. I do my job, but he not do so much for me. I am sure he have thousands of Yuan in his bags. He can make my life easy. Like Western women do for boys in India. Marriage gifts for my future wife's family not enough for a smart man like me. I want brand name clothes, too. I not get any with little money he pay me.

He not even interested in India boys. When I try to tell him funny India stories, he say be quiet, there are more important things to discuss. Mr. Kai Lun say, "Norbu and Madame Erzebet sneaking off to spend time together again."

I know this true. My ratting on Norbu to his parents went nowhere. I hear Norbu in tent with her the night we come back from mountains. I think police catch him when they come to camp. But he already leave Erzebet's tent. He lucky. Mr. Kai Lun tell me make sure Norbu know Madame Erzebet keeps secrets from him. She is here to find her husband's documents. When I tell him, Norbu act surprised. But this is just big show for me. Of course, she already tell him this.

"Want to keep working for me?" Mr. Kai Lun say. "You'd better come up with a good plan to keep them apart. If she gets the documents, you're the one who will be in trouble, not me. "

The arrival of boys from India make it easy. In morning, over *tsampa* and tea, I tell them about Norbu and Madame Erzebet, how they are staying together in the tent. I have embarrassment to say more, but they nudge each other and laugh, so they know what I am talking about. That afternoon at river, larger boy hit Norbu in arm and say, "Hey, brother. Dhondhup told us you have Western woman taking care of you! So you know already what a good thing it is." Norbu glare at me. Boys from India idiots. I never think they will tell him how they know.

"Yes, it's a good thing. . ." Norbu have fake excitement on his face, like clown in carnival traveling through village. He not tell them he is still a child and his parents get angry and make him leave her tent.

"Show us what she's bought you, brother. Did she bring things from Europe? They have best radios. What about brand name clothes? Where are your brand name clothes?"

"Expensive jacket and good radio stashed up on mountainside. I'll show you another time." Norbu face is red. I know he get no riches from her. She give him nothing.

"What about visa to get out of China? If she's from Europe, easy for her to help you go there. You'll be living the best life in Paris or London."

"What is this word visa they are saying?" Norbu whispered. "What does visa have to do with leaving China?" I didn't know either, but it sound very important.

India boys run off to the river and Norbu follow me. "Why did you tell them about Erzebet?" he ask. I'm afraid he attack me like when we in the mountains, so I start to race away. I still have scabs on head where he pull my hair out with the slingshot rubber.

"I didn't know it is secret anymore," I say over my shoulder. "Besides, you not even stay in her tent. Boys don't need to know that. If you tell, they think she kick you out because she done with you."

I stopped running—he only wanted to yell at me. "She didn't kick me out--my parents forced me to leave because of Kai Lun. Because of you and your big mouth."

"But what about papers so you can go to West? You weren't tricked by her, were you? If she cared she would give you money and arrange papers, right? Hmmm-is that what visa means? Is visa papers so you can go the West?"

"I need to talk to her," Norbu say. "Maybe she didn't know she could help me. Will you come with me? You spent more time with boys from India than me. You know how she could have helped me, if she wanted to."

"Remember to tell her you are naïve Tibetan boy. She is old woman. She make you think she love you, but really this just to confuse you," I suggest to Norbu. It work in my favor if she think Norbu no longer love her. She trust me instead of Norbu. "She used you. Right?"

"I guess so," he mumbled as we go together to Madame Erzebet's tent.

We enter tent. He give her quick kiss on cheek and take cup of tea. I afraid he not ready to get tough with her after all. He say nothing. Only turn cup around and around. He run his finger back and forth through steam.

"Did you need something Dhondhup?" she say.

"No, Norbu want me to come with him." I take my tea and sip it, looking around tent.

They sit next to each other on corner of bed. I play with yak string ball in corner. I can wait all day to see fireworks. After several minutes, she touch his hand. Hand lay without moving under her fingers.

"What's happening?" she say. "Are you upset?"

"I'm not spending time with you anymore. You've used me." It happen so fast. He spin his body toward her. Half of mouth change into ugly sneer with teeth showing, like crazy nomad dog.

"Used you? What are you talking about? Why are you saying this to me?" she say. "And what is Dhondhup doing here? Leave, Dhondhup."

I never see Norbu or Erzebet like this before. Try not to get in middle of what come next. I start to get up, but Norbu stop me. "He's with me. I can trust him." I sit back down and pick up yak string ball again. Watch out of corner of my eyes.

"You used me for love and sex," he say. His eyes small. Space between his lips narrow slit. "You promised to help me leave here."

"I never promised you that." Her eyes flit over to me. Then she continue talking. "You're angry at me because I'm no more superhuman than you. No more capable of taking you out of here than I'm able to stay here myself."

"Don't talk to me. You're trying to confuse me," he sputter, pacing in tent. She was rabbit cornered by dog. His back stiffen and he turn with snarl to face her. My gentle friend is gone. "You can't turn this around. I'm the man here. You don't tell me what's happening. I tell you."

All at once, I can tell this coming for days. Not my fault. Their love start to break long ago. I only need to make small push to make it happen.

"I'm naïve Tibetan boy. You're older woman. You have all the power."

She laughed out loud and for so long I thought she no longer angry with Norbu. But then laugh stop short and she screech. "Power to do what?" I slide my tongue over inside of my teeth, one by one, trying to think about something else than what is happenng in front of me. I feel sick in stomach. Want to go out into sunshine.

"Get out of here before I take a rock and slam you in the head," she scream at Norbu. "You can lie to yourself or your friends, but I won't listen to your lies about our time together." She jump off bed and fly toward him. Her fists stop just before they punch his white face. "Both of you. Get out of here. Now."

Norbu look scared. I afraid she strike me. But she not even remember I there. She look around like wild woman, eyes dart back and forth, then grab photograph from painted chest. I remember the picture. She and Norbu stand in wildflowers at summer's beginning, smiling at camera. Heads together. His cheek rest against hers. She rip photo and throw pieces in his face. Then she push us out of tent. Her fists beat Norbu's back as he run across meadow. Norbu go with me to my tent. Climb under sheepskin blanket and cover his head. I think he cry. But I never hear man cry before, so maybe I wrong.

Hours later, I go out and bring in the last sheep. Madame Erzebet walking in marsh area next to river. She move as if sleepwalking, look at ferns. I look in that direction, too. Ferns glow in golden-green sunlight. Hawks fly over tall grasses. Hunt for signs of life. Listen for movement in rustling reeds. Prairie dog peek at me from burrow and whisk to gather food for winter. It die before my eyes. Squealing, delicious meal for hawk.

Madame Erzebet stay in grasses until end of day steal all color and meadow turn to ink.

After lights out in all of tents, I hear woman call from tent boundary. I rush out. Madame Erzebet. I afraid she come to talk to Norbu. Afraid he be pulled back into her life. Then Mr. Kai Lun angry with me and cut me off--no more money, maybe even bring trouble for me with police.

"Is Norbu here?"

"He doesn't want to see you," I say.

"I don't want to see him. I want to talk to you. We don't need Norbu—either of us. We can help each other."

"How? How can we help each other?"

"I know where my husband's documents are. I'll make it possible for you to get them to Kai Lun, if you help me. Make a deal with him for more money—he has it. He'll give it to you when you produce the papers."

"What do I have to do for you?" I look uneasily toward tent. My parents just return from mountains. If they hear, they beat me and kick me out. Where I go then? My marriage finished. No one take me for son-in-law if they find out I am traitor.

"I'm looking for information about the people who killed my husband when he was in Tibet. If you get me those names, I'll get you the documents."

"I have to think."

"You have until tomorrow morning," she say. "If you're too cowardly to do this, if you don't want the money, I have someone else who does."

"Alright, tomorrow I tell you."

As she turn to go, she suddenly hold out her hand with envelope. "Norbu forgot this." I take it without speaking. Not sure if I give it to him or not.

Inside tent, I light butter lamp and open envelope. Between two watercolor paintings are Norbu's hand-written notebooks. The books he work on when his parents not around. Each page filled from edge to edge with different languages. Small drawings.

Norbu always acting like he smarter than me. Smarter than any of us. What can I do with this evidence of his big, fat brain? Burn it and destroy lessons? I can cut it into little pieces. Then each character stand on own scrap of paper. No meaning at all. Rip book until pages fall apart? Then notes make no sense. Soak in water until ink dissolve and no words left? A blank book.

I hold book in hand, not knowing what to choose. In end, I not have mind to get back at Norbu by destroying his book. Don't even know what I get back at him for. What he do to me that I want him to feel pain? Maybe because Father talk about him like he is hope of village. He teach himself to read and write. Is that why I hate him? I turn the pages of book one more time.

Stuck inside is photograph. So rubbed and faded I barely make out separate figures. People in front of blue and white picnic tent in meadow. Glacier shine white behind them. I take out magnifying glass Madame Erzebet leave in our tent one day and look more closely—who are those people? Group of children from camp squat next to yellow-haired man with cameras around his neck. There is my older sister, Lhamo. Next to the man is young boy, five or six years old. Tall child with eyes shaped like gentle waves on the sacred lake. He lean with one arm around man's shoulder. He prop his foot on man's leg.

It is Erzebet's husband and Norbu.

# CHAPTER 36

## *Mirror of My Karma*

| | |
|---|---|
| *Shi te nyel pa'ee yool gyee* | *Residing in the realm of healing and death* |
| *Cho gyel lay gyeei me long* | *Mirror of my karma* |
| *Tee na thrik thrik meen dook* | *Here you cannot see what has been done* |
| *Te nae thrik thrik nang zhu* | *But there you see exactly what is right* |

*- Sixth Dalai Lama*

### Kai Lun's Story

At the bend in the river where it left the lake, I heard splashing. It was Lhamo Sangye washing clothes. I stood up in a daze and went to the woman who had bathed my body when I was ill, changed my stinking blankets and sent her children on a perilous journey in the night to bring back a doctor to save my life.

I meant to thank her and leave, but instead blurted out, "Where is your husband? Don't you have a husband?" Lhamo Sangye placed the wet clothes on a granite boulder and dried her hands on the edge of her chuba. She pursed her lips and looked at me for a long time before she answered.

"You not want to hear my husband story." I nodded yes. I did want to hear it. I needed to know who this woman was and gauge my emotional courage against hers.

"Authorities take husband away years ago. Punish him for speaking out at village meeting."

"But what did he say?"

"He protest way soldiers beat elderly monks who carry photos of Dalai Lama. So they beat him with clubs. Take him to prison. We travel three days each way to see him. Take him food. Otherwise, he starve in cell. Each time we visit, he worse. After five years, we hear he will be released. Come home in rags. Blood run from nose and bowels. He lay in tent unconscious. Monks pray over him. I feed him meat broth and hot water. On third day, he stop breathing. Spot of blood on his head tell us soul left body. We take him to mountains. His body cut apart. Vultures cry in sky and carry him away."

The blood drained from my face. "Then why did you help me?" Putting my hand in my pocket, I felt the satiny sheen of the amulet given to me by the monks, sliding it back and forth between my thumb and forefinger. "Why did you care for me when I was ill?" I pushed the words out, feeling light-headed as if I might topple into the reeds.

"Did you personally hurt my husband?" Lhamo Sangye pulled more wet clothes from the river and spread them on the hot boulders on the bank. "You're a human being just as I am. A human being who was suffering. If I can't help a man who is dying, then what kind of human being am I? What kind of people will my own children become?"

"The men who took away your husband. The people who beat him. Do you hate them still?"

"I forgive them long ago. Without forgive them, better to just die like my husband."

"Come with me." She led me across the field to the tent where the twins had lived with their mother.

At the tent, Lhamo Sangye took me inside. The mother was snoring in her bed, lying under heaps of sheepskin blankets even though the weather outside was furnace warm.

"Ama-la, Ama-la," said Lhamo Sangye, waking up the woman. She rolled over and her face sagged to the bed until it was lying almost in a puddle on the blankets. "I bring Chinese man. Tell him his brother's story."

"My brother?" I was confused. "What do you know of my brother?"

"You not see your own blood in twins?" said Lhamo Sangye. "You blind to humans who live here. Not even see own flesh and blood walking in your midst."

"The twins? My flesh and blood?" I was still confused. What did the twins, my bumbling spies, have to do with my family?

"Your brother," said the twins' mother, her body shaking with each explosion of spittle. "His name Zhang Haitao?" My head spun. Impossible. How could this woman living in a yak hair tent know the name of my brother?

"I continue, Ama-la?" said Lhamo Sangye. The old woman choked out yes. I wanted to run out of the tent away from these insane women who were ready to tell me lies.

"Your brother come to Manigango. March with army. Arrive with official documents with red seals. He given right to have tent, three yaks, three sheep, horse. Right to say who correct. Authority to punish those in error.

"He organize struggle sessions. Try to flush out those with poisonous ideas to work against Party goals. Doctors. Teachers. He must banish them to countryside. However, in Yi-Lhun Latso, Cultural Revolution upside down. Who professional? No doctors or professors here. No university. No hospitals. No one educated. No one to reform for acting smarter than common man. Everyone common man."

"This is my brother you're talking about?" I interrupted. "Are you sure? They are many men named Zhang Haitao." But even as I spoke, I knew it was true. The twins. They were my brother's children.

"He is the one," continued Lhamo Sangye. "He try to do job for many months. Remove photos of Dalai Lama. Beat and send owners to prison. Yet they continue to pray for Dalai Lama blessings in private. He order them to stop. Stop chanting *Om Mani Padme Hung.* Our old men and women look blank and continue on. Reform useless. Send these people to countryside? No further countryside to go to."

"So what?" I said. "He was an army functionary, just trying to do his duty."

"Zhang Haitao not know what to do with yak, sheep, tent," interjected the old woman in the bed. She had raised herself up one elbow and was eager to add to the story. "No idea how to use chula stove. What to do with people who eat roasted barley at every meal? People who gnaw mutton off bone while squatting next to fire? No foreigner books to destroy. No Big Letter Posters speaking out against Party."

"I've heard enough about my brother," I said.

The old woman had one more thing to say, "Take him to the sacred lake."

"Not a good idea. . ." Lhamo Sangye began.

"Better once to see than many times to hear. He must go to lake," said the old woman.

"What is she talking about?" I paced in the small tent, the old woman's smell filling my nose, while Lhamo Sangye tucked the blankets under her and ushered me out into the blinding sunlight.

We walked without speaking over small hills to the lake edge where she took off her shoes and rolled up her leggings, and gestured at me to do the same. We waded from the shore. My legs looked like peeled alabaster bamboo through the clear water. Colored fish nibbled at them and small bubbles lined up in rows on my shins.

As we worked our way further out, Lhamo Sangye said, "Your brother not a bad man, but his karma caused him to do bad things to the people here. He forced that woman to have sex and live with him. But he also cared for her."

We moved slowly past the first mound of mani stones, until the water was as deep as my thighs. This could be a trap, a plan by the nomads to get rid of me. I couldn't swim. I could easily be pushed over and drowned. I clutched at the amulet in my pocket.

"But then army return," Lhamo Sangye continued. "March back through camp. They say they free village people from monks and say yellow-haired foreigner they left behind write lies to newspapers in his home country. Government say he had to be stopped."

"What foreigner—are you talking about Pelletier?" My legs were freezing in the lake, but the skin on my back and arms was crawling with anxiety. "What does this have to do with my brother?"

Lhamo Sangye didn't answer. She kept wading. The water got deeper, up to my waist and then my chest. I looked back over my shoulder. The shore was close enough to call for help to anyone who might be in the meadow. There was no one there.

"Why are you bringing me here?" I said, as we moved between two large boulders rising out of the lake. The lower part of the stones was visible through the turquoise green water like half-submerged icebergs. "Why did you bring me here?"

She pointed at the largest stone. Only the first line was visible out of the water. I read the inscription, which faced toward the sacred glacier. Tibetan characters carved into the stone said:

**ON THIS DAY APRIL 22, 1959**

I ducked my head under the water, my open eyes blinking in the cold, green expanse. Through the bands of sunlight rising and falling in the lake, I saw several more lines carved into the stone.

**THREE MEN KILLED FOREIGNER**
**NEAR THIS SACRED LAKE**
**HAN FAICHEN**
**GAO ZHINGZHAO**
**ZHANG HAITAO**

**ZHANG HAITAO BRING DYING MAN**
**TO YI-LHUN LATSO FOR FINAL PRAYERS.**

**PRAYERS ALSO SAID FOR MEN**
**WHO KILLED FOREIGNER**

I lifted my head from the water, my clothes drenched, and my hands shaking. "Why is my brother's name written on a stone in a lake?" I asked. "This is a lie! He could not have killed a man."

"Your brother go out one evening in bad rainstorm. With two other men. Come back hours later, bloody and weeping. The foreigner, Erzebet's husband, shot. Army Jeep push his car off road."

My mind scrambling to make sense of all the tragedy I had heard today, I sank into the water until it was lapping at the edge of my neck. Lhamo Sangye reached out her hand and pulled me back to the surface and I leaned against the mani stone, my fingers tracing the letters of Haitao's name.

"The twins' mother beg your brother to take foreigner body to hermit. Then to monastery for final prayers. Until soul pass out of body. Until soul begin travel looking for positive rebirth. Your brother do that for her. He do it for himself. To balance terrible karma of killing a kind man.

"Not long after, army start to drain lake. Force us to dig trenches from lake shore to meadow," Lhamo Sangye said. "Mani stones exposed as lake went down. Your brother ask hermit to carve story to what happened here on stone. Brother's own confession written in stone. After hermit finish, Zhang Haitao tell his superiors that nomads now love Chinese army. Reform of nomads at Yi-Lhun Latso and Manigango complete. Then he go away. We never know what happen to him after that.

"Twins' mother bring me here after girls born. Their misshapen bodies reminder of dual nature of man. Cruelty and kindness in one human being. That spring, army man sent here to study lake. He demand they stop draining water. Lake fill again, until only top of stones can be seen."

I again ran my fingers along the characters, blessing my brother who had been caught in evil as we all had been. These were the names Madame Erzebet was looking for. As if I had said it aloud, Lhamo Sangye, spoke.

"Should I bring Erzebet here? This is what she need to know to bring peace to her life."

"Do you want her to leave Tibet safely?" I answered. "Then keep this to yourself. She is a headstrong woman. She could go back to Derge with this information and try to meet with the authorities again. There is nothing she can do with these names that would not put her life in danger and bring disaster to the camp."

# CHAPTER 37

## *Before A Great Lama*

| | |
|---|---|
| *Tsan den la ma'ee droong du* | *Before a great lama* |
| *Sem tree zhu bar cheen pa'ee* | *I asked for holy help* |
| *Sem pa gor kyang mee thoob* | *But my thoughts* |
| *Jam pa'ee chok la shor song* | *Went back to my beloved* |
| | *-Sixth Dalai Lama* |

### Erzebet's Story

The scene with Norbu in the tent opened up a hollow in my heart that brought to mind my darkest days after Girard disappeared. His accusations came out so easily there had to be pieces of the truth embedded in his tirade. It was more than a charade for Dhondhup's benefit. In the beginning weeks, when he had mentioned going to the West to become educated and I questioned him, he had laughed at me and dismissed it.

In the end, I was complicit. I knew it was eating at him and that, despite our tender time together, he saw me as his only link to a future out of Tibet. Did I have the right or the responsibility to squash those hopes and dreams whenever they surfaced? After all, who was I to say this nomad would never have the chance to go to the West? Just because I might not have the will or the way to make it happen, did I have the license to tell him no one ever would?

The relationship with Norbu was only one part of my conundrum. My time in Tibet was drawing to a close, and my options for finding out who had killed Girard were fast diminishing. I was not willing to bring the nomads any further into my search than they already were—their lives were perilous enough already. But there was one person I wasn't concerned about. Dhondhup. Dhondhup was a betrayer—willing to backstab his friends and society for his own gain. I could use Dhondhup, just as he had tried to use Norbu.

I forced down my breakfast and went out to walk along the river, waiting for him to tell me his decision, and waiting for a signal from Lhamo Sangye that I should go to the monastery to get the documents. I didn't let myself think about what would happen afterwards.

Dhondhup found me first. "Yes, I do it. But first, you give me papers. Then I give you names." He left, singing the song of King Gesar and shooting stones from his slingshot at a rabbit running through the field.

Lhamo Sangye appeared not long after. "Time to go to TriSong. Now." she said. "Norbu go with you. Not safe to go alone. We have word tonight police search monastery again. Tell Lama Lobsang Phuntsok. I bring Tashi

Choegyal's horse. Norbu meet you along trail at backside of lake."

Within the hour, I was on the trail heading toward Manigango. Past the stupa, past the cove, Norbu rode up next to me and we continued on. We didn't speak, riding as fast as we could along the stony paths, out of sight of the villages and the main road. By noon we were there. We tied the horses in the stable behind the main buildings and went directly to Lobsang Phuntsok's room. He sat on the floor, reading from a rectangular loose-leaf book that had thin wooden covers with brocade insets.

"Lhamo Sangye said to tell you it's time," Norbu explained, as he sat down on the floor. "Police are coming."

"We've already been informed. We have a few hours."

"Lama-la, how did Erzebet's husband's papers end up here?" Norbu asked.

Lobsang Phuntsok turned to me. "The last thing your husband did before he fled the monastery was to place the papers under the main Buddha statue in the temple. He told the Abbot. I believe he thought he might come back one day and retrieve them. The Abbot took them for safekeeping. Hid them in the monastery without telling anyone."

"When I arrived in the camp, was it your plan that I would take them to Europe when I left?" I asked.

"It was a possibility. A risky one."

"Was a possibility? Have things changed?"

"This morning, the Abbot threw the three dice of the *Mo* to see the future. It's too risky to give you the documents."

"I want to try." Footsteps in the hallway halted outside the door. Lobsang Phuntsok signaled to us to be quiet and when the person walked on, he picked up my bag and gestured for me to follow him. We walked to the hillside above the monastery, where we could see the green hills of Manigango and the snow covered Qu'er Mountains above Yi-Lhun Latso.

"If your tent was secure, you could take the papers," he said. "But it isn't. Mr. Kai Lun is desperate to find the documents."

"What if I copied the pages and planted them so Kai Lun could find them? The PSB would destroy that copy, but the original set might make it out of Tibet."

"Too dangerous for you," said Norbu.

"Kai Lun needs the notes. I'm safer if he finds them than if he doesn't."

"They'd have to be good," Norbu continued. "If Kai Lun found out he'd been fooled, he could have the camp and the monastery burned to the ground."

Lobsang Phuntsok was quiet. "We have no choice; we're running out of time. Norbu, stay out of sight and be ready to help. I'll take Madame Erzebet to the temple. We have to wait until the monks have finished their prayers." We walked from the hillside to the main temple complex. In the hall, I slipped unnoticed into the darkened Medicine Buddha shrine room and slid down against the wall. It left cool circles all along my spine. The monks chanted from the main temple. I closed my eyes and the vibration ebbed and flowed.

*Om-mani-padme-hung. Om-mani-padme-hung. Om-mani-padme-hung.*

The clear, high-pitched sound of the bells brought an image of Girard holding a new baby he named Lilia. The bell rang again. A candlelight dinner in Paris before his departure to China. A blue poppy protected by thorns. A giant nomad on a cinnamon stallion who had the light of recognition in his eyes when he met me.

"Are you ready?" I jumped at the sound of Lobsang Phuntsok's voice. A pigeon flew in the rafters, bringing food to a nest in the eaves. The flutter of wings perforated my consciousness. I opened my eyes. Norbu was with him. I had no idea how long I had been there.

He led us into the main temple hall. The monks were gone and it was pitch black, pierced only by the glow from a single butter lamp burning before a statue of the Buddha. The dense smell of frankincense brought to mind my father's funeral. I wished him peace.

"Norbu, stay at the door. Listen for anyone approaching. We have to be fast," Lobsang Phuntsok said.

Following his lead, I skirted the wall with the wrathful deity murals and squeezed behind the central Buddha. Craning my neck upward, I could not see the top of the statue. My face next to the metal figure felt cold. Lobsang Phuntsok slid his hands over the statue's surface and signaled for me to light a butter lamp and hold it near. In the yellow light, simple wooden joints in the platform revealed themselves as a series of small drawers set into the base.

He spread his fingers and measured from the edge of the statue: *chik, nye, sum, she, nga.* At the tenth joint, he stopped and tapped on the wood. A small door opened, exposing a lock. Chanting under his breath, Lobsang Phuntsok reached inside his robe and brought out a gold key. Reminiscent of a fleur d'lis, it was forged in the shape of a *dorjee*, the Buddhist thunderbolt of active compassion.

Inserting the key into the lock, he jiggled it back and forth until it fit. There was a crusty scraping as the key dislodged years of accumulated smoke and grit. Bits of soot fell from the keyhole onto the floor. One final turn and the drawer slid open. I held the butter lamp high above the rectangular box. Lying flat inside was a red leather folder. Lobsang Phuntsok reached in and placed the folder with yellow tissue-thin documents in my outstretched hands while he held the light.

I recognized the backwards slant of the handwriting, the unusual loop of the letters below the line. Running my fingertips over the letters, my throat ached as I willed contact with the writer. *Girard, I am in Tibet to find you. . .* I quickly leafed through the pages, filled with names and numbers. Lobsang

Phuntsok put the folder inside his robe, closed the drawer and removed the key. He gestured for me to follow him.

"Sssh," Norbu whispered from the door. Muffled footsteps thudded at the end of the wooden corridor. He dragged a wooden bench against the main doors, each sound hammering through the hall, and then ran and hid behind the brocade tapestries hanging from the rafters to the floor. Lobsang Phuntsok blew out the lamp and we melded with the statues themselves, holding our breath in the darkness. There was banging on the temple doors. The doors flew open, knocking over the bench and scraping it across the floor. A beam of light from a torch swept through the room. The wrathful deities rose up as monsters, the shadows lurching back and forth in the smoke of the incense. I looked down. A sliver of light reached under the cabinet and squarely illuminated the toe of my shoe. Leaving my foot planted, I shifted my body to fit Lobsang Phuntsok's.

Shouting filled the room, Kai Lun's voice unmistakable among the others'. The yelling seemed to be directed at him and his response was confused, conciliatory. There was the smack of flesh hitting flesh and a groan. The torch swept the temple again and the men moved back out into the corridor. Doors to the monk's small quarters ground open and we heard voices as monks were rounded up in the hallway, and then sent back to their rooms, one by one. We waited for hours in the darkness. When the monastery was quiet and the roar of vehicles ricocheted off the hillside, we crept from behind the statue. Lobsang Phuntsok took a grass broom and swept away our footprints from around the Buddha, as we all backed toward the main doors.

"The papers?" I said. "What should I do?"

"Go to my room. I'll follow you. Norbu, go to the stables. Get the horses ready."

I ran down the empty corridor, slipping inside his room. He followed a few minutes later, pulling the red folder out of his robe.

"Work fast. You have to get out of here. You don't have time to copy them all." He handed me a pen and a sheaf of thin, ancient paper that clearly had been folded and stuffed in the back of his drawer for years. On it, I copied dates, names of monks, numbers of soldiers and the description of their uniforms, injuries to monks, and deaths.

*January 12, 1959: Lobsang Tenzin, 25 years old, beaten with a rifle butt. Appears to have broken jaw, possibly lost his eye.*

*January 17, 1959: Kalsang Tenzin, 20 years old, beaten with club on the head, broken arm. Dawa Dondhup, 48 years old, shot in the leg. The monk's quarters at the rear of the monastery have been set ablaze and burned to the ground. Statues of the Buddha broken with sledgehammers and the pieces run over by army trucks.*

*February 22: 25 monks arrested and taken away in a truck. Don't know where.*

*April 26: They've beaten the Abbot of TriSong, broken his arms and hung him on a hook in the main courtyard. His shoulders appear to be ripped out of the sockets. Other monks were thrown off the balconies onto the stone floors below.*

No wonder Girard thought it was crucial to hide his notes. It was now 1978 and the world still didn't really know what had happened in Tibet. Had this been posted in 1959, world opinion might be in greater sympathy and Tibet might now be a free country.

I wrote automatically, filling page after page, shifting the paper so I could purposefully imitate Girard's familiar backhanded script. I was almost finished when Lobsang Phuntsok returned.

"The Abbot is worried. You have to leave the monastery immediately." I yearned to have a token that was directly connected to Girard—something his hand had touched. I chose a paper from the middle of the stack and tore off a corner with a scribbled observation about the intensity of the Tibetan blue sky. Reaching in my pocket, I slipped it into the tiny box with the remaining two poppy petals from Tro-La Pass, now dried into crepe paper, unrecognizable as the flower except for a tinge of aquamarine. Folding the copied papers, I put them back in the red folder, and ran out to the back stables.

Norbu had the horses saddled and waiting. We mounted and spun the horses around, ready to return to the camp.

"When you go back to the camp," Lobsang Phuntsok said, "continue to do your paintings. There's only a week left until the official car returns from Chengdu to take you back. We'll find a way to bring the original documents out. They've been safe here for almost twenty years. They can wait longer."

He threw his robe over his thin shoulders in the cool, post twilight air. The swirling robe was the beating wings of a giant red bird folding in for a long night. "Madame Erzebet, don't come back to the monastery. If you need me, send for me. It would be very dangerous for you to come here again."

The road through town was empty, the stores dark. We veered off at the foot of the hill and crossed the empty festival grounds to the river. Mid-way to the camp, we alighted to let the horses drink from a stream. My ears throbbed with the echo of cars on the main road paralleling the river path, coming from the direction of Yi-Lhun Latso. They left the roadway, stopping every few minutes to direct their headlights into the trees. Sparks shot into the air as the carriage of the cars scraped through the rocky pasture. Small patches of dry grass ignited, flared and burnt out. Voices carried through the thin night air. One was the distinctive voice of Kai Lun.

The men clomped into the reeds, searching with flashlights along the riverbank, and then climbed back up the bluff. Following Norbu, I grabbed the reins and waded across the river, leading the horses to a stand of pine trees. I stroked the sorrel's neck and muzzle as it nervously shifted from leg to leg, snorting and backing into the trees. Dry branches cracked like a rifle shot. I picked at straw stuck in the horse's mane as its hot breath warmed my face and arms. Norbu stood quietly, his arm around my shoulders, idly running his fingers through my hair. The men roamed the pasture, the red of cigarettes zigzagging in the air as they yelled back and forth, and then they got into the cars. Driving back across the field and onto the main road, they headed towards Manigango.

"This is bad. We need to hide the papers," said Norbu, his voice shaking. "If they come back and catch us. . ."

"We can't leave them here. We have to get the papers to the camp for Dhondhup."

I took the folder from my pack, rolled it into a tube and wedged it under the saddle between two blankets. Then we rode more quickly toward the camp, taking a mountain goat's stony trail on the river's west side. The clopping of the hooves rang in my ears, and I guided the horse to the soft dirt to mute the sound. In the freezing night, I leaned into the horse flattening my chest and arms against its neck to absorb the animal's heat. Hours later, we rode down the hill, around the lake on the stupa side. I couldn't spot vehicles in the pasture or along the road, but still I dismounted, afraid to approach the camp. The Jeeps could be camouflaged in the trees.

"Wait here," said Norbu. "It's too quiet for there to be strangers in the camp. The dogs would bark if the police were there. I'll go ahead and signal if it's safe."

I thought of sleeping at the stupa, but the temperature was dropping by the hour. I was already chilled to the bone and in the morning, if I hadn't died from hypothermia during the night, I would have the same fate awaiting me.

Norbu came back on foot, waving for me to continue into the camp. He led the horse down the dirt trail, and headed straight for Tashi Choegyal's tent. The dog growled and I picked up a rock to chuck at its head if it attacked. Who chained the dog in the middle of the night when it should be guarding the tents?

"Madame Erzebet?" Tashi Choegyal's voice came through the tent walls.

"Yes, it's me."

"Are you alright?" He came out and peered at us while he unsaddled the horse, tossing the sweat-drenched felts with the papers inside against the logs. "Go to your tent right away."

We ran across the meadow. In the tent, Norbu opened the brazier and stuffed in hay, yak dung and a match, while I climbed under the sheepskin blankets with my clothes on, curling into a fetal position to collect my body warmth. My entire body wrenched in spasms. Within moments, Lhamo Sangye appeared.

"Police came earlier in evening." She got under the blankets with me, wrapping her chuba around my freezing arms and legs. "Looking for you. Mr. Kai Lun in rage when he found out you and Norbu both gone. Did police go to monastery?"

"They were there. Where are they now?" The words shuddered out through my chattering teeth.

"Two cars dropped off Mr. Kai Lun hour ago. Police shot Jamyang and Yangchen's dogs before they could be chained. Police gone for now, but Mr. Kai Lun somewhere here in camp."

"Where?" Norbu asked.

"Not sure. No lights anywhere. Everyone scared to see what happens."

Nyika's bark halted the conversation. Norbu jumped up and grabbed for the stick at the entrance flap, just as Kai Lun burst into the tent. He motioned for me to get out of the bed.

Norbu shifted from foot to foot, both hands gripping the club, while Lhamo Sangye moved next to me.

"Get over there. Don't get involved in this. It has nothing to do with you." Kai Lun said to Lhamo Sangye. He ignored Norbu's weapon and turned to me. "Take off your clothes and throw them to me."

Without a word, I unbuttoned my jacket and started to take it off.

"Don't," said Norbu. "Erzebet, don't do it."

"Then we'll start with you. One of you is hiding the papers I want. Take off your clothes and throw them to me." Norbu stripped until he was naked standing there in front of Kai Lun. Kai Lun went through the chuba and the pants, finding nothing.

"Now you," Kai Lun said turning to me. Norbu grabbed his chuba from the tent floor and put it on, stepping forward.

"Get back, Norbu. Think of your parents before you get even more involved in this," said Kai Lun. He fumbled in his pants pocket and took out a pack of cigarettes and a lighter. He lit the cigarette and inhaled as if it was his last breath on earth. In the light of the oil lamp, I noticed his lip swollen out over his teeth and a blue-black swelling on the side of his head and remembered the groan of someone being hit as I hid in the temple.

Moving into the shadow next to the cabinet, I took off my jacket, dress, sweaters, and leggings, tossing each to Kai Lun who caught them with one hand and threw them on the bed. When I was done, he flung a blanket in my direction and reached inside the leggings, socks and shoes, shaking out the dress with the hummingbirds. He took my silver box from the pocket of my jacket and pried it open. Inside were the poppy petals and the yellow triangle of paper with Girard's description of the mountains. He stared at the pieces for several seconds, his hand covering his mouth. Sighing, he threw them aside.

Lhamo Sangye sidled over to me and wrapped me in a chuba as Kai Lun stubbed out his cigarette on the brazier and ripped the bed apart, layer-by-layer. He punched the pillows, sorted through the blankets. When he was done, he went through the cabinet holding the kitchen supplies. He took the kettles, pots and pans, lined them up and reached inside each, dumped the *tsampa* flour from the bag into a heap on the table, and ran his hand through it. Then he roughly gathered up my paintings and sketchbooks. I let out a sob. Kai Lun continued without speaking, but turned each painting delicately by the corner.

Walking the tent perimeter, he kicked at the bottom where it reached the ground, pushing it back and forth. Cold air surged in. I shivered and without meeting my eyes, he threw me another blanket from the bed and pushed out of the tent.

"Norbu, I stay here with Erzebet," Lhamo Sangye said. "Go to your parents'. Make sure they're safe."

She put more yak dung on the fire while I crawled on the floor, holding a candle in one hand, rummaging between the packs, searching for the objects thrown out of the box. The poppy petals were stuck in a crease in the blanket. The paper with Girard's writing was under the table, a shoe print ground into the corner.

"What happen at monastery?" Lhamo Sangye gathered clothing from the piles, set the bed upright, and arranged the blankets.

"I got my husband's documents."

She wrapped the chuba tighter around my shoulders. "You brought them to camp?"

"I copied them. The original documents are still at the monastery. I need to hide the copies here, where Dhondhup can find them." My teeth still vibrated from the cold. Grabbing a sweater and a jacket from the pile of clothing I settled in for the night, huddled next to the brazier.

Well before dawn, Norbu and Tashi Choegyal came to the tent. Tashi Choegyal handed me a tanned yak skin, the red folder with the documents rolled inside.

"I know the right place to hide them," said Norbu. "The place where my I hid my knowledge when I was a child."

"Go now," Tashi Choegyal said. "When through, Norbu, get out of camp for few days again. Get far away from Mr. Kai Lun."

Norbu led me to the giant, cottonwood tree by the river. White fluffy seed casings drifted in the air, the morning sun glowing through their silvery angel hairs. At the base of the tree, Norbu took a thick branch and dug into the ground, unearthing a box decorated with the flaming sword of wisdom. The box was empty. I placed the red folder with the false papers inside, fastened the lock and dropped the container back in the ground. We kicked earth over the spot, scattering grass and leaves until the area was camouflaged as the land surrounding it.

On the way back to the tent, Norbu turned abruptly and veered toward the hills, whistling for the dogs to follow him. I watched him go, my throat constricted. We had not said good-bye. I called to him to wait and started to run after him. He turned and gestured with his head toward the river. I looked to the clump of trees along the inlet and there was Dhondhup and Kai Lun peering through binoculars. When I turned back toward Norbu, he had already disappeared over the first rise.

# CHAPTER 38

## *Shameless in Your Thoughts*

| | |
|---|---|
| *Tan rok khyo la sem pae* | *Eternal friend* |
| *Khrel dang ngo tsha me na* | *If you are shameless in your thoughts* |
| *Go la gyab pae tsuk gyu* | *The turquoise on your head* |
| *Kae cha rae nee mee shae* | *Would not know how to tell* |

*-Sixth Dalai Lama*

### Lhamo Sangye's Story

Erzebet find me in the high fields on mountainside. She run up. Grab me by waist. Dance in circle around me. Maybe terrible night with Mr. Kai Lun forgotten. Everyone digging for *yartsa gumbu*, caterpillar fungus. Erzebet get down on knees with us, parting plants that grow next to *yartsa gumbu*. She dig around in soil for the orange fungus. Middleman take *yartsa gumbu* to sell in Chengdu for hundreds of Yuan. None of us very good at finding fungus, but even small amount of Yuan make big difference in our lives for entire year. Whole time, Erzebet happy chatter. Tell poems from Sixth Dalai Lama. I had not seen Norbu since they came back from the monastery, but now I wonder if he sneak back into camp and they find way to spend time together again.

Late in afternoon, we walk back to camp.

"What happen with you today?" I ask. "You so happy. Different woman today!"

"Look," she hand me folded piece of paper. "On this paper are the names of the men who killed my husband."

I have shock. After the day at lake, maybe Mr. Kai Lun change mind about giving her names. Why? He in big trouble if she take those names and go back to officials in Derge.

While we drink tea, she talk. Tell me her family and husband's work partners try for many years to get information about his death. They run into problems every time they think they make progress. Even her own government not able to find out what happen to husband.

I take paper from her and read names aloud.

Ma Yi
Wei Liang
Ying Liangzhi

"Where did you get this?" I ask. "Is this what make you so happy"

"Dhondhup brought it to me. We made a deal," she say, her eyes shine as she look over my shoulder at paper. "And yes, I am more at peace than I've been in many years."

"Erzebet. . ."

"With this information, I can ask the French Government to re-open the investigation about Girard's death," she continue. "Nineteen years later, I've managed to do what an entire investigative team failed at."

"Erzebet, these names of young men who work on crew building road past lake."

"I don't understand," she say slowly as she blow the butter to the side of tea, and reach again for the paper with the names. "They were working on the road, but they were also with the police?"

"Only one year ago. These boys work here last year. Friends of Dhondhup's. Not even born when your husband at Yi-Lhun Latso."

Her face go dark. Her body crumple into my arms and like the day at the Gesar Festival, I feel ribs of her thin body through her blouse. Her body and heart not made to live hard life like we nomads. Not made to have disappointment and tragedy come everyday of her life. The moon grows darker as it gets nearer to the sun.

I take Erzebet back to my tent to spend night Lotse, Dolma and me. Not good for her to be alone. It quiet in the meadow for hours when I hear dog's happy snuffling. Visitor to my tent. Lotse and Dolma bundled together asleep on carpet next to stove. Erzebet in deep sleep in my bed.

"Who is it?" No answer. I have shiver of terror. Like when I child and afraid of wolves leopards, and bandits. Afraid of own mind.

The dog growl. Tent wall push in. Someone lean against other side.

"Who's there?" I pick up club at entrance.

"Lhamo Sangye?" I not recognize the strangled voice.

"Lhamo Sangye?" It Mr. Kai Lun.

"What do you want?" Voice thick. I not understand his words.

I strain ears toward tent wall. "What did you say?"

"My wife died." He weeping. "The police came to question her. They were going to arrest her for something she wrote in a letter years ago. A statement against the government. She jumped out of a window in Shanghai. They took our son to an orphanage."

I fumble untying strings of tent flap. "Come in."

"No, leave me here."

"How you know? It can be mistake." I start to go out. Then pause. Not right I talk to Mr. Kai Lun at night. Not when he cause so much trouble in camp. Not when Erzebet in my tent, and Mr. Kai Lun try to hurt her not so many days ago.

"A truck driver brought the message from my colleague in Chengdu."

I speak again through tent walls. "Mr. Kai Lun, you have family who can go to your son?"

"No one. My only brother is in prison in Chengdu."

I must see this man. I lift flap, but he already gone.

When Erzebet wake in morning, I tell her what happened to Mr. Kai Lun's family. I tell only her, but entire camp feel something strange in air. He no longer write notes in his book. Before, he play with children at river. No more. He leave early in morning when meadow still sparkle with dew. Return after dogs unchained at night. Easy to attack him. He not care. Tsering see him hike up mountain to Tro-La Pass. He carry a pack. Lhamo see him lying in meadow's dry grass in middle of day. Sun beat down with no black grease or shade on face.

One evening, I see light through seams of Mr. Kai Lun's tent. I take dog on chain, cross pasture and stand outside. Not sure what to do. I hear talking inside. I relieved. He spending time with friend. I listen more closely. No other voice. He talk to himself. He say words from hermit's prayer book.

*When all who are close turn against us as enemies*
*This is the Wheel of Sharp Weapons returning*
*Full circle upon us from wrongs we have done.*
*Till now we've held grudges inside us with anger*
*With thoughts of sly methods to cause others pain*
*Hereafter let's try to have less affectation*
*Nor pretend to be kind while we harbor base aims.*

I softly call his name. No answer. I call again louder and reach for tent flap.

"Don't come in here," he said. His voice no longer follow rhythm of words I hear coming through tent walls. Voice flat. Dead.

I stop, dog squirming at end of the leash. "Is there anything I can do?"

"Nothing. Please go." He begin to murmur again.

*All of our suffering derives from our negative behaviors*
*All of us share in this tragic misfortune*
*From selfish delusions we heed and act out*
*This is the Wheel of Sharp Weapons returning*
*Full circle upon us from wrongs we have done*

I stand and listen again. Big breaths with sadness. Despite everything that happen in camp during summer, my heart care about this Chinese man. I take leash and pull dog to its feet to leave. Then I remember. I go into Mr. Kai Lun's tent weeks before and find him dying alone. His karma linked to mine. I quietly untie tent flap.

Mr. Kai Lun sat on bed. Legs folded under him. Wrapped in maroon monk's robe, he read from small book open on his lap. Butter lamps burn on table next to bed. Throw shadows across his face. Rest of tent in gloom. I confused.

"Mr. Kai Lun," I not understand what in front of me. His glasses reflect light of butter lamps. Make eyes look like steady, amber flames. "Sorry to come in. . ."

"There's nothing you can do. There's nothing anyone can do," he said. "Please leave."

His voice creep from hollow shell and he tell me tale I not believe. "Two thousand years ago, Confucius said, 'Incomparable indeed is Kai Lun. A handful of rice to eat, a gourdful of water to drink, living in a mean street. Others would have found it unendurable and depressing, but to Kai Lun, cheerfulness makes no difference at all. Incomparable indeed is Kai Lun.' " He bend his head. Return to reading.

I stand silently for few moments. Then back out of tent, leading dog across meadow, I swallow hard. Remember how friends and family try to help me through grief after husband's death. Vultures carry away my husband. Without my Lama to teach me and my children to care for, I would have been lost.

# CHAPTER 39

## *My Lover Has No Shame*

| | |
|---|---|
| *Dru shen sem pa me gyang* | *The ferryboat has no feelings* |
| *Da goe che meek ta joong* | *But its horse-head still looks back* |
| *Threl shung me pae jam pae* | *But my lover, without shame* |
| *Nga la chee meek lha* | *Will not even glance back at me.* |

*- Sixth Dalai Lama*

## Norbu's Story

I came down from the mountainside just days before Erzebet was to leave the camp. I had spent the last days thinking about all that had happened in the summer and where it had gotten confused. Where I had gotten confused.

When Dhondhup and I went to Erzebet's tent and I said the terrible things to her, I thought I was play-acting. I thought it was to fool my devious friend, Dhondhup. But, when I rushed from Erzebet's tent, Uncle Nyima Rabten caught up with me in the pasture and I began to see it differently.

"What happen, Boy," he asked. "Why you run?" I tried to get by him. I didn't want to explain my plan with Erzebet to trick Dhondhup. It suddenly didn't make sense.

"Boy, what is this crazy behavior?" I squirmed under Uncle's gaze. "What have you done?"

"I pretended in front of Dhondhup that I hated Erzebet. I pretended I was angry at her for not buying me expensive things." I shouted the final words, "For not taking me to Europe when she leaves."

"You pretended? Erzebet knew you pretended? Then why are you upset?"

And then, I understood. She knew I was not pretending. The words I had spoken had truth in them. She could hear the ugly truth in my voice. I had hoped she would take me to Europe. I had hoped for more time with her. I was jealous of her husband, even though he had been gone for years. In my heart, I knew better than to tell this to Uncle. But I took a chance.

I told Uncle the fake conversation with Erzebet, with Dhondhup standing there. Dhondhup so happy to hear our anger. Uncle listened. When he spoke, his voice was as taut as a sling cord as it zipped through space. He was doing everything in his power to keep it under control.

"You get these stupid ideas from reading? Don't you know only way anyone can leave is escape over mountains? You think only of yourself. What you think that poor foreign woman can do for you?" He shook his head and walked away. He left me alone to drown in my selfish thoughts in my thick brain.

The next day Uncle called me from the flock to the family tent. "Norbu, you must leave camp. Go to India to be educated." A simple statement, said as if it was a call to dinner.

"But how can I go? I'm a shepherd, not a scholar. My duty is to take care of the animals and my parents when they're old."

"Don't worry about such things," said Uncle. "I'll take over these responsibilities."

"But Uncle, it isn't necessary for me to leave," The thought of actually leaving my homeland made me fidget like a toddler. I wasn't ready to leave. It had been a dream. One I never thought would become a reality. "I can live the same way I always have. I'm a nomad, who just uses reading and learning as a pleasurable thing in my life."

"No," he said. "It's too late. You've changed. No longer a simple nomad. If you have courage, you must take next step." Over the next days, Uncle went to the neighbors and borrowed the money for my escape. He didn't tell them why he needed this money, but I think they knew. He combined it with a sheep here, a yak there, extra mutton sold over the summer. Money collected in a box secreted in the tent's dirt floor. He packed the bags for me, his beloved nephew, himself.

Uncle also gave me a large paper packet sealed with red wax. "Do not open until you sit in front of Dalai Lama himself." In a serious night by the fire, alone, he gave me instructions. If I was captured by the Chinese on the escape over the mountains, I was instructed to destroy the papers. Throw them into an icy stream, burn them, tear them to pieces if need be and eat every last one. Ne

"I'm afraid I will get sick and die going over the mountains. What if I'm too weak to make the trek?" I admitted to Uncle. I had already chosen five of my little notebooks to take with me. I thought of Erzebet's husband and his courage to help my people when he had come from the other side of the world. It was my turn to try and be as noble. But I didn't think I could do it. I clung to Uncle like a child who has fallen from a pony, sobbing into his arms.

"You afraid now. You be more afraid if you stay." He smoothed my hair and patted my heaving back. "Your life worth nothing in this camp. Erzebet leaving. Police come to question you soon after. When they come, trouble for everyone. During summer, you make decision as man to be with Erzebet. Now you must be a man and protect village. Time for you to go. Do not cause parents more sadness by saying good-bye. I will tell them later that you are safe with Dalai Lama in India."

I spent my final days memorizing the meadow and the mountains, fearful

I would wake up in a foreign land and be unable to recall the details of my home. I paced the shoreline of Yi-Lhun Latso Lake, prompting myself. Had I noticed the way the ripples broke against the loaf-shaped mani stone? Had I remembered to admire the fish as they swam through the reeds, gold streaks forming a latticework of light on their orange backs? Had I absorbed every inch of the meadow, inhaled the fragrance of every wildflower, and imbibed the dip and sway of the eagle, the hawk and the vulture as they circled looking for dinner on the ground? Would I be able to recall the heartache of the mountains, the hushed snowfall on the rocky outcropping, the luminous green of summer calling the nomads and their sheep to the high pastures?

The Jeep arrived at 8:30am to take Erzebet and Kai Lun back to Chengdu. Lhamo Sangye, Tashi Choegyal and the rest of the nomads were there to bid them good bye. I hung to the side out of sight of Erzebet, but able to hear the farewells. Tashi Choegyal had told me to let them get on their way, to not give Kai Lun an excuse for delaying their departure or turning against me in these final hours.

I wanted to hear her voice one more time. As on the first day in the camp, Erzebet was soon covered in the drapery of white *khatas*. She gave her friends presents of small drawings that featured their tent, dog, children, or the wildflowers they had brought her to paint. Lotse and Dolma received the magnifying glasses, small tubes of colors, brushes with Chinese calligraphy on the handles, and squares of her most expensive watercolor paper.

"Don't forget to do the correct shading on the leaves and the roots," she said. They clung to her dress, digging their shoes in the soft dirt near the road, and she wiped at her eyes with her shirt sleeve. "And don't make anything up. You must paint the flowers just as they are in real life."

"Will you come back to see us, Madame Erzebet?" they asked.

"I will try. But if I cannot come back, you must know I will never forget you."

I stepped out of the way as Lobsang Phuntsok ran past, carrying a small bag. When he got to the Jeep, he asked Erzebet if he could ride along.

"You can ride next to me." She didn't even bother to ask Kai Lun's approval. He lingered near the edge of the crowd, three *khatas* from Lhamo Sangye and her children around his neck.

The driver piled their baggage on the rooftop and tied it down with ropes. Erzebet looked around the crowd, talking while her eyes darted back and forth across the field, gazing up to the hills. I knew she was looking for me. I stayed hidden behind the tent, just a few feet away from her, my heart pumping with anxious blood, wanting to hold her and say good-bye.

When the driver placed the last bags in the Jeep, I turned and slipped behind the stone boundary wall and walked in a trance state to the far side of the pasture. There I stood on an earth shelf overhanging the river where it coursed the fastest. My eyes traced the water's path as it melted out of the glacier and traveled through the meadows. What if the soil gave way at the shoreline as I balanced here, gazing in a reverie into this deep pool? The dark earth held together with roots and decaying leaves was vulnerable to collapse and I would be carried away in an instant. Today, at this mountain stream, if the ground folded beneath me, would anyone notice at all?

I heard faint shouts and laughter and the sputtering of the Jeep starting up. Car doors slammed, horses whinnied and the pounding of galloping hooves carried over the meadow. While the engine revved as it pulled onto the dirt road and headed on the journey to Chengdu, I gathered the backpack and the blanket I had stowed behind the boulders during the night. In the pack, I carried water and food for several days.

I listened as long as I could to the Jeeps' motor reverberating off the hills, the horn growing fainter and fainter, then I turned and walked into the mountains.

I hiked to the ridge above the camp. From behind boulders and rock outcroppings men, women and children appeared, dressed as herders, but carrying packs on their backs filled with food and clothing to last for weeks or months. Most were strangers, but one man, Tenzin Jamyang, I had seen at festivals. He was a champion archer. The man always joked and played tricks on his friends and family. Now he sat to the side, not a smile escaping from his grim face. While we waited for the guide, the group split up and wandered in the hills on the pretext of finding lost animals or bringing back yak herds.

At the end of the afternoon, a man with a large backpack wended his way up the mountainside. He was a weathered stranger from Chengdu who spoke Chinese, Tibetan and Nepali.

"We travel at night," he said, "when less chance of meeting border patrols. Everyone must keep up."

"What about the children?" three monks asked. "What if someone becomes ill?"

"Pace not set by slowest person in group. Everyone must carry own food and water. Eat little. Drink little. Maybe days when no food." The adults looked at the tiny children already bent over by the size of their packs. They divided the children's food among them to lighten the loads.

"If someone ill and can't continue, they'll be left behind. Can make way back to their village if they have strength. We'll go on." I stared at the mountain peaks in front of us. Used to climbing and running in the mountains, now the trails ahead seemed filled with peril. It was my last chance to return to the camp and try to make amends. But even as I watched from the hillside, I could see the faint scrim of dust in the air from a vehicle approaching the camp. It could be a trader, a bus heading to Derge or the police.

I handed the guide the remainder of the money due, a summer of hardship for Uncle who had saved and scrounged from every possible source. Each person stepped forward after me, handing over money wrapped in newspaper and stuffed in yak skin bags.

Twenty-three in all, we trekked over the first hill and just kept going.

As the light fled from the sky, we made camp under rock ledges and rested for a few hours. The guide passed through the group after nightfall. "Let's go. Now. On your feet." Two nuns tried to wake the sleeping children by whispering to them, but as the group headed up the trail leaving them behind, they resorted to shaking and pleading. The children dragged themselves after the guide, the monks and nuns following next.

We followed a rocky trail in the moonlight. It wasn't long before we came to a wide river, the moon shining on the ripples. We waited for only minutes on the bank before we forded. The human line across the silvery water alternated taller men and women with those who were shorter. The current was too strong to swim against, but only a few people knew how to swim anyway. The guide told us to walk out as far as we could, until the water was up to our waist and then lie down, outstretched, and kick as fast as possible, floating to get to the other side. There was no other way to proceed. The cold penetrated my chuba and the water soaked my food supplies, although I tried to hold them high above my head. The strongest men carried the children on their shoulders. On the other side of the river, we spread the wet blankets on the ground and tried to sleep. For some it was impossible. For others it was the sleep of the dead, and they had to be shaken and kicked to move again before dawn.

For three nights, we trudged through snowdrifts skirting the edge of recent avalanches. The snow cast a strange blue light onto the travelers, moving in single file along the escarpment. Despite freezing wind, without benefit of lights, we stumbled on, yearning for the daylight when we would spread out wet chubas in the first light of day and huddle together in wooden huts and under rock ledges.

By the end of the first week, we knew how to cross the rivers with our clothing and food on our heads, how to link arms and make a bridge for the children to be passed along, how to hang onto the person's robe in front of us if we were too weak to stand against the current ourselves. By then many people had fallen ill. Cheeks that had been fat and rosy days before were sunken and cadaverous. Eye sockets were dark pits of misery. Children's noses ran with mucous night and day, caked and dried on their cheeks, in their hair and on the sleeves of their chubas. There was no sense in cleaning them up; we would just have to repeat it later.

Some of the skinniest people were the strongest, trudging ahead without complaining, even carrying the packs for others. Some who spent their time in the mountains, herding sheep and yaks or doing hard labor building stonewalls turned out to be the most vulnerable. I was one of these. Maybe it was the dried yak meat. Maybe the curd in the tin jar hauled out of the depths of a monk's bag. Maybe it was grief. I vomited everything I ate and lagged far behind the group. Just when I would drag my body to the rocky ledge where they rested, they were up on their feet, swinging packs onto their backs and moving on. I forced myself to keep going even though they were often specks in the snow, far up the mountain ahead of me. If not, I would be lost, food for the bears and wolves.

One night, I reached the group just as they were laying out food for the evening meal. I felt a rush of hot diarrhea running out of my bowels, down my pants legs, into my socks and shoes. I ran from the fire in embarrassment and changed my clothing behind a rock. The yellow, stinking clothes I rubbed in the snow and jammed back into my pack. When I returned to the fire, the group was gathering up the food, and preparing to leave. They handed me bread and *tsampa* and I ate as I walked. A half hour later, my bowels let loose again with a great eruption. There was nothing to do but walk on. By the second day, I ignored the rush of shit as it coursed out of my body and so did everyone else. I was not the only one.

I scrubbed my clothes in streams or in the snow when we stopped at dawn and laid them out in the sun. Though the air and the hot sun got them nearly dry before it was time to trek again in the night, the energy it took to wash the clothes exhausted me. After I rested, I could hardly manage to right myself again to continue. The others forced me to my feet. After two weeks I was sure I was dying and gave away all my food. I was too weak to carry it and nothing I ate stayed in my body anyway.

I was far behind when I saw the group waiting at the top of an embankment, looking out into space. Struggling the last steps, I heard a steady roar and looked down to see a raging river on the valley floor. The guide had said those who were ill would be left behind. I prayed they would leave me behind to die. Instead, they pulled me forward, down the rocky slope to the water.

I waited my turn to cross the muddy roiling river, planning to be last. I would refuse to enter the water. The guide would insist they go ahead, continue without me. "Norbu," they called, "Come now. Time to cross."

This would be the last river I would ford. Next time I would turn back.

I stumbled to the shore and walked straight into the water, my legs floated from underneath me and I immediately fell to the side, bobbing like a bloated fish which rose to the surface of Yi-Lhun Latso Lake. As the people on the shore drifted away from me, I turned on my stomach and swam mid-way, my arms barely emerging above the water. The stream carried me down, away from the people on the bank. I saw fur hats and sheepskin coats covering tiny bodies huddled on the shore.

"You are a Khampa. Keep trying!" they called after me as they dashed along the bank, thrusting long tree limbs in the direction of the water. My feet traveled ahead of me down the river, slamming against rocks, and tangling in river grasses. The water was surprisingly warm under my chuba. I hoped the current would carry me away and the journey's torture would be over.

"Don't give up. Pray to Dalai Lama to protect you," voices carried over the choppy waves. "Don't be weak."

The churning water echoed the words from the shore. *Khampa, Khampa, you are a Khampa, Khampa.* My head sank under the water and then lifted to the surface again, water streaming from my nose. I choked and tried to turn face down, needing to sleep, but the river threw me from one eddy to the next. *Khampa, Khampa, you are a Khampa, Khampa.* The roar of waterfalls was just around the bend and the river picked up speed, throwing me into tree branches and against boulders that caught my legs and arms and tried to twist them out of the sockets. A figure with a shaven head waded into the river and grabbed my arm. Seconds later, the river spat the monk and me out on a gravel strand. I tumbled and rolled head over heels, until I was crawling on my hands and knees over the rocks and the stickers. "You looked dead out there," my fellow travelers said. "Your skin blue. Your lips color of yak meat."

"We wait one half hour," said the guide. Everyone collapsed into a pile and tried to sleep while I dug in my bag for dry clothing. There was none.

The next day, we plodded toward an ever-receding rocky ridgeline, eventually coming to a view of a huge snow-filled amphitheater. "Oh, this so smooth," an old woman said. "No more dangerous than bowl of dri milk." We laughed and since we had spotted no patrols for several days, decided to cross the snow bowl during the daylight hours and camp on the opposite ridge at night.

The day was sunny. Everyone pulled their hats down over their eyes. As I had in the winter mountains when I helped with a neighbor's yaks, I tied a scarf over my face to prevent the snow from searing my eyes and blinding me. An old man was already blind from the snow's shocking glare and had to be led by the others. They took turns, but after several hours they tired of coaxing the old man along and the group tied him with a rope to a teenage boy's belt. They walked single file in the hip-deep snow. The children looked like an army of marching heads with fur hats, sinking with each step up to their necks. Just before noon, the sky glowed golden-grey and it began to snow. It was impossible to see anything. In thirty minutes, we moved less than twenty feet. I forced myself to stay close to the man being dragged by the teenage boy, but if they moved beyond my arm's length, they were gone. Muffled voices drifted through the snow curtains.

I thought we must be nearing the bowl's edge when there was an alarming, dull "whoomph." Everyone clutched at the hand next to them and froze on the hillside. The ground cracked and shifted and a wall of snow slid down the mountain. The trekkers were swept away, tumbling head over heels, screaming and crying. A body flying past kicked me in the side and I fell on my back. Facing downhill, I couldn't right myself. I scrambled to turn my body and stand up, but was pulled down again, as if by quicksand. I twirled inside a silent cocoon. When the spinning stopped, I couldn't tell if I was on my head or feet, but the exhaustion and illness of the past weeks receded from my mind. The hollow white shell was safe as a blanket made from lambs' wool.

From far away, pinched voices called from their snowy graves. "Help me! Help me!" Those who surfaced first checked for broken bones and then excavated for the others. Scratching and digging was all around me. They were coming up from the cold underworld, sputtering, spitting snow from their mouth and nose, coughing and sneezing to clear their air passages.

I hoped they would not find me, that I would be able to remain there and drift into unconsciousness, not forced to march along into more of the unknown. For the first time since we started the trek, my thoughts about Erzebet and the blue poppy seeds never found on the mountainside were not filled with shame. I watched with fascination as my breath warmed the snow. Crystal by crystal, the snow dissolved in front of me and then froze into a hard shell just above my face. It was like looking backwards through a mirror. The ice got thicker and I realized my fate. I would not die in a white soft blanket of snow, but with my face and head encased in a hard frozen mask. Panicking, I tried to kick my way out, but the snow enclosed my legs and arms in a suit of armor. Now I was also one of the people in the underworld, crying out for someone to find me, pleading to live. I wiggled my hands and feet until I carved a tunnel that ended in a diffused blue light. I was the last to swim through the snow to the world of living creatures.

We counted a nun, an elderly man from Derge, the children of Pema Tsering of Ganzi, and a shy young woman missing, now under meters or kilometers of snow or swept to the valley below to be carried by the spring thaw river to the nomad pasturelands. The trek started again. This time we chose the snowfield edge, rather than crossing the center, marching as before, in single file, terrified to make a sound that would bring on another avalanche. I fell in behind the men and women from Ganzi and the guide. The children holding the monk's hands and the elderly woman lagged far behind. When I reached the top of the pass and looked down at the bowl, I could see uprooted trees and boulders piled on top of each other. Spots of red and blue were hats and gloves ripped off heads and hands, or the signal of an arm or leg buried under the snow.

If I could survive this avalanche, I could endure whatever happened in the future. I was not a coward after all. I had survived death more than once already, so I must be at least as brave as the children who clung to the monks' hands and continued without whimpering or crying. I turned to face the next mountain range.

Thirty-four days later, we crossed the last pass before the Nepalese border, guided by the crystal moon. Eight people had died. Eleven were seriously ill. I staggered the final kilometers and my companions followed, frostbitten and starving, debilitated by the stress of the journey.

On top of the mountain, we pulled crumbled paper prayer flags from our backpacks and pockets and threw them into the air, greeting the gods and goddesses and giving thanks for the journey.

"*Ki ki so so, lha gyel lo!*" we yelled. "What a great view! What a great distance we have come!"

# CHAPTER 40

## *I Think About My Love*

| | |
|---|---|
| *Sem pa dee la dro dro* | *I think about my love continuously* |
| *Tam pa'ee cho la cheen na* | *If I meditated upon the dharma as much* |
| *Tshe cheek lu cheek nyee la* | *In this one lifetime* |
| *Sang gyay thob pa dook goe* | *I would attain enlightenment* |

*- Sixth Dalai Lama*

## Erzebet's Story

Dark vapors escaped as I breathed. The summer's promise had ended in a confused morass. I fell in love with a nomad as simple as that, playing out a clichéd, archetypal story of privileged white woman meets uneducated tribal man. The only difference being, this man yearned for me to take him to a bigger life—a journey and a task I did not know how to do. My heart cringed over the final conversation with Norbu and Dhondhup despite the fact it had been a sham. I was afraid Norbu had not known we were living in a time capsule, separate from everything that came before and everything that would come after. Had I known?

I attempted conversation with my fellow passengers, but they said little. Coiling into a corner of the Jeep, I closed my eyes, obsessively reviewing the summer. Every step of the search for Girard's murderers had met with an obstacle I was too slow-witted to overcome. I was living right where Girard had been, but had not been able to find the names of the men who killed him. I was tricked by both Kai Lun and Dhondhup. I should have stood up to the official in the musty room in Derge, had the courage to demand that someone lead me through the maze of bureaucrats who would have answers. I had been scared off by Lhamo Sangye, Tashi Choegyal and Lobsang Phuntsok and their dire predictions of catastrophe, but unwilling to test them and place the nomads at greater risk than they already were. There was solace at having seen Girard's documents, touched his handwriting, and torn off a shred of a paper I would give to Lilia to cherish. There was not a chance I would ever get another visa to China, much less be allowed into Tibet.

I had even botched the search for the elusive poppy seeds. Mountains full of poppies and I wasn't able to get there at the right time to harvest a handful of pitiful seeds. So what if I had completed the paintings? They were never truly the point of this journey—not for me or for the Chinese Government.

The car heaved over the rutted road back to Chengdu. I dozed off and awoke only when the driver slammed on the brakes just a few hours past

Manigango. In front of us, a road crew was shoveling away piles of dirt, sawing up tree limbs and hooking chains to the bumper of a truck, the other ends encircling a gigantic boulder. The driver jumped out of the car and came back with the information that the road crew had been blasting ahead and the boulders had broken off the cliff above. It would be at least 24 hours before the road would be cleared. He suggested we drive down a side road that would take us back toward Yi-Lhun Latso, but would then double back to the main road.

Two hours later, we came again to a road barrier—tree limbs and boulders being removed by a road crew dressed in rags. This one would be cleared in an hour or less. We all got out of the car, carrying bottles of water and wandered along the road. The sun beat down. My cheeks were on fire from the heat. I watched a herder with his animals coming out of the valley between the hills.

"Why do Tibetans write that prayer on the hillsides?" Kai Lun asked"I've kept meaning to ask that question all summer." He was staring at the mountain across from us. Both Lobsang Phuntsok and I followed his gaze to white characters carved into the hillside at the peak of the next hill. The huge, curved strokes said *Om Mani Padme Hung* Gouged into the exposed earth, they were outlined with new emerald green grass.

"Nomads paint the *Om Mani Padme Hung* stones on the hillside the first days of spring," said Lobsang Phuntsok as we continued to move down the slope. "It's part of the spring picnicking."

My eyes moved inch by inch down the mountain until the grass ended in a narrow dirt road weaving in and out between the hills and the ravine beyond, the view of the hillside characters broken by the tree branches in front of us. I put my hand up to my mouth. My mind transposed the bright colors to the black and white of a photo from years before—the photo sent to us from the Chinese Government after Girard's death. The photo with the marks on the hillside beyond a ravine. Keeping my eye on the hillside, I ran.

"Madame Erzebet," Kai Lun yelled. "Are you alright?" I hurtled myself toward the road and the ravine. Lobsang Phuntsok and Kai Lun followed, jumping over the incline and onto the road. In front of us was the steep embankment that went down to the river, the hillside covered with shrubbery, fern glens and skinny-trunked trees.

I held on to the branches, letting myself down the muddy slope, slipping into brush, following the narrow animal trails that zigzagged down the hill. Halfway down I could see the glint of metal through the shrubs. My heart was pounding. We all saw the fender of the car half-submerged in the river.

I pushed on through the bushes. The river gurgled, flooding over the hulk of the car, an odd juxtaposition with the silent rusted vehicle. The door had been wrenched open, a thick branch still wedged in the hinge. As we approached, a flock of sparrows flew out, chirping and heading into the flowering bushes next to the river. Clematis vines twined through the broken windshield, moss greened the dashboard and I imagined I could smell the lingering odor of burning brakes. Dark stains mottled the yellow foam of the seat cushion. I stared in wonder at three tiny blue eggs with brown speckles nestled in a hollowed out area where a man's head might have rested.

Blood thumped deep in my ears in rhythm with the creek flowing by. Gathering flowers from the riverbank, I placed them in crevasses in the vehicle. Both Kai Lun and Lobsang Phuntsok helped me until the car was covered with ferns and flowers and the river was running like ink reflecting the falling night. We climbed back up the embankment and walked in silence to the Jeep.

Back on the road, I gave up any hope of falling into forgetful sleep and stared blankly out the window, as the car bounced over the ruts and stones. Hours later, I felt a tap on my shoulder and in the dim light of the dashboard, Lobsang handed me a package with my name written in Tibetan calligraphy on the cover. I managed a smile as I unwrapped a small book with many pages. The hand-drawn images were almost exactly the same from page to page.

I flipped the pages and in front of my eyes, two hands moved smoothly back and forth, crossing and arcing, flowing like the current in a slow moving river. The hands closed, thumbs extended upwards, symbolizing burning, purifying incense. Then they opened with fingers raised to offer flowers of compassion to the Buddha. Fingers snapped out to the world and then snapped in toward the heart: spirits called in and sent away again. These were the hands of the TriSong monks gesturing in prayer, in the midst of their magic rituals, carrying blessings to end suffering for all sentient beings.

"Lobsang-la," my voice caught on each syllable. "You made this beautiful book for me?"

"I did. I drew five different ones before I got it just right. I got hair from the horse's tail and wrapped silk thread around it to use for binding. The other monks laughed at me because I made mistakes and threw one after another away."

Kai Lun turned around in the seat and I handed him the book. "Nice. Very interesting," he said turning again to face the road and lighting up another cigarette. "Your head," he said over his shoulder. "Is my smoking bothering you?"

"I'm fine. Go ahead." His face was pinched and his brow knitted in a deep furrow.

We stopped at small hotels so we could all sleep comfortably. My room had a hard straw mattress and a thin sheet, so I slept in my clothes for warmth and padding. After an hour of tossing and turning, I got up and removed the rolled thangka from the Abbot of TriSong from my bag. Unfurling it, I hung it from a nail lodged in broken plaster in the wall. The

Thirty-Five Buddhas of the Forgiveness of Sins.

Holding the thangka closer to the dim light, I inspected each of the figures. I hadn't noticed their different positions: some with hands folded in their laps, some with one hand raised or extended to touch the earth. They had auras of gold or rainbow and bodies of white, yellow, red, blue and green. I guessed there was a Buddha to match every type of indiscretion. Some robes were decorated in intricate gold floral designs, others painted to appear patched and worn. The gold designs caught the light and radiated off the thangka. Passing my hand over the painting, I stretched to lower and smooth the protective drape again and my eye caught a shadow on the edge of a green Buddha figure. It sat with the left hand open and the right hand raised, holding a *dorjee*, the shape of the key that opened the drawer with the hidden documents. There seemed to be a defect in the thangka, even a slight tear from age or the rigors of traveling.

Running my finger along the edge, I caught a nail on the torn fabric. It lifted, an entire section rising up like the door of an Advent Calendar. Something was written on the back of the Green Buddha. I took out a magnifying glass and looked closer. It was a name in both Chinese and Tibetan script. *(Gao Zhingzhao, Deceased-Shanghai; March 27, 1963)*

It was unlikely that it was the name of the man who painted this thangka. It was Chinese, not a Tibetan name. Rubbing my eyes I tried to imagine what the name meant. Gao Zhingzhao. Suddenly I was wide-awake. Gao Zingzhao. Was this one of the men who killed Girard, his name delivered to me in a container infused with compassion—a holy thangka.

My hands searched for another figure--another name. Scattered throughout the painting, hovering next to jewel-laden trees, more Buddhas sat on lotus pedestals, the corners of the images only lightly tacked down. Taking a razor blade out of the supply box, I carefully worked the corners of the small figures. In all, I lifted three Buddhas off the painting: three Buddhas, each with different colored skin, each with a different name on the back. I took out my book of Tibetan symbolism to read about the colors and the meaning of the hand gestures.

The right hand of Ratnasambhava, the Yellow Buddha, touched the earth and the left was held in the meditation pose. Ratnasambhava transformed pride into wisdom. Was it my pride and not my love that pushed me to come to Tibet? Pride that would not let me stop until I had triumphed over my husband's alienation. It was both love and pride that drove me to find Girard's murderers, to do better than the police, better than the French Government, better than Marie-Heléne Cartier. Behind the yellow Buddha was the name (*Zhang Haitao Chengdu, 1962-* ).

The Red Buddha, Amitayus, held its hands with the palms open in his lap. The text described this as the meditation pose and recommended acting with the speed of fire. Act to turn desire into wisdom. Had I learned anything from this journey with Norbu? If I had seen the Red Buddha at the beginning of the summer instead of at the end, would I have been more prudent with Norbu's desires and my own and transmuted lust and passion into the wisdom to solve the mystery of Girard's disappearance? *(Han Faichen, Deceased in Harbin; September 12, 1964).*

I was scanning the pages for the description of the green Buddha when I heard a scratching in the ceiling. My shoulders clenched. An animal scurried in the rafters. Shivering, I reached for a blanket. My eyes traveled across the transom. The shadow of a man's hat reflected from the hallway. I stared, barely breathing. Picking up the pen, I scratched out the names I had begun to write in my notebook. I blackened the letters, writing over them from every direction, until they were rectangles of ink. Pressing down the images on the painting, I slowly rolled the thangka and placed it in the suitcase, surrounded by sweaters. The sound of the zipper closing ripped through the room.

I fixed my eyes on the transom, my neck tense and temple throbbing, afraid to blink. Stowing the bags under the bed, I went noisily to the door, scuffling my feet to alert anyone in the hallway I was coming. At the door, I listened and heard nothing but my own thick breathing. Rattling the chain, I slipped the bolt from the door and stepped out. A pile of cardboard boxes teetered in the corridor, the top one casting a fedora-like shadow against the transom window.

The next morning the driver, Lobsang Phuntsok and I shared butter tea, hot water, *momos*, and bread. Kai Lun sat off by himself. I held my suitcase on my lap the whole day, afraid someone would steal it from the Jeep when we stopped. At night I went to my hotel room, refusing rooms that did not have a secure lock and chain on the door. When settled, I unrolled the thangka and again copied the names into my notebook.

I remembered back to what Lobsang Phuntsok had said to me, what would I do with the names if I had them? I didn't know. Gao, Han, and Zhang were all common Chinese surnames, held by hundreds of thousands if not millions of people. Kai Lun himself shared the last name of Zhang.

The closer we came to Chengdu, the warmer the weather, the better the roads, the quieter our group. I found it impossible to hold on to my toxic feelings. I sat in the backseat at rest stops and started a painting for Kai Lun. At first, I hid my project, but quickly realized he was beaten down, only interested in being by himself. He would not be coming over to talk or inquire about what I was doing.

After eight days, we drove past the last range of snowy mountains, through the rolling malachite hills and down the last stretch of highway. Thousands of people in blue pants and shirts rode bicycles into the city to work and school.

Turning on to a street filled with vegetable and fruit sellers, people carrying skinned animals hanging by their necks from bamboo rods, we pulled up in front of a grey cement building with a sign over the door. Lobsang Phuntsok read it aloud: Public Security Bureau. Kai Lun looked up dully and reached for the door handle. We got out and stood alongside the car as he gathered his bag from the top of the Jeep. We said good-bye. His face was a contrast--tanned with dark, vacant eyes. He wore the same blue jacket and pants he had on when we arrived in Tibet, but now they hung off his body, several sizes too big. He was a Chinese police official once again. Without emotion, he nodded at Lobsang Phuntsok. Looking briefly at me, he paused before he continued up the steps into the cement building.

"Kai Lun," I said, "Wait. I've something for you."

He turned from his superiors who stood on the landing, awaiting his report from the summer investigation and the hand-over of my husband's documents. He came back to the Jeep and I gave him the small painting of Yi-Lhun Latso Lake, jade in the sunlight, wildflowers on the surrounding hills, mani stones erect along the shoreline. Nodding his thanks, he went back up the steps without a word.

A few blocks further down the street, a belching bus thundered into view heading back to the West. Lobsang Phuntsok asked the Jeep driver to pull over, took his bag and moved to the roadside, flagging down the crowded bus.

"Where are you going?" Jumping out of the Jeep, I dodged a bicycle and followed him to the side of the road. "We've just gotten here."

"I'm going to the monastery," he said as he boarded the bus. "The Abbot sent me to make sure you arrived safely and had no problems. Have a good journey home. I will not forget you, Erzebet." He waved from the window. The bus spewed out a cloud of black smoke and pulled back out onto the roadway and within minutes had rounded the bend and was gone.

# CHAPTER 41

## It Is Not for the Turquoise Bee to Mourn

| | |
|---|---|
| *Me tok nam da yel song* | *About the flowers that fade in the fall* |
| *Yu trang sem pa ma gyo* | *The turquoise bee does not grieve* |
| *Jam pa lay tro se pay* | *It is the fate of lovers to part* |
| *Nga nee gyo gyu meen dook* | *And I, too, shall not lament* |

*- Sixth Dalai Lama*

### Norbu's Story

In Kathmandu, staff from the Tibetan Exile Government helped the new arrivals. They gave me medicine for diarrhea. I lay down on a cot in a cement room with hundreds of other refugees and thought I had never been so tired. After two days I woke, went to the clinic and watched as doctors bathed the frostbitten feet of the children and two nuns in warm water. Their black swollen toes detached and floated away in the bloody water. Some of the people in my group went out to see the big city. I was afraid to cross the busy streets by myself. I waited at the road edge until people who knew more darted across and then I followed behind.

"What are your plans?" the staff of the Reception Center asked me.

I didn't know. I didn't have any plans. "I want to see His Holiness the Dalai Lama," was all I could think of to say. I didn't tell them my Uncle had given me a special package that must go only into the hands of Dalai Lama himself.

"What languages do you speak?" A young man born in India who worked for the Tibetan Exile Government asked.

"Tibetan."

"Read? Write?"

"No. No." I didn't want anyone to know. Reading had caused me a lot of trouble already. But in my pocket that morning I had stuck a paper with seven new words to learn. Learning five words each day would not be enough in my new life. Refugee. Signal. Sewage. Cement. Option. Grumble. Intrigue.

"Relatives in India?"

"No."

They arranged for me to travel with my group on to India by bus. A translator escorted us, a man who could speak English, Hindi and Tibetan.

We arrived in Delhi and they sent us by another bus to Dharamsala, where the Dalai Lama lived. The bus was filled with refugees who had come to Delhi to shop. They arrived from the north at night and returned home the next day. They carried shoes, t-shirts, jackets, and burlap bags full of goods to sell or trade in the small town at the foot of the Himalayas.

The first days in India, I wandered the streets looking at the cows and the few cafés and shops owned by refugees. My countrymen walked in a daze, their bright red cheeks a signal they were "newcomers" just like me. The buildings were brick covered by cement. Not warm like the mud houses along the road at Yi-Lhun Latso. Those houses had walls so thick they were warm in winter and cool in summer. My room in India had sunlight for only an hour a day. Then the sun dropped behind the other buildings. We had to put on wool socks and our sheepskin chubas. Sewage streamed down the sides of the street. It formed a stinking mass when garbage was trapped with sticks and old newspapers in the culverts.

We trooped to the forest to use the toilet. Someone hung a blanket from a tree limb for privacy. It was close to the path going up to the village and open to the Dhaladhaur Mountain Range—a spectacular view while emptying your bowels. After three months, the Reception Center staff in Dharamsala gave me the option: move to South India to a settlement being constructed in the steaming jungle or make my own way in Northern India.

I moved into one room of a small house with six other Khampa men. We slept on thin blankets on the floor and cooked rice with meat broth on a two-burner gas stove. We told each other we were better off than being in Tibet. We talked constantly about what would become of us in India. I missed my parents. I missed my Uncle. Even Dhondhup. I yearned for the freedom to run in the mountains and play in the wildflower meadows. I had found out that school in the refugee camps was only for children. I was considered an adult. My education would have to continue as it had started, on my own.

"What are we doing here?" grumbled one of my roommates one night after drinking cups of *chang* and smoking cigarettes. "I'm going back to Kham. This place is a prison cell."

"How will you go?" I said. "You don't have money."

"Same way I got here," my roommate said. "Over the mountains. I'm homesick. This country isn't for me." Two days later, he packed his bag, took his blanket and was gone. He headed back to Nepal to find a guide to take him over the same passes on which he had nearly lost his life just a few months before.

That same afternoon, there was laughter in the hallway. Kalsang, one of my roommates, sauntered into the room. Two Western girls followed him. One was from Canada, the country north of America.

"These are my new friends, Katie and Carolyn," Kalsang said. "I met them drinking tea. They're helping me learn English."

The girls sat on the edge of the bed and asked questions. Where was I from? What did my family do? How had I escaped from Tibet? The questions reminded me of the first day I met Erzebet on the mountain at Yi-Lhun Latso Lake. Then I had been intrigued by these questions and the boldness of a Western woman to ask them. Now I found it disturbing. They took photos of themselves with their arms around Kalsang. They wanted me to be in the picture too, but I refused. Why should I be in a photo with these strangers? I didn't want to know these girls. They were too friendly. It scared me.

Two days later, I saw Kalsang on the street in a new down jacket. "Where did you get that?" I felt the thick puffy jacket with the elastic binding at the sleeves.

"Where do you think?" said Kalsang. "Katie and Carolyn got it for me. New socks, too." He lifted his leg and pulled up his pants so I could admire the wool socks. That night Kalsang didn't come back to the room. He stayed with Katie at her guesthouse. In the morning, they both showed up before I was even fully awake. They held hands and laughed together, while I fixed them bread and tea. Kalsang threw his clothes into his small backpack and was out the door. When he left, I sat in the small square of sunlight. I warmed my hands on a cup of steaming butter tea and tried to study my English lessons. More new words today. Courage. Asphyxiate. Beg. Toilet. Captivate. Wrinkle. Entangle.

When Katie left town, she gave Kalsang rent money for the next three months until she returned. He moved back in with me and the other boys.

"Now what?" I found the courage to ask him one night when we were huddled in our chubas. A coal brazier warmed the room, nearly asphyxiating us at the same time.

"I'm in love with her," Kalsang said, rubbing his hands together over the coals. "She's in love with me. She's going to take me to the Canada."

Three letters came over the next weeks. Each with more money for Kalsang. He bought good shoes and meals for all of his friends, including a thick wool sweater and an English book for me. Then he heard nothing. The money ran out. Kalsang had to borrow money from me for the third month's rent.

"Why don't you get a job at the café?" I had gone and begged for a job and had been hired to wash dishes there for a few hours everyday.

"No need to do that. Katie will be sending me more money soon."

Two months later, Kalsang and I were standing on the dirt road running through town, when Carolyn ran up.

"Remember. . . me? Katie's. . . friend. I. . .am. . . back," she said in slow, drawn out English. She didn't need to talk like that. I could understand perfectly well. "How. . . are. . . you?"

We had tea. Katie had a boyfriend at her university. They were both political science majors. Kalsang frowned and his mouth dropped. She looked at his face and shrugged. Didn't Kalsang know about that? Two days later, he came to the room with Charlotte from the United States. They met having tea. She was teaching him English. He wore brand name athletic shoes. He carried a small radio with foam earphones.

I kept to myself. The thought of meeting a Western woman made my skin quiver with shame. Made my body ache with desire for Erzebet. I remembered the smell of her hair and how she held me when I told her I was confused about my life. I was more confused now than I had ever been then. Kalsang and Charlotte moved to America three months later.

"Read this," said Migmar. We drank tea in the café as the monsoon pounded the tin hut and the streets overflowed with sewage water. I had just stepped into a drain hole and filthy water soaked me up to my knees. "It's a letter from Kalsang." We clustered around as he read. Charlotte worked as a teacher. Kalsang stayed home, watched television, and listened to music. There were photos of the house they lived in, a bathroom with a hot water shower. A black arrow drawn on the photo pointed to a toilet that wasn't a hole in the floor. *Guess what this is?* was scribbled next to the toilet. Another picture showed him leaning against to the fancy red car he had learned to drive. *Me!* announced the black arrow.

"Is this the good life or not?" the boys whooped and hollered. "I'm next! I'm next!" I fixed my face into a grin and laughed along with them. After that, I stayed in my cement room for days at a time and refused to go out. I was afraid such a woman would captivate me. I didn't trust myself. I didn't find Western girls very beautiful or interesting, but I might try to get one to fall in love with me, so she would take me to the West.

Everyday, I took out the packet given to me by Uncle, but never pried open the red seal. It was my responsibility to make the delivery, but I hesitated to go to Dalai Lama. A nomad boy going to see this great teacher? I was afraid Dalai Lama would read my mind. Discover my devious thoughts from the past summer.

I was making my way up the cow path on the hillside beneath the town when a boy from Kham passed me sprinting up the hill. "Dalai Lama is giving an audience," yelled the boy. "All newcomers are invited." I hurried back to the village. Everyone was talking about it, rubbing stains from pants and shoes. They heated a heavy iron over the brazier to take the wrinkles from their best clothes. My roommates took out their cleanest shirts and chubas. I went to a street stall to buy a white *khata.*

"I want your best *khata,*" I said to the street vendor.

"They go from one rupee with no design," said the vendor. "Synthetic. Silk ones are eight rupees. Take your pick."

I counted the change in my pocket, thirteen rupees, and chose the most beautiful one there. A *khata* with ivory designs and an ivory fringe. Back in my room, I dressed in my best grey wool chuba and put the packet with the red seal inside my shirt. I lined up with a hundred other Tibetans with red, windburned cheeks in front of Dalai Lama's Namgyal Monastery. One by one, we moved forward through the metal detector and the search line. Men on one side, women on the other. When the man with the rifle waved me through, I showed him the package for Dalai Lama. Told him I had been instructed to deliver it personally. An important looking man with wire-rimmed glasses approached in a grey chuba. One sleeve hanging down showed a very white shirt buttoned to the side. He was Dalai Lama's Private Secretary and held out his hand to shake mine. I had seen him in town and watched as he rode by in an official car with Dalai Lama in the backseat. He looked at the red seal of TriSong Monastery and motioned me to the side. He told me to wait.

The newcomers filed through and looked at me curiously. Then the Private Secretary took me through a garden at the top of the forested hill and into a small room, decorated with thangkas and flowering plants. They served me tea and biscuits, but I was afraid to eat with my nomad manners in Dalai Lama's quarters. After a few minutes, Dalai Lama himself came in. Weeping, I fell to the floor before him, outstretched my arms and pressed my forehead against the ground.

"No, no," said Dalai Lama. "Stand up." He put out his hand and touched me gently on the head and shoulder. I stayed crouched down, my shoulders bent and my hands clasped in respect. I was trembling, afraid to look up. It was not correct to look into the eyes of this leader. But the Dalai Lama lifted my head until I had no choice.

I handed him the package and watched as he pried off the seal. Yellow papers were folded inside. Each one had a story about a man, woman or child who had been beaten, arrested, or tortured by the Chinese army or police. Dalai Lama called in the staff from the Security Office and the Human Rights Office. They interviewed me right there, pouring more cups of butter tea, and asking everything about how I had received the papers. They had a tape recorder and took notes.

What did I remember hearing from my parents about the situation in Tibet during the years when these were written? What was the situation now? Were there Chinese people living in the community? How many? Were people arrested for speaking out? What was the monks' status at TriSong Monastery? Was the Abbot alive? Dalai Lama wept when I told about the many people in the village who walked with crippled legs and lifted tea to their lips with mangled hands.

He went out to do the blessings of the newcomers and then came back, listening to everything I said. When the interview was finished, they thanked me for bringing the packet, wished me well and escorted me to the front of the complex. It was then I remembered the silk *khata*. I ran back up the path and asked if I could see Dalai Lama one more time.

"Of course, of course," he laughed as I explained I had forgotten to present the *khata*. "I thought you came back for more biscuits." Dalai Lama took the silk scarf and draped it over my neck. I bent half at the waist with my hands pressed together in front of me. The Secretary brought out a camera and took my photo. I could pick it up at the front desk in two weeks time.

Taking the *khata* home, I folded it into a small square and placed it in the box with my tiny books from Tibet. I would save it for the day when I saw my mother again in the nomad camp at Yi-Lhun Latso. She would listen to every detail of how Dalai Lama looked and what he said. She would ask me to repeat every word. She would be so proud of her son who had the good karma to meet Dalai Lama. My promise to Uncle Nyima Rabten and my society was completed.

The days dissolved one into the other. Red starbursts of azaleas grew in the forest. Rain flooded the hillsides and mold grew on every shoe, shirt and book. Foreigners traveled in and out of the town. One day, a group of laughing Western men and women were eating breakfast at the café where I worked and I timidly tried out my English on them.

"We love your accent," they said. "Where did you get a British accent? Were you born in India?" I explained as carefully as I could how I had come to India. I used all the words I remembered from my talks with Erzebet and from the books I read, leaving out the complicated details of the summer.

"What are your names?"

"I'm Christopher. This is my colleague, Katherine. We need to hire a translator while we're here." They explained their plan to interview refugees who had just arrived from Tibet. They were lawyers working on the issue of Tibetan independence. "Can you get time off to work for us?"

That night I plunged back into my dictionaries. I wrote down key words I thought I would need: demonstration, torture, escape, prison, guns, beating. How would I explain my own journey over the mountains? I found all the words describing my ordeal and that of my fellow travelers: avalanche, river, frostbite, terror and diarrhea.

Day after day, the team knocked on the doors to cement houses where six people lived in one room, one person working to support the others. They stayed late into the night at the Reception Center where 300 people slept on battered cots lined up in a hall during the night, ate soup ladled from giant metal pots onto steel plates, and aimlessly walked the hills during the day.

"My father was killed by the police for praying to Dalai Lama," a young man wept into his chuba sleeve. I encouraged him to go on. "The police dumped the body in front of our tent. Demanded we give them money for the funeral. My mother never recovered. She committed suicide and we were raised by our neighbors."

"I was in prison for ten years for raising a Tibetan flag," said another. He showed us burns on his arms and legs from cigarettes and scars on his back from beatings. His leg had holes a knuckle deep where bullets had entered and never come out. Nuns talked in low voices of being raped. Forced to walk naked down the streets of their towns. I felt fortunate I had left Tibet before I became entangled in the brutal consequences of my summer liaison.

I became friends with Katherine and Christopher, spending long nights sharing tales of our families, and the countries where we grew up and lived.

"You're more than a translator to us. You're helping us understand your culture and the truth of the newcomers' lives. We want you to come to England and study," the lawyers said near the end of their time in India. "We'll arrange your immigration papers so you can enroll in a university."

"How could I go to a university?" I asked, wary of false hope. "I've never been to a real school."

"For people like you, there are special rules," they said. "You can take tests to establish what you know and you'll receive school credits just as if you had attended."

For people like me? They had no idea what kind of person I was. I was a man who had fallen in love with a foreign woman and dreamed she would take me out of my country. My face flushed with shame at how I had betrayed my love for Erzebet by pretending to Dhondhup that all I cared about were expensive clothes and her ability to get me out of Tibet.

A year later, the papers were in order. The team from England sent me funds for airfare. I balked. I told them it was too soon to go. I had responsibilities to translate for other foreigners in the town. I hid the money in my pack, as it was not really mine to use. Maybe in the spring I could travel. Spring came, the apple-pear trees blossomed white flowers. The rhododendrons clung like red balls to the mountainside bushes above the village. I wasn't ready. Summer came and the snow on the mountains between India and Tibet melted. The rivers coursed brown torrents through the valley, slowly drained off their seasonal mud and turned glass clear, a window to the fish and colored stones below. Hundreds more people escaped over the Himalayas into Nepal and came on to India. I was too busy translating for other foreigners in the town to go to England.

After my days were finished at the café, I studied on my own. I wrote notes in large blank books that I bought on the street for one or two rupees. From time to time, I took out the tiny notebooks from my first years of learning. I caught a mistake here and there--no, giraffes did not live in the United States, except in zoos. There were more planets being discovered all of the time. Men had traveled in a spaceship and landed on the moon.

Months later, the lawyers came back to our refugee town. Again, they hired me. They took me to dinner, bought me new warm socks and good leather shoes. They kindly reminded me they had arranged for my papers. I could come to England to school whenever I was ready.

"Do many people travel to England from France?" I had looked in the geography books to see how far it was from London to Paris. 343 kilometers. A very long distance.

"Yes, indeed," they nodded and patted my shoulder. "You'll meet a lot of people from France. There are French students at the university. You can go to France yourself if you want. We can fly there on vacation."

That was all I needed to hear. I made a new excuse not to go. I was afraid I would see Erzebet on a street in Europe. What if I walked down the street of her city and she told everyone what I had said to her in the ugly conversation with Dhondhup. What if part of her believed me and had forgotten that we were making it up? What if she hated me and never wanted to see me again? They would send me back to India because I was the kind of person they didn't want in their university.

The attorneys left for home and wrote to me. "Norbu, we think you don't want to come to England, but are afraid to tell us. Please let us know if this is true, as we'll offer the opportunity to someone else in your community. Don't worry. We'll always be friends, but tell us the truth."

The truth? The truth was that every cell in my body wanted to go to Europe and be educated. My feet were stuck in centuries-old mud in this town. People's lives were small and getting smaller. They wished only to return to Tibet. They built houses of tin and plastic sheets saying, "Why do we need to do more? We are going home to Tibet very soon."

The streets were filled with trash and cow shit was everywhere. Lepers congregated at the temple to beg money from foreigners who came to see Dalai Lama. Old men and women trudged over the dangerous mountain passes in the dead of winter to see their great teacher. Then they turned right around, and went back again. They wanted to die in Tibet. Foreigners told me how lucky I was to live in this rich, traditional community. They wished they could move here themselves. But they had houses and jobs in other countries. They must return to the university. They had the same dreams for their future I had for mine. To be educated.

A second letter arrived in late summer. I had been in India for two years.

*Dear Norbu,*

*Our team needs to know your decision. The university semester will start in January. If you come to Europe in November, you will be well situated by then. We will pay for your ticket, as well as all of your expenses for the time you are in school. We have arranged your visa. We await your decision and hope you will join us.*

*With Warm Regards, Christopher and Katherine*

I packed my small bag, took the tiny notebooks, special mani pills blessed by Dalai Lama, and bought a bus ticket to New Delhi. My friends saw me off on the muddy road far below the refugee town. Through the bus windows, they handed me meat *momos* wrapped in newspaper with a packet of chili for the fourteen-hour trip. Good-bye white *khatas* billowed around my neck. I waved from the broken window, settled into the torn seat and tried to sleep. Wind whistled through the holes in the bus and the broken windows rattled. Neither was as loud as the din in my own mind.

In Delhi, a British Embassy representative met me at the bus. The official dressed in a suit with a white shirt and tie and rode in an expensive car driven by a man in a uniform. The official took me to his grand home to spend the night. In the bathroom were bottles of perfume. I pulled out the stoppers and smelled them, hoping to sniff the fragrance Erzebet had worn. Not finding it, I put the bottles away, trying to remember exactly how they had been placed on the shelves. The next day, after a breakfast of more food than I had seen in months, and many kinds I had never tasted in my life, the embassy officials handed me my travel documents and escorted me to the airport, helping me navigate the lines. They waved good-bye at the gate, wishing me good luck and handing me a small British flag to carry wth me.

I walked down the ramp alone. On the flight, I spoke to no one.

"*Ki ki so so, lha gyel lo!* What a great distance I have come," I murmured to myself hours later as the plane landed with a thud on the London runway.

# CHAPTER 42

## *Better to Seal One's Heart*

*Gyab pa'ee nak choong thay'oo*
*Soong keh chon nee mee shay*
*Tril thang shoong gee thay'oo*
*So so'ee sem la gyon thang*

*The small black seal when stamped*
*Cannot utter a word in witness*
*With the seal of justice and truth*
*It is far better to seal one's own heart*
*- Sixth Dalai Lama*

### Erzebet's Story

Upon my arrival at the Chengdu hotel, the European coordinators for the educational exchange greeted me in the lobby.

"My God, Erzebet," they said, "you smell like you've been camping all summer. Your hair and clothes are saturated with wood smoke!" Everyone hugged me and laughed. "We look like mushrooms--your skin is permanently tanned."

They were anxious to see the paintings and sketches from the summer and arranged to meet in my room later on in the evening. That night we traded adventure stories of our summer research missions. One group had studied the effect of small dams on tributaries of the Yangtze River. Another visited all the local Chengdu prisons and studied the economic value of using prisoners as labor--for their own rehabilitation as well as to generate income for the prison itself. All of the teams were ready to leave China except for the prison labor analysts. They would do one more round of interviews and inspections the next day. The main interviewer, Pauline Cadot, was ill with diarrhea and a severe headache. She wouldn't be able to accompany them on the last round of interviews.

There was a knock at the door and a smartly attired bellhop delivered a sealed envelope with the appointment times and names of twenty-four prisoners to be interviewed. I leaned over the table and idly browsed the list. The name Zhang Haitao leapt off the page. One of the three names on the back of the Buddha painting given to me by the Abbot. How many people named Zhang Haitao could there be at Chengdu Prison?

"Can I go to the prison in place of Pauline?" I said as I gathered up the wine glasses and dessert plates. I kept my back to my colleagues, afraid my face would reveal my frenzied excitement.

"But why? You just got back from days of traveling." They stood and collected their papers for the next day. "Take a rest. We'll be back by late afternoon."

"I'm interested in the prison labor project. I don't want to stay at the hotel tomorrow. I'd rather go with you. Since I already have official clearance from the Chinese Government for my project, it shouldn't be a problem."

My colleagues agreed. It might be good to have a fresh perspective in the interview sessions. I would work as a member of a two-person team. "We'll check with the Chinese coordinator and see if there's any problem."

"Why do that? Pauline and I have the same color hair, minus the white streak, of course, and we're approximately the same height. I'll just go along."

They looked at each other and shrugged. "You're right. It's set. We'll see you in the lobby at 8:00am. The car picks us up right out front."

When my colleagues departed, I went to the front desk and arranged to have the English-speaking receptionist call the PSB office where we had dropped Kai Lun.

"Please tell Mr. Zhang Kai Lun I would like to meet him in the Lotus Dragon Hotel lobby tomorrow. I need to return the French-Chinese dictionary I borrowed during the summer."

Kai Lun arrived just before 8:00am, the same time my associates from the university entered the lobby to leave for Chengdu Prison. I introduced them and accompanied Kai Lun to the door.

"Kai Lun," I said in a low voice, "during the summer, you told me you have a brother. I need to know his name."

"Zhang Haitao." His head nodding, he let out a giant puff of breath. "Why are you asking me this?"

"Where is he?"

"Chengdu Prison. He's been there for many years."

"Why is he in prison? Tell me quickly."

He lowered his voice. "He spoke out against the government's treatment of the minority groups--the Tibetans."

"What? Why did he care?"

"He was in Tibet a long time ago. I don't want to say too much. When he came out of Tibet, he fell out of favor with the PSB and was imprisoned. He's been in Chengdu Prison for more than fifteen years." He looked around cautiously at the people in the lobby, dropping his voice to a whisper. "Madame Erzebet, I am sorry I could not tell you this before. He was implicated in your husband's death. But he also tried to save him."

We continued walking to the door where an official car waited for him at the curb, just behind the Jeep for the university team. "Have you seen him?"

"Not for ten years. A demonstration happened in the prison. We heard he was severely injured, but we were never allowed to see him after that." I handed him the dictionary and said good-bye. We shook hands and when I took away my hand, there was a small folded square of newspaper in my palm. Did it have to do with his brother? There was no time to go back to the room. I carefully placed it in my purse to be opened later.

We arrived at the prison after an hour's drive. In a dreary cement room, a stocky woman in khaki pants and shirt frisked me and poked around in my bag, pulling out each piece of tissue and my notebook. She opened the pens, emptied the film out of the camera and put it all in a separate tray. The bag was checked at the main office. What was in the newspaper packet? I broke out in a sweat; it could contain information that would compromise either Kai Lun's future or my own. I weighed the advisability of asking to have my purse back and then going to the restroom to see what was in the packet. I rejected the notion. There was nothing I could do now that would not appear suspicious. I couldn't afford to take the chance.

The hollow sound of our voices and footsteps boomed as we were led down the corridors and through a series of locked steel doors, each with a small window covered with chicken wire mesh sandwiched between glass. After a final patdown search, the team was shown into a cinderblock room with three tables and four chairs at each table. A clouded window was cut high into the wall. Bare light bulbs hung down in the center of the room and buzzing fluorescent tube lights lined the ceiling. Hanging on the wall at a careless angle was a calendar from 1974 with a photo of a woman with a red armband marching across a field. She held aloft a large stalk of wheat and workers with big smiles plowed in the background.

A translator stood at each table despite the fact that my colleagues spoke fluent Mandarin. The prisoners were brought in three at a time for a twenty-minute interview. Most were chosen based on their high production statistics in the machine tool unit, one of the main labor units in the prison.

The fifth set of prisoners to enter the room included Zhang Haitao. He swayed to the table next to mine looking like a recent survivor of a car accident. His head was misshapen, dented on the left side. One eye was either swollen shut or missing. His left ear was shaped like a pulverized winter vegetable. He dragged his leg; reminiscent of the monks I had seen at TriSong as they moved through the monastery corridors. Zhang Haitao sat down with a blank stare, repeatedly rubbing his fingers together.

I listened with half attention to my own interview and half attention to the questions being set to Mr. Zhang at the table next to me. "Tell me, Mr. Zhang," said my colleague. "How long have you worked here in the machine tool unit?"

I glanced over as Mr. Zhang looked at the translator and the guard, a question on his face. He was remarkably like Kai Lun, but was missing several teeth and appeared to be thirty years older.

"He's worked here sixteen years," said the translator.

"Thank you very much," said my colleague. "It would be excellent if you could let Mr. Zhang answer for himself. If that's alright, of course."

"Of course," said the translator with a smile.

"Mr. Zhang, What are your primary duties?"

The translator repeated the question again in Chinese. Mr. Zhang said nothing. Out of the corner of my eye, I glimpsed him, again smoothing his fingertips.

"Well then, what about the number of hours per day that you work?"

There was no response after the translator completed speaking. Mr. Zhang just lifted his hand and traced the outline of his face; starting at the forehead and continuing down over his nose, lips and chin, following every indentation and bulge.

"Please, Mr. Zhang, It would be most helpful as we study how China has succeeded in boosting its economy," the team member looked beseechingly at the guard and translator. "If you can answer just a few questions for us."

"Of course he wants to do that," said the translator. "Ask him again."

"May I help?" I said getting up from my table. "Perhaps I can ask a question he will answer." My colleagues looked between the translator, the guards, and me.

"Why not?" my colleagues said. "There's no reason not to try." They directed a question to the guards. "Is it alright if she changes tables?" The guards and the translators conferred and nodded.

"Maybe we could start with some other questions," I said. "Mr. Zhang, were you ever in the western area. Beyond Chengdu—on the Tibetan Plateau?"

The translator hesitated, but then I heard him say the Chinese word for "Tibet," Xizang, in his sentence. They were going to let me go ahead.

"Yes," said Mr. Zhang.

"What was your work there?" I lifted my pencil as if I were ready to record his answer on my notepad.

"Yes," he said, nodding his head.

"I mean, what type of work did you do while you were in Tibet?"

"Yes," said Mr. Zhang.

I called the translator over. "What's happening?" I said. "Can he answer my questions?"

"He has full permission to answer all questions put to him. Continue."

"Did you see a foreign man in Tibet? A tall man with blond hair?" My colleague reached over and placed his hand on my arm, pressing my arm down into the table.

"Yes."

"Does he understand what I'm asking?" I said again.

"We don't know if he understands," said the translator. "He hasn't said more than 'yes' for ten years. He fell and hurt his head. He's an excellent worker, but unable to talk. I'm happy to answer for him, but I am sorry I don't know anything about Xizang, so can't answer those questions. Would you like to know something more about his work schedule?"

I shook my head and gathered up my few pages of notes. My colleagues started again with their own line of questioning, the translator answering each query for Mr. Zhang. In the car, they turned to me. "Erzebet, who were you asking about? Did your questions have to do with Girard's time in Tibet? What if that man had said something that went against the Communist Party?"

"There was no risk for them," I said. "They knew exactly how much information we'd get out of that interview."

Alone in my hotel room, I remembered with a start the newspaper packet from Kai Lun. I emptied out the purse on the bed, sorting through the papers and notebooks. The packet was missing. I sorted the items and leafed through the notebook in case it had slipped inside. Finally, kneeling down, I moved aside the bed skirt to see if it had fallen out when I upended the purse. There was nothing under the bed but old tissues from a past guest and feathery balls of dust and lint. Picking up the purse again, I pulled it inside out and then saw the rip in the lining. Two pens, some change and the folded packet had fallen between. I let out a long whistle of air and collapsed back on the bed. How long I had been holding my breath I wasn't sure.

Picking up the packet, I looked at the newspaper envelope, wondering if the wrapping itself was the present, a message to me I would have to decipher. It contained bits of stories and advertisements printed in Chinese. Only a few of the characters were familiar to me. There were no marks other than the printing itself.

I slid a nail file under the tape and unfolded the paper. There seemed to be only dirt inside. On closer examination, I saw nestled inside the creases of the newspaper hundreds of black seeds, no bigger than pinheads.

*Meconopsis horridula,* the Tibetan blue poppy.

# PART III

# CHAPTER 43

## *My Flesh is Lifeless*

*Rang la ga ba'ee jam pa*
*Zhen la dun mar lang song*
*Khong nang sem pa'ee tsong gee*
*Lus po'ee sha yang gam song*

*My love who admired me*
*Has married another*
*Misery gnaws at my heart*
*And even my fleshis now lifeless and dry*

*- Sixth Dalai Lama*

## Erzebet's Story

### Paris, France: October 2, 2008

Mist hugged the shoreline of the Seine, undulating upward toward the spires of Notre Dame Cathedral on Ile de la Cité. A far-away foghorn let out a mournful blast. The discordant clang of metal striking metal rang out and voices carried up from boats passing below. I could just make out the lights of Pont de Archeveche glittering in the gathering darkness. A generation of poets had written that these bright lights were like stars. To me they were the Tibetan wildflower, *Stellera chamejasme*, so utterly white they harvested moonlight and reflected it back to all who cared enough to see. From far beyond the planet, the *Stellera's* meadow display might be mistaken for an ancient constellation, a star bouquet releasing a heady fragrance into the crystalline night air of Tibet.

"Misery gnaws at my heart and my flesh has become lifeless. . ." I ran my fingers through my hair, brushing back a wisp of white escaped from iris obsidian clasps purchased by my husband in China nearly fifty years before. My sigh seized the attention of my companion, Anja Schumann. Anja shifted her eyes from admiring the view from the hotel terrace and glanced in my direction. On the steps below, a couple argued. A high-pitched question was followed by the rapid clicking of heels that faded in the distance.

"What did you say?" asked Anja. My friend was a striking woman of 80 years, dressed casually in linen pants, a silk shirt and simple gold jewelry. "It sounded a bit tragic, frankly."

"Say?" I'm sure I looked perplexed as I stared into space for a few seconds. "I was thinking about Tibet. About the Sixth Dalai Lama's poetry." The disturbance in my mind cleared and I turned to face my friend. Anja leaned across the table and kissed me on the cheek. We touched goblets, "Well then, To a Long Life! To France! And to Tibet!"

I was two inches shorter than in my prime, my toned arms from years of tennis and swimming transformed to velvet bags. Yet, at 78 years, I was still considered attractive with a model's posture. Tonight I wore Italian shoes and a Vietnamese [illegible] silk pants. On my right hand was a gold ring engraved with the Tibetan prayer, *Om Mani Padme Hung*. Cast the first winter after I returned from Tibet, it was a self-prompt to be mindful in dealings with others, a way to heal a ruptured heart.

We lounged in armchairs on the familiar terrace of the Hotel Relais Christine, drinking Chateauneuf du Pape, and trading memories of the stupendous and horrific in travels together over five decades. Each glass of wine encouraged a roar of laughter and a new round of arguments about the proper sequence of events or even the actual locales.

"When Lilia was small, her friends and their families relaxed at vacation cottages in Provence while you hauled her off to near-death adventures on the other side of the world." Anja said, swaying her shoulders to the notes of a Franz Liszt tribute floating over the terrace.

"Because of those adventures Lilia can also recite a Tibetan poem today," I countered. "Not something everyone can do."

*Not something everyone can do.* I once again retreated into memories that transported me to the nomad camp, trying to communicate with my neighbors. Attempting to put foreign words on the days' events. Practicing Tibetan by reciting the poems of the Sixth Dalai Lama. Being with Norbu as he pursued his own course, attempting to translate his world into the language of the West.

*"What's the best way to learn your language?" he had asked.*

*"Do you mean the best way to learn my language or the best way to learn any language?"*

*"Any language, I guess."*

*"I'd say the best way to learn any language is to learn words that have to do with your own interests."*

*"Me, I'm interested in kissing. I want to learn words that have to do with kissing," he'd announced.*

A simple statement from a young man, is that when it had all begun? A young man who wanted to learn words that had to do with kissing. A statement that provoked, drew me in and pushed me through a door that had been ajar since Girard's disappearance. Who should be blamed for that transgression that summer? Blamed? Taken aback by my own question, I reprimanded myself for wallowing in thoughts about events thousands of kilometers and a generation away and pulled myself back to my friend. Our talk meandered between two languages and covered several continents, a crazy quilt of travels that careened from Asia to South America and back again.

"And then there was the beetle..."

"What beetle?"

"You've forgotten that night of terror?" Gesturing to show the creature's size and how it flew and ricocheted off the hotel room walls, I knocked a wine goblet from the table and it shattered on the stone floor.

"Now you've done it," said Anja. "They'll kick us out of here before the night is over."

"I'm sorry Louis," I said as the waiter rushed over. "Anja's making me laugh talking about how I tortured her and Lilia on vacations."

"Please don't worry about the glass, Madame Pelletier." He swept up the pieces and replaced the goblet with another. "May I bring a tray of vacherin? We still have some left in the kitchen."

"Thank you Louis, we'd love it," said Anja. He bowed slightly, crossing the room to attend to another table of guests.

Anja resumed gazing out over the Seine and I slipped back into my own reverie. I stared at my hand as I lifted my wine glass. The thinned skin, blue veins and age spots were like Italian marbled papers. So, I could look at my aged hands and think of Italy. Is that what all the traveling added up to in the end? Had living with people halfway around the world made me any more capable of facing my own aging? My own death?

"Did traveling give me any answers I wouldn't have gotten anyway through staying at home and gardening?" I said to Anja.

"Hmmm, so that's what's spinning around in your brain tonight." Anja leaned from her chair and patted my arm. "When you look back, do you think your world adventures changed you? From my perspective, you were often different when you returned."

I drew in a long breath, studying my oldest friend. "Change me? It made me an intrepid traveler, if that's what you mean. After the first years, when I was just out of college, I knew I could go anywhere on my own if I wanted."

"I wasn't thinking about that. You often seemed sad when you returned," said Anja. "Excited about your time away, but pensive."

When I spoke again it was halting. "If I'm truthful, those first trips also stamped a bit of an air of depression on travels. Confusing. I equated traveling with working things out. When it was time to take a hard look at relationships, my work, the family, I pulled out my passport."

"I don't believe I've ever heard you say that before," said Anja. "You and Girard changed continents like other people move between cities. You were a matched set in that regard."

"After he died, I was convinced Lilia and I would gain relief by traveling instead of stewing in our own melancholy. It was pretty clear, though, that healing for Lilia meant staying put--familiar streets and faces, a language she recognized."

"At this point in my life, all this traveling to work out tribulations makes my head swim," said Anja. "A street in China is not so different from a street in Italy. It's the people you meet. Or is it actually the opposite? Is it that the people are not so different and it's the streets that make the experience? A new geography brings its own set of problems."

It was midnight and we had been talking for hours. The mist on the river lifted. We leaned on the balustrade to soak in the lights of Notre Dame reflected in the Seine.

"Erzebet, you've been preoccupied all night," said Anja. "Is there something else you wanted to talk about?"

"I've been invited to speak at the Royal Horticultural Society about the 1978 Tibet botanical illustration expedition."

"How wonderful! When is it?" said Anja. "I'd love to be there."

"It's tomorrow night, as a matter of fact."

"What do you mean it's tomorrow night? I would think you would be in London already. I know you like to arrive days early for any such event."

"I sent Lilia in my place. I didn't care to go. I don't have the energy to leave Paris again this year."

When I had asked Lilia to go in my place, she had hesitated, wondering aloud why I had chosen her instead of one of the English botanists. I reassured her she was, indeed, the best person to speak for me about the trip. I had shared Lilia's apartment in Montparnasse as I studied botanical illustration to prepare for Asia that year. She was the first person to hear the stories and see the illustrations when I returned from Tibet.

"So you sent Lilia in your place because you're too tired, and we have just spent the entire day walking the banks of the Seine?" Anja rolled her eyes. "Tell me one thing. Did they invite Norbu Tenzin and is that why you didn't want to go?"

I could feel the corner of my mouth pucker in annoyance.

"That face answers my question," said Anja. "Did Lilia know he might be there?"

"Yes, she knew."

"I hope she did know and you didn't set her up for a possibly unpleasant surprise."

Anja and I each remembered in our own way the clash that occurred after I returned from Tibet and told Lilia about my short relationship with Norbu Tenzin.

"I don't want to hear this," Lilia, just a few years older than Norbu, had cried as she leapt out of her chair at an outdoor café. "It's disgusting you've been involved with a man as young as me. You're a fool."

"How dare you talk to me like this," I had countered in an icy, decisive tone that startled Lilia. And if I am to be honest, it startled me, too. "My own daughter doesn't give a damn about my happiness. Do you believe you can decide whom I should care about?"

A month after that exchange, Lilia moved out of Paris to Barcelona, entered the university to study architecture and fell in love. When we saw each other again, it was through a reunion orchestrated by Anja under the pretext of helping Anja deal with her own mother's estate. Only then could I admit that my daughter had touched a raw nerve with her comments. I did feel like a fool. My final moments with Norbu had swept away love and left tangled rubble in its place.

"Erzebet," Anja bit into a strawberry vacherin and wiped the crumbs from her lips, "You should have gone to London, not sent Lilia in your place. You've things to say to that man."

"If I do, I'll find another way to say them and that's the end of that."

"Don't wait too long, my friend," Anja countered. "The saying goes: none of us is getting any younger."

I flinched. "What if Norbu came to the presentation, and saw me as an old woman, not the woman he fell in love with years ago?"

"What do you imagine--he isn't older, too?" asked Anja.

"Of course he's older, but not much older now than I was then. He'll be handsome and youthful, but I. . ." I had always told myself our relationship was rooted in intellectual companionship and friendship. There was no denying the passion--the magnetism from the first day I met him in the nomad camp--his shoulder-length hair and teasing gaze. From time to time over the years, I had envisioned a reunion through the romantic lens of the mountain air of Tibet. I couldn't stand it if that beautiful memory evaporated right before my eyes. Before his youthful eyes.

"Look at these crepe papery arms. I see them out of the corner of my eye and it scares even me."

"Stop," said Anja. "He'd be shocked at how you've aged? What would he expect--that you're still 48 years old, running through meadows, jumping on horses, daring the Chinese police with your defiant behavior. That was a long time ago."

It was a long time ago, but aging was only part of my anxiety. For thirty years, I held hope the chance would come to reframe the harsh words that defined our last days in the camp. Now that the possibility was near, I couldn't face it. What if I were the only one with regrets for the emotion that fired our last conversation? I had to consider that Norbu had none and had closed the door on our time together as quickly as it had opened.

"I may not look like it here, telling stories and knocking wine glasses onto the terrace, but I'm in the last stages of my life. With Lilia there in my place, the dream is intact. Don't I deserve to have that memory stay as it was?"

"Forgive me for being blunt, but I think the memory is causing you pain not joy," said Anja. "I don't know what you blame yourself for, but it's been an undercurrent in your relationships for years."

"That's what I get for sharing my fears. You always force me to see things I'd rather be blind to."

"I agree we all deserve to keep our dreams," said Anja. "But frankly, you're not giving Norbu Tenzin much credit. And, by the way, it's not as if you've lived a life of despair mooning about him ever since you left Tibet."

The waiter appeared and stood quietly to the side, indicating we were the last to be enjoying the night air and drinks on the terrace. Looking up, we saw the other tables had been cleared, chairs had been discretely stacked on the side, and lights dimmed at the bar. We called for the check and gathered our purses to leave.

"Anja, I don't know if they invited Norbu," I said, taking my friend's arm as we crossed the terrace. "If he's there, I've asked Lilia to extend my greetings to him."

"That's probably as innocuous a request as one could think up," said Anja. "Lilia knows you well. You should hope she has the good sense to take it a step further if she gets the chance."

# CHAPTER 44

## *Sleepless in the Night*

| | |
|---|---|
| *Sem pa phar la shor nay* | *Because love has overtaken me* |
| *Tsen mo'ee nyee theb chok gee* | *I am sleepless in the night* |
| *Nyeen mo lak hu ma lon* | *When day does not bring my beloved to me* |
| *Yee thang che rok yeen pa* | *I am discouraged, overwhelmed* |

*- Sixth Dalai Lama*

## Norbu's Story

**London, England: October 3, 2008**

Rolling to the left in bed, my eyes locked with Greta studying me.

"Thinking about her, aren't you?" she said. She extended her finger and wiped across the thin sheet of perspiration prickling my forehead.

"Greta, let me sleep," I turned over and the clock's green glow blinked back at me. "It's 5AM and I'm not having this conversation again. Let me sleep."

"You weren't sleeping," she said. "You woke me up. I felt you thinking about Erzebet. What's going on?"

Thinking about Erzebet? I had been dreaming about her--her wild animal laugh, her legs wrapped around mine while a lightning storm in the mountains electrified the air around us. But long ago elation had been pushed away by a flush of shame, by the memory of my performance intending to convince Dhondhup that I was happy to break her spirit and humiliate her.

It was disheartening to know that a grown man could still regret something he did as a youth. It made feel stalled in time.

"Norbu?" said Greta, her bronze and grey streaked hair splayed out against the white of the pillow. "Don't go back to sleep. Talk to me."

I didn't want to talk. I wanted to savor in secret the fact that, in my desk drawer at the law office, lay the gold-edged invitation with today's date. The Tibetan blue poppy, *Meconopsis horridula* was engraved on the front. A red square in the corner depicted the Chinese characters of the artist's name, Erzebet Pelletier. The vellum insert read:

*The Royal Horticultural Society of England*
*Cordially Invites You to a Lecture and Slide Show*

*Wildflowers in Tibet*
*Exhibit and Presentation by the Botanical Illustrator*
*Mdme Erzebet Pelletier*

*October 3, 2008*
*7:30PM*
*School of Oriental and African Studies*
*Vernon Square Campus, Penton Rise*
*London*

"Can't I have a moment's peace?" I said. "I'm thinking about work. I have an important meeting in Amsterdam today."

With a look of disgust, she got out of bed and headed to the bathroom. Pausing at the bathroom door, she turned, "How long do you think I'm going to go through this?"

At breakfast, our two grown sons noted their parents' tense jaws, grabbed their food and slipped from the room. I feigned more patience with the situation than I felt, just to keep the second round of the argument at bay. The last thing I needed was a fight this morning, but Greta's jealousy gnawed at the back of my mind. It was three years since our last confrontation about Erzebet, the phantom lover from the past. I had been able to delude myself that I had conquered my demons and it was all behind me. Now, here I was, gutless again. I couldn't even admit to my distraught wife that she was right on target. Instead, I had grasped at just a few more minutes to sink into the memory of Erzebet and the knowledge that tonight I would see her again.

No wonder Greta was picking up on my anxiety. I had been too depressed to tell her about last night's meeting with the law firm. My twelve closest friends and colleagues had sat around the massive cherry wood table, their grim expressions a mixture of empathy and concern.

"Norbu, we need your help on this," began Harold Bryant, my senior partner. "We hope you know we have two priorities--your mental health and the firm's credibility."

"I know I've been distracted lately. . ."

"Norbu," my friend had shaken his head, "there's no need to go into explanations. Let me finish. We want you to take a well-deserved paid sabbatical. Right after The Hague presentation. Go on vacation. Get a good physical examination. Do whatever you have to do to pull yourself back. We want you here, but we can't afford the feedback about your distraction from these cases. Take as long as you need--and this is the hard part for all of us--we're prepared to negotiate your release from the partnership if you can't come to grips with whatever it is that's dogging you."

I'd wanted to argue, but just the day before, it had been a whiff of incense on a juror's jacket that transported me to a seat alongside monks praying at TriSong Monastery temple. In that case, the opposing lawyer had thrown up his hands in frustration and the frowning judge bided his time, his mouth pulled to the side, tapping out a drumbeat of annoyance on the podium. I wasn't even sure how long I'd been stumbling through my words, was it seconds or minutes?

"Norbu, your office will be intact, waiting for you," Harold continued. "Let us know if we can do anything to help." My partners had stood up and shook hands with me one by one. Some averted their eyes, and others reached out to pat my shoulder or hug me, as they would a teenage son who had been given an ultimatum about doing better at school. "Good luck."

If I thought I could go to Erzebet's slideshow tonight without a crisis at home, I was kidding myself. I had to talk to Greta. If she found out I had met Erzebet without telling her, it would start a barrage of well-deserved accusations that would end, once again, in a nasty argument and threats of divorce. And all because of my fraying the fabric of truth. Thirty years without seeing Erzebet had not dulled her ability to rattle me, and my family knew it.

"Greta, I'll be home for an early dinner." I ran through the drizzle to the waiting limousine and rolled down the window for a final good-bye. "Please be here."

At The Hague World Court, I presented the legal implications of recent cartographic discoveries that clearly defined Tibet as a country independent from China. The maps, drawn over the past two hundred years, might spark renewed interest in international support for a free Tibet, an issue I had worked on for almost three decades.

I filed the report and the Chinese delegation left in a huff, which was expected, even planned for. Focused on the task at hand, nothing disrupted my lawyer's outward calm. Not always the case. Unbidden memories could overtake me at the most inopportune times. Meadows like confetti-strewn party tables competed for my attention while I counseled clients. Leopards hungering after lambs edged out my concentration while I argued cases before high court judges.

Relaxing in the town car on my way back into London, I cringed remembering my last admonition from an exasperated judge. "Excuse me, Councilor Tenzin; do we have your full attention here today?"

"Yes, Your Honor." A client with a crease at the mouth's corner had evoked my stubborn aunt in the nomad camp. Her face was a wrinkled *momo* the whole two years she fumed at Uncle Nyima Rabten because he sent their daughter away to school. I had pulled my mind back to the courtroom, catching a chastising glance from Harold who sat, tense jawed, at my table.

I returned home from The Hague with an hour to spare. Greta waited for me at the dinner table, the food steaming in stainless steel warmers. I had practiced easing into the conversation, but blurted it out as soon as I walked into the room. "I've received an invitation. A showing of Erezbet's work from the Tibet expedition. I'm going. I have to lay this to rest."

"Lay what to rest?"

"I have to make peace with Erzebet. I don't care if it was thirty years ago. I don't care if I was naïve. I have to get this out of my head."

"You mean your heart."

"Please don't make it into a big deal." She flinched and I wished I could take back the demeaning tone. Unable to face my own confusion, I belittled Greta's anxieties.

"Big deal?" she said. "You're bent on insulting me today, aren't you? How could you seeing Erzebet possibly be of any consequence to me? To us?"

"Greta, are we ever going to be through with this?" It struck me that I was asking myself, not Greta that question. I loved her, but would I ever allow her to actually replace my memories, my fantasies, of a time and a relationship long over? "Erzebet was one summer on the other side of the world. Years before I even met you."

"It may have been years before you met me, but she's been a living presence in this relationship since Day One and you can't deny that."

"You're jealous of a woman old enough to be your mother."

"And your mother, too. Have a nice evening." She stood up from the table, walked out into the garden and stood in the rain.

How had I grown into a man who so held his emotions at bay—from myself as well as the people who adore me?

Two hours later, the limousine pulled up across from the School of Oriental and African Studies Library just as a pack of animals charged around the corner, crashing into litterbins, spraying saliva. Their necks yanked back as broken teeth snapped the air and nicked throats on the way down. They careened into evening walkers who jumped out of the way, flattening themselves against walls and display windows in defense. A woman in a velvet cloche was knocked to one knee and dazedly grabbed the arm of her elderly companion. She righted herself and then limped away. Were those yaks running in a pack on London streets?

"Damn mongrels are terrorizing this neighborhood. Wreaking havoc," muttered the chauffeur. He tapped his fingers on the seat and waited for me to give an indication that I was ready to exit the limousine. Instead, I continued to stare out the rain-blurred window.

I shifted position and saw the chauffeur staring at me in the rearview mirror. "Mr. Tenzin, Sir, are you alright?" Was I going to sit out here the whole evening? My eyes re-focused and the yaks morphed into street dogs, chasing each other, barking in an irritating cacophony. I gazed across the street just as the chauffeur handed me the mobile phone.

"Norbu," said the familiar voice on the phone—Harold from the law firm. "I know this has been a long day for you and I hate to interrupt your evening. We just heard from Judith at the Tibet Justice Center. Your presentation at The Hague didn't go as well today as we thought. Your argument had holes TJC thinks the Chinese will drive a truck through."

"Harold. . . "

"Norbu, no need for discussion now," he said. "The word is you're a sitting duck for the Chinese. You're on the verge of giving them the ammunition to undo all you've accomplished for the Tibet issue in the last three decades. I want to make sure you know what you're up against."

"Thanks, Harold." I handed the phone back to the chauffeur and looked across the street. People hastened up the steps to the building where light from amber sconces gleamed through the windows and illuminated the bushes outside. I saw Francesca Lennox and Sir Walter Harrigan inside the main room talking, drinks in their hands. I would have the chauffeur take me home.

Before I could tell him to drive on, the chauffeur opened the door and held out an umbrella. I took a last glance at the dog pack lounging on the sidewalk bothering no one and crossed the street, passing between the pillars at the building entrance. A small sign announced the meeting of the Royal Horticultural Society, one of the oldest and most famous botanical societies in the world.

I entered the room. Embarrassingly, heads turned and a murmur of recognition spread over the guests. More than fifty years after the Chinese takeover of Tibet, Tibetans living in exile in the West were still a novelty for Europeans and people were fascinated with my work as an attorney in the international community. I knew I captivated men and women alike, an individual who appears to bridge successfully both ancient and modern cultures. If they only knew the truth. I was a man on the brink of personal and professional disaster.

The Savile Row pinstriped suit I wore tonight told one facet of my story. Only my tailor and Greta knew the other. Embroidered in the seam of every article of clothing was a delicate insect. A turquoise bee. The angular veins in the wings were stitched with the finest black silk thread; the spaces in between appeared glassy and transparent. The body was exquisite, worked in the exact color of turquoise and lapis lazuli stones ground to powder and mixed by the old school Tibetan thangka painters. A glance at the bee when I buttoned my shirt was all I needed to be reminded of friends and family left behind, when days and nights moved at a slower pace, when I wore sheepskin robes to work, not expensive three-piece suits. A reminder of Erzebet at the lake, the air thick with the fragrance of wildflowers. A time when dogs were never mistaken for yaks.

Walter approached across the library foyer, his hand extended, "My friend, we were hoping to see you. You're looking a bit worn tonight. Are you okay?"

"I'm fine, just a busy week," I said.

"I believe this event will bring back many memories for you," Walter continued. "Francesca and I were trying to recall what year you first came out of Tibet. Was it before or after Erzebet Pelletier was there on her botanical journey? You were a young man at the time, but we wondered if your paths ever crossed."

"Walter, aren't you provincial after all. Tibet is a huge country and my friends always expect me to have met everyone who ever crossed through." I leaned away from Walter and kissed Francesca on both cheeks. "Your shawl is stunning, Francesca. Let me refill your glasses. I need a drink myself. Wine, Francesca? Scotch and water, Walter?"

Walter turned and greeted an elderly man navigating the room with a walker. "Charles, have you met Norbu Tenzin? He's a consummate spokesperson for the Tibetan independence issue."

"Really?" said the man. "Sorry to be so ignorant, Mr. Tenzin, but I guess I've lost track over the years. Are Tibetans still trying to get their country back? Hasn't it been over fifty years since the Chinese invasion?"

"Yes, it has, but the independence issue has never died."

"I thought the Dalai Lama had given up and even settled in the West."

"Sir, pardon me for being so direct, but you're misinformed. . ."

The call lights blinked. I nodded my regrets for the quick end to the conversation and took a glass of wine from the waitress. The crush of guests moved through the curtained entrance into the intimate theater. I slipped into a seat near the back, as the heavy doors closed with a muffled thud. I needed to relax and didn't want anyone watching me, asking questions and requesting my comments on the slide show. My heartbeat was irregular, speeding up, skipping a beat here and there. Maybe I shouldn't have come. I was a fraud. These people saw me as a calm, assured professional--unruffled by speaking before the United Nations or The Hague.

I dabbed at my palms with a handkerchief. The Tibetan damying's high-pitched music drifted through the hall, and a slender woman strode across the stage toward the podium. I gasped. It was Erzebet, moving with an easy air, smiling and gesturing to people in the front rows, acknowledging friends and acquaintances. She dressed in a jet-black and azure Mandarin dress, slit up the side, worn over satin pants. She wore no jewelry. She carried no notes. The familiar white streak swept the front of her hair. But, there was something wrong. Erzebet would be almost eighty by now and the age of the woman on the stage had to be close to my own.

I looked closely as the moderator stepped to the microphone, "I am sorry to say that Madame Pelletier could not be with us this evening, but we are honored to have Mademoiselle Lilia Pelletier, her daughter."

Her daughter--a relief. There'd been no need to go through the hysterics with Greta. She might have even accompanied me tonight. I might leave early to patch things up at home. Or perhaps I would stay and introduce myself to Erzebet's daughter at the end. Just a small greeting. Was it possible the daughter wore the same perfume as the mother and her hair might even smell like Erzebet's?

Lilia spoke. "Thank you for coming. It's a privilege for me to be here at this esteemed school as a guest of the Royal Horticultural Society. My mother has asked me to share with you the slides she took on her first trip to Tibet. Many of you know if she were standing here herself, she would have you laughing uproariously as well as holding back your tears with her storytelling about Tibet."

She held a book that, even from a far away seat, appeared weathered and tattered. The sight dislodged memories of rainy afternoons in Erzebet's tent, lying on a sheepskin bed reading. Always reading with a dictionary by my side, and notebooks waiting to be filled with facts, stories and questions. Passages penned by Erzebet wrapped around miniature sketches of flowers and watercolors of snow-covered mountaintops. Erzebet had been the catalyst as I strained to move beyond the confines of the nomad world. But the seed had been planted long before she ever arrived in the village.

*I wasn't more than six or seven years old. The late summer camp was set at Yi-Lhun Latso. The yak and sheep were close by the tent. The dog prowled, patrolling for strangers and predators out for a meal on a chilly night. I sat with my grandparents, mother, father, sister, and uncles in the tent. A fire burned in the center of the room, smoke filled the air, twirled upwards to the stars and then escaped into the purple sky. We drank butter tea and hot water, talked, laughed, and spontaneously sang songs of love and war and Buddhism.*

*The adults squatted near the fire and talked about the weight of sheep and the strongest yak. They told stories about the fastest horses and reminisced about who had won the festival races. They talked about picnics and the government and traded news of the Chinese on the border, in the camps and in Lhasa. They spoke about life.*

*"Pa-la," I had addressed my father with a respectful greeting and burrowed up the sleeve of his massive sheepskin chuba. "Why do some children learn to read and others don't?"*

*Pa-la's eyebrows had collapsed in furrows; the radiant fire and butter lamps glowed on his cheeks and bathed his forehead. The beads hanging from his neck were silver pools of light. "Who learns to read? Tell me who you're talking about."*

*"Tsangyang Gyatso, the Sixth Dalai Lama. He could read." I ventured.*

*"Boy, you ask too many questions. Tsangyang Gyatso was reincarnated from a long line of Dalai Lamas. He was our leader. He needed to read. We don't. We herd yaks and sheep all the day and sit by the fire at night. Meat momos? Sister, serve the boy. Enough of silly talk about reading."*

"I hope to bring a piece of life in Tibet to you," Lilia continued, "as I show the land and the people my mother loved, as well as the flowers she painted. With her permission, I'll read a few passages from the diary she kept during those months."

I stifled a cry. Was it possible she would read out my name? Thank God, Greta wasn't here. Yet surely, Erzebet's daughter was judicious enough not to reveal her mother's affairs of the heart to an audience of strangers.

"Preparing for this evening," Lilia said, "my mother and I rummaged through the contents of a hand-painted trunk from Tibet. It had been stored in the attic for years. The diary was wrapped in a traditional offering scarf and tied with a red cord. It was among amulets, a small book of hand-written love poems of the Sixth Dalai Lama, bone knives, prayer flags, a bag of sheep's wool and rosaries. Remarkable treasures packed from halfway around the world."

Beside Lilia hung the thangka of the Thirty-Five Buddhas of the Forgiveness of Sins. I blushed at the memory of the day Erzebet came back to the camp from visiting TriSong Monastery. She was hanging the thangka in her tent, excited to tell me about her visit to the monastery, but I couldn't appreciate it. I was jealous of the monks who gave her this beautiful present. I was a spoiled child in those years.

Lilia gestured toward the painting, "My mother believes personal and societal redemption lie in forgiving ourselves and others. No program about her time with the Tibetans could be complete without me saying this and without this beautiful painting to remind us of that intention."

Lilia's comment called to mind a conversation with Greta years ago. I had lamented my reluctance to seek out Erzebet and ask for forgiveness for the way I had attacked her in the final conversation. The way I had been maneuvering to convince her to take me out of Tibet, without her knowing.

"Ask forgiveness?" Greta had said, disgusted. "My God, Norbu, she was a woman twice your age. Don't you think she knew what she was doing? Maybe she should be asking for your forgiveness, not the other way around."

The lights dimmed. Lilia stepped to the side of the stage and turned to the first slides. I checked my watch and settled deep into my seat, steeling myself for a further onslaught of emotions.

A hum moved through the audience as three photographs lit up the screen. I leaned forward. In the photo on the left, two dark-skinned children dressed in traditional Tibetan clothes smiled for the camera. The boy wore a cowboy hat. The girl held a small Tibetan doll, also dressed in traditional clothing: a tiny chuba-robe folded across the chest, hair braided with red yarn, a necklace of small turquoise and coral beads. Lotse and Dolma. My head buzzed as I recalled them drawing pictures of yaks, following Erzebet from river to lake and back again like playful puppies.

Ten years after this photo was taken, I had already immigrated to Europe and was studying in the university library when a colleague sought me out with the BBC news printout. Five people had perished during an escape from Tibet. The news stated the names and ages of two of the dead: Lobsang Tsering (Lotse) and his sister, Dolma, of Manigango, Ganzi Prefecture, aged seventeen and eighteen. They had suffocated in an avalanche as they trekked over a mountain pass in winter, moving at night to avoid the Chinese border patrols. The guide had proceeded despite the mountainside danger in the freezing night. As I read, I had almost fainted in my chair at the library table. I had stood up unsteadily and weaved my way out of the building to sit with my head in my hands, staring for hours at crumpled leaves in the park's dry stone fountain.

Lotse and Dolma, smiling and happy, eager to learn. Gone. Their deaths had marked a before and after flash point in my life. It took me six months to recover and begin to focus again on the job in front of me--to become an educated man. Daily I weighed the wisdom of leaving the university and returning to Tibet. In the end, I made a conscious decision. I would not, could not, allow such information to undermine the momentum of my new life. The suffering and deaths of people with whom I had laughed, eaten and played were relegated to the past. Only years later, now that my career was established and my future assured, had the memories percolated their way to the surface.

*"Norbu, we want you to take a well-deserved paid sabbatical. Norbu, we want you to take a well-deserved. . ."*

I shifted my eyes back to the slide show: Yi-Lhun Latso Lake. The lake shone pale green in the sunlight. Buttercups, gentian and lupine covered the surrounding hills. The images to the left and right faded away dramatizing the startling Tibetan blue poppy in the screen's center. All eyes in the audience riveted on the tissue-like sapphire blossoms protected by a thick stem covered with sharp thorns.

Lilia spoke: "Finding the Tibetan blue poppy was my mother's obsession. From the time she first heard of it she yearned to paint this flower.

"She's traveled and lived in many countries, gravitating to places where people struggle with poverty, politics and cultural preservation. She tends to emphasize the strange and the humorous, glossing over the grueling aspects of travel to the other side of the world and making it all sound like a romp.

Here's a short passage from a postcard I received from her on that first trip to Tibet.

*May 14: "We're traveling through the most spectacular scenery, rushing rivers, yaks, sheep and deer running up and down the hills. Went over a 16,000 foot pass yesterday, glorious wildflowers. I am having a lovely time. . ."*

"Later I found out she had altitude sickness during that part of the trip--ill for hours with a migraine headache and vomiting. They almost had to turn back. We have a joke in our family that my mother tells such stirring stories about her travel that unsuspecting dinner guests clamber to sign up to accompany her on the next grand journey, blind to the hazards. We feel we have an obligation to say, 'Please, before you buy your ticket, remember who is telling this story!' Let me read another diary passage."

*June 25: We've gone to the mountains with the sheep and today he showed me the Lady Slipper Orchid growing against the rocks on the mountainside. We climbed for hours, over rocks and along muddy paths. I saw the first cluster, and then realized they were hidden in crevices, clinging to the rocky slopes. The color was brilliant, purple with stripes. Near them were magenta peonies and Dresden Blue delphinium.*

Indeed, the photos on the screen were stunning, but I could not take my eyes away from Lilia. A memory rode the wave of her voice and the damying's faint melody. I had trouble believing this was not Erzebet herself. Her familiar French accent; the way she moved her hands in arcs as she talked and casually brushed the lock of hair off her forehead. I smiled now, remembering Erzebet perched on the rocks outside Manigango. We had recited a love song dreamed to life by the Sixth Dalai Lama 300 years before. Leaning against each other in the sun, I had breathed the words into her heart. My lips quivered against the soft down on her childlike, delicate ears. She had shuddered; digging her nails into my hand so fiercely the crescent moon marks remained the rest of the afternoon.

The slides clicked through: the wildflowers, the mountain pass heading to Derge, the horse races, the river, TriSong Monastery. With each click, I hoped for redemption. I had wanted a slide show to magically discharge me from memories and regrets I could not release on my own in thirty years of trying. How exactly had I imagined that would happen? Did I think photos of Tibet would make me happy--seeing a glimpse of home? Did I think seeing Erzebet as an old woman would wash the memories out of my cells? Or did I think she would rush down from the stage and tell me she understood, that she forgave me?

The river. *Click.* Tro-La Pass. *Click.* Lhamo Sangye at the fire. *Click.*

# CHAPTER 45

## *The Jewel is Lost*

| | |
|---|---|
| *Nor bu rang la yor dook* | *When the jewel was mine* |
| *Nor bu'ee nor nyam ma cho* | *I did not care and ignored its value* |
| *Nor bu mee la shor dook* | *Now the jewel is lost to others* |
| *Nying loong to la tsang joong* | *I am overtaken with sadness* |

*- Sixth Dalai Lama*

## Lilia's Story

The lights went on. The audience applauded. I felt I had represented my mother well. The announcer stepped to the stage, thanking me and then led another round of applause. He said goodnight, warning the guests a storm was brewing in London and to be careful on the drive home. The majority headed to the lobby and the blustery streets. On the stage, I greeted friends who inquired after my mother's health and recalled their own stories with her after Tibet. When they slipped away, I reached to the easel top to unhook the painting of the Thirty-Five Buddhas. Out of the corner of my eye, I saw a man walking down the aisle and up the stairs at the side of the stage.

"A wonderful presentation, Mlle Pelletier," he said. The man looked familiar, but I was unsure as to whether we had met before. "May I help you?"

"Thank you. You can help me roll this thangka if you will. If you'll hold the top part, I'll roll it from the bottom. Have we met?"

"No we haven't, but I'm a friend of your mother's. I knew her in Tibet. My name is Norbu Tenzin."

He was just as handsome as my mother had said, years ago. Probably more so now, with the slight graying at the temples. I set the thangka down and he held out his hands to grasp mine. The tenderness of his gesture almost brought me to tears. "Mr. Tenzin, I bring greetings to you from my mother. She'll be thrilled to know you were here this evening."

As we began again to roll the thangka, Francesca Lenox and Sir Walter Harrigan approached. "Mlle Pelletier, fascinating stories and slides. A first rate presentation. We'll help you get things together here. The members of the presentation committee are looking forward to taking you out for a late dinner. Norbu, perhaps you would like to join us?"

I met Norbu's eyes and turned to Walter, "Is it possible to take a rain check on dinner? I appreciate your kindness, but I'm tired and I must leave for Paris on an early flight tomorrow. Perhaps we could do it another time when I'm back in London."

"Of course. I'll tell the others. They'll be disappointed, but we know you have a busy schedule," said Walter. "May I drop you at the hotel?"

"Actually Walter," Norbu interrupted, "I'm going that way myself and would be happy to have my driver give Mlle Pelletier a lift."

An hour later, we were relaxing in the intimate bar of Claridge's, ruby glass lights illuminating the dark corners of the room.

"My mother told me about your drive to become educated and about your trips to the mountains carrying books on the back of yaks." I turned my goblet in the light, watching the wine travel up the sides of the glass. "These have always been some of my favorite stories of her travels."

"It started when I was a child," he said. "All summer, while the sheep grazed, I read. My grandfather and uncle were in collusion. They taught me. My father didn't know I took books from the local school. The years crawled by and I continued to study. Finally I refused to hide my books anymore and carried them openly wherever I went."

He shook his head, apparently remembering the struggle of learning on his own. "When your mother came to the camp, we studied together. She was as obsessed with learning as I was."

"Tell me more. I'd like to know how you came to Europe."

"We all knew people were going to India to be educated, but for us it seemed like a fantasy." He signaled the waiter to bring a menu. "Forgive me Lilia, you must be starved. I've forgotten my manners in the midst of this reverie."

We ordered light snacks and I asked him to continue with his story.

"A person here or there disappeared and sometimes came back, but no one we knew could afford to do this. It was expensive and besides I had the duty as the son to tend the sheep and take care of my parents and grandparents.

"When your mother left Yi-Lhun Latso at the end of the summer, I fled just an hour later. My Uncle helped me escape; knowing if I stayed I would be imprisoned and the safety of the whole village would be jeopardized."

"Your parents didn't know where you'd gone?"

"No one knew except my Uncle. When I disappeared, my parents even went to the government to file a missing person report. After four months, they received my letter telling them I was in India.

"When I got to India, I lived with other young Tibetans. I was unsure about what I was doing in India and if I should stay. I kept a packet of papers given to me by my Uncle inside my bag. One morning I woke and felt fully recovered and it struck me. I have something for the Dalai Lama. I had promised I would deliver it in person."

"Were these my father's notes?" I asked.

"How did you know?"

"I didn't. I never really got the straight story on what happened with those papers. We didn't know how or where they surfaced. When I turned thirty, my mother gave me a gold locket set in turquoise. Inside was a scrap of paper. She had torn it from the original documents. Now my own daughter wears it along with a rabbit-shaped pendant I had given my father before he went to Tibet."

"You probably know the entire reason for your mother's expedition to Tibet was a ruse to see if she could surface the papers."

"She was never after the documents--at least not in the beginning. She went there searching for the names of the people who caused my father's death. She wanted them brought to justice. She wanted to know she had taken the investigation as far as it could go."

"I read in the London Times that your mother turned the names over to the French authorities after her return from Tibet. I hope it brought her a sense of closure. The papers along with the names helped re-open the international conversation about China and Tibet. The Tibetan Exile Government sent the documents to human rights groups around the world. Your father's research became an integral part of the ongoing campaign to free Tibet. You both should be proud."

I felt spent, ready to wrap up the evening. Yet, what we had not discussed in the car or while drinking wine was my mother's and his relationship. The topic hung in the air between us, a palpable entity.

"I can't continue without speaking about your mother," he said, letting out a sigh. "Do you know about your mother's and my relationship when she was in Tibet?"

"I've known for many years," I said. "In fact, when my mother told me, it caused one of our biggest fights and one of our biggest reconciliations."

"The reason it was so imperative for me to leave Tibet was because of my relationship with her. It was certain I would be arrested after she left. Of course, I knew this as a possibility all the way through the summer. I couldn't stop myself. I was falling apart. Loving your mother and wanting to leave Tibet. How could I not love your mother? She was a shining presence in the camp. Everyone was indebted to her because of what your father did for us by saving the Abbot of TriSong Monastery, but by the time she left, she had carved her own niche in our lives. She taught me to be alive that summer, to care about my dreams. She showed me what it was to act with integrity and follow through on a mission years after the fact."

"Could she have helped you leave Tibet?"

"I don't think so. It would have been impossible in those years. The borders were closed. I couldn't figure out which way to turn and needed to blame someone. Your mother appeared as a convenient scapegoat. My Uncle saw what was happening to me and got me out. I imagine your mother never forgave me for how it ended."

"She understood the conditions there." I shifted in my chair and had a shiver of remembrance as I brushed my hair off my forehead. It was as if my words to Norbu came from my mother herself. "She knew what you were going through and what was at stake for everyone in the camp. I'm quite sure she wouldn't want you to blame yourself."

"Thank you for that assurance. I was young and confused, said many things I shouldn't have. I've never had the courage to contact her to make it right."

"My mother talked to me once about her own role in what happened that summer. She didn't take it lightly. She feared she had encouraged you to enter into a situation that was too difficult, too extreme for you as a young man."

"I wish it was that simple," he said, gesturing to the waiter to pour more wine. "My life-long regret is that I was the one who pursued your mother. At first, I only wanted an education and to leave Tibet. I thought your mother could help me do that. In my mind, she was my only hope. Early on, however, I fell in love with her. It became much more complicated."

"She was dealing with her own struggles." I rested my chin in my palm as I gazed at him. "It was just after the death of her father and she was a woman approaching middle age, without her husband, whose death was assumed, but the body never recovered. These weren't simple times for her, either. As her daughter, I thank you for expressing your regrets."

"There's more, unfortunately." The muscles of his jaw tensed and he took a deep breath. "She wanted so badly to find the blue poppy seeds; I've regretted not being able to help her do that. In the final days in the camp, I could have gone back to the high mountains to find the seeds, but I never did. I never saw my own family again after I left Tibet. I can only imagine her sadness at not being able to realize her dream to give a gift to her father's friend."

"The blue poppy seeds? But, she got them."

"She. . .what?"

"She got them anyway."

"But how?"

"The Chinese spy."

"Kai Lun?" he laughed. "Well, I guess I owe him a debt of gratitude. He was a better man than me. I think your mother turned out to be more than he expected to handle."

I laughed. "To tell you the truth, I don't know that my mother has changed so much over the years."

I shifted in my seat, getting ready to leave. "I have a present for you from my mother." I opened my purse and took out a small packet wrapped in kingfisher-blue silk brocade, tied with a red blessing cord. "She sent this in case you were here tonight."

I handed it to him, and he slipped it into his pocket. "If you don't mind, I'll wait to open it until I reach home." He kissed me on the cheek and then walked with me through the lobby to the elevator. "Please tell your mother thank you for me. Give her my love. It would be my pleasure to see her again."

After spending such a lovely time with Norbu, I went to my room and called Paris. My head was light with the conversation and my happiness to relay to my mother what he had said. In fact, it had healed something for me, too, believing all of those years that he had only used my mother for his own purposes, and never knowing just what those purposes might have been. Anja, not my mother, answered the telephone. "Bonsoir, Anja. It's Lilia."

"How did the evening go, dear?" Anja's voice was strained.

"It was wonderful. I'm still here in London. Leaving for Paris tomorrow. May I speak to Maman?"

"Lilia, she isn't feeling well. I'll put her on, but I'm not sure she can speak to you." She whispered into the phone, "Lilia, if you can get a night flight, you should."

"What do you mean? What happened?" I quickly moved to my suitcase and gathered my clothes off the bed and the chair and placed them inside, the phone cradled between my chin and shoulder.

"Your mother appears to have had a stroke. Just moments ago. The ambulance is on the way. I'll hold the phone for her."

"Maman," I said, tears flooding my eyes, trying to maintain calm in my voice. "Maman, can you hear me?" There was a soft, slurring sound and whispering in the background. "Maman, I'm coming home. I love you. I'll be there in a few hours."

"She nodded her head, Lilia," said Anja. "Don't worry. I'll be with her."

"Please hold the phone for her again. I need to tell her one more thing."

There was a shuffling and the sound of slow, labored breathing in the phone. "Lilia," said my mother, her voice was thick, dragging out the syllables.

"Maman, Norbu Tenzin was at the slide show and he sends his love to you." The phone crackled, a drawn out exchange happened between the two women in Paris. Anja came back on.

"Your mother wants to know, were you able to give him the gift?"

"Yes. He has the gift. He said he would open it in private at home." I called the bellhop to retrieve my suitcases, reached up and closed the curtains against the lights of the city.

# CHAPTER 46

## *From Lithang, I Shall Return*

| | |
|---|---|
| *Cha de trung trung gar mo* | *White crane* |
| *Nga la shok tsel yar thang* | *Lend me the power of your wings* |
| *Tha ring gyang la mee tro* | *I will not fly far* |
| *Lee thang gor nay leb yong* | *From Lithang, I shall return* |

*- Sixth Dalai Lama*

## Norbu's Story

It was past midnight when I arrived at the house. The sidewalk still wet from the early evening storm, a breeze shook water out of the locust tree and caused a second rainfall as I stepped onto the porch. It occurred to me I was emerging out of a trance, and had woken to a part of my life I had forgotten while asleep--an angry wife I had left in tears just a few hours before. I entered the foyer and headed for the study at the end of the hall. As I passed the formal living room, lights and voices spilled out into the hallway.

"What's happening here?" I asked, standing in the doorway. Greta and our two sons lounged on the sofa and in the armchairs. "What are you three doing up?"

Greta stood and came over, kissed me on the cheek, and took my arm, "Would you join us? We're finishing a little cognac and waiting up for you. How was the evening, Norbu? Did it go well?"

I looked at her with curiosity. She smiled. My trepidation over returning home dissipated in her calm. It was as if the evening's reflective mood had drifted from the slide show and the hotel where I spoke with Lilia and alighted here, in this drawing room. My family had been privy to too many nights of anxiety as I mused over my life in Tibet. Now they waited for me to recount the evening.

"I'm too tired to talk," I said. I was afraid if I related the evening too soon, the relief would retreat from its tentative resting place in my cells. I wasn't ready to be so exposed. "I promise I'll tell it all to you inquisitive people in the morning. I will say it was a wonderful event even though it stirred up many painful memories. Erzebet was not there. Her daughter gave the presentation. She is much like her mother."

Greta handed me a glass of cognac, I kissed her again and retreated down the hall to my study. "Norbu," she followed me and took my arm. "Erzebet called tonight from Paris. She talked to Tsetan and Nyima and then to me."

"I'm sorry," I said, reaching out to take her hand. I searched her eyes for anger, but there was none. "I had no idea. . ."

"It wasn't like that. I was still so upset, but hearing her voice. . . For the first time I could feel how long ago it all was. It wasn't easy for her to call me, a stranger married to you. She said she had thought to pick up the phone many times over the years, but didn't want to disrupt your life. Her openness shifted something heavy out of my heart. Our conversation was cut short. She wasn't feeling well, but we'll talk again."

Erzebet, who asked so many questions and pried into the nomads' lives, getting them to talk about their families and their hopes and fears. She sent her daughter to me and now bridged the divide with Greta. I hugged my wife and continued down the hall. She went back to be with our sons.

In the study, I fell into the leather wingback chair, my eyes traveling over the wall in front of me. Bookcases filled with law journals and legal texts stretched from the floor to the ceiling, a rolling ladder accessing those near the top. In a frame on my desk were photos of me and Greta in Paris; me as a young refugee in Dharamsala; standing next to the XIVth Dalai Lama in San Francisco at a World Peace Conference in the 1990's; Greta and the boys on a beach in Greece.

It was on that vacation in Greece I had fallen in love with Greta all over again. That night I had admitted I was ashamed of the tiny notebooks I had kept in Tibet. Before that lovely evening I hadn't shown them to a soul except for Erzebet. I feared someone might ask where I was educated and I would have to tell them I'd never been to school before I arrived in Europe. Greta marveled at their precision and complexity. She'd exclaimed at the breadth of knowledge they contained. "Norbu, your lack of formal education as a young man is your hallmark," she'd said. "What you accomplished living as a nomad, educating yourself, should be your greatest pride. Not your greatest shame."

Nyima and Tsetan had run in from the sand and the ocean and cuddled on my lap while I reminisced about the Tibetan sky, the winter cold and the eagles stalking the spring lambs. Greta had listened from a nearby chair. "Read to them from the little books," she said. I removed a special book from the wooden chest with the dragons and flaming swords of wisdom carved on the sides and read.

"The kangaroo had thick fur." My hands had caressed my sons' silky hair. It was the beginning of a nightly ritual that carried on until my sons were far too old to be read to. "Strong back legs for jumping and the female kangaroos carried the babies in a pouch in the front. The kangaroo is extinct."

"But Dad, that's not true," they'd jumped up and down on the bed in protest. "Kangaroos aren't extinct, they live in Australia. We saw one at the London zoo."

"It was true then. In that different world."

I turned in my chair in the study, my eyes drifting from the photos to two maps on the wall behind me. The sepia-toned antique map drawn in the late 1800's depicted Tibet as large as contemporary China. The other drawn in the 1970's showed Tibet two-thirds smaller and the letters CHINA stretched from Changthang in the West to Shanghai in the East.

As a boy growing up in Tibet, I had scoffed at family and neighbors who governed their days by incantations and thousand-year old proverbs. They lived in a myth. The world was passing them by and they didn't even know it. Now, a half century later, I lived surrounded by educated people, anxious and burdened in their daily lives. And I was one of them. Only with the passing of time had I come to appreciate the precious nature of life in Tibet.

One entire spring I'd come home from the law office in the late afternoon, ate an early dinner with my family, and then sat in this same chair harshly reviewing the decisions that had led to this point in my life. Night after night I watched wrens dart in and out of the pomegranate tree beside my window. I knew them from the time they were eggs in a nest until they flew away as glossy-feathered adults. Greta would slip into my study carrying trays of Tibetan *momos* and tea, place them on the desk corner and linger while I re-considered the boundary map of old Tibet. There were nights when I attempted to reach across the chasm, imagining I was recovering from the early death of my parents or maybe from a terrible accident, and she had held out her hand to me. It was impossible to complete the link, my despair was too deep.

"Maybe I didn't have a right to leave," I'd said one night to Greta. I'd put the boys to bed and we sat alone in the study. "Is it possible education spoiled me for Tibet? Can I ever go back and be that person again?" I knew these questions had no answer.

"You're too hard on yourself," she had stifled her tears before she disappeared to the bedroom alone.

A sound at the door brought me out of my reverie. Nyima stood in the doorway, leaning against the frame, watching me stare into space and study the maps.

"A call for you, Dad." He handed me the telephone. Twenty-three years old, Nyima was tall and handsome. Prominent cheekbones, coal black hair and dark skin gave him the exotic Asian look. Startling blue eyes rooted him in Greta's Germanic ancestry. I gestured to him to come over while I took the call.

"Hello," I said, "Who's speaking? The connection is bad."

"It's Lilia," said the voice on the phone. "I'm at the airport on my way to Paris. My mother had a stroke."

"My God, is there anything I can do?"

"There's nothing. Norbu, she didn't make it. It happened quickly. I talked to her while I was still at the hotel, but just got word she died on the way to the hospital. I have to go. The flight is boarding now."

"Please be in touch. Let us know if we can help."

"Dad?" Nyima bent over the back of the chair, peering at my stricken face. "What happened, Dad?" He encased my shoulders in his arms, his cheek pressed against my hair.

"I need some time alone." The packet from Erzebet smoldered in my pocket. "Tell your mother I'll be out in a minute." I walked automatically to the shelf with the bronze butter lamps that framed the photo of His Holiness the XIVth Dalai Lama. I lit the wicks and the prayer of *Om Mani Padme Hung* welled up from my heart as if it had been reciting itself inside me for all of the forgotten years.

Removing Erzebet's gift from my pocket, I untied the red cord. Sliding my fingers over the brocade cloth, I delayed the awareness of the gift itself, admiring instead the woven design of the auspicious golden fish swimming in the clear water of the mind.

I held the package next to the soft glow of the butter lamps and unwrapped the brocade. Inside was a book of handmade paper, only 2" X 2", the binding fastened with horsetail, wrapped round and round with orange silk thread. Drawings that changed only slightly from page to page filled the tiny book. When I turned the pages quickly, the image moved. A turquoise bee rapidly beat its transparent wings and flew across the globe from Tibet to Europe and back again. I flipped the pages repeatedly watching the story unfold: a dream brought to reality by a person I had not seen for more than half my life.

On the last page was one word written in both Tibetan and English.

*Seh pa.* Forgiveness.

Taking a silver filigree box from my desk drawer, I undid the clasp. Inside was the ivory silk *khata* blessed by the Dalai Lama. I had meant it to be a present for my mother but she had now been dead for more than two decades.

My moist eyes fell on the large oil painting that hung between two bookcases. My cells breathed in the panoramic landscape of rolling hills, wildflower meadows and the never-ending sky of Tibet, so little atmosphere between the painter and the deep space of heaven. It was time to take my family and go home.

*Ki ki so so, lha gyel lo!*
*What a great distance we have come.*

## In Support of the Tibetan People

10% of sales from this novel, *The Dream of the Turquoise Bee*, and 10% of sales from Dianne Aigaki's original scientific botanical illustrations, prints and greeting cards from the exhibit, *The Dream of the Turquoise Bee: The Search for Wildflowers in Tibet,* are donated to projects that benefit the Tibetan people, both those living on the Tibetan Plateau as well as Tibetan refugees the world over.

These projects provide continuing and emergency healthcare for frail, elderly Tibetans; support for nunneries and monasteries; food and medical care for political prisoners and their families; school fees and supplies for children in Eastern Tibet; and scholarships for higher education for young men and women.

If you would like to make an additional, tax-deductible donation, you may do so through the 501(c)(3) nonprofit organization:

Companions in Compassion
215 10TH Ave. South, Unit 1013
Minneapolis, MN 55415

www.companionsincompassion-us.org

***May all beings be happy***
***May we all dedicate our lives to make it so***

## ACKNOWLEDGEMENTS

The following people entrusted me with their stories, their hopes and dreams, and their memories of a life and loved ones left behind in Tibet. Without them, this book would have never come to life: Ama Adhe, Bumchung Tsering, Norbu Damdul, Palden Gyatso, Pasang Dorjee, Pema Mehto, Pu-Druk, Rinchen Tsering, Sonam Yangchen, Sonam Wangdue, Tsultrim Gyatso, Tashi Gyaltsen, Dr. Tenzin Choedak, Ven. Lobsang Jigmey, Ven. Lobsang Tenzin, Ven. Lobsang Tsering, Ven. Jamyang Choedak, Ven. Dawa Dhondhup, Ven. Kalsang Tenzin, Ven. Leksok, Ven. Pema, Ven. Lobsang Tenzin (Apay), Ven. Lobsang Dhondhup, Ven. Lobsang Tenzin (Tehor), Ven. Samdhong Rinpoche, Ye-Ga, and Yong Lha.

Other accounts came from the scores of friends and family who hold the line in the Tibetan homeland, dreaming that one day their sons and daughters, wives and husbands, fathers and mothers will walk back across the Himalayas, coming home. With great sadness, I omit their names here to protect them from repercussions that might come from having shared their stories.

A special debt of gratitude goes to all those who gave me insight into the poems of the Sixth Dalai Lama. Many people pored over the poems, translating and discussing the true meaning, the literal meaning, the historical meaning, and the emotional meaning.

Thank you to everyone who heard this story from the beginning, listened to a hundred revisions, challenged the flow and my skills and encouraged me to keep at it: Wren Aigaki-Lander, Gary Felder, Hollis Fulmor, Nora Joanne Gerber, Liz Graham, Ruth Hayward, Michael Lander, Miki Hsu Leavey, Cindy McLeod, Eileen Morrow, Barbara Morse, the San Miguel de Allende Writer's Group, Rebecca Scott, John Scherber and Rhonda Slota. This book would not have been possible without the support of Paula Amen-Schmitt who critiqued, edited, and fielded letters and phone calls in the United States, while I was in India; Jan Baross, who has a brutal, but keen editing knife; and Fleur Wood who alloeed me to sit at her kitchen counter in Sydney, Australia for three months, as I obsessed over adjectives, verbs, and punctuation.

Season Harper-Fox at Gotham Writer's Workshop gave me the initial courage to think I could write this story.

Marilyn Garber of the Minnesota School of Botanical Art gave me the visual vocabulary of botanical painting and encouragement to do the first botanical illustrations in Tibet.

*Dianne Aigaki*

Many decades ago, Han Kai Lun, came to the United States from China and opened my eyes by his obsessive drive to communicate in a new language and forge heart bonds with new friends and a new culture. This is his story, too.

## A BOOK GROUP GUIDE

### Interview with Dianne Aigaki

***How is that someone who grew up in a small town in Colorado ended up writing a book of fiction about Tibetan nomads?***

That's a mystery all on its own. I had lived in California since the mid-1970's, working as an artist and a consultant for non-profit organizations. Someone I knew was traveling to Dharamsala, India with a group of Tibetan Buddhists, and they were going to have an audience with the Dalai Lama in 1996. I didn't know much about the Tibetans, wasn't Buddhist, and had never thought about going to India, but I decided to go along. It was very spontaneous. When I got to Dharamsala, I felt an instant kinship with the environment and the people and moved there not long after. I built a home there in 1999. In 2004, I started traveling to Tibet, visiting the families of people I knew in Dharamsala. In many cases, I was visiting families my friends in India never expect to see again.

***What was the impetus for writing this epic story?***

I wanted to write a work of historical fiction that would tell the Tibetan story without pounding home the recurrent themes of cultural obliteration, human rights abuse and environmental devastation on the Tibetan Plateau. I'm a story collector, so I was keenly tuned in to the personal stories of the Tibetans I met—about the homes they had left behind and their lives as refugees in India. I hoped to write a novel that would capture the attention of people who know and care about Tibet, and maybe many more who know nothing about it, but would like to learn, or will learn as a side experience while reading the novel.

***Did you feel a responsibility to tell the Tibetan story in a certain way?***

Of course, I was anxious to tell the story accurately and yet make it compelling for the reader. I wanted to get it right—I had to get it right—it's my responsibility to the people who have shared their lives with me. All of the novel weaves between the stories of scores of men and woman, children and their families I have met. So it is a collective history of a people. For me, it was much more than just writing a story that had been percolating in the back of my mind—I had a social mission, too.

If the Western reader believed, but the Tibetans said, "This isn't us," then I would have failed in my mission. Fortunately, that hasn't happened. Tibetans come up to me and say, "You captured my Grandfather and his lessons to me." "You brought my aunt back to life." "That was my story you told in the escape over the mountains."

That confirmation was the biggest gift I could ever receive and made this whole journey worth it.

***Is this the first novel you've written?***
Yes—in a few writing classes I wrote short (very short) fictional pieces and enjoyed it so much, Ithought I might be able to make the leap from nonfiction writing. I've been a grant-writer for many years, so am used to always having to tell the truth in preparing funding proposals. So to write a novel was a huge change—and a fun one. When you're writing a funding proposal, it's all backed up by facts. When you're writing a novel, if it isn't convincing to you or a reader, you can just change the situation, the dialogue or even the character's motivation. It's liberating!

***How did you start?***
I signed up for a Gotham Writer's Workshop fiction class online. Once I started writing, I was at it for 20 hours a day—I couldn't stop, all of the stories kept pouring out of me. Of course, over the next eight years, I wrote and rewrote many, many times—chasing adjectives and clichés and tired plot lines and everything else I could root out that seemed banal. I analyzed my favorite novels and tried to figure out, with fresh eyes, why they had kept my interest and how they were different from books I had just tossed to the side after the first five minutes. I had friends and other authors tear it apart and encourage me to keep going, and all of that kept me on track.

***Are you Erzebet?***
Well, I guess I am Erzebet in that it generally seems to be impossible to write a work of fiction without some of you bleeding through into the characters. But, no this isn't my story—it is the story of many, many Tibetans who over the last two decades have confided their personal stories to me—both in India and in Tibet.

***But aren't you a scientific botanical illustrator?***

Yes, that's true, but all of that came to be when I first started traveling to Tibet. I went to the Minnesota School of Botanical Art and the director, Marilyn Garber, encouraged me to start the documentation of the wildflowers growing at 11,000-18,000 feet altitude. That "side project" definitely put another layer on the themes of the novel. When I got to Tibet, and saw my first Tibetan Blue Poppy, I was hooked by the transparent blue, by the magic—just like explorers have been for centuries, just like Mr. Cline was in the novel. There's an exhibit (*The Dream of the Turquoise Bee: The Search for Wildlfowers in Tibet*) of the botanical paintings I've completed in Tibet over the last years; it not only tells the botanical story of the Tibetan Plateau, but also the story of the people who have been part of that project.

### *Is there a sequel planned?*

We'll have to wait and see—I'd have to sort through a lot of tales still running in the back of my mind and the lives of the people I know. I've thought about Erzebet's illustrated diary. We know she kept one—it would be wonderful to see what was in there—what flowers did she paint? Did she do landscapes of Tibet? What did she say about her days in Tibet and about her relationship with Norbu and Kai Lun? I think I've still got a few possibilities.

## QUESTIONS FOR BOOK GROUPS:

1. Describe the relationship between Erzebet and her father. Is it believable that she would still be trying to please him and seek his approval when she is a middle-aged woman?

2. What were Erzebet's greatest strengths as she pursued the investigation into Girard's disappearance—both directly after it happened and twenty years later?

3. Did you have sympathy for Kai Lun and his dilemma as a spy?

4. What plot twist was the most unexpected?

5. How realistic were the characterizations of the main people in the novel? Could you see yourself, or others you have known, in these fictional characters?

6. Is Erzebet's journey a triumph or a pointless tragedy?

7. This is a story with many layers. Discuss how the Sixth Dalai Lama's poems foreshadowed or deepened the chapters they introduced.

8. Was there a time in your life when you went through a life crisis, and then, because of a child, or your own health, or other mitigating circumstances had to "move on"—perhaps before you actually felt ready?

9. What was the ultimate life lesson that Norbu learned in this journey? How did he triumph?

10. If one (or more) of the characters made a choice that had moral implications, would you have made the same decision? Why? Why not?

11. How does the setting figure into the book? Is the landscape a character? Does it come to life? Did you feel you were experiencing the time and place in which the book was set?

12. How would the book have been different if it had taken place in a different time or place?

13. Did the introduction of Erzebet's botanical illustration career and quest to find the blue poppy make the novel more interesting or was it a distraction? Did it add a layer of complexity to her as a character?

14. Would you recommend this book to a friend?

Made in the USA
Lexington, KY
30 March 2013